Ab...

Two-time Golden H... has been reading ... writing for even lon... gallons of iced tea a... one of her favourite things – convincing two characters they deserve their happy-ever-after. When she's not writing, she spends time at the lake, hangs out with her family and reads. Ami lives in Michigan with her four kids, three cats and very supportive husband.

Award-winning author **Louisa George** has been an avid reader her whole life. In between chapters she managed to train as a nurse, marry her doctor hero and have two sons. Now she writes chapters of her own in the medical romance, contemporary romance and women's fiction genres. Louisa's books have variously been nominated for the coveted RITA® Award, and the NZ Koru Award and have been translated into twelve languages. She lives in Auckland, New Zealand.

Leah Martyn comes from a long line of storytellers and finds writing comes to her as naturally as breathing. As well as her medical romances, she has written and published short stories. She insists her characters must have a sense of humour! She loves holidaying in Queensland and browsing in bookshops is high on her list of enjoyable things to do. Consequently, each year around Christmas, she breaks the budget, buying an armful of new releases to read over the holidays.

A Surprise Family

LS.

A Surprise Family: Baby Makes Three

AMI WEAVER

LOUISA GEORGE

LEAH MARTYN

MILLS & BOON

All rights reserved including the right of reproduction in whole or in part in any form. This edition is published by arrangement with Harlequin Books S.A.

This is a work of fiction. Names, characters, places, locations and incidents are purely fictional and bear no relationship to any real life individuals, living or dead, or to any actual places, business establishments, locations, events or incidents. Any resemblance is entirely coincidental.

This book is sold subject to the condition that it shall not, by way of trade or otherwise, be lent, resold, hired out or otherwise circulated without the prior consent of the publisher in any form of binding or cover other than that in which it is published and without a similar condition including this condition being imposed on the subsequent purchaser.

® and TM are trademarks owned and used by the trademark owner and/or its licensee. Trademarks marked with ® are registered with the United Kingdom Patent Office and/or the Office for Harmonisation in the Internal Market and in other countries.

AN ACCIDENTAL FAMILY

AMI WEAVER

For the Wicked Muses: Chelle, Jodie, Marcy and Rae.

Thank you for all your help. I love you all.

And for Dale, who believed. xo

CHAPTER ONE

THE STICK WAS pink.

Lainey Keeler squeezed her eyes shut, lifted the test with one trembling hand, then peeked with her right eye only.

Yup. Definitely a pink line. Maybe she needed to check the instructions to be sure....

Oh, God. How had this happened?

Okay, so she knew the technicalities of the how. In fact, she knew the when. Lord help her, that was the kicker.

Her eyes swam and her stomach rolled as she reached for the test box anyway, knowing what she'd see there. Knowing the result would read the same as the four other sticks—all different brands—in the garbage.

Knowing she'd been screwed in more ways than one.

So this was the price she paid for one night of lust infused with a heavy dose of stupidity. She slumped on the cold tile of the bathroom floor and let her head thunk on the vanity door. Hysterical laughter bubbled in her throat and she pressed her fingertips to her temples. Did it count, fifteen years after graduation, that she'd finally bedded the star quarterback? The same one she'd nurtured a killer crush on all through high school?

And managed to conceive his baby?

"And here I thought I had the flu," she said to her calico

cat, who observed her from the doorway. Panda's squinty blink in response could have meant anything. "Why didn't being pregnant occur to me?"

Single and pregnant. Right when she was starting a new business and her life couldn't be more unstable.

What would her parents say? She winced at the thought. At thirty-three, she was supposed to be burning up the career ladder. Instead, much to her family's chagrin, she burned *through* careers.

Chewing her lower lip, she took a last look at the pink line, then tossed the test stick in the trash with the others. Five pregnancy tests couldn't be wrong, no matter how much she wished it. She needed a plan.

"A plan is good," she said to the cat in the doorway. Panda meowed in response. Shoot, what was she going to do? She stepped over the cat and hurried into the small hallway, facing straight into her pocket-sized bedroom. Panic kicked up a two-step in her belly. She'd need a bigger place. The cozy one-bedroom apartment above her shop, The Lily Pad, worked beautifully for one person and an overweight cat. But adding a baby to the mix…? Babies needed so much *stuff.* She laid her hand on her still-flat belly. *A baby.*

Good God, she was going to be a mother.

She clenched her eyes shut and willed the tears away. What kind of mother would she be? Her ex and her family told her over and over she tended to be flighty and irresponsible. A baby meant responsibility, stability.

What if it turned out they were right? She certainly hadn't demonstrated good judgment on the night of her reunion.

The thought sliced her to the core and she took a deep breath. No time to cry. Not when she had a shop to open in a few minutes. Beth Gatica, her friend and employee, was already downstairs. She swiped at her eyes, tried to think.

"Where do I start?" she wondered aloud, trying to get her head clear enough to think.

A doctor. She'd need a doctor. Her usual doctor happened to be a friend of her family's, so she'd definitely have to head over to Traverse City. Since she felt better with something to do, she reached for the phone book.

"Lainey?" Beth's voice came through the door connecting the apartment to the shop. "Are you okay?"

Lainey fumbled the phone book and caught sight of herself in the small mirror next to the door. Dark blond hair already escaping from her ponytail? Check. Dark circles under her eyes? Check. Pasty skin? *Yikes.* Wasn't there supposed to be some kind of pregnancy glow? "I'm fine," she called. "Be right there."

"Okay, good. Because we've got a problem."

Well, of course they did. Lainey marched over and yanked open the door, almost grateful for the distraction. "What kind of problem?"

"Come see." Beth turned and hurried down the stairs, long dark curls bouncing. The fresh, cool scent of flowers hit Lainey as they entered the workroom. Beth tipped her head toward the older of the two walk-in coolers. "It's not cold enough, Laine. It's set where it's supposed to be, but it's nearly twelve degrees warmer in there."

"Oh, no." *No.* She needed the cooler to last another year—like she needed the van with its iffy transmission to last another six months. Preferably twelve. A headache began to pulse at the edges of her brain at the thought of her nearly empty bank account. Using only one cooler would mean reducing inventory, which meant possibly not being able to meet the needs of her customers. Which meant less income. And she couldn't afford to lose a single cent at this point.

To say The Lily Pad operated on a shoestring budget was to put it optimistically.

She pulled open the door, even though she didn't doubt Beth. She could feel the difference as soon as she walked in. She tapped the thermostat with her finger. Maybe it was stuck somewhere? She should be so lucky.

"Call Gary at General Repair," she said to Beth. "See if he can get us in today."

"On it." Beth hurried to the phone.

Lainey headed to the working cooler to do some rearranging. Some of the more delicate flowers would have to be moved over.

She tamped down the spurt of fear and worry that threatened to explode. No point inviting trouble, and Lainey figured she had enough to fill her personal quota. She closed her eyes and inhaled the fresh, green scent of the flowers, with their overtones of sweet and tangy and spicy. It always, always relaxed her just to breathe in the flowers.

But not enough, today, to rid her of her worries. About choking coolers. About babies. Lainey smothered a sigh. If she'd stayed home two months ago part of her predicament wouldn't be here. She'd invited trouble. Or, more accurately, trouble had invited her.

Of course she hadn't turned him down.

"Gary will be here at eleven," Beth said from behind her. "Want me to help move things?"

Lainey glanced at her watch. An hour and a half. "Sure. We'll just move a few for now. Let's group them by the door so we can open it a minimum of times." The colder it stayed in there, the better for her bottom line. She couldn't afford to lose a cooler full of flowers.

"Are you okay, Laine? You're awfully pale," Beth commented as she lifted a bucket of carnations out of the way.

Lainey sucked in a breath. Should she tell Beth? They'd been friends for years. Beth wouldn't ridicule her for her mistake with Jon. It would feel so good to tell someone….

"Lainey?" Beth's head was cocked, her brown gaze worried. "What's going on?"

"I'm pregnant," she blurted, and burst into tears. Beth hurried over to her, nearly knocking a bucket over in the process.

"Honey, are you sure?"

Lainey nodded and swiped at the tears. "Pretty sure." Five separate pink lines couldn't be wrong. Could they? "I'll have to go to a doctor to confirm it, though."

"Oh, Laine." Beth hugged her, stepped back. "How far along? I didn't know you were seeing someone."

Lainey closed her eyes. *Here we go.* "Well, I'm actually not. I'm about eight weeks along." She'd let Beth do the math.

"So that's—oh." Beth drew out the word and her eyes rounded. "Your class reunion."

"Yeah." Lainey couldn't meet her friend's gaze. Her poor baby. How could she ever explain the circumstances of his or her conception?

"So who's the daddy?"

"Jon Meier." Lainey could barely say his name. "We… ah…hit it off pretty well."

Beth gave a wry chuckle and opened the cooler door, a load of calla lilies in her hands. "So it seems."

"I have to tell him, Beth, but he lives so far away. Plus the whole thing was pretty forgettable, if you know what I mean. We used protection, but obviously…" She shrugged and swiped at her leaking eyes again. "It didn't work." An understatement if she'd ever heard one.

"He's not father material?"

"I don't know." It wasn't as if they'd discussed things like personal lives. "Plus he lives in LA. He's in some kind of entertainment industry work. He's not going to pull up and move back to Northern Michigan." He'd made his contempt for the area crystal-clear.

"Sometimes having a kid changes that," Beth pointed out.

"True." Lainey didn't want to think about it. "But I think we were pretty much in agreement on how awkward the whole thing was." So much for sex with no strings attached. The baby in her belly was a pretty long string. The length of a lifetime, in fact.

She wanted to bang her head on the wall. What had she been thinking, leaving with Jon that night? Was her self-esteem so damaged by her divorce she had to jump on the first guy who smiled at her?

Best not to answer that.

"I think you'll be a wonderful mom," Beth said, and Lainey's throat tightened.

"Really?" She couldn't keep the wobble out of her voice. Beth's confidence touched her. Her family would look at her being single, pregnant and nearly broke and lose their collective minds. She shoved the thought aside.

"Of course. You're wonderful with my kids. Now, let's get this finished before Gary gets here."

"It could go at any time?" Lainey could not believe she'd heard the repairman correctly. A year—she only needed twelve measly months. Why, oh, why was that too much to ask? "Are you sure?"

"Yes. We can cobble this along for a few more months. But you are definitely going to need a new unit." Gary's lined face wasn't without sympathy.

She took a deep breath. "Do what you have to, Gary. I need it to last as long as possible."

The repairman nodded and returned to the cooling unit.

Beth stood at the counter, ringing up a large bouquet of brightly colored carnations. A great sale, but not nearly enough to buy a new cooler. Or even a used one.

"Thank you. Have a great day," Beth said to the customer as he exited the shop. To Lainey she said, "What's the news?"

"We're going to need a new cooler. Sooner rather than later, probably." Exhaustion washed over her and she sank down on the stool behind the counter. "Even used, that's not something I can swing yet." Or possibly ever. No cooler, no business. No business, no cooler.

No business, no way to provide for the baby.

A wave of nausea rolled through her at the thought. Another failure. This one could be huge.

"Oh, man." Beth leaned on the counter. "Well, let's see. We've got the Higgins wedding coming up. We need more weddings. The funeral business has been picking up. That's good. Maybe...."

She hesitated, and Lainey knew what her friend hadn't said.

"Maybe if my mother sent business my way we wouldn't be in this predicament," she finished. "I know. I agree. I've asked." The answer, while not in so many words, was that the florist her mother used had been around a lot longer and wasn't in danger of folding. The implication? Lainey would fail—again.

Beth winced. "I know you have. I just wish she'd support you. I'm sorry I brought it up."

"It's okay. It's the truth. I don't know what will change her mind." Lainey stood up. "Let's finish getting the deliveries ready."

As Lainey gathered flowers and greenery she wondered if she'd let her business go under rather than ask her parents for a loan. They'd give her one, with plenty of strings attached, and she'd have to crawl to get it. This was supposed to be her chance to prove she could make something of her life without advanced degrees or a rich husband.

Right about now it didn't seem to be working.

Gary came out of the cooler, toolbox in one hand, invoice in the other. "You're all fixed up, Ms. Keeler. Can't say how long it'll last. Could be one month. Could be six. I'm sorry I don't have better news."

"The fact it's running right now is wonderful," Lainey said. "Thank you. I appreciate you coming on such short notice."

"Anytime. Have a good day, ladies." He left the store and the bell above the door chimed, its cheerful sound mocking Lainey's mood. She looked at the amount on the invoice and sighed.

She'd known when she bought the shop nine months ago there were no guarantees on equipment. Even in her current financial bind she didn't regret taking the plunge. This shop felt right to her in a way none of her other jobs ever had. Right enough, in fact, that she hoped to someday buy the building outright.

Working steadily throughout the morning, they completed their orders. The repair seemed to be holding for now, thank goodness. Lainey slid the last of the arrangements into the back of the van and closed the door. "All set, Beth. Hopefully we'll get more this afternoon."

"Fingers crossed." Beth climbed in and turned the ignition. She leaned back out the window. "I'll stop at Dottie's Deli and grab lunch on the way back. I think we've each earned a cheesecake muffin after this morning."

"Mmm." Lainey perked up at the thought. Everyone

knew the calories in Dottie's heavenly muffins didn't count. "Sounds wonderful. Thanks."

She held her breath as Beth thunked the old van into gear and drove off. Relief washed over her. After this morning she'd half expected the thing to go belly-up out of spite.

"Don't borrow trouble," she reminded herself as she turned and went inside.

The chime of the door caught her attention and she hurried to greet the customer.

Fifteen minutes later she started on a new arrangement, this one for a new mom and baby at the hospital. They really needed more of this kind of business—more happy occasions like...

Babies.

Pregnant.

Lainey gulped and gripped the edge of the worktable, her eyes on the array of delicate pastel flowers she'd gathered. She only had about seven months to stabilize her shop and get ready to be a new mom herself. A *single* new mom.

Seven months.

No one could ever accuse her of doing things the easy way.

Ben Lawless pulled into the driveway of his grandmother's old farmhouse and stared. Same white paint, black shutters. The wide porch was missing its swing, but two rockers sat in its place. The two huge maples in the front yard had dropped most of their leaves. Funny, he'd been gone for so many years but this old house still felt like home.

He frowned at the strange car parked behind his grandmother's trusty Buick. Last thing he wanted was to talk to anyone other than his grandma, to deal with friendliness and well-meaning questions. Acting normal was exhausting.

He pushed open the truck door, stepped out and scanned the layout of the front yard. Plenty of room for a ramp, though some of the porch railing would have to be removed, and it would block one of the flowerbeds lining the house's foundation. He kicked at the leaves littering the cracked walkway. The uneven concrete posed a hazard even to an able-bodied person. Why couldn't Grandma admit she needed help?

Why did you assume she didn't need it?

His self-recrimination didn't get any farther as the front door opened and framed his beaming grandmother in her wheelchair. He tried not to wince at the sight. She'd always been so tough, strong and able, and now she looked so small. He moved up the walk and the stairs to the porch.

"Grandma." He bent down to give her an awkward hug in the chair, afraid to hold on too tight. "How are you?"

She hugged him back firmly and patted his face. "I'm good. Making the best of this, I hope." She studied his face for a moment, her clear blue eyes seeing too much. "I'm so glad you're here. Not sleeping well?"

He straightened, not surprised by the observation. "Good enough."

She gave him a look, but dropped the subject and rolled back into the house. "Where are my manners? Come in, come in. I want you to meet a very good friend of mine."

Ben braced himself as he followed her across the familiar living room to the kitchen. Hopefully this friend wasn't one of the mainstays of Holden's Crossing's gossip mill. Last thing he needed was word getting out and people asking him questions or making accusations. He stopped dead when he looked into the cool blue gaze of the gorgeous—and young—blond at the kitchen table.

"Ben Lawless, meet Lainey Keeler. Lainey, this is my grandson. The one who's a firefighter in Grand Rapids." The pride in Rose's voice made Ben's stomach twist. "Lainey was a few years behind you in school, Ben."

No way. *This* was his grandmother's friend? Long dark blond ponytail, a few strands loose around a heart-shaped face. Clear blue eyes, smooth creamy skin. Full breasts a snug pink tee didn't hide. He gave her a brief nod, forced the proper words out. "Nice to meet you."

Her smile curved, but didn't reach her eyes. "Same here. Rose has told me so much about you."

"Did she?" He tensed at her comment, then forced himself to relax. It didn't mean she actually knew anything. He rested his hand on his grandmother's thin shoulder. "Grandma, I'm going to bring in my things, okay?"

Lainey rose. "I'll walk you out." She leaned down to plant a kiss on his grandma's cheek and gave her a hug. "I'll see you in a couple of days, Rose."

"Don't work too hard, honey," Grandma said, and Ben nearly laughed. If he remembered correctly, none of the Keelers had to work. They'd been given anything and everything on the proverbial platter.

Ben caught a whiff of her scent, something floral, as she moved past him. Since he'd gotten boxed in, he followed her out into the cool early October night.

Once on the porch, she turned to him with a frown. "She's glad you're here."

"And you're not."

Those big blue eyes narrowed. "I'm not sure. She's been struggling for months now. Where were you then?"

Temper flared at the accusation in her tone. He'd felt bad enough once he'd realized how much help his grandma needed. He didn't need this chick sticking her nose in, too.

No matter how hot she was. "She isn't big on admitting she needs help." Seemed to run in the family.

Lainey gave him a look that said he was full of it and stomped off the porch. "She's in her eighties. How could you not come visit and check on her?"

Guilt lanced through him. "She always said she was fine, okay? I'm here now." Why did he care if this woman thought he was a total heel?

She shrugged. "You still should have checked on her. How far is it up here? She's so proud of you. But you never bothered to visit."

Even in the dim light he saw the sparks in her blue gaze, the anger on his grandmother's behalf. "I'm here now," he said, his own temper rising.

"Till you leave. Then where will she be?" She spun around and strode across the yard.

God help him, he couldn't pull his gaze off her tight little tush. She climbed in the little car and slammed the door. The spray of gravel that followed her out to the road said it all.

Well, great. He'd managed to tick off his grandmother's hot little friend.

Ben shook his head and stepped off the porch, walked to his truck to get his bags. He'd done something far worse than that. His best friend was dead, thanks to him, and any problems with Lainey Keeler were not even on his list of important things. It made no difference what she thought of him.

Back inside, his grandma frowned at him. "Why were you rude to Lainey?"

But of course it would matter to Grandma. He scrubbed a hand over his face. "I'm sorry. It's been a long day. I didn't know you two were friends."

"We are. We met awhile back when she volunteered

for Senior Services and just clicked, as you young people say. She comes out every Wednesday. More if she can. I didn't think you knew her." His grandmother's eyes were sharp on his face.

"I don't. Just knew *of* her. She was four years behind me in school, as you said. How are you feeling?"

She studied him for a second, then seemed to accept the change of topic. "Every day is a little harder. I'm so glad you're here and can make this old house a little easier to live in. I don't want to leave it."

These last words were spoken in a soft tone. Ben knew this was the only home she'd lived in with his grandfather, her husband of fifty years. Her best friend.

The kind of love and relationship he'd ended for Jason and Callie.

Pain pounded at his temples and he closed his eyes. He shoved it down, locked it back into the deepest part of him he could. Thing was, that place was nearly full these days.

"You won't have to leave, Grandma. You'll have to tell me what you'd like done besides the ramp. Even in the dark I noticed the walk out front has seen better days."

Her smile was rueful. "A lot around here has seen better days, Ben."

"We'll get it fixed up, Grandma. You won't have to leave," he repeated.

"I know. I'm very grateful to you." She maneuvered the chair toward the living room. "Let me show you to your room. Well, partway anyway."

Ben started to say he knew where it was, but of course she'd have taken over the downstairs bedroom after the arthritis in her hip got too bad. "Which one?" There were three upstairs.

She stopped at the base of the stairs and looked up, the sorrow and longing clear on her face. "The back bedroom.

It has the best view and is the biggest room. Lainey freshened it up for you. Dusted, clean sheets, the whole shebang. The bathroom is ready, too."

His grandparents' old room.

"Okay. Tell her thanks for me."

Grandma backed her chair up and gave him a little smile. "You can tell her yourself. Didn't I mention she visits a lot?"

He stared at her. *Uh-oh.* "Grandma. I'm not interested."

She slid him a look and her smile widened. "No one said you were."

He'd walked right into that one.

Smoke filled the room, smothering him, searing his lungs, his eyes, his skin. God, he couldn't see through the gray haze. A cough wracked him, tearing at his parched throat. He couldn't yell for his friend. Where was Jason? He couldn't reach him. Had to get him out before the house came down around them. A roar, a crack, and a fury of orange lit the room. The ceiling caved in a crash fueled by the roar of flames. He spun around, but the door was blocked by a flaming heap of debris. Under it, a boot. Jason. Coming to save him.

Ben woke with a start, his eyes watering and the breath heaving out of his lungs as if he'd been sprinting for his life. Where the hell was he? Moonlight slanted through the window, silver on the floor. The curtain stirred in the faint breeze. He sat up and pushed himself through the fog of sleep. Grandma Rose's house. Had he cried out? God, what if she'd heard him? Shame flowed over him like a lava river. He stepped out of bed, mindful of the creaky floor, and walked down the hall to the bathroom near the landing.

No sound came from downstairs.

He exhaled a shaky breath and went into the bathroom.

He'd been afraid of this—of the nightmare coming. He had no power over it—over what it was, what it did to him. No control.

He turned on the squeaky faucet with unsteady hands and splashed cold water on his face. There'd be no more sleep for him tonight.

CHAPTER TWO

LAINEY WALKED INTO Frank's Grocery after closing the shop and pulled out her mental shopping list. Nothing fancy. Just sauce, pasta, shrimp, some good cheese. If she had more energy she'd make the sauce from scratch, but not tonight. So far the hardest thing about being pregnant was being so tired at the end of the day. She grabbed a basket from the stack and headed for the first aisle.

She came to a dead stop when she spotted the tall, dark-haired man frowning at the pasta sauce display.

Oh, no. Ben Lawless.

She didn't want to chat with Rose's grumpy grandson. He'd made it pretty clear he wasn't interested in being friendly. Since he stood smack in front of the sauce she needed, though, she'd have to talk to him.

He glanced up as she approached. For a heartbeat she found herself caught by those amazing light green eyes, by the grief she saw searing through them.

What the heck? She cleared her throat. "How are you?"

He tipped his head in her direction, his expression now neutral. "Fine, thanks."

His uninterest couldn't have been clearer, though his tone was perfectly polite.

"I just need to get in here." She pointed to the shelves in front of him. He stepped back, hindered by a woman and cart behind him, and Lainey slipped in, bumping him in the process. A little shiver of heat ran through her. "Sorry," she muttered, and grabbed the jar with fingers that threatened to turn to butter.

She managed to wiggle back out, brushing him again, thanks to the oblivious woman behind him who kept him penned between them. She plopped the sauce into her basket and offered what she hoped passed for a smile. "Um, thanks."

"No problem," he murmured.

She turned around and hurried out of the aisle, unsettled by both the physical contact and his apparent loss. So Ben had a few secrets. That flash of grief, deep and wrenching, hit her again.

Rose had never mentioned anything. Then again, why would she? She'd respect her grandson's privacy. It was one of the things Lainey loved about her friend.

It only took a few more minutes to gather the rest of the ingredients. Her path didn't cross Ben's again, and she unloaded her few purchases at the checkout with relief.

Outside, she took a big breath of the cool night air, and some of the tension knotted inside her eased. Fall was her favorite time of year. A mom and small daughter examined a display of pumpkins outside Frank's and her thoughts shifted back to her baby. Next year she'd be carving a pumpkin for her five-month-old. Oh, sure, he or she would be too small to appreciate it, but despite the precariousness of her position the idea gave her a little thrill.

She deposited the bags in the trunk and slipped into the driver's seat to start the car.

Click. Then nothing.

Oh, no. Maybe if she tried it again....

Click.

She leaned forward, rested her head on the steering

wheel, and fought the urge to scream. Not owning any
jumper cables, she'd have to go back into Frank's and find
someone who did. While she was at it she'd hope like crazy
the problem was simply a dead battery, and not something expensive. She yanked the keys out of the ignition,
grabbed her purse and got out of the car. One thing was
for sure—she'd push the stupid car home before she'd ask
her parents for help.

She nearly collided with Ben coming out of the store.

"Whoa," he said, checking his cart before he ran her
down.

Before she could think, she blurted, "Can you help me?"
Her face heated as he stared at her. "Ah, never mind. I'll
find…" She gestured vaguely behind him but he shook
his head.

"What do you need?"

"My car won't start. I think the battery's dead. The
dome light's been staying on longer than it should and it
didn't go off at all this time. I don't have any jumper cables." Realizing she was babbling, she clamped her mouth
shut.

He nodded. "Where are you parked?"

She pointed. "There. The silver one." Which he no doubt
already knew, since he'd seen her in it the other night. "The
space in front of me is open."

"Okay. Give me a minute. I'll pull around."

He walked off and she stared after him. *Shoot*. Why
hadn't she found someone else? On the other hand, the
whole process wouldn't take very long. Then she could
be on her way back home to fix her dinner and curl up
in her bed.

The wind picked up, skittering dry leaves across the
parking lot, and she tucked her hands under her arms
to keep warm as she went back to her car. She propped

the hood open as a big black truck rumbled into the empty spot.

Ben got out, cables already in hand, and went to work on her battery. Even though she knew how to hook them up—her mother would be appalled—she let him do it, because it was easier than having his carefully bland gaze on her.

He glanced up. "Do you know how to do this?"

Something in his tone made her bristle. She lifted her chin just a bit. "Actually, I do. I can even change a tire."

His mouth twitched in what could have been a prequel to a smile. "Good for you."

Before she could reply, a voice shrilled nearby. "Lainey? Lainey Keeler, is that you?"

Ben returned to the battery and the fragile moment was shattered. Lainey internally groaned as she turned to see Martha Turner, one of her mother's best friends, hurrying toward her.

"Hi, Mrs. Turner."

"Goodness, what are you doing?" The woman peeked around Lainey and frowned. "Do your parents know you have car trouble? I just left your mother at the Club. Have you called her yet? I'll never understand why you traded in that cute little coupe your husband bought you for—for this." She fluttered her hands at the car.

Not offended, Lainey bit back a laugh. She had to be the only person who'd ever traded in a new car for a used one. "Of course I didn't bother either of them, Mrs. Turner. It's really not a big deal. Just a dead battery."

Behind her, Ben cleared his throat. "Sorry to interrupt, but I need to start the truck now. It's loud."

"Okay." She gave Mrs. Turner an apologetic smile. "It was nice to see you."

Mrs. Turner's gaze went to Ben, reaching into the cab of the truck, then back to Lainey. "You too, dear. Take care."

Lainey could almost see the wheels turning in the other woman's head and imagined her mother would get a phone call before Mrs. Turner even made it inside Frank's. She sighed. She'd get her own call in a matter of minutes after that, and spend a half an hour calming her mother all over nothing.

So much for a relaxing evening.

Ben came back around and stood, hands in pockets, staring at her engine. Finally he lifted his gaze. "What did you trade in?"

Not exactly sure how to interpret his tone, she spoke carefully. "A Mercedes. After my divorce."

She didn't mention the sleek little car had been a bribe—an attempt to keep her in the marriage. Getting rid of it had been a victory of sorts. One of the very few she'd managed.

She caught a glimmer of amusement in his eyes. "That's funny?"

He rocked back on his heels. "Not the divorce. The car. I wouldn't think—" He stopped and she frowned.

"Think what?"

He looked at her, amusement gone, and seemed actually to see straight into her. The full effect of his gaze caused a funny little hitch in her breath. "I think you can start the engine now," he said, and she swallowed a surge of disappointment.

Which was crazy. She didn't care what he thought of her.

She slid into the car and tried not to notice when he braced one arm on the roof of the car and the other on the top of the door. When he leaned down she got a tantalizing glimpse of the smooth, hard muscles of his chest through the gap in his partially unbuttoned shirt.

Her mouth went dry.

"Go ahead and see if it'll start."

His voice slid over her skin and she gave a little shiver. She caught a whiff of his scent—a yummy combination of soap and spice. A little curl of heat slipped through her belly. She reached for the ignition and hoped he didn't notice her shaking hand. The engine turned over on the first try.

"You should be all set now," he said, straightening up. "Drive it around a bit to let the battery charge up."

"I will. Thank you," she said, and meant it. "I appreciate it."

He shrugged and stepped back. "No problem. I'd have done it for anyone."

Her little hormonal buzz evaporated. Of course he would. After all, she'd practically attacked him when he came out of the store.

"Well, see you around," she said, and he gave her a nod and then disappeared around the front of her car.

She sat for a moment, waiting for him to unhook the cables, and gave herself a reality check. She was two months pregnant. Being attracted to a man right now couldn't be more foolish—and she'd learned the hard way what a poor judge of men she was. She'd paid dearly for that mistake. Her focus was her shop, her baby, and making her life work without her parents hovering over her, waiting for her to fail.

Clearly these pregnancy hormones threw her off balance.

The hood of the car dropped with a thud and the sudden glare of headlights made her blink. With a little wave, in case he could see, she put her car in gear and backed out of her spot, then drove the long way through town back to her apartment. Ben stayed a respectable distance behind, but the thoughtful gesture gave her an unwelcome frisson of warmth.

Under his gruff exterior, Ben Lawless was a gentleman. Somehow that made him more dangerous.

Lainey let herself in to her apartment, not allowing herself to glance after Ben's truck as he drove on by. Her phone rang. She dug it out of her bag and checked the display. Ah, here was the call she'd been dreading.

"Hi, Mother," she said into the phone, as a purring Panda wound between her feet.

"Hi, dear," Jacqui Keeler trilled. "I'm almost there. Let me in, love."

That hadn't taken long. Mrs. Turner must have really run up the alarm if she was getting a visit, too. Lainey dumped her bags on the counter with a little more force than necessary. "Here? Why?"

"Can't I simply visit with my daughter?"

Oh, if only. "Of course, Mother. I'll be down in a sec."

She dropped the phone back in her purse and glanced around her cozy space. Her apartment was neat, for all the good it did. It would never meet her mother's standards, no matter what. She'd learned that years ago.

She hurried down the front stairs to unlock the street-level door just as her mother walked up.

"Lainey." Jacqui kissed her cheek, her usual cloud of sweet perfume tickling Lainey's nose. "You look tired."

She bit back a laugh. If her mother only knew. "Thanks," she said dryly as the trim older woman swept past her up the stairs. Jacqui, as always, was impeccably groomed. She wore a pale pink suit and her smooth blond hair swung smartly at her chin. Lainey ran her hand down her ponytail and tried not to feel inferior in her non-branded jeans and tee shirt.

Damn it. She'd given that life up. But, oh, sometimes she did miss designer clothes.

"Have a meeting tonight, Mother?"

"I did." Jacqui tucked her monster-sized bag securely under her arm, as if she expected to be robbed right there on the stairs. "For the Auxiliary at the hospital. The gala."

No surprise there. For all their differences, Lainey still admired her mother's energy. "When is it?"

"Two weeks. Don't forget you are expected to be there."

Right. Just what she wanted. "Who did the floral arrangements?"

"Gail, of course. She does a lovely job."

Implying that The Lily Pad didn't. Disappointment clogged her vision for a moment. Lainey opened her mouth, snapped it closed. Frustration rushed through her. She'd never get through to her mother until the woman took her seriously. When would that be? What would it take?

"You really should move back home, honey," Jacqui said, her gaze drifting around the living room. "We have plenty of space. You could have your old room back. We'd love to have you."

Lainey stifled a sigh. More like they'd love to micromanage her life into one that met their standards. Been there, tried that, failed spectacularly.

"I know you would. I'm very happy here, though." Lainey saw her mother's hand twitch, as it did when she was stressed. "Can I get you something to drink?"

"No, thank you." Jacqui perched on the edge of the sofa, the monster bag set primly on her lap, and Lainey sank down on a nearby chair. "Now, I received a disturbing phone call from Martha this evening. You had car trouble? Why didn't you call?"

Lainey smoothed her hand on her jeans. "It was nothing. Really. A dead battery. Not worth bothering you over. Rose's grandson Ben helped me out."

Jacqui's tone turned chilly. "Yes, Martha said you were with a man."

Lainey nearly choked. "Standing in a parking lot while someone was kind enough to jump my battery is hardly being with a man." Though she'd certainly had visions of another kind of jumping, but those were best kept to herself.

"If you'd kept the car your husband bought you—"

"Ex-husband," Lainey said through clenched teeth.

Unperturbed, Jacqui continued on. "If you'd kept the car, and the husband, you wouldn't need strange men to help you in the parking lot. Men who may have less than honorable intentions toward you."

Lainey tried to count to ten and gave up at three. "Excuse me? How does being nice equal intentions of any kind?"

Jacqui glared at her. "Do I need to spell it out for you? Your father's political connections are extremely valuable. Some people will use you for them. You don't always have the best judgment, Lainey."

Ouch. Direct hit. "Like Daniel did?" Lainey shot back. "You weren't concerned then, about my judgment *or* my connections, since he came from the right family. I can't see what need Ben Lawless would have for political connections, or how he thinks he'd get them when we only had ten minutes together."

"Martha said you looked awful cozy."

"Martha was wrong," Lainey said flatly. "Trust me, Mother. Please."

Jacqui made a noise in her throat. "I talked to Daniel earlier."

Betrayal sliced through her, sharp and quick. "What?"

Jacqui sent Lainey a look full of reproach. "He said you never call him. Why ever not, Lainey? He's a good man."

Lainey sucked in a breath. She'd worked so hard to get free of her ex-husband. "I can't think of any reason I'd ever have to call him." Not even if hell froze over. Twice.

Her mother looked at her as if she were a bit daft. "He misses you, dear."

Not a chance. She knew Daniel. Her ex-husband missed the perceived gravy train.

Lainey had never filled her family in on all the reasons behind her divorce. She'd been afraid they would take his side—a fear only reinforced as she looked at her mother now. Her parents adored Daniel. She'd dated him in an effort to be the daughter they wanted. They'd been over the moon when she'd succumbed in a weak moment, perhaps blinded by the three-carat princess-cut ring, and agreed to marry him. She'd thought she could make it work and earn her parents' respect in one fell swoop.

She'd been wrong.

"Why would he miss me now? We've been divorced more than a year," she said, and wasn't totally successful at keeping the bitterness out of her voice. Jacqui didn't seem to notice.

"I gave him your cell phone number and I've got his for you," she said, fishing in her bag. "He said he'd give you a call."

Anger propelled Lainey to her feet. "What? Mother, how *could* you? I don't want to talk to him. Ever. My life is none of his business now." He'd never cared when they were married. Why would he now?

Surprise crossed her mother's face. "Lainey, you were married for seven years. Those feelings don't just go away. He can help you out of this mess you're in. You're barely hanging on. Everyone knows it. You need his help."

Nausea rolled over Lainey. There lay the crux of the matter for Jacqui—the possibility of another public shaming by her wayward daughter and the offer of salvation by a man deemed worthy, no matter the cost.

"I most certainly do not." Telling her parents the truth of her marriage to Daniel would only prove how good she was at failing. "I don't need him or anyone else to make this work. I'm doing perfectly fine on my own." Well, except for the fact her shop was in the red and she had a cooler and a van on the fritz. Oh, and she was about to become a single mom. Still… "I'm happy, Mother."

Jacqui sighed, shook her head, and gestured around the apartment. "Oh, honey. You can't possibly be happy living like this, after how you were raised and how well you married. Talk to him when he calls. Maybe you'll get lucky and he'll give you a second chance."

Lainey shuddered. God help her. "I'm not interested." Those years she'd spent with Daniel were ones she'd never get back. She wasn't going to repeat the mistake of chaining herself to a man. No matter what.

"You should be." Jacqui glanced at her watch. "I'd better get going. Lovely to see you, dear. Come visit us soon."

Lainey bit back a sigh. Typical. Her mother would act as if nothing had happened. "I'll walk you out."

The next evening Ben looked up at the crunch of tires on the gravel drive. He recognized the silver car, and he already knew Lainey Keeler was coming over to visit his grandmother.

He wondered again at her modest choice of car. Somehow that intrigued him. He'd bet there was more to that story than she'd let on.

It would be flat-out rude not to make sure the car was running okay after he'd helped her yesterday. He'd be polite, then get back to his prep for the wheelchair ramp. He leaned the piece of wood he'd been about to cut against the wall and walked out into the twilight.

As he approached the car the door opened and he watched as Lainey planted one slim denim-clad leg, ending in a high-heeled black boot, on the ground. He tried not to notice how long that leg was. She appeared to be struggling with something so he went over to help.

"Evening," he said. She jumped, yelped, and nearly lost her grip on what he could now see was a pizza box. Big blue eyes swung his way and a pretty pink stained her cheeks. Her lips parted slightly and his gaze zeroed in on her mouth. *Very nice.* He shoved the unwelcome thought away. "Can I get that for you?"

She shook her head and her long hair shifted silkily on her shoulders. "I've got it. Thanks."

He stepped back to let her exit the car. "Is it running okay?"

She glanced up at him. "Yes. Thank you again." Her tone was cool, polite. She bumped the door shut with her hip, but her keys fell to the ground. Ben bent and retrieved them for her, pressing them into her palm. A quick zing of heat flashed through him at the contact. He pulled back quickly. *Hell.*

"Um, thanks," she murmured.

"You're welcome." He turned toward the garage. He needed to get away from her before he started to *feel*.

"Ben." Her voice—hesitant, a little husky—flowed over him. He turned back and she tipped the pizza box slightly toward him. "There's plenty here if you want to join us."

"No, thanks." The words came swift, automatic, but he caught a flash of hurt in her eyes. *Damn it.* "I'm in the middle of a project," he amended. "I'll try and grab some in awhile." Why did he feel the need to soften the blow? Since when had big blue eyes affected him? Since last night, when she'd narrowed her eyes and told him she could change a tire.

She shrugged. "Good luck. Rose and I love our pizza."

He slid his hands in his front pockets. "I'll keep that in mind."

She turned to go and he couldn't tear his gaze off the sway of her hips as she walked up to the house.

Double hell. He couldn't risk forging any type of connection. No way would he allow himself the luxury. How could he, when he shouldn't be the one alive?

Turning, he headed back to his project, tried to ignore the feminine laughter floating through the kitchen's screen door. Lainey's throaty laugh carried, teasing at the edge of something he'd shut down after Jason's death.

His phone rang before he could start the saw. A glance at the display revealed the caller to be his boss. Nerves jolted through him, but he kept his voice steady as he answered.

"Hi, Captain."

"Ben." The concern in the older man's voice carried clearly and Ben shut his eyes against the guilt it stirred up. "How are you, son?"

"I'm getting by," he replied.

"Just getting by?"

"Pretty much." Ben paused. He didn't need to paint a rosy picture for his boss. He'd already been ordered to take leave due to the stress of Jason's death. It couldn't really get any worse than that.

"Still having the symptoms, I take it." Not a question.

"Yeah." When the dream stopped, would he be free of the pain? Did he want to be? Wouldn't that be disloyal to the friend he'd loved like a brother?

After all, Ben was alive. Jason wasn't.

The Captain sighed. "It won't do any good for me to tell you again that it was an accident and not your fault, right?"

"With all due respect, sir, you're wrong." The words caught in Ben's throat. "It was my call. I made a bad one, and a good man—a family man—died because of me."

"That's not what the investigation found," the Captain reminded him softly.

It didn't matter. The investigators hadn't been there—in the inferno, in the moment. "I don't give a damn." Ben shut his eyes against the waves of guilt and pain that buffeted his soul, tried not to see Callie's grief-ravaged face. "I know what happened."

"Ben—"

"Please, don't."

There was a pause, then another sigh. "Then I won't. This time. Son, when you heal, come back and see us. There will always be room for fine firefighters such as yourself and I'd be honored to have you."

Heal. Ben swallowed a lump in his throat. He didn't know if it was possible. "Thank you, sir. I'll keep it in mind."

He disconnected the call and the emptiness he'd been battling for the past six months constricted his chest. He could never work as a firefighter again. He no longer trusted his judgment, his ability to read a situation and respond appropriately.

Without those skills he was nothing.

"Ben?"

He looked up sharply, feeling exposed. Lainey stood in the open door with a plate, uncertainty on her beautiful face. He cursed silently. How much had she overheard?

"Rose thought you might be hungry." She lifted the plate slightly.

He rubbed his hand over his face, afraid the rawness of

his emotions showed too clearly. He needed to get them back under control—fast. "Thanks." He shoved the phone in his pocket and walked over, not wanting to look at her and see pity. Or disgust. He'd seen plenty of both over the past couple of months. She handed him the plate wordlessly, then laid her hand on his forearm before he could move away.

His muscles turned to stone even as the heat from her simple touch sought the frozen place inside him. His gaze landed on hers, despite his best intent. He saw no pity, only questions, and he couldn't take the chance of her asking them. Not now, with everything so close to the surface.

He cleared his throat and she stepped back quickly, taking her warmth with her when she removed her hand. It was a much sharper loss than he'd like. "Thanks for the pizza."

"Sure." She hesitated and he held his breath, afraid she'd ask. Perversely, he was almost afraid she wouldn't. She gave him a small smile. "Eat it before it gets cold."

Then she turned and walked into the night before he could tell her how very familiar he was with cold.

And what a lonely place it was.

CHAPTER THREE

AN IMPERIAL SUMMONS was never a good thing.

Lainey had long thought of her mother's invitations to dinner as such a summons—and more often than not they included some well-meaning but completely off-base idea of her parents' to "improve her life."

She'd met her ex at such a dinner. And apparently she was the only one who saw it for the farce it had turned out to be.

Now, if Daniel had been a man like Ben maybe things would have been different. The thought wasn't as shocking as it might have been, considering she'd been unable to get Ben and the haunted look on his face out of her mind for the past two days. She hadn't overheard enough of his conversation to find out what was eating him alive, but she'd heard the pain layering his voice, each word laced with more than the last.

Still, Ben struck her as a fundamentally honorable man, not one who would marry for money without dumping his long-time girlfriend first. Like, say, her ex-husband. The good thing was her heart hadn't been involved—but her pride and self-worth had taken a beating.

Lainey sighed and turned through the thick stone columns into her parents' driveway. Since her parents were expecting her, the black iron gate stood open. She wound her way up the drive and parked in front of the massive log house that managed to be both rustic and majestic.

Lainey turned the car off and got out. On the plus side Grace, the cook, always put together fabulous meals, so she'd make sure she enjoyed that even while avoiding the bombs that were likely to be lobbed over the table. The front door opened even before she made it all the way up the carefully landscaped walkway.

"Lainey!" her father greeted her in his big voice.

"Hi, Dad." She allowed herself to be drawn into a hug. Tall and trim, Greg Keeler cut a handsome picture with his dark, youthful looks, a perfect foil to Jacqui's petite blond paleness. Even in their late fifties, they looked every inch the power couple they'd been for as long as she could remember.

"Come on in. We're in the family room."

He turned and Lainey followed him into the large room off the foyer, with its high ceilings, thick carpet and fireplace. While the outside screamed North Woods, inside the only concession to the house's rustic roots were the thick beams soaring overhead.

Lainey walked across the luxurious carpet, its velvety pile the color of cream, with nary a stain in sight. She tried to picture a baby crawling around in here and failed. Nothing about this room said *family*—even with the professionally shot family photos on the mantel. She vowed to make sure she raised her baby in an environment that was warm and welcoming, not precious and impersonal.

Her mother perched on the edge of a chair near the fire. A manila folder lay on an end table next to her.

"Hello, dear." Jacqui rose and offered her cheek to Lainey, who came around the end of the sofa to place the obligatory kiss.

"Hi, Mother."

"Have a seat." Her dad gestured toward the sofa and turned to the mini-wet-bar. "Can I get you anything to drink?"

Well, no. I'm pregnant. She swallowed the words. That would get this little pow-wow off to a roaring start. In fact it might create stains on the carpet from dropped or flying liquor. "No, thanks."

He raised an eyebrow but said nothing as he mixed his drink quickly and took the seat opposite Jacqui.

Lainey flicked her gaze between both of them. There was no reading her parents. Whatever they'd done, they wouldn't be smug, since they'd consider it a necessary move. She might as well get it over with. "What's going on?"

Jacqui frowned a little. "Wouldn't you rather eat first? Grace has a lovely roast chicken prepared."

Lainey's shoulders tensed at the deflection. "I'd like to know what's going on." She looked at her father but his expression was unreadable. "Dad? Please?"

He down set his drink—a screwdriver, no doubt. "Might as well cut to the chase. Lainey, we want to help you."

Oh, no. Her stomach lurched. She threaded her fingers together in her lap to keep from shaking. She kept her tone measured. "Help me how?"

"With your little shop, honey." Jacqui reached for the folder and the hairs went up on the back of Lainey's neck.

"My little shop? What have you done, Mother? Dad?" She heard the note of panic in her voice. She'd been safe, had rented the business from Esther Browning, what could they possibly—?

Jacqui beamed. "We thought you'd be pleased to know we bought your building."

The room tilted a little and Lainey gripped the arm of the chair, struggling to focus on her mother's clueless face. She couldn't have heard correctly. "I'm sorry—what? Why?"

"You're having such a hard time getting this going, and Esther was worried about making ends meet. You know she needs the rent to live on, dear."

My parents are now my landlords. The realization swept through her, followed closely by rage. "I've never paid late. Not one single payment." She bit off each word. If nothing else, she prided herself on that. She knew her elderly landlord depended on that income, and made absolutely sure those payments went out on time.

Her father cut in. "Of course not. But there's reason to believe you might have a hard time making them, so we thought this would help both of you out."

Lainey sucked in a breath. Poor Esther. The prospect of having the building all paid for, most likely in cash, must have been powerful. She'd done what was best for her, and Lainey refused to fault her for that.

Keeping her voice even, she asked, "But you didn't think maybe you should ask me? See how I'm doing?" Of course the documents would have been anything but reassuring, but still… Betrayal rose in her throat, the taste bitter, and she swallowed hard. Why was it too much for them to think to include her in the decision making?

Jacqui looked surprised. Or would have if the Botox hadn't been working so well. "Well, we already know how you're doing. The whole town does. We've got your best interests at heart, dear. Always."

Lainey shut her eyes. How often had she heard that little line? When would it actually prove to be true? "How exactly does this help me?" She braced herself for the kicker.

"Well, you won't have the monthly payment anymore. We won't make you pay rent. And you can live here now. We'll rent out that little apartment." Her mother sounded pleased, as if she'd truly solved a problem. Her father nodded in agreement as they exchanged a look.

She sucked in a sharp breath. "No. I can't live here." *How am I supposed to puke in private every morning? Hide my rounding belly? Raise my child here?* Panic seized her and she jumped up as her father's phone rang. He checked it, and rose.

"I've got to run. Lainey, we'll talk more later. But for now we feel this is the best thing for you."

He kissed her cheek and strode out of the room. Lainey stared after him, floored because both of her parents seemed to think this was a done deal and hadn't bothered to truly consider *her.* "Why did no one ask me? Has no one noticed I'm an adult? I'm not moving back home." Where she'd go, she didn't know. But it wouldn't be here.

Jacqui set her snifter on the table. "Of course you are, dear. That little place isn't good for you. We've got plenty of room. We can remodel your suite if you'd like. Daniel agrees you should be here."

Lainey whipped around so fast she nearly got dizzy. "He has no say in my life. None. We're divorced, remember?"

Jacqui leaned forward, her gaze earnest. "You were wrong, Lainey. He loves you and he's willing to give you a second chance. What is so bad about that? Now you don't have to struggle anymore. We've taken care of it."

Lainey stared back. Her mother really believed it. She could see the sincerity in the other woman's gaze, hear it in her voice. They didn't understand it was Lainey's problem and she wanted to be the one to solve it—or not. That had been the whole point of taking over the shop—to make it work by herself. Now the choice was gone.

She lifted her chin and met her mother's expectant gaze. "I'm not coming home." Each word came out crystal-clear and Jacqui's eyes widened. "I'm happy where I am. I love my job, my shop. My apartment. I'm not going to give it up, give you control of my life, because you can't accept I'm an adult and haven't chosen the path or the man you wanted for me."

Jacqui frowned. "Lainey, please be reasonable. You needed help. We gave it to you."

"Yes, but at what cost to *me*?" Despair rose and Lainey fought it back, preferring anger. There was really only one option here, since she wasn't going to walk away from the shop she loved. "What do I have to do to get it back?"

Jacqui sat back. "Pardon?"

"I want it back," she repeated. "I'll buy the building flat out from you. And you'll have to completely butt out of my life."

Jacqui frowned, as if this wasn't going the way she'd planned. "I don't think—"

Lainey stood up, the words she should have said years ago boiling out of her. "I'm not letting you force me into this. And there's no hope for Daniel. You have no idea what my marriage was like. *None.* I'd hope you'd want better for me, even if it's not what you would have chosen." She picked up her purse with shaking hands. "I'm going, Mother. I'll find somewhere else to live. And don't worry. I will make those rent payments on my shop. They will be on time. I'm never late."

Pulse roaring in her ears, she walked away before Jacqui could say anything else.

The nerve. Lainey pulled over a couple of miles past the house and sat for a minute, tears of rage pouring down her face. *The nerve.*

Poor Esther. Lainey hoped they'd at least given the woman a fair price. But while apparently not above blackmail, her parents weren't cheats. One small thing in this whole mess to take comfort in.

What she needed was a plan. One that could get her the money, and the time, to solve this herself—which was all she wanted. Just to prove she could do it—run a business, be successful on her own terms without any help from her family.

To show them she wasn't a screw-up, but just as worthy of being a Keeler as they were.

She fished a napkin out of the glove box and wiped her face. Crying wasn't going to solve anything. She put the car back in gear and headed for the public park at the lake. She'd spent many hours here as a kid, and later as a teen when she'd needed space. Sure, there was a private beach at her parents' home, but the park had swings and a playground, now upgraded to a fancy plastic playscape. They'd kept the old metal merry-go-round, her favorite thing in the park.

The gathering twilight and chilly breeze off the water ensured the park itself was empty, though a couple cars parked nearby indicated joggers still out on the loop that ran next to the water.

Lainey pulled the hood of her jacket up and settled on a swing. She scuffed her feet in the wood chips, then backed up, ready to swing. Back and forth she went, pumping her legs, stretching out in the swing until her hood slid off and her hair fell in her face when she leaned forward. The moon hung over the quiet lake, full and incandescent, a bright star to its left. *Star light, star bright, first star I see tonight.* A small laugh escaped her, followed by more tears. She'd gone way beyond childish wishes, even if as a kid she'd believed in the power of the first star. The tensions of her parents' betrayal slid away in the stinging wind, into the encroaching darkness. Finally she stopped pumping, let herself glide through the cool evening air, slowly coming to a stop.

A motion to her left caught her eye and she turned her head.

Ben Lawless sat on the merry-go-round, watching her. Her belly clutched. Oh, no. What was he doing here?

"Did it work?" Despite his low tone, she heard him clearly.

Caught, Lainey forced herself to meet his gaze. "Did what work?"

"The swinging. The tears. You looked like you were trying to get rid of something."

She tilted her head so it rested on the chain. No point in denying it. She didn't want to. "For the moment, maybe." Though the ache under her heart hadn't gone away.

Her parents had bought her building. She squeezed her eyes shut as another wave of betrayal washed over her. How had she not seen it coming?

When she looked back over at Ben he stood up from the merry-go-round, gave it a small shove with his hand. It wobbled in a slow circle. "For the moment?"

Lainey scuffed her foot in the wood chips. Was that an opening for her to talk, no matter how reluctantly issued? She almost laughed. Where would she start? With her parents? With her baby? With her ex-husband? With the father of said baby? "I don't know. Can we not talk about it?" The very thought of trying to explain the twisted mess her life had become exhausted her.

Ben laughed—a quick deep flash that sent tingles though her body. "As long as we don't talk about me."

His grief-stricken face flashed across her memory. "Deal." She hopped out of the swing and her balance shifted a bit. No doubt an effect of her pregnancy. She started toward the water, simply needing to move.

She was surprised when Ben caught up to her. He walked beside her, his arm almost brushing hers. Even without the contact she could feel the heat from his big body as hers seemed to be *way* too tuned in to him.

This was bad.

Distracted, she stumbled a bit on the uneven sand. He caught her arm—pure reflex, she was sure—especially because he let go of her almost as soon as he touched her, as though she'd burned him somehow.

"Careful," he said, his voice low.

"Thanks," she murmured, keeping her eyes on the ground. His scent, a yummy mix of soap and fresh air, drifted over to her. She curled her fingers into fists and shoved them in her pockets so she didn't do something stupid—like reach for him and bury her face in his chest.

Even as the urge confused and scared her she knew Ben wouldn't lie to her, use her, or treat her like a wayward child. Even with his secrets, he came across as sincere in a way she so wanted to believe in.

Except she was done with believing.

They stopped when they reached the lake. The water was almost mirror-still. Perfect for skipping rocks. When was the last time she'd done that? The moon was bright enough that she could see pretty well, so she started to hunt for flat stones. She didn't look at Ben, but could feel him watching her.

Strangely, not talking felt right. She didn't feel she needed to fill the night with chatter—after the bombshell her parents had laid on her that was a good thing—and he seemed to be quiet because he was more comfortable without words.

She picked up a rock—a flat disk, smooth and cold in her hand. She lined up and let it fly over the still water, counting twelve skips. She couldn't resist a little fist pump. She still had it after all these years.

"Not bad." Ben fingered his own rock. "My turn."

"Good luck," she said politely. She'd always been a top-notch rock-skipper. One of her many under-appreciated talents. She couldn't smother a small sigh. No doubt her mother would be appalled.

His rock flew over the water. Thirteen skips.

"Hmm." Glad for the distraction, Lainey narrowed her eyes when he turned to her, eyebrow raised. "I can beat that."

A small laugh escaped him and he looked surprised at the sound. Her heart tugged. Had he really gone so long in sorrow he'd lost laughter?

He leaned toward her, not close enough to touch, but close enough to see the challenge in his eyes. "You're on."

His warm breath feathered over her cheek and her little shiver had nothing to do with the chill in the air. "Good luck," she said again. The words came out a little husky, and she turned away quickly to look for more rocks. What was wrong with her? What was it about Ben Lawless that drew her in? It was wrong on so many levels. She was pregnant, for God's sake. And her life was a mess. There was no room for a man. Especially one with issues of his own.

It took everything Ben had not to ask why she'd been crying. The tracks from her tears were dry now, but even in the light of the moon he could see her beautiful blue eyes were red-rimmed. An unwelcome protective surge caught him off-guard and left a sour feeling in his stomach.

He couldn't protect anyone. He knew that. But tonight he'd been drawn in by her obvious distress. Since she was a friend of his grandma's it had seemed wrong just to walk away until he knew she was okay.

Yeah, that was all it was. A favor to Grandma.

Riiiight...

Choosing to ignore his inner voice, he let his gaze follow her as she searched for rocks along the water's edge. The moon's light turned her hair to silver as she lifted potential candidates, weighed them in her hand, then discarded some and slipped others into her pockets. That unfamiliar smile tugged at his mouth. She took this seriously. He'd do the same.

He picked up a few rocks of his own and was ready when she came back. Determination sparked in her eyes. He swallowed hard. "You ready?" If she noticed the rasp in his voice she didn't show it.

"I'm ready. I'll go first."

She stepped forward to the edge of the water and Ben allowed himself to admire her slender figure as she let the rock fly and stood, as if she were holding her breath, until it sank, leaving an expanding ring of ripples on the water's surface.

"Ten skips."

"Not bad." He moved up next to her. "But let me show you how it's done."

He was rewarded with an eye-roll. He bit back another grin.

He took his turn and after nine skips she turned to him, her glee barely contained. "*That's* how it's done?"

In spite of himself he laughed again, the feeling foreign after so many months of not being able to. It felt—good. But scary, too. Here in the moonlight, with a beautiful woman who wanted nothing from him, playing a silly game, he was almost relaxed.

Back and forth they went, and after six stones each Ben sent her a look. "This is it. Winner takes all."

She arched a brow and pulled out her final stone. "Really? What does the winner get?"

"Bragging rights."

"Good enough." She pulled out her final stone and readied herself. She let it fly and Ben watched it, counting the skips until it sank.

"Fifteen skips." Triumph filled her voice. "Beat that, Ben."

He took his turn and they both watched as his rock sank after twelve. "You win."

She did another fist-pump. "Yay. I like to win." Then frowned. "No offense."

He shook his head. "None taken." He hesitated. "Better?"

She nodded, but he saw the shadow that fell over her features. "Yes. Thank you for staying."

He turned with her to walk back. "No problem. You're my grandma's friend."

There was the tiniest of hitches in her step. "Right. Of course."

He forced himself to ignore the hurt in her tone. He needed to build the distance between them back up. But when she turned those big blue eyes on him something long buried inside him cracked. "Lainey—"

She gave a little shake of her head as she reached her car. "Thanks again."

To hell with it.

Ben turned her around as she fumbled in her pocket for her keys. Her eyes widened and her lips parted, but before she could say anything he dipped his head and covered her mouth with his.

After a heartbeat her cold mouth opened and let him into her warmth. God, it had been so long since he'd felt anything, *anything*, and she was warm and soft and so, so sweet. He fisted his hand in her hair, to angle her head so he could go deeper, and her moan lit fires inside him that had long been dormant.

For a reason.

He broke the kiss and stepped back, his ragged breath catching in his chest. God, what had he done?

She blinked up at him, her gaze smoky and slightly confused. Then her eyes cleared and a look of pure horror crossed her face.

"I've got to go," she said, yanking her keys out of her pocket.

"Lainey, I'm sorry." As soon as the words were out he knew they were the wrong thing to say.

Her back stiffened as she unlocked the car. "It's forgotten." She got in the car and slammed the door.

He stood in the cold and cursed as her taillights disappeared out of the park. Hell. He'd just made a huge mess of something he had no right even to start.

And he had no idea how to fix it.

CHAPTER FOUR

"THEY DID WHAT?" Beth's words ended on a small shriek. The look on her face would have been comical if Lainey could muster the energy to laugh. "No way. Is that even legal?"

"Unfortunately," Lainey said as she selected a few silk 'mums for the centerpiece she was working on.

"They're kicking you out," Beth breathed. "I never thought—"

"It's not technically a kick out," Lainey corrected her. "It's a very strong suggestion I move in with them." And a heck of a way to do it, too. Though where in the budget she'd find the money to rent a place plus continue to pay her parents she didn't know.

How had it not occurred to her parents that their "helping" would put her in this kind of bind?

Beth frowned. "Are you going to? How would that work with the baby?"

A chill ran through Lainey. "I can't think of anything I want less than to live there. Especially since my mother is apparently in cahoots with Daniel. I'm going to ask Rose if she knows of any rental houses. I know she owns a couple."

Maybe she'd get lucky and one would be open. On the other hand, that would make Rose her landlord, and she wasn't sure she wanted to risk extra contact with Ben.

The kiss flashed through her mind and a delicious little shiver ran through her. It had been a mistake, which he'd acknowledged. She had to agree. But a small part of her was hurt. She'd spent much of her adult life being made to feel everything she did was a mistake. To hear it after something as sweet as that kiss, on top of her parents' antics, had cut deep.

"Wow." Beth shook her head and cut a length of ribbon. "I'm just floored."

"Yeah, me too." Lainey fitted the 'mums into the floral foam and stepped back. "These look nice. Let's get them in the window."

It took a nice chunk of time to redo the front windows with a fall theme geared toward Halloween. Lainey was pleased with the result. She glanced at the clock. Almost noon. "I need to call Jon and tell him."

Beth came around the counter. "Do you need me there?"

Lainey gave her friend a hug. "Thanks, but, no. I'll be fine. I just need to get it over with."

She climbed the stairs to her apartment with butterflies roiling in her stomach. She and Jon hadn't even bothered to exchange contact info. It had been pretty clear how forgettable the whole thing was—or would have been except for the baby.

Her hands shook as she sat down at the computer and pulled up the website she'd found for Jon's company. Since California was three hours behind Michigan it was early morning there, so she hoped she had a chance of catching him at his office.

It took two tries to dial the number correctly, but amazingly she got through. His assistant sounded about twenty and possessive, and Lainey bet Jon valued looks over work ethic. How could she have such poor judgment when it came to men?

"Jon Meier." His crisp voice sent a chill over her skin.

"It's Lainey Keeler. We—ah—met at the reunion." She stumbled a bit over the words. How exactly did one phrase *one-night stand* for polite company?

A pause. "Lainey. What's going on?" His tone was wary.

Lainey stared at the ceiling of her living room. It seemed there was only one thing to say and one way to say it. "I'm pregnant."

The silence roared in her ears. She gripped the small phone tighter.

"Jon?" she ventured after a few seconds.

"I'm here," he said, sounding slightly strangled. "Are you sure it's mine?"

Indignation spiked. "Of course it's yours. Who else's would it be?" Like she was some slut.

He said a clear and succinct curse word and Lainey winced.

"I'm sorry," he said, his voice low. "But there's something you should know."

Her heart kicked up in a pattern of dread. Those words never meant anything good. "What's that?"

She heard him exhale roughly. "I'm married."

Nausea hit Lainey like a freight train. Oh, God. *Married?* How had she not known? He was just like her ex-husband. Her stomach rolled and she sank down on the floor, hand pressed over her mouth. *Oh, no. No, no.*

"Lainey? Are you still there?"

I'm married. The words almost physically crawled over her skin. She'd played a role in the betrayal of a marriage. *What Daniel did to me.* "Oh, my God. How could you? You cheated on your wife." She couldn't keep the horror and disgust out of her voice.

There was a rustle of paper. "Well, in my admittedly weak defense, we were going through a rough patch. She doesn't—she doesn't know. I can't have her know. I can pay to take care of it, though, if you'd rather not have it."

It took her a second to sort through the numerous atrocities in those sentences. "Are you—are you offering to pay for an abortion?"

"You're what? Eight weeks? Early enough. Listen, Lainey—"

"No." The word came out furious and flat. Temper rose like bile in her throat, a sharp burn.

"I can't be a father to that baby, Lainey. My wife—she's pregnant, too. I can't risk—"

"Can't risk what? Her finding out what a slime you are?" She couldn't help the angry words. Not because she wanted him in her life, or the baby's, but because she'd given her child this kind of man for a father. The same kind of man her ex was. She pressed her hand over her eyes, willing the tears of anger and frustration away.

He let out a sigh. "Something like that. Listen, I haven't been the best husband, okay? I get that. But we are finally getting on the right track again. I can't—I just can't risk it."

Lainey sucked in a breath. The depth of his deception hit her hard. She couldn't get involved in his mess, though. She and her baby would stay above this.

She couldn't keep the disgust out of her voice. "I want you to sign off on all parental rights. I don't want you in my child's life."

"I'll talk to my lawyers," he said after a moment, and she allowed herself to breathe again. "I don't see how I could be involved even if I wanted to be. My wife..." His voice trailed off. Then, "I'm sorry, Lainey. I really am. But—you understand?"

Your poor wife. Lainey truly felt for her. She could see her own ex-husband pulling this exact same stunt. For all she knew he had. The thought made her even angrier.

"What I understand is you are a cheating, lying bastard. When will I hear from you?"

"End of the week," he said, apparently unfazed by her description of him. "I'll need your contact info. I'd prefer to communicate through email, if we need to discuss anything further."

"Fine with me." She gave him the relevant information and hung up, mind whirling. The sick feeling wouldn't recede. Most likely she'd get what she wanted, but at what cost? What could she tell her baby? The loss here was truly Jon's, but her baby deserved a father.

She dropped her face into her hands. Given her track record with men who seemed great on the surface but were total losers, she wasn't sure she could trust herself to know a good man when she met him. She pushed herself off the floor and went to get a glass of water.

Ben flashed across her mind. He was a good man. His kiss. His quiet playfulness last night. Even though it had seemed as if he was coming out of a deep shell, for that scant hour she'd spent with him he'd been more real than her husband or Jon had ever been. Maybe it was because he hadn't wanted anything from her. Maybe it had to do with the other two men being cheaters. Another wave of nausea flowed over her and she put her head back in her hands. She'd been with a married man. How had she not known? How could she know, with no ring and no mention of a wife?

She went back downstairs. A couple of months ago her life had been pretty simple. Keep her shop open and stay out of her parents' line of fire. Period. Now she was looking at single motherhood and her parents buying their way into her life and pulling her ex along—not to mention her odd connection to Ben.

Maybe one of these days she'd do something the easy way, instead of somehow making everything as difficult as possible.

* * *

Lainey called Rose that evening and at her friend's invitation went over to her house. She didn't want to see Ben, seeing as how the awkwardness level there would be epic, but she wasn't going to avoid her friend. Plus, being with someone who didn't want to manipulate her sounded wonderful.

She didn't see Ben's truck, which was both a relief and an unexpected disappointment. Ignoring the disappointment part, she saw he'd been busy. The framework for the ramp was already in place. It touched a little sweet spot in her that he took his grandma's issues so seriously.

Rose opened the kitchen door with a concerned look. "Hi, honey. Come on in. Everything okay?"

She stepped in with a smile. "Yes. Just a little tired." She didn't ask where Ben was as she slipped her jacket off. She told herself she didn't care. Not to mention it was very important that Rose did not realize Lainey's conflicted emotions regarding Ben. She didn't want any matchmaking attempts, and she doubted Ben would appreciate it, either. Possibly less than she did, if his aloof manner was any indication.

But, oh, the man could kiss.

"Dear, you look a little flushed. Are you sure you're okay?" Rose wheeled over to the table.

Her face heated even more. She couldn't very well tell the older woman she'd kissed her grandson, so she took a seat at the table and filled Rose in on her parents' bombshell.

Rose frowned when she'd finished. "I'm sorry, Lainey. I understand they mean well, or think they do, but they really don't take you into consideration, do they?"

Lainey stared at the table, a small knot in her throat. It was the truth. "Not really."

Rose reached over and squeezed her hand. "Well, as it happens I've got a little place you can rent." Her surprise must have shown on her face because Rose chuckled. "I do. I've got a little rental house over by the lake. The same couple has rented it for—oh, goodness—decades. Thirty years or so? Anyway, they moved out a couple weeks ago. Decided to retire in Florida."

Lainey opened her mouth, then closed it. Hope surged through her. "I—wow. Really?"

"Of course. Two bedrooms. Nice backyard. It's a little Cape Cod. Not real large, but plenty big for you and your cat."

Relief rushed through her. "It sounds wonderful."

Rose reached for the phone. "It needs a little work. Nothing major. Just some freshening up and some minor repairs. Why don't you go take a look? Ben's over there now, assessing what all needs to be done. He seemed to think it could be ready in around a week or so. You can even pick your paint colors."

Ben was there. Anticipation zipped through her, too quick for her to stifle. She didn't see a way to refuse without raising Rose's suspicions. "All right. I'd love to see it, if you're sure?"

Rose waved a hand. "Of course I'm sure. I can't think of anyone I'd like more to have for a tenant than you. Let me call him real quick and you can head over."

Lainey followed Rose's directions to the house, which was on the other side of the lake from her parents' place, a block from the water. The little white house was charming, from what she could see as she pulled in the driveway behind Ben's truck. It had a garage, a front porch, and the backyard was fenced. A little shiver of excitement ran though her.

"It's very cute," she said aloud as she walked up to the front porch. The light was on. She knocked, then stuck her head in. "Hello?"

She'd been hoping somehow that Ben wouldn't be here, or that someone else would be here, too. Anything but just the two of them. Not that she couldn't control herself—of course she could—it was just the last thing she needed was another complication in her life. As Ben appeared in the living room archway she couldn't help but wish all complications could be so hot.

"Lainey?" Ben said, looking behind her. "I'm sorry. Grandma said there was a potential tenant coming to check the place out."

In spite of her nerves, Lainey laughed. *Oh, Rose.* "It's me. I'm the tenant."

"You?" His brow shot up. "I thought you lived above your shop."

Lainey closed the door behind her and unzipped her jacket. She couldn't quite keep her voice steady. "Not for long."

She saw understanding dawn in his eyes, but all he said was, "I see."

Awareness sparked between them, hot and deep, and she knew while he didn't mention it he was thinking about *the kiss.* Lainey pulled her gaze off him and focused on the wall behind him. He looked so good, even with the wary expression he seemed to wear perpetually. Except the other night, when he'd actually laughed. And kissed her.

Darn it. She shut her eyes. *Not helpful.*

"You okay?"

She opened them again and gave him a small smile. "Peachy." She gestured with her hand. "Can I look around?"

Ben stepped back out of the doorway. "Sure. Kitchen—

dining room through there—" he pointed to his right "—bedrooms. Bathroom that way. I'll be in the kitchen if you need anything." Then he disappeared.

She took a minute to wander around the room she stood in—a good-sized living room, with two large windows and a fireplace, flanked by two smaller, higher windows over built-in bookcases. The former tenants' drapes remained, but otherwise the room was bare. The floor was hardwood, scuffed and worn and in need of being redone. She rubbed the toe of her shoe on it. How would a hard floor be with a baby? Maybe she could get some thick rugs. The paint color was an odd shade of pinkish tan, but maybe that was the light from the overhead fixture, which was a little harsh. Still, it had charm and lots of potential.

She walked across the floor and it creaked under her feet. She heard banging and swearing from the direction of the kitchen, so she detoured that way down the short hall.

Ben was on his knees, bent over, half in the cabinet under the sink, and her gaze locked on his very fine butt and flexed thigh muscles. The back of his shirt had ridden up, exposing an inch or so of an equally nice back. She blinked and forced herself to refocus.

"Is there a problem?" she asked.

He scrambled back out from the cabinet, whacked his head and muttered another choice word. She winced.

"Sorry," she said. "Are you okay?"

"Fine." He stood up and rubbed the back of his head. "Need something?"

"Um…no. I heard some noise and thought I'd see what was going on in here." She looked at the array of tools and wet towels on the floor. "Maybe you need a plumber?"

Ben stared at her, then let out a sharp bark of laughter. "What I need is another wrench." He bent over and she tried very hard to keep her eyes off his butt and failed. She very much wanted to chalk it up to pregnancy hormones, except for the little fact she wasn't attracted to any other man but this one. He pulled out two pieces of what had been a wrench and held them up.

"Oh. That's not good."

"No kidding. Are you parked behind me?"

He was going right now? The little stab she felt couldn't be disappointment. It had to be relief. "Yes. I'll move my car."

He turned away to wipe his hands on the towel lying on the counter. She glanced around the room, noting the old but serviceable appliances, the Formica counters that were a bit worn, the old linoleum on the floor. The cabinets were in good condition. It was a nice size. It would work well for her.

"Not what you're used to, I'm sure," Ben said and she blinked at him.

"What isn't?"

He swept his hand out, indicating the room. "This."

It took her a second, then anger spiked. "Oh, for God's sake. Why would you think that?"

He just looked at her and she shook her head, sadness chasing the anger away. Just because she'd been raised in a wealthy household it didn't mean those things mattered to her. "You don't know me. At all. I'd appreciate it if you'd keep your judgments to yourself. I'll go move my car to the street."

Ben shut his eyes as she stomped off. He'd achieved his goal, which had been to drive her away, but he felt no sense of victory. Only shame. She'd looked way too hot, standing there in her jeans, boots and sweatshirt, with her hair up in a ponytail. None of it was even particularly form-fitting, but it was enough. Worse, he'd wanted to touch her, to feel her hot, responsive mouth under his again. That was dangerous. *Wanting* was something he tried to keep a lid on, along with feeling. He saw her headlights flash across the wall as she backed out of the driveway.

Now he needed to apologize. Whatever had prompted last night's crying jag had brought her here today, and it wasn't right for him to make it harder for her just because he was attracted to her. Or to lose a tenant for his grandmother.

So he went into the living room and didn't back down under the cold glare she leveled at him when she came through the door. "I'm sorry. I was out of line."

She considered him, her blue eyes cool. Finally she nodded. "You were. But I accept your apology. Next time don't assume you know anything about me."

I know how you kiss, he wanted to tell her. *I know how you feel in my arms, how soft your skin is under my hand. I know how your breasts feel against me.*

She must have read his thoughts on his face because her gaze skittered off his and she jingled her keys in her hand. He cleared his throat, trying to bring his thoughts back around.

"Okay, then. I'm going to go. If you leave before I get back you can lock the door behind you. Also, if you're considering renting this place, start thinking of paint colors. The sooner you can get them to me, the better. I can get started as soon as I finish a few repairs."

She nodded. "I will. I like it. So far I think it'll suit us just fine."

"Let me know." As he escaped out into the night, he wondered, *Who's us?*

CHAPTER FIVE

LAINEY SHUDDERED OUT a deep breath when the door closed behind him. There had been no mistaking the look on his face when she'd said he didn't know her. Odd that he could know her a little physically but not at all as a person.

It seemed to be a pattern. Her ex-husband had never attempted to really get to know her. He'd had his secretary take care of gifts and things. She'd allowed herself to pretend it was because he was busy, but she knew it had been because he'd never cared enough to find out.

Lesson learned.

She shoved all the thoughts away and walked down the hall to the bedrooms. Two of them, both of which were bigger than her bedroom at the apartment, plus a decent-sized bathroom. Another door led to an open and clean attic.

She went back to the kitchen, where she found a small pantry, an entryway by the back door with hooks for coats, and stairs to the basement. A quick scout revealed it to be clean and apparently dry, and she found the laundry hookups. At some point the space might make a good play area, if there was a way to cover the cement with carpet.

Back upstairs, she mused over paint colors as she went back to the bedrooms. She hadn't decided yet if she wanted to know if she was having a boy or a girl. Then she frowned. Either way, probably better to go neutral. That way she could forestall any questions for longer.

With a groan, she rested her head on the doorjamb. It wouldn't matter. Her little secret would out itself in a matter of weeks. Her pants were already feeling a little snug, and she had taken to wearing slightly baggy tops to cover up.

That wouldn't work much longer.

Her phone rang and she fished it out of her pocket. Seeing Rose's number, she answered.

"What do you think?" There was excitement in Rose's voice and Lainey had to smile.

"I love it."

"I knew it." The smugness in her friend's tone made Lainey laugh. "Come on back tomorrow and we'll sign a lease."

Lainey hesitated. "How much are you asking?" She'd told her parents she'd make rent payments anyway, and to add house rent on top of it would seriously stretch her already tight budget even more.

Rose named an amount that Lainey knew had to be way low, considering the size of the house and the location. "Rose, are you sure? That's not much."

"The house is paid for," her friend said, then added impishly, "And don't you dare argue with your elders."

Lainey laughed and flicked the light switch off in what would be the baby's room. "Well, when you put it like that…"

"You can help do some of the work if you want," Rose said. "Painting and such."

"Sure," Lainey said. How would that work with being pregnant? She'd have to make sure it was safe before she cracked open a paint can.

They talked a few more minutes, then Lainey hung up.

She locked the door behind her after one last look around. She would make a home here, for herself and her baby. But to get it she'd have to work with Ben.

Ignoring the little thrill that gave her, she started her car. She needed to remember Ben would leave. She was going to be a single mother. He was clearly struggling with some kind of issues of his own. None of that held hope for any kind of relationship.

And the very fact she'd even thought the word *relationship* in regard to Ben was troubling.

"So, I've found a place to live," Lainey told Beth as she carefully unpacked the latest shipment of flowers the next morning.

"Really? That was fast."

"Yep. It was perfect timing. Rose has an empty rental house."

Beth snipped the ends off a handful of lilies before plunging them in the water bucket. "Hmm. Will this put you in contact with her very appealing grandson?"

Lainey's face heated. Of course Beth *would* make that connection. "I wouldn't call him appealing," she hedged. *Liar.* "She wants me to help with the cleaning and painting and stuff. Which Ben is doing."

Beth set her scissors down, arched her brow. "Hmm. Is there something you're not telling me, Lainey?"

Lainey busied herself breaking down an empty box. Then she gave up. Her friend would figure it out anyway. "He kissed me."

Beth's mouth dropped open. "Holy cow! When? Was it amazing?"

Amazing? Lainey recalled the tender yet hot way his mouth had moved over hers and her whole body buzzed.

"Um… After the thing with my parents. And, yes, I guess it was."

"You *guess*?" Beth's eyes bugged out. "He doesn't look like the type to rate 'I guess' on the kissing scale."

She had a point. "Okay, yeah, it was amazing."

Beth grinned. "I knew it. So. Spill. What happened?"

Lainey filled her in on her visit to the park and finding Ben there. She finished with, "But it was a mistake. It won't happen again."

Beth shook her head. "Why not?" The front doorbell jingled and she pointed a finger at Lainey. "Don't go anywhere. We're not done here." Then she hurried out front and Lainey heard her greet the customer.

Lainey's phone buzzed in her pocket and she pulled it out. She didn't recognize the number, but answered anyway, tucking it under her chin as she reached for the next box of flowers. "Hello?"

"Lainey?"

Her blood froze. She'd recognize that smooth voice on the other end of the line anywhere. Flowers forgotten, she gripped the phone so hard it hurt.

"Daniel." His name fell like a razor off her tongue. "What do you want?"

He chuckled—a low sound that sent chills up her spine. How had it ever thrilled her? "Why, to talk to you, baby. It's been a long time. Can't I talk to my wife?"

"Ex-wife," she corrected, because it had been hard-won and it mattered.

"Whatever," he said, and she pictured him waving away her words with a sweep of his hand, like so many pesky flies. "It's just details. Can we get together soon? I'd love to see you."

She nearly dropped the phone as rage rolled through

her. "No. Way. I've got nothing left to say to you." As if he'd ever listened, ever heard her.

"Laine. It's been so long. I miss you. I made a mistake." The seductive tone of his voice made her skin crawl and she shivered.

"Yeah, so did I," she muttered. Her marriage had been one big fat mistake from start to finish.

"Lainey, please." Now he sounded almost pleading.

"No." Oh, it felt so good to tell him that. "I can't talk right now, Daniel. I'm at work."

He sighed. "So I've heard. Some little flower shop, right? It's not going well. Your mother said you're having some problems—"

"Having some problems?" she sputtered. His condescending tone had her teeth grinding together. This was the Daniel she knew. "It's a new business. I'm still getting it off the ground."

"Yes, but it's been—what?—nine months? It was an honest try but it's not getting better, Lainey. You need to face reality."

Hearing him voice her own fears made her stomach churn.

His tone turned slightly wheedling. "I'd love to help. I think we could make it work this time."

"Did she dump you?"

A beat, then, "I'm sorry? Who?"

"You don't want me, Daniel. You never did. You want what you think I stand for. Calling me and belittling my shop and the life I've built without you is not going to change my mind. Nothing will," she qualified. Fueled by her chat with Jon, she added, "You cheated. You used me. Don't call me again."

"Lainey, for God's sake, just listen. You can't do this."

His anger snapped through the connection and for a heartbeat she froze.

"I am doing it. Goodbye, Daniel." She clicked the little phone shut as hard as she could. Oh, for the days when a phone could be slammed in a cradle.

She dropped the poor phone on the worktable and leaned forward on her palms, head down, tried to settle. He was right. It had been nine months and she was still struggling. Hearing him voice her fears, in that awful tone, had tears burning her eyes. What if the scumbag was right?

More than that, couldn't he see if he'd really loved her he'd want her to succeed? Couldn't he see she knew what he really was?

More than all that, though, *what if he was right?*

Beth came in and started toward her in alarm.

"Lainey! Are you okay?"

"I'm fine," she said, and wished she meant it. "Daniel just called."

Beth sucked in a breath. "What? Wow, he's got some nerve."

She gave a sharp laugh. "Daniel's got nothing *but* nerve."

Her feelings must have shown on her face because Beth leaned in. "Listen to me. Don't you dare let him get to you. Look at what you've done here. It took a lot of guts to divorce him and buy this place. To keep your parents at arm's length despite their meddling. It hasn't been easy but you're doing it. Don't let them derail you now."

Lainey stared at her friend. "I never—you see it that way?"

Beth leaned over and gave her a one-armed hug. "Of course. And you should, too."

Lainey had never thought of it that way. Oh, she did what needed to be done, but usually well after it should have been done to begin with. Long after she'd been taken for a fool. It didn't strike her as something to be proud of.

The chime of the front door saved her from answering. "I'll get that," she said, and slipped past Beth.

Her friend's words were kind, but Lainey could only hope she was right. There was too much riding on her being able to make this work.

Ben wouldn't admit it to anyone, but he'd been listening for her car.

When he saw her park at the curb he tried to squelch a completely inappropriate spurt of anticipation. He told himself he didn't want this, didn't want her, but every time he saw her it got a little harder to believe it. So he'd rather be anywhere than here, having her help him paint. Just having her in the same house made his skin feel too tight.

Before, he would have asked her out. Seen where it went. But that was—before.

Now he needed to keep his distance—something he wasn't doing very well at.

He heard her come in the front door and turned his attention to finishing taping the bedroom so she could paint. Heard her quick, light steps coming down the hall. He tensed even more as she came in the room.

"Hi." Her voice was slightly tentative, as if she expected to be shot down.

He turned and simply took in the sight of her in old jeans, an oversize sweatshirt, her hair pulled up in a ponytail. She plucked at the sweatshirt uncertainly and he realized he was just standing there, gaping at her like a fool.

He cleared his throat. "Hi. You ready?"

She moved into the room a little farther. So as not to spook her, and to give himself some space, he busied himself popping the top off the paint can.

She came to stand beside him. "I can't wait to see this."

She'd gone to the hardware store on her lunch hour to pick the colors. He'd gone in later to pick them up. Efficient.

She made a little humming noise in her throat. "That's a little pinker than I thought."

"It'll look different once you get it on the wall. It will dry darker. They all do." He set the can off to the side. "You know how to do this?"

He looked up in time to see her shake her head.

He stood up. "You can change a tire, but have never painted a room?"

She looked a little sheepish. "Ah. No. My skills are a bit scattered, I'm afraid."

He didn't want to find that sweet. Or charming. *Damn it.* He turned back to the paint cans and cleared his throat. "Lucky for you, it's easier than changing a tire."

She laughed. "I hope so."

He stirred it and tipped the can to pour into a paint tray. He handed her a paintbrush. "This is pretty simple. You'll do around the trim first. I taped in here already."

He explained the method and showed her how to make small, careful strokes, taking care not to touch her. But she seemed to take equal care not to touch him. She smelled so good it was hard not to give in to temptation.

"When that's done you can do the rest. The roller's pretty simple. Just don't get too much paint on it. You'll be okay in here? I've got some other things to finish up."

Translation: he needed some space. Quickly.

She gave him a small smile and moved the ladder over by the open window. "I'll be fine. I'll call you if I need you."

Dismissed. He walked down the hall toward the kitchen, rubbing his hand over his face. He needed to get this house finished quickly, before the woman in the bedroom back there drove him out of his mind.

When Ben returned to check on Lainey it had only been a half-hour. He'd stayed away as long as he could, which was pitiful. He found her on the ladder by the window, carefully painting under the crown molding. He took a moment to admire the long, lean lines of her legs and the curve of her ass, which was hugged nicely by her soft jeans. Her sweatshirt lifted when she extended her arms up to paint, but not quite enough to give him more than a small but tantalizing glimpse of skin. He tried to shut the feelings down—kissing her had been a mistake because it had unleashed a whole torrent of feelings he didn't want. Couldn't afford. And he was now swamped with them.

This was bad.

She shifted then and he stepped fully into the room. The last thing he wanted was to get caught staring and make things even more weird. "Lainey—"

She turned quickly on the ladder and upset it enough to lose her balance. With a little cry, she fell awkwardly on her rear on the hard floor.

He crossed the room in about two strides. "Lainey! Are you okay?"

She twisted to sit up, wincing. The floor was hard and he imagined it had been quite a landing. She grabbed her ankle with a sharp hiss.

He knelt beside her, worry clouding his vision. "Honey. Are you okay?" When she shook her head he pulled up her jeans leg to see her ankle starting to swell. "We'd better get that checked out. You might need an X-ray."

Her gaze swung to his and he saw the horror and worry there. She shook her head. "No. No X-rays." She gave a forced little laugh. "I'm just clumsy."

"Your ankle—"

"No."

He sat back. "Lainey, listen—"

"I'm pregnant," she whispered and he drew back to stare at her.

The word rang in his head. *Pregnant.* And he'd been kissing her and wanting her—someone else's woman.

She must have seen the expression change on his face because she grabbed his arm. "The father—he's not in the picture. I'm in this alone. My balance is off. That's why I fell. And X-rays might be bad for the baby."

"What kind of man walks out on his responsibility?" he said, not really expecting an answer, but outraged on her behalf.

She gave a humorless little laugh. "One who misrepresented himself. I'll be fine." She tugged her pant leg back down. "I have to ask—no one but my friend Beth knows this yet… Please—don't say anything to Rose. I'll tell her, but…" She hesitated. "I didn't mean to tell you."

"I understand. I won't. But the father—" For some reason he seemed to be stuck on that fact more than anything.

She cut him off with a slash of her hand. "He knows. He's not on board, so to speak."

A surge of anger welled in Ben. A baby should have a father. And here was a man, apparently alive and well, not willing to take on the responsibility for the little life that he'd created. A responsibility that a good man, like Jason, hadn't been able to keep even though he'd wanted to. "His loss."

Her gaze shot to his and she grimaced slightly. "Damn straight. Can you help me stand?"

"Let me check that ankle first." At her confused expression, he added, "I'm a firefighter and an EMT. I'm not a substitute for a doctor or an X-ray, but I may be able to tell if it's broken."

"Oh." She extended her leg slowly and inched up her jeans.

He removed her shoe carefully but didn't miss her wince. With careful fingers he probed her slim ankle. Her skin was smooth and soft and he was a total heel for his completely unprofessional physical response to touching her.

"I don't feel anything broken," he said. "Let me help you stand."

He got to his feet and took both of her hands in his, trying not to feel the heat her soft touch generated in him. He gave a gentle pull and she hopped up on one foot, overbalanced, and landed on his chest. His arms went around her before he could stop them and he looked down into her beautiful, upturned face. There was confusion and pain and heat and wanting in her blue gaze, and his groin tightened at the press of her breasts against his chest.

He cleared his throat. Kissing her was *not an option. Not an option, not an option,* chanted the loop in his brain, but he wanted so badly to lose himself in it, in her, in this—

Pregnant woman.

He cleared his throat and loosened his hold but didn't let her go fully. "So…um…how's the ankle?" His voice was a little rough.

She rested it on the floor and pulled back a bit, putting a little weight on it. Her wince spoke volumes and he steadied her with his hands on her waist. "Lainey. Please. I know I didn't feel anything broken but some types of breaks I wouldn't necessarily feel. Do you need to go to the hospital?"

She gave a little hopping motion and moved backwards.

"No. I'm okay. It's sore, but I can take acetaminophen for it. I want to finish this."

Somehow she hadn't upended the paint when she fell off the ladder, even though she'd dropped the brush on the drop cloth. He took the tray off and poured the paint back in the can so he wouldn't reach for her again. She'd felt far too good in his arms.

But she was pregnant. And even with the father out of the picture he couldn't risk a relationship with her or her baby. He wasn't that kind of guy. Not anymore.

"We'll finish tomorrow. Right now you need to get that ankle up with ice on it. Don't argue," he added when she opened her sexy little mouth to do just that. "And I want you to promise me you'll go in tomorrow if it's worse or not getting better."

She pressed her lips together, then nodded. "Okay. You're right."

"I'll drive you home. You'll need help up to your apartment, right?" He'd get her home, get her settled. It was the least he could do for her, for his grandma's friend. "Tomorrow I'll bring you your car. Leave me your key."

He saw all the arguments cross her face. "I don't want you to go to any trouble—"

"No trouble." He caught her chin, unable to stop the action. The surprise in her eyes licked him like fire. "Lainey. You need a little help. You need to be careful so you don't hurt the baby."

That got her attention and she nodded. "Right. Okay. Thank you."

He swung her into his arms. She let out a little, "Eeep!" and her arms went around his neck.

He gave a little chuckle, surprised by the sound. "Relax. I've got you."

The scary part was how damn good she felt in his arms.

How right. How oddly protective he felt of the baby. He hadn't seen the swell of her belly, but her sweatshirt prevented that.

He cut his thoughts off right there. There was nowhere for this to go that could end well. He would be leaving as soon as he had his grandma squared away and his confidence back. He'd only hurt Lainey and he couldn't bring himself to risk it.

CHAPTER SIX

WHAT WAS SHE thinking?

Lainey winced as she buckled her seat belt and Ben walked around the truck to get in. Holy cow. She'd just blurted out her secret to this man, and she hadn't even told his grandma—her friend—yet. Somehow her filter kept shutting off and then her mouth took over.

"I'm not the type who sleeps around," she blurted as soon as he got in the truck. *Ack!* There went the filter again. Maybe it was the pain in her ankle? Yet for some reason it was very important he understand.

He fitted the key in the ignition. His jaw was tense. "I didn't say you were. Things happen."

Yes, they did. She was living proof that *things* tended to happen to some people more than others. She stared out the window, not wanting to see him even in profile, lit by the dash lights. It wasn't his fault he kept showing up when she was falling apart, though it had happened with alarming frequency since she'd met him.

The drive home was tense but Lainey had no desire to talk. Her ankle throbbed and she tried to focus on that rather than the fact she'd told Ben about the baby. Told an almost perfect stranger who'd kissed her, for God's sake. There was a kind of intimacy that they were both pretty good at ignoring. And she'd just added to it by blurting out that she was pregnant. A little panic raised its head. It had been far, far easier to tell him than it should have been. What was it about him that made her spill her secrets? Was it because he was so different from her ex-husband? She frowned. Even that didn't fully make sense, since she barely knew him. But something about him spoke to her, soothed her. Almost as if she recognized him somehow, on a deeper level.

She gave herself a mental shake. Wow. That really didn't make sense. Maybe she'd somehow managed to hit her head when she fell. Or the pain in her ankle was making her a little crazy.

Ben pulled in front of the shop and she reached down to unbuckle the seat belt. "Well. Thanks for the ride," she said brightly. "Sorry to put you out."

He caught her hand. In the dim glow of the streetlights, he looked as surprised as she was at the contact. "You could never put me out. Stay there. Please. Let me help you down."

"I can—"

"Of course you can," he interrupted. "But you don't want to risk a fall that might hurt the baby or further damage the ankle. And you might need some help navigating those stairs."

Darn it. He was right. "Okay."

He gave her a small smile before he slipped out of the truck. "It's okay to need help, Lainey."

She watched him walk in front of the truck through the wash of the headlights and couldn't help but think he wasn't totally correct. Needing help didn't make her weak, but it left her open to people like her parents and their manipulations. It was safer to rely on herself than sort through the motivations of others.

He opened the door and reached for her. It was a little

awkward to slide out into his arms, and she was surprised when he didn't put her down, instead settled her into his arms. She didn't want to admit how good the hardness of his chest felt against her side, how incredibly good he smelled.

"This is easier if you relax a little," he said close to her ear.

She looked up to see humor spark in his eyes. The humor died, though, when his gaze fell to her mouth and his arms tightened perceptibly around her.

She caught her breath at the dark heat she saw there and an answering one rose in her. It wouldn't take much, just a slight shift…

A car drove by and the spell was snapped. He cleared his throat and started for the door.

Her face burned. Good Lord, what *was* this?

She forced herself to relax into his solid chest. Weird moments aside, it felt good to lean on someone. Just for a minute. His heart beat faster against her ribs. Its rhythm matched that of her own and she wondered if it was from the moment they'd shared or the exertion of carrying her. The coolness of the evening did nothing to counteract the warmth he generated in her.

He got her upstairs and she unlocked her door.

"Sit," he said as he steered her gently toward the couch, and she sank down gratefully.

He put a pillow under the ankle. She couldn't help but notice how he sucked all the air out of the room and made her small space seem even tinier.

"I'll get you ice and some acetaminophen. Where do you keep it?"

"Bathroom, in the medicine cabinet," she said, adjusting the pillow. Not because it needed it but because then she didn't have to look at him and see—what? Or maybe, more accurately, he wouldn't see what kind of effect he had on her.

"All right." He went in the kitchen. "Hey, kitty," she heard him say, and her heart tilted just a bit. Then, in a louder voice, "Where are the glasses? And do I need to feed the cat? She's looking at me like she expects something."

She swallowed a laugh. "She does. There's a can of food in the fridge. You can put the rest of it in her dish. And glasses are in the cupboard to the right of the sink."

She listened to the sounds in the kitchen, the low murmur of his voice as he talked to the cat, the opening and closing of the cupboard, the rattling of ice. She rested her head on the back of the couch and shut her eyes. No one had ever taken care of her before. Such a little thing—ice for her ankle, feeding the cat, water for the pills. Not earth-shattering. Yet it was somehow.

He appeared with the items and placed ice, wrapped in a towel, over her ankle. "That okay?"

The gentleness of the action nearly undid her. She swallowed hard. "Yes. Thanks."

"Here's the water. Hold on while I get the pills."

He headed down the hall, looking first to the left—her bedroom—then to the right—her bathroom. Where she'd thrown bras she'd hand-washed over the shower rod. She shut her eyes in mortification. There was a brief pause as he entered the bathroom—no doubt he'd gotten an eye-ful—then the rattling of the pill bottle. When he came back down the hall he didn't actually make eye contact. Then again, neither did she.

"Here you go." He plopped the pills in her palm. Was it just her, or were his fingers slightly unsteady? "Can I call anyone for you?"

She almost laughed. "No. I'm all set, thanks."

He cleared his throat. "All right, then. I'll bring you

your car tomorrow. If you need anything, call me. Where's your phone?"

She tugged her purse over and pulled the phone out. He took it from her and added his number. "Now you have no excuse. I'm serious. Especially if you need help with those stairs in the morning." He handed the phone back and this time their fingers lingered for a heartbeat.

Breathless, she tried to smile. "I will. Um…thank you. For everything."

He stepped back. "No problem."

When the door shut behind him she flopped back on the cushions and pressed both hands over her eyes, unsure if she should laugh or scream.

She was in way deeper trouble than she'd thought.

Ben stared at the game on the TV above the bar. He couldn't have told anyone who was playing, much less the score, and he was only vaguely aware it was a hockey game. All he could see was Lainey's perfect mouth forming the words *"I'm pregnant"*.

They still packed a punch. It wasn't even his kid, and he'd never meet the baby—no doubt he'd be long gone by the time Lainey gave birth. In fact, it was most likely he'd never talk to her again, unless they ran into each other though Rose somehow. So why the hell did it matter?

He shifted on the stool. Lainey was dangerous. The kind of dangerous that made him want what he couldn't have. It wasn't fair to Jason—or Callie, for that matter. What right did he have even to think about pursuing a woman—Lainey—when Callie's husband was gone?

He took a swallow of the beer he couldn't even taste. He was pretty sure the bitterness in his mouth came from his own feelings rather than the drink in his hand.

Pregnant.

He'd felt a stab of jealousy straight to his soul when she'd looked at him with those big blue eyes and whispered those words. No use passing it off as anything but that.

What could he offer her? He didn't even know if he could do his job anymore. That anxiety was ever-present, hovering in the back of his mind. Shading everything he did. It mixed with guilt into a potent brew of shame and sorrow.

So, no, he wasn't in any shape to pursue her. Therefore, being jealous was a complete waste of time and energy. Still, he'd felt a roaring protectiveness when she'd fallen. And far more than that when he'd walked in her bathroom and seen those lacy, sexy bras lined up on the shower rod.

God help him. He was getting in way over his head and all he'd done was help her. But something about her drew him in and he couldn't seem to walk away. All those feelings he'd walled off…? Yeah. He was in danger of drowning in them if he didn't get them under control fast.

It didn't matter. He set aside his half-empty beer, since he couldn't even taste it, and signaled for his bill. He wasn't getting anywhere having a pity party and it was a waste of time anyway. Might as well go home, where there were at least projects he could do to stay busy.

He entered the house quietly, but his sharp-eyed grandma was in the living room, knitting. He couldn't tell what it was but her hands flew and the needles clicked together sharply. She looked up when he came in.

"So. How was it?"

Ben sat down opposite her, since it seemed rude to stand and talk when she was all settled in. He outlined the progress he'd made on the house, then hesitated.

Rose arched a brow. "What?"

He debated how much he could say and keep Lainey's secret safe. "She twisted her ankle," he said finally. "Stepped wrong off the ladder."

Rose's hands stopped moving. "Is she okay?"

"I checked it out," he said. "She was adamant about not going to the hospital."

"She needs an X-ray," Rose muttered and Ben sighed.

"I suggested it but she shot me down." True enough.

Rose sighed and her needles started moving again. "I bet."

"I offered to call her mother, but she said no." He wasn't fishing, exactly, but he was curious as to why Lainey seemed to think she was on her own when she had family nearby.

Rose snorted. "That woman doesn't have a maternal bone in her body. And that ex of hers—" She pressed her lips together tightly. "Well. Anyway. I'd better call her— make sure she's okay. I wish you'd brought her back here."

Ben was pretty sure Lainey didn't want Rose to figure out about the pregnancy. As Rose dialed Lainey's number he took a good look at the knitting project on her lap. The soft colors and small size looked an awful lot like a baby blanket. But he wasn't going to ask any questions.

They'd each keep Lainey's secret.

He hung around, fixing himself something to eat he really didn't want in the kitchen, but he wasn't going to admit that. When he went back in the living room Rose was hanging up and frowning.

That protective instinct reared back up and he forced himself to keep his voice level. "Is she okay?"

Rose's gaze flicked to his. "She's hurting."

Ben started to stand. "I can go—"

Rose shook her head. "She won't come. Thinks she has to be strong." She gave him a pointed look. "Like some-one else I know."

He opted not to touch that comment. "I've got to get her car to her tomorrow."

"That's good. Then you can see if she's okay in person. She's likely to not admit it over the phone."

She had a point.

He cleared his throat. "Sounds good. You need anything before I go take a shower?"

Rose shook her head, her hands flying once more over the blanket. "Thank God for DVR. Got one more show to watch. I'm all set, thanks."

He chuckled and walked toward the stairs. She said his name softly. When he turned, she looked at him, her faded blue gaze serious.

"She needs someone like you."

Ben froze as the words pinged around in his heart. "No. No, I'm not what she needs."

"Ben." Her voice was sharp. "You are exactly what she needs. Don't sell yourself short."

He had nothing to say to that. As he went up the stairs his heart was heavy. He wasn't what Lainey needed. He was too damaged to be enough for anyone.

Still. He regretted not being able to have the chance.

Where there's smoke, there's fire.

Ben could see the black plume of smoke the next morning from the front porch of his grandma's house, where he'd been working on the ramp. It was coming from the other side of town. *Lainey's side.*

That thought bumped him into action. He'd go check on her, make sure—just make sure. Since he had to take her car back anyway, this gave him the excuse. And she wouldn't be moving real fast after that fall, so no one would think twice if he checked on her.

"I'm going to take Lainey's car back," he told his

grandma, who was in the kitchen with her Sudoku book.
"You need anything while I'm out?"

She tipped her glasses down her nose. "Everything
okay?"

He hesitated. "There's a fire."

She gave a small nod. "We've got good people here,
Ben. Maybe you should be one of them?"

He opened his mouth, then shut it again. He shook his
head, grabbed his jacket from by the back door and hurried to his truck.

It only took a few minutes to drive to the other house.
From this angle it was hard to tell precisely where the fire
was, but he could smell the smoke. He flexed his hands
on the wheel as he turned onto the street and pulled into
the rental house's driveway. He started Lainey's car and
headed for downtown.

He whipped the car into a spot down the block from
Lainey's shop and jogged across the street toward the
smoke. He needed to see, to know if he could handle it.
Now he could see ash floating in the air, and he heard the
wail of sirens. Tension built in his shoulders and he rolled
them in an effort to release it.

He took a deep breath of the smoky air and coughed as
he turned down a side street to see a fully engulfed building. He stayed well back from the cordoned-off area. Fire
didn't fascinate him the way it did other people. It was an
enemy, a force, a beast to be tamed and conquered. Seeing
it lick gleefully at the building gave him no thrill.

He watched the firefighters doing their job—*his* job—
and swallowed hard. This was what he was born to do, but
he wasn't sure he could ever go back. God, but he missed
it. He missed it like he'd miss his arm if he'd lost it. Missed
the adrenaline, the teamwork. The battle. It could be grim

work—messy, and damn hard—but, hell, there wasn't anything else he'd rather do.

When the roof caved in with a shower of sparks and the flames leapt higher he shut his eyes as nausea rolled over him. For a second he couldn't breathe. Finally he turned and walked away, disappointment lodging in his gut like a rock. He'd wondered—now he knew. He wasn't ready. Would he ever be?

He stopped in front of The Lily Pad, its bright windows and festive decor drawing him like a beacon through the cool, smoky air. He didn't want to examine his relief at finding her shop okay or his anger at himself for his reaction to the fire. Or the real reason the shop pulled him: the woman inside.

Every step closer tangled everything tighter inside him.

He pushed it all away and walked through the door.

Lainey looked up and gave him a small, startled smile. He didn't miss the flash of pleasure that crossed her beautiful face.

"Ben."

He tamped down his own reaction and pulled her key out of his pocket. "Thought I'd stop by and give you this." He moved forward and shook his head when she started to get up. "No, sit. How's the ankle?"

"Better today." She held out her hand and he pressed the key into her palm. Her skin was warm under his cool fingers. Her eyes widened slightly at the contact and he wondered if she felt it, too. The heat, the spark.

Sparks.

"Did you see the fire?" She shook her head as she slipped the key into her pocket. "Of course you must have. I can smell the smoke on your jacket. You said you're a firefighter, right?"

He cleared his throat, suddenly having trouble breathing. "Yeah. I did. I was." *Was.* His voice stuck a little on the word. Was he or wasn't he? Could he ever go back? What if he couldn't?

"Ben?" The concern in her voice made him wince. "Are you okay? You looked a little lost there for a moment."

Lost. That was a good word for him. "I'm fine. Sorry."

She studied him, and for a second he thought she'd ask him more questions. But her phone rang. She glanced at it, then at him.

"I'll get out of here." So he wouldn't touch her, he put his hands in his pockets. "Your car's down about half a block."

"Thank you," she murmured as the phone rang. "I appreciate it."

He didn't hang around as she answered the phone, but he did pause at the door and look back. Her eyes were on him and she blushed just a little as her gaze caught his. He swallowed hard and walked out into the smoky fall air.

Lainey let out a shuddering breath as she hung up the phone from an order. She'd managed to get all the information, but it had been hard, seeing Ben through the windows as he'd walked, slightly hunched against the wind, past the windows of her shop. She'd hoped—foolishly— he'd look back at her one more time. *Silly.*

She entered the last of the order information into the computer and stretched. While her ankle needed to be propped up, the position was uncomfortable for her back.

Beth breezed back in, to-go bag from the café in hand. She shook her head as she placed it on the counter. "Was that Ben I saw walking by? Was he here?"

Lainey took the offered sandwich and set it carefully on a napkin. "Just for a minute. He brought my car up here."

Beth waggled her eyebrows. "Is that all?"

Lainey sighed. His face—so closed up today, after how sweet he'd been last night. He'd shut down even farther when, in her apparently misguided quest to make conversation, she'd asked him about being a firefighter. Clearly a sore spot. "Yeah. That's all."

Beth clucked her tongue. "Too bad. He's hot. And the two of you would be so cute together."

She thought of how easily she'd fit in his arms last night, and the heat in his eyes, and a little shiver passed through her. "That's silly."

Beth shrugged and snagged a French fry. "Maybe. Maybe not. But you have to start somewhere, Laine."

She stared at her sandwich. No, she didn't. Not really. And Ben wasn't interested in her. Well, actually, that wasn't true. He was clearly interested in her. But he wasn't willing or able to take it anywhere.

And neither was she.

CHAPTER SEVEN

THE DOOR CHIMED and Lainey walked carefully out of the back room, not wanting to admit the little skip in her pulse was the hope it was Ben coming back, no matter how unlikely that was. She'd decided to ask him to her mother's gala, and didn't want to lose her nerve.

It was a complete surprise to see her brother. "Kevin?"

"Hey, little sis," Kevin greeted her with a smile. "What's going on? Mom said you're moving."

Lainey looked at her brother, still in his scrubs. He looked tired, and there were definite lines around his blue eyes, but his smile was warm.

She gestured to him. "Come on back. You stopped in to ask me that?"

"Well, I was on my way to Mel's Café for lunch and thought I'd stop in." When Lainey opened her mouth, he held up his hands. "No, I'm not here to convince you of anything. I'm just asking."

Lainey moved to the worktable and pulled out a length of pumpkin-colored ribbon she was using for a silk centerpiece. Kevin had rarely, if ever, been on the receiving end of their parents' ire. He was a surgeon, lived in an appropriate condo, and drove a nice car. No wife yet, but that wasn't held against him. "Did they tell you what happened?"

Kevin leaned on the table. Now his expression was concerned. "No."

She took a deep breath. "They bought this building."

Kevin cocked his head. "Doesn't it help you out?"

She stabbed a floral pin in with a little more force than necessary. "Kevin. They didn't ask me. They showed me the deed and said I had to move back home."

Kevin swore softly under his breath. "I'm sorry, Laine. Did they say why?"

"Of course. I'm not doing well here. Yet. It's been a struggle. And I guess they don't think that reflects well on them." She didn't mention Daniel. No point in muddying the waters.

"Are you?"

"Am I what?"

"Moving back home?"

She gave a sharp little bark of laughter. "God, no. I found a nice little house a friend of mine owns. I'm moving there—this weekend, in fact."

He chucked her under the chin, a gentle and brotherly gesture. "Good for you. I'm glad you stood up to them."

Emotion flooded her. She'd never really expected him to watch her back. "Thank you."

He stepped back. "Do you need help? I'm on call this weekend, but I can come over if I'm around."

She hesitated. Why not? Beth and her husband were helping, but she could use the extra pair of hands. "Sure. That'd be great."

"All right." He turned to go. "I'll be here at nine unless otherwise noted. That okay?"

"See you then," she said, and watched as he disappeared through the workroom door. Strange to have him in her corner. Maybe she'd walled herself off from her brother with her own feelings of inadequacy and inferiority. If so, shame on her. It seemed Kevin might actually be an ally.

God knew she could use one.

That evening, Ben looked up from the whine of the saw to see Lainey standing there, her eyes hooded in the dim light of the rental house's garage, her hands twisted into knots in front of her. He hit the switch on the saw and silenced it.

"Hey."

She swallowed hard. "Hey."

He came toward her and she tipped her head back to look at him. He saw anxiety swimming in her eyes and he closed his hand into a fist to keep from stroking her face.

"Let's go outside—out of the dust." He took her elbow and lightly steered her toward the porch.

"What are you doing in there?"

"Repairing one of the cabinet doors. Do you need some help with the painting?"

She shook her head and her hair bounced lightly on her shoulders. He caught a hint of a lightly fruity shampoo. "Actually, I need you."

The words stopped him cold, even as a spear of heat shot through his belly. It would be no hardship to have her need him, but of course she hadn't meant it that way. He cleared his throat. "For what?"

She paced across the front lawn, kicking at the leaves. "I feel so stupid. I wouldn't ask you if I wasn't desperate."

Ben was pretty sure that was his ego, flying away in shreds. "Desperate?"

"Oh!" She spun back around and her cheeks were bright pink—a huge improvement over the paleness they'd held a few minutes ago. "I didn't mean— I just meant—"

"It's fine," he interrupted. "What do you need?"

She stared at the sky for a minute and he wondered if she was looking for a lightning bolt.

"A date."

He couldn't have heard her right. A date? He didn't date—even casually. If he did date, it definitely wouldn't be a woman who was in danger of making him feel things again. He opened his mouth to tell her so but she rushed on.

"My mother hosts this fundraiser gala thing at the hospital every year. I need to go, and I don't have a date. I was hoping maybe you'd come with me."

"When is it?" God, was he actually considering it? He'd meant to say *no way*.

"Next Thursday." When he said nothing she turned even pinker and turned to walk away. "You know…this was a bad idea. I'm sorry. I'll just go alone."

He crossed to her in two steps. "Black tie?" Hell, he hated black tie.

She swallowed. "Yes."

"I'll go." Holy hell, what was he thinking?

"It's okay—" she started, then stopped as his words sank in. Her eyes widened. "You will?"

He nodded.

"Oh, thank you," she breathed, and flung her arms around him for a brief, tight hug. "Thank you."

He couldn't resist teasing a little. "Only because you're desperate." Hell. He was getting soft. He couldn't possibly be letting her get to him. Right?

She pulled away, but he looped his arms around her back and held her against him, wanting to feel her for a moment. Her gaze caught his and the world fell away for a minute. Heat wove around them, lazy and slow, and his gaze dropped to her mouth. The memory of that kiss in the park hung between them—her warm, sweet mouth and hungry response. He wanted it. Especially now, with her pink cheeks and slightly parted lips tempting him to claim them.

She made a little sound in her throat and he let her go, setting her away from him. Her gaze refocused, then bounced away, landing anywhere but on him.

"So…ah…I'll get going," she said, edging toward her car. "I'll see you later."

"Yeah." He marshaled his thoughts away from kissing her. It took way more effort than he wanted to admit. "What time for the gala?"

"It starts at seven—so say, six-thirty?"

"All right," he said, and she hurried to her car and hopped in. As he watched her drive down the road he wondered where the hell he'd find a tux by next Thursday night.

He strode back to the garage. Then he fished his cell out of his pocket. First things first. He wouldn't let Lainey down.

It seemed the harder Ben tried to keep his distance, the more he was drawn to Lainey.

It wasn't good.

He locked the little house up behind him. Lainey had gone home after painting. They'd managed to avoid any more awkward moments like they'd had outside. It seemed the best thing he could do was bump up his timetable. He'd finished the ramp for his grandma just today, and he was nearly done with this rental house. So there weren't any real reasons to stick around once he'd gotten his grandma squared away. It would be best to get away from Lainey before he got any more involved with her.

Which was why it had floored him when he said he'd go with her to that party. That wasn't the way to keep his distance.

He scrubbed a hand over his face with a sigh. While he wasn't ready to go back to firefighting yet, there was really no reason not to go back to Grand Rapids.

Well, there was Callie and her broken family. He blew out a breath. He couldn't go back yet. He wasn't ready. He couldn't even return Callie's phone calls. Eventually she'd quit trying. One more thing to add to the morass of guilt.

He'd finish up the house, go to the gala, and that would be the end of the contact he had with Lainey. He'd make excuses and leave when she came to visit. It would be easier on both of them. She wanted to see his grandma, anyway, not him.

He cleaned up his mess and drove back to his grandma's house. As he got out of his truck a car turned in the driveway behind him. Grandma—coming home from her knitting group, he thought. She had a very full social calendar, which amused him no end. And pleased him, too.

He walked up to the car and opened her door. She beamed up at him. "Hello, Ben."

"Hi, Grandma."

He went around back when the driver popped the trunk and pulled the wheelchair out. Then he held it steady as his grandma moved from the car to the chair. As much as he hated to see her like this, he had to admit she handled it with grace and humor.

"Thank you," she said, and waved at her friend. Ben helped her wheel up the ramp into the house.

"This ramp is wonderful," she said as they came in the door. "I can't tell you how much easier it is going to make my life. I appreciate it so much."

Ben shut the door behind them, uncomfortable with her gratitude. He didn't deserve it. He'd been gone for too long, and she'd needed him. Lainey had been right about that when they'd first met. "I'm glad," was all he said.

She wheeled around to face him, a frown on her face as she put her knitting bag on the floor by her favorite chair. "It was an honest compliment," she said quietly. "It's okay to accept it."

He shoved his hands in his pockets. "I know. I just feel like I should have been here long before now."

She sighed. "I could have let you know, Ben. I was very clear that I didn't want to worry you. This isn't all on you. As you can see, I've got a very solid support system. I've been managing. And I am very grateful you took this time to help me out. That is all I meant."

He knew that, but it was hard to let go of the self-recrimination. He'd held on to it like a shield for the past week or so, using it to keep his distance.

"So," she said. "Is the house ready for Lainey?"

Grateful for the topic-change, he said, "Pretty much. I'm still working on some minor repairs. But, yes, it's otherwise ready."

She gave a little nod. "Excellent. She's moving this weekend, then?"

"Far as I know." He opted not to mention yet that she'd asked him to the gala. That might put ideas in Grandma's head he didn't want her to have. She liked Lainey, and he didn't want to get her hopes up.

Or your own?

Choosing to ignore that particular thought, he shoved his hands in his pockets. "It'll be all ready for her. You can call her and firm up the date and time."

Rose cocked her head. "You've got a truck," she said thoughtfully. "It might go faster if you offered to help."

Ben swallowed hard. Of course it would. Lainey's car wasn't nearly big enough to haul furniture. And he wasn't going to *not* help her because he was so damn terrified of her. "When you call her, tell her I offered."

She didn't push. "I will. Thank you, Ben."

"Sure," he said, not adding, *I'd do it for anyone.* Because he was afraid that wasn't true.

Lainey's cell buzzed. The number was the same area code as she'd dialed for Jon. Her stomach instantly fell. Beth had left for deliveries so she was alone. She took a deep breath and answered.

"Hello?"

"Lainey. It's Jon." His voice was crisp. "Wanted to let you know we've drawn up the paperwork to begin the process for me to terminate my rights. It's been overnighted to you."

Lainey froze for a moment. This was what she wanted, but somehow saying *thank you* seemed both wrong and inadequate. "I—okay. I'll look out for it."

There was the slightest of pauses, then he cleared his throat. "Best of luck to you, Lainey."

She turned and stared out the window at the cars passing by. "You too. You're going to need it far more than I will."

He barked a laugh, even though she hadn't been trying to be funny. "Don't I know it? From here on out if you have any questions refer them to my lawyer."

"I can't imagine I'd have any need," she said. "But okay."

She clicked the phone shut in her hand. Slowly the import of the conversation began to sink in. She was well and truly a single mother now. Relief mixed with sorrow that it had gone this way. That she'd given her baby a man like Jon for a father. A man who would sign his rights away rather than tell his wife. Instead of a man like Ben.

She sighed and slipped the phone in her pocket. Ben would leave, too. He'd been clear that he was only here for a short time, and even more telling, that his attraction to her was reluctant at best. Something he couldn't help rather than something he actually wanted.

She'd do well to keep that in mind.

"Geez, sis, what do you have in these boxes?"

Kevin's grumbled question on Saturday morning made Lainey smile.

"Rocks—just for you," she teased, and saw Kevin frown out the window. "What?"

"You expecting someone? Big truck. Tall guy. Wait— is that Ben Lawless?"

Lainey's heart skipped. "Yes." It was a good thing he could help, since Beth and her husband hadn't been able to come after all.

"Our job just got easier. He's got a lot of room in that truckbed. Let's get these boxes out of the way so we can move the furniture."

Ben came up the stairs and Lainey tried very hard not to flush or otherwise react in case her brother picked up on anything. As it was, she'd taken care to dress in clothes that hid her slightly rounded midsection, without being obvious about it. She couldn't take the chance that Kevin's doctor eye would spot what she wasn't ready for him to see.

Ben's greeting was a nod, before he turned his attention to Kevin and they launched into a moving strategy discussion. Feeling oddly left out, Lainey slipped into her bedroom, where she'd left a couple boxes of fragile items she didn't want mixed in with the rest of her things.

It only took a few trips. It was a little depressing that her life had been reduced to a couple of car and truckloads, including the furniture. Now it was all in her new house, somewhat willy-nilly, though the guys *had* asked her where she wanted things. Kevin had left after the last trip, and Ben was coming back with a few miscellaneous items.

Lainey went in the kitchen. If she started in there she would be able to at least eat a bowl of cereal or soup. When the front door opened her pulse kicked up. She'd managed to keep Kevin between them. Not too hard, considering they were the ones doing the heavy lifting. But now she and Ben were alone.

She ripped open the box closest to her and found her dishes. She heard Ben's steps in the hall and rose from the floor to greet him. He leaned on the wall and surveyed the mess.

"You've got your work cut out for you," he observed, and she took the opportunity to turn and examine the chaos.

"Yep. It will take me a couple days, but I'll get it all done." Not sure what to do now, she hesitated, then stuck out her hand. "Thank you. I appreciate your help."

He paused just a heartbeat before he took her hand in response. His palm, warm and rough, sent shivers up her arm. What would it feel like on her skin?

She released his hand and stepped back, willing the thoughts away. He shoved his hands in his pockets. She didn't know how to make the awkwardness stop—wasn't even sure it was the best thing to do.

He cleared his throat. "Grandma's invited you to lunch at Mel's Café. She'll be there—" he glanced at his watch "—in about fifteen minutes."

"Oh. That's wonderful, but I think I need to get cracking on this." Practically on cue, her stomach growled loudly and he arched a brow.

"What are you going to eat? One of these boxes?"

Humor glimmered in his eyes and it took her breath away because she knew how rare it was to see it.

"I—well, yeah. Maybe with peanut butter?" She grinned at him and was rewarded with a small smile. Which for him was an ear-to-ear grin.

"We can do better than that," he said dryly. "Come on. I'll drive you."

Unable to think of a suitable excuse—and really she didn't want one, she was hungry—she grabbed her purse and followed him out the door, which she locked with her new key. He opened the passenger door and she climbed in.

"How is Rose getting there?" she asked when he got in the other side.

"A friend took her to get her hair and nails done this morning. She'll drop Grandma off."

Lainey frowned. "How will she get home? This truck is awful high." His expression was shuttered and she realized he'd taken it as a criticism. "I didn't mean that as anything other than a statement of fact," she added stiffly.

He didn't touch her comment. "She's got something else going on after lunch."

"Oh." Lainey stared out the window, mentally kicking herself for her thoughtlessness. It seemed every step they took forward was quickly followed by three back. Such an awkward dance they were doing—trying to be ultra-polite while pretending there was nothing between them.

It was exhausting.

She unbuckled when he'd parked at the café, just down from her shop and her now-former apartment. Once they entered the café she saw Rose at a table by the window. The older woman waved and Lainey waved back. She slid into the seat across from Rose and was surprised when Ben sat next to her. Until she realized Rose had taken over the second seat with her coat and purse. In spite of herself, she wondered if it had been intentional. Was Rose match-making? She wouldn't put it past her friend.

"Love your hair," Lainey said, admiring the soft curls, and Rose patted it.

"She did a good job, didn't she? Makes me look good."

Lainey laughed and caught Rose's hand. "What color is this?" It was a deep pink, a perfect shade for her skin and her silver hair. It occurred to her *she* hadn't had a manicure since she'd divorced Daniel. Not that it mattered, but was one more sign of how much her life had changed.

"I can't remember exactly. It had peony in the name."

"Did you order?" Lainey asked, and Rose shook her head.

"Not yet. But I know what I'm getting."

The waitress came over and Rose ordered a club sandwich, Lainey a turkey sandwich, and Ben something big with roast beef.

Rose sat back. "So. Did you get it all moved?"

She glanced at Ben. "Yes. Ben and Kevin made it look easy. I guess it helped I didn't have that much stuff."

Ben stretched his legs out in front of him and bumped her thigh in the process. She sucked in a breath.

"Sure seemed like a lot for one woman and a cat."

His low, teasing tone gave her goosebumps. She smacked him lightly on the arm, trying desperately not to respond to him. *Rose is here.* The mental reminder didn't work.

"Not that much," she said with a laugh, and saw Rose watching them with an expression that could only be described as thoughtful. Lainey sighed inwardly. The undercurrents between them were on full display.

So much for not feeding the matchmaking fire.

CHAPTER EIGHT

LAINEY'S WEEKEND PASSED in a flurry of unpacking. While the end result was a little sparse, she wasn't worried. One thing she'd always loved was finding treasures at places like thrift shops and garage sales. One more thing her mother had never understood. So she'd keep an eye out for what she might need.

Well, after baby needs, of course. That was her next project. Setting up the nursery.

In fact she stood in the room in question right now. Nothing was in here yet. She'd left it empty on purpose. She needed a crib, a changing table… Maybe she could find a dresser that could do double duty. A rocker for the corner. A bookcase for toys and such. She left the room, a smile on her face, and walked back though the house. Being here felt right. Panda sat in a spot of sunlight on the kitchen floor. While the cat hadn't been pleased about the car ride, she'd settled in once she'd found her food and water bowls, as well as her litter box. Lainey was hopeful come spring she could let the cat out into the fenced-in backyard.

She padded into her bedroom to get dressed. And frowned when her low-rise jeans didn't snap. Yesterday they'd fit—albeit a bit snug. Today, no dice. That meant two things.

One: full-time maternity clothes.

Two: telling her family.

Lainey shut her eyes. The moment of truth was here. Her father was out of town, so she'd have to tell her mother alone. She'd do it after work, when she returned the apartment keys.

She left the house with a little fizzle of joy as she used her new key to lock it up behind her, and drove to the shop. As was her habit now, she checked the cooler temperature first thing. It was running a tick above where she wanted it, but it had been holding fairly steady.

Beth walked in a few minutes later. "Hey, Laine. How was the move?"

"Pretty smooth," she answered.

"Was it just you and Kevin? Aw, Laine. I'm so sorry we couldn't be there. We should have—"

"You should have gone to visit your father-in-law, just like you did. It all worked out. Ben helped, too," Lainey said quickly. "I think Rose asked him to."

A small smile tugged at the corners of Beth's mouth. "Really?" she said, drawing out the word. "How was that?"

Lainey rolled her eyes and stomped over to open the cash register, pretending not to catch her friend's meaning. "A lot of work—what else?"

Beth's low laugh followed her across the room. "Mmm-hmm. Do you think Kevin noticed anything? Lainey, it's pretty obvious there's chemistry with you guys."

Oh, she hoped not. "I don't think so. He's a guy, so he can be pretty oblivious. Plus, I really didn't see Ben that much. They just loaded and unloaded. They were together more than we were." Then she realized what she'd just admitted. "Oh—"

Beth wrapped an arm around Lainey's shoulders and

squeezed. "Now all you have to do is stop fighting it. Let yourself just give in."

She stepped away, her point clearly made, and Lainey busied herself with the cash drawer. It wasn't as easy as *just giving in*. There was too much at stake to *just give in*. Why couldn't Beth see that? She wasn't sure she could give in if she wanted to. She was aware of how quickly things could go wrong. Once you'd had your wings clipped, it made it awful hard to get off the ground.

And she was scared to try and fly again.

Lainey turned down her parents' street and her stomach fluttered. Silly, really, since she was an adult. But those old habits of wanting to be a good daughter were hard to break. She'd decided to go in quick, say her piece, and get out. She'd send for the housekeeper if her mother passed out.

The thought made her giggle just a little hysterically. The unflappable Jacqui—completely flapped.

Her mother's car was parked by the garage—a sure sign she'd be heading back out later. Lainey parked in the circle and took a second to brace herself. While it was time, it would be nice if she had someone to back her up, and she almost wished she'd asked Kevin to come along. He'd know how to manage their mother.

She rang the bell and waited. Jacqui answered after a minute, brow arched high. "Lainey. This is a nice surprise. What brings you here?"

She stepped aside and Lainey entered the foyer.

"I need to talk to you for a minute." Her voice was calm, not betraying her nerves. Good.

"Of course. I've got a meeting in a half-hour. Will this take long?"

"I don't think so," Lainey said.

She followed her mother's trim form into the living

room and took a deep breath. Once again she tried to imagine a baby on the floor, or pulling itself up on the velvet-covered furniture. She couldn't picture it. Was that because she was afraid her parents wouldn't want her and the baby in their lives? Wasn't that part of what had made her so reluctant to tell them?

It didn't matter now. She took a deep breath. "I have something important to tell you."

"I see." Jacqui crossed to the mini-wet bar. "Well, then. Something to drink? Will you be joining me for dinner?"

Not likely. "No, Mother."

Jacqui turned, a can of ginger ale in her hand, an expectant look on her face. "Well, then, what do you need to tell me, dear?"

There was no point in beating around the bush. "I'm pregnant."

Jacqui gasped, and the color leached from her face as the pop can slid from her hand and landed on the carpet with a fizzy hiss. The golden liquid splashed all over her legs and feet. Frozen for a heartbeat, Lainey leapt up and grabbed a handful of paper towels from the wet bar, almost grateful for the distraction.

"Are you sure?" Jacqui's voice was faint.

Lainey didn't look up from blotting at the mess. She wasn't sure she could look at her mother just yet. "Positive. I'm a little more than two months along." Her hands shook as she dropped the first mass of sopping towels in the garbage under the bar.

Jacqui let out a long exhale. "Good God."

That about sums it up.

"Are you getting married? Who's the father?"

Lainey winced. "No. And the father is no one you know." True enough. Jon wouldn't have been on her parents' radar.

"Ben Lawless?" Her mother nearly spat Ben's name.

Lainey bobbled the paper towel roll. What did her mother have against Ben? "No. Of course not. He'd *want* to be involved in the baby's life." The truth of those words batted against her heart.

"And the father doesn't?"

Lainey couldn't speak over the wave of shame that rose in her. She pressed her lips together instead and shook her head.

Jacqui sighed and stepped out of her sticky heels. "Oh, Lainey. You need to get married, pronto. I wonder if Daniel would be willing to marry you with you carrying some-one else's baby? Lainey, *damn it.* I think you just ruined any chance you had with that man!"

Lainey sat back on her heels, temper snapping at her throat. "I already told you I don't care, Mother. I'm not get-ting married. I will be a single parent. I don't give a damn what Daniel thinks. I'm sure he has kids somewhere. He did enough sowing of the seed, as they say."

Jacqui gasped. "Lainey!"

"Well, he did. If it wore heels, he chased it. He almost never slept with *me*, thank God—who knows what I could have come down with?—but he did with other women. At the end he was bringing them into our home, did you know that?" The humiliation burned though her all over again. "I'd be gone, or maybe not. The basement was his little playboy cave. He could have cared less about me—about our marriage. He married me for you and Dad—for your money, for where your name could take him. So when I grew a spine and divorced him it really threw him. He's not back here for *me*, Mother. He wants to get back in your lives."

Jacqui stared at her, jaw dropped. "Lainey—" she said finally, then lapsed into silence.

"But you knew, didn't you?" Lainey said softly. "Some of it, anyway. And it was okay, because he had the right connections, the right amount of money. You were willing to look the other way, like you've done with Dad." The truth arced through her, sharp and hot.

Jacqui stood very still. "Be very careful, young lady. You're on dangerous ground now."

Lainey couldn't stop. It was too important. "He's always been very discreet—unlike Daniel. I'd have thought you'd want better for me than you had. I know I do."

The truth hurt. She loved her father, but she knew his weaknesses. Daniel was just like him, only without the intelligence or compassion. She also knew her father loved her mother, despite his failings. And that was between them. Not her business.

She stood up and threw away the last of the paper towels. "I'm going to go now," she said quietly. There was nothing more to say. It wasn't as if her mother was going to embrace her and squeal with joy at the thought of grandchildren. So the lump of disappointment in her throat was useless. She turned and walked toward the door.

"Lainey—wait."

She paused and turned.

Jacqui asked, "Who else knows about this?"

Lainey laid her hand on her belly and saw Jacqui flinch. "Only Beth knows about your grandchild." There wasn't any reason to tell her Ben knew as well. It would only make things worse.

"Okay, good. We need to make this spin positive somehow. I'll get on it and let you know the plan." Jacqui, clearly perked by the thought of something to do, padded across the carpet on sticky feet.

"No."

Jacqui stopped. "Excuse me?"

Lainey shook her head. "You can plan all you want, but it's not going to make it go away. Not going to make it any more or less than it is. I'm not going to go along with any plan. My baby. My life."

Jacqui's mouth flattened. "Your store—"

"I know. It's at your mercy." Lainey grabbed her purse. "You keep telling me. Now you know why I won't let it go under. I need to succeed so I can support myself and my child. Can I call anyone for you before I go?"

Jacqui shook her head. "No. I don't—I need to talk to your father first. He's going to be so disappointed," she added, more to herself than to Lainey. "Plus it's an election year."

Lainey stared at her. "Mom, I'm thirty-three. Not a teenager. Not even close. So what if I have a baby on my own?" She nearly laughed. As if it was such an easy thing to do. Maybe she was crazy. "Women do it all the time."

"But not women in *your* position," Jacqui said.

She kept her voice steady with effort. "And what position would that be?"

"Women whose lives are under scrutiny," she said, and Lainey's jaw nearly dropped.

"I'm hardly under any kind of scrutiny. Besides, I don't think this is any worse than my divorce," she said dryly. "And it's a much happier occasion."

Jacqui shook her head. "Don't make a joke of it. You don't understand. You never have."

Lainey hesitated, then simply turned and walked toward the door. There wasn't anything else to say. Behind her, she heard her mother on the phone with the housekeeper, telling her to come clean up the mess.

Outside, she took a deep breath as she got in her car and drove out of the driveway. Then she pulled over. She reached for her cell and called her brother.

Amazingly, Kevin answered.

"You're not in surgery today?"

"Nope. Office visits all day. I've only got a few minutes, though. What's up?"

Lainey fiddled with the steering wheel. "I just came from home."

"Oh? How's Mom?"

Lainey stared out the window, not seeing the rain on the windshield. "I kind of shocked her, Kev. She's not happy."

"You told her you're pregnant?"

Tears stung her eyes. Even though she'd suspected he knew. "How did you know?"

He sighed. "I can just tell. Where are you going for your OB?"

Lainey filled him in on the details.

"Is Lawless the father?"

Oh, she wished. Of the few men she'd been involved with, he was the most honorable, hands down. "No," she whispered.

He made a noise that could have been anything. "I caught him looking at you a couple times on Saturday. Really looking. Not how a brother wants a guy to look at his kid sister."

She nearly laughed, and tried to ignore the spurt of pleasure and pain his words caused. "Wow. I'm pretty sure you're wrong. And don't ask me any more about the father, okay? It's not—he's not interested in being a father."

"That's too damn bad," he growled. "Do you need me to hunt him down?"

Now she *did* laugh, at the vision of her respectable surgeon older brother beating the hell out of Jon. It would be quite a match, but her money would be on Kevin. "No. But, thanks."

A pause. "That's not right, Lainey. He shouldn't leave you—"

"It's okay," she interrupted him. "We're better off without him."

Kevin sighed. "All right. And, little sis? You'll be a hell of a mother."

His words and his faith in her warmed her. It was so nice to have him stand up for her. But still... "I don't want to be like our mother," she whispered. There it was...her deepest fear.

Kevin snorted. "You won't be. She somehow flat-out missed the maternal gene. You've got it in spades. You feeling okay?"

"Yeah. Just a little tired. Thankfully I don't have much nausea."

"Okay, good. I've got to run. I'll stop by and see Mom after I get out of here. Let me know if I can help, okay? You don't have to do this alone."

His words brought tears to her eyes. "Thanks, Kev. I will," she promised, and disconnected, feeling a little better. Kevin would smooth out what Lainey couldn't, but she doubted either of them could make Jacqui see this as a good thing.

She tucked the phone back into her purse and sat for another few moments. Her mother's reaction hadn't really shocked her. Jacqui would spin and spin, but in the end it was what Lainey did that mattered, and she'd make it work on her own. Again, if things were different— But they weren't. Whatever was going on with Ben, it had him clearly reluctant to make even the slightest commitment. She needed someone reliable.

So far the only reliable one was herself. The irony of that wasn't lost on her.

* * *

Lainey stood in her new backyard the next day after work and stared up into the nearly empty oak tree, then down at the ground where she stood ankle deep in yellow-brown leaves. Yesterday they'd all been on the tree. Today they were all on the ground. Clearly it was time for a trip to the hardware store to buy a rake.

She trudged through the leaves, hearing the crunch under her feet, on her way out front to her car. Her trip to the hardware store, where she purchased a rake, leaf bags, and a pair of work gloves, took less than half an hour.

She went out back, rake in hand, and tilted her face to the sun. She had a couple of hours before it would be too dark. Might as well make the most of it.

She hadn't been going for more than ten minutes when Ben's big truck pulled in the driveway. Her pulse kicked up and she gripped the rake a little harder. She walked over to the gate to greet him.

"Hi," she said, when he emerged from the truck and turned her way. She tried not to devour him with her eyes. She wanted to curl herself into his embrace, feel his warmth through the black fleece jacket he wore—

Wait. No, she didn't.

"Hey," he said, coming closer, his expression neutral. His gaze dropped to her belly. "Is this okay, in your condition?"

"Of course. I'm not doing any heavy lifting, so I'm fine," she said. "I can do pretty much anything as long as I don't overdo it."

He lifted his gaze to hers. "I can see you overdoing it."

She smiled and shook her head. "I'm very careful. I'm not going to put the baby in any danger."

"Of course you won't. I'll help."

She tried not to stare at the rear view as he walked to the

bed of his truck. How could she not notice how those worn jeans hugged his rear and thighs just right? She cleared her throat. "Do you just carry a rake in the back of your truck for emergencies?"

"I was here earlier and saw what had happened," he answered as she stepped aside for him to come through the gate. Before she could ask, he nodded to the garage. "The light in there was out. I put in a new bulb."

"I'm going to get spoiled—all this personal landlord service," she teased, and saw his back stiffen. "Not to worry. I can change my own lightbulbs."

He sent her a grin. "Does your mother know?"

"Shh," she murmured. "She'll hear you."

He laughed and started raking.

They worked in relative silence for a bit. Lainey kept sneaking glances at him. He'd unzipped his jacket and, while the tee shirt he wore underneath wasn't exactly skin-tight, she could still see the play of muscles underneath it when he raked.

She exhaled. It had certainly gotten hotter out here since he had shown up.

They raked a big pile over the next little while, and a slight breeze stirred the remaining leaves on the tree and several came floating down. He reached out and plucked a piece of one out of her hair, his fingers lingering on the strands. Her mouth went dry at the intense heat in his gaze and her pulse kicked up when he dropped his gaze to her mouth. Lainey stopped herself from leaning forward, from pressing her mouth to his. He stepped back and offered her the leaf with a small smile.

She took it and twirled the stem in her fingers. "Wow, thanks." She held it up, looking at the red and green threaded in with the yellow. "Pretty, isn't it?"

He closed his hand over hers. She looked up into his gaze.

"Gorgeous," he murmured, drawing her closer and she knew, with a flutter deep inside, that he wasn't talking about the leaf anymore.

He settled his mouth over hers. With a sigh, she melted into him, opening, letting his tongue slip in. When the kiss became deeper, hotter, she fisted the front of his jacket and he gripped her hips, drawing her closer, before plunging one hand into her hair, angling her head to thrust his tongue even deeper.

Fire skipped through her veins, burned along her nerve-endings, sent heat arrowing into the depth of her belly. She pressed closer, feeling his hardness against her and the answering heat of her response.

Suddenly he broke the kiss, though he didn't pull away from her, but rested his forehead on hers. Their breath mingled as she tried to calm her breathing. Every time he touched her she craved more. It wasn't enough. But it was all there was. Frustration welled and she squeezed her eyes shut.

"Lainey," he murmured, his voice raw and rough. "I told myself I'd stay away, but..." His voice trailed off as he stepped back, and she shivered from the loss of his heat. "We'd better get to work."

Shaking, Lainey bent to retrieve her discarded rake. She needed to pull back, keep this kind of thing from happening.

But the real question was, did she want to? In her heart, she feared the answer was no.

CHAPTER NINE

IT DIDN'T TAKE all that long to make a huge pile. Ben pulled some sticks out. "When was the last time you jumped in a leaf pile?"

Shame flushed Lainey's cheeks. "Well, never."

He stared at her. "No way? All those trees on your parents' land and you never played in a leaf pile?"

"No. My mother—you'd have to know my mother. She's not big on dirt." That sounded sad, but it was the truth.

"Oh." There was a wealth of understanding in the word. "I see."

She looked at him in surprise. "You do?"

He nodded. "You need to experience it before the baby gets here. Let me make sure all the sticks are out."

He poked in the pile and she watched with a combination of amusement and exasperation. After extracting a few more sticks, he fluffed the pile with his rake and turned, the satisfaction on his face making her laugh.

"Does it pass muster?" she teased gently.

He nodded. "You're not too far along for this, are you?"

On impulse, Lainey unzipped her vest and ran her hand over her very slight baby bump. The tenderness in his eyes as he watched made her breath catch. "Am I jumping out of a tree?"

His gaze jerked up. "Of course not."

"Then I'll be fine." She leapt lightly into the pile, landing on her knees. The crackle of the leaves and their fresh scent invigorated her. She laughed and threw an armful of leaves in the air, then tried to cover her head when they came raining back down.

"Incoming!" Ben called, and before she could scramble too far over he came crashing into the pile with her. He gave her a big grin—the first she'd seen with no shadows, no pain in his eyes—and tossed a handful of leaves at her. "So, what do you think?"

She threw some back at him. "It was worth the wait."

He laughed. "Yeah? Awesome." He turned and flopped back, folding his hands under his head. "I'm guessing you never looked at cloud shapes either?"

"Stop reminding me how deprived my childhood was," she scolded him with a laugh, and he snaked out a hand and pulled her head down to his. The sweetness of this kiss after the passion of the earlier one threw her.

When she pulled back, searching his face with her gaze, he touched her cheek, twining his fingers in her hair. "I'm sorry," he said.

She arched a brow. "For what?"

"For all you missed. I assumed, growing up as you did, you had everything."

She shrugged and pulled a leaf out of his hair. "I had everything material you could want. Only I didn't actually want it. I didn't get time with my parents. But I see now my mom didn't know how to raise us. She was so caught up in perceptions that just letting me be a kid wasn't possible. She meant well, but…" She sat up in the leaves. "We turned out okay, Kevin and I. Him more than me," she added with a little sigh, thinking of her struggling shop, her pregnancy and her money woes.

Ben frowned. "Don't do that."

Startled, she looked at him. "Do what?"

"Put yourself down like that. You're living life on your terms. How is that not okay?"

"Oh." She nibbled on her lip while she thought. "You're right. I hadn't thought of it like that. I guess I just want to prove I can do it."

"You are. You will." He stood up and extended a hand to her.

His quiet confidence warmed her down to her toes and her heart tipped dangerously.

"Let's get this done."

She grasped his warm, callused palm and let him draw her to her feet. "Okay."

They managed to load about half the leaves into bags before it got too dark. Lainey's arms and back were screaming, and it was with an incredible sense of relief that she dropped her rake on the ground to stretch her back.

"Did you overdo it?" The concern in his voice made her smile.

"According to my back and arms, yes. But none of that will hurt the baby."

"Go on in," he told her. "I'll put these things in the garage. I'll finish tomorrow."

She hesitated before starting toward the house. "Do you—do you want to come in? For coffee or something?"

"I'd like that," he said softly. "If you think you aren't too tired?"

"No, I'm fine. Come in when you're done."

She hurried into the house and started the coffee maker. A quick trip to the bathroom revealed wild hair and a nose bright red from the cold.

Oooh. Sexy.

Though Ben clearly hadn't minded. He'd kissed her. Twice.

Would there be a third time?

She shook her head at her reflection. *Stop it.* She detoured to the living room to switch on the fire. While the walls were bare in here, as she hadn't had a chance yet to deal with artwork, she'd gotten the furniture arranged like she wanted and unpacked pillows and a couple throws. It was comfy enough for the moment. Ben would understand.

When she got back to the kitchen she caught a glimpse of him coming out of the garage. For just a heartbeat she was a wife and a mom, waiting for her man to come in.

The thought threw her. She'd been a wife, and had given up waiting for her man to come in pretty quickly. She was going to be a mom—and that terrified her. But she'd never felt for her ex-husband what she felt for Ben—and she wasn't even in love with Ben.

Not yet.

Reeling from that thought, she opened the cupboard to take out coffee mugs as Ben came in through the back door. She gave him a bright smile. "It's decaf. That okay?"

"Sure," he said, and shrugged out of his jacket.

She poured his and handed it to him. "Let's go in here," she said and led the way to the living room. She settled on the couch with him across from her.

"Something wrong? You look a little pale."

Ben's casual comment threw her. She certainly couldn't tell him *he* was part of what was worrying her. "I'm not ready to be a mother," she blurted. "But I'm committed now."

He looked genuinely surprised. "Why do you think you're not ready?"

"I'm still getting my shop off the ground. I'm not in the best place financially." He just looked at her and she shut her eyes. "I'm not. My parents are wealthy, yes, but there was no trust fund or anything. It was kind of understood

I'd either get a fantastic career or a loaded husband. Or both." She stared at his shoulder, unable to meet his eyes. "I managed to do neither."

"You say that like it's a bad thing," he said softly.

She looked at him and the misery in her eyes nearly had him reaching for her. He wanted to tuck her under his arm and hold her against his chest, where he already knew she fit perfectly.

"I know it shouldn't be. And my ex-husband is a real doozy. Seven years of my life I'll never get back. But somehow it is—in my family. I'm happy where I am. I'm just—"

She stopped and he saw the sheen of tears. "Just what?"

"So worried. Because I don't want to be a bad mother," Lainey blurted, and covered her face with her hands.

Now he did reach for her, and caught her wrists and gently pulled her hands away. "Why would you think you would be?"

She gave a harsh little laugh and looked down in her lap. "My mother has no maternal genes. None. Zero. We aren't close, even though it seems like I see her all the time. I don't want my baby to feel like he or she doesn't matter."

Anger washed through him. "You feel like you don't matter?"

She stood up and walked over to the fireplace. She stared into the dancing flames. "I— Yes. I've never really been a part of the family. I always felt like just a prop, I guess. The black sheep."

He came up behind her and slid his hands down her arms. "You are going to be a wonderful mother, Lainey." When she shook her head, he leaned down and pressed his cheek to hers, inhaled her sweet scent. "Listen to me. I haven't known you long, but what I see is a warm, compassionate, giving woman who cares deeply about those who matter to her. You're strong. You're sweet. You're funny. All of that is going to translate naturally to motherhood."

She turned in his arms and looked up at him, her eyes huge in the soft light of the lamp and the fire. The uncertainty in her eyes killed him.

"You think so?"

He'd meant every word. He touched her face, unable to stop himself from feeling her soft skin. She leaned into him just slightly, eyes closed, and he swallowed hard but couldn't step away even if he wanted to. Which, God help him, he didn't.

"No. I know so."

Her eyes fluttered open and he gave in, lowering his mouth to hers, hearing her sharp inhale. He hesitated at the last second. Her breath feathered over his and she closed the gap, coming up to meet him. He slipped his hands in her hair, even though they really wanted to roam farther south. All he wanted to do right now was feel.

Lainey. Only Lainey.

The kiss grew more urgent quickly, and she opened to him with a little growl in her throat that only served to fuel his internal fire. When her arms went around his neck and she pressed her length against him he was lost.

No. He was found. He hadn't wanted to be, and he wouldn't be able to stay. But she'd managed to lay waste to all his defenses.

He broke the kiss before he accidentally toppled her into the fireplace and rested his forehead on hers. She didn't move away, though he felt the tension return to her body. "I didn't want you to end up in the fire."

She blinked at him, then a small smile curved her mouth. "Thoughtful of you."

"Isn't it, though? Gentleman through and through." He savored her laugh as he took her hand and led her to the couch. If she knew how badly he wanted to take her to bed, to feel her move beneath him, to make love to her, she'd know he wasn't any kind of gentleman.

And those thoughts weren't helpful.

Trying to bring them back around, he asked, "How are your shoulders?"

She rolled them and winced. "I'll be feeling this for a couple days, I think."

He pulled her down on the couch and sat so he was behind her. He began to knead her shoulders gently. "Wow. You *are* tight. Relax and let me see if I can help with that."

She let her head fall forward. "Mmm. That feels wonderful."

Yeah. It did. But touching her like this, on top of the kisses earlier, was sending all his blood south. And when she moaned his breath shortened. He leaned forward and kissed her neck, still massaging, but letting his hands slip over her shoulders to brush the tops of her breasts through her shirt, then moving them back up to her shoulders. Her little inhale prompted him to do it again, this time slipping his hands under her breasts to cup them in his hands, brush his thumbs over her nipples. Was this one of the lacy, sexy bras he'd seen that day in her bathroom?

"Lainey..." he murmured against her neck, and she tilted her head to the side, her breathing shallow. He kissed her neck one more time and she shifted out of his arms. He let her go, instantly feeling her loss, but she just turned around and settled on his lap, wrapped her arms around his neck.

"Stay," she whispered. "Please."

"Lainey." He rested his forehead on hers, struggling for some semblance of control. "Are you sure?"

She slid off his lap and held out her hand. It was trembling slightly and he could see uncertainty warring with desire in her eyes. She was offering him a gift and she was afraid he wouldn't take it.

This might be his only chance. A few hours of heaven he knew he didn't deserve.

But Lainey did.

He took her hand without ever breaking eye contact and stood.

Smoke filled the room, smothering him, searing his lungs, his eyes, his skin. God, he couldn't see through the gray haze. A cough racked him, tearing at his parched throat. He couldn't yell for his friend. Where was Jason? He couldn't reach him—had to get him out before the house came down around him. A roar and a crack, and orange lit the room. The ceiling caved in on a crash fueled by the roar of flames. He spun around, but the door was blocked by a flaming heap of debris. Under it was a boot. Jason coming to save him.

Ben woke up, gasping, to find Lainey's terrified face over him.

"Ben?"

The concern, the worry, was too much for him, and he clamped both hands over his face so she couldn't see the pain, the anger, the shame seeping from him like tears.

Her hand was soft on his arm. "Ben?"

He shook her off. "Lainey—don't. God. I—it's just a dream." He sat up, cursing himself for falling asleep, for allowing the intimacy at all, for thinking maybe it would be okay.

She drew back, a sheet pulled up over those glorious breasts, her gaze steady and worried. "If it's just a dream why are you so rattled?"

She saw too much. Too damn much. He was stripped

emotionally bare after their wonderful night together—all that emotion which he hadn't expected.

"I can't explain it now," he said, weary. "Go back to sleep. I'll see myself out."

Her quick intake of breath lanced him. No point in telling her he wouldn't sleep anymore, anyway. Better she knew as little as possible. Better he didn't give her the chance to soothe him, to connect, while he was vulnerable.

She said nothing as he pulled on his pants in the dark, fumbled with his wallet.

"What ever it is, running isn't going to make it go away."

Her words, though soft, hit him as hard as if she'd shouted or thrown glass shards at him.

"It's not going to make it stop."

"I'm sorry," was all he could say, while he thought, *Yeah, but all I can do is run.* If she knew what he'd done she'd never speak to him again. Bad enough now she'd see him as weak.

He paused in the doorway, looked back. She'd lain down again, her back to the door, covers pulled all the way up. He ached to go back to her, but he knew it was for the best.

"Go if you're going to," she said, her voice raw, and he did, leaving her in her warm bed and slipping into the chilly night.

Beth stopped in her tracks as soon as she entered the shop the next morning. "Wow. You look tired. What happened?"

Lainey winced, then sighed. It was true. Between Ben keeping her awake and then leaving after the nightmare she'd gotten pretty much no sleep. "Ben happened."

Beth cocked her head. "If you were glowing, I'd guess the lack of sleep was due to happy times with Ben," she said. "But I'm guessing not so much?"

"It ended badly," Lainey said finally. "I'm not sure what happened. We were—well, we…" She paused as her cheeks heated and Beth's brow rose as a grin stole across her face. "I guess I don't have to explain it to you. But he just left." She shrugged as if it hadn't hurt. After how wonderful everything had been, she couldn't *help* but be hurt.

It infuriated her.

"Just walked out as in thanks and bye?" Beth's tone was incredulous.

"Not quite that crass, but, yeah." Lainey couldn't tell Beth about Ben's nightmare. He seemed to be ashamed of it, and it wasn't her place to tell anyone. "I really don't want to talk about it."

Beth sent her a sympathetic look. "Love is messy."

Lainey nearly dropped the bucket she held. No one had said anything about love. Especially not with a man who was clearly keeping something from her. "We've just got really good chemistry."

"Chemistry is good," Beth said cheerfully. "And, all told, this is a huge improvement over last week, when I told you to go for it and you looked like I'd kicked a puppy." Her voice sobered and she threw an arm around Lainey's shoulders. "Seriously, though, I see more than just chemistry. The way you say his name—"

"Oh, Beth." Lainey interrupted before this got any worse. "I do *not*. Obviously I like him a lot but that's all. There's no more than that."

Except the slight twist in her belly told a different story. The way he'd loved her, cherished her. The way he made her feel important. The way he stood up for her, even to herself. How crushed she'd been when he shut her out last night.

Oh, no.

Beth looked at her steadily. "If you say so."

Lainey forced a smile. "I do say so." As she forced herself to walk casually to the back room, gripping the bucket handle so hard it hurt, she was afraid Beth was right. This whole thing, at least for her, had tipped well past mutual chemistry and into dangerous emotional territory.

Clearly she'd learned nothing from her past.

But Ben wasn't Daniel or Jon. And, really, how would she know love? She'd never been in love before. It most certainly couldn't happen this quickly.

Could it?

Ben sat at the Rusty Hammer bar, a burger with all the trimmings before him. Best damn burgers anywhere, but it could be cardboard for all he could taste it. Still, the owner was looking at him, so he gave it a shot.

Someone settled on the bar stool next to him. A quick glance revealed Kevin Keeler. The other man nodded in acknowledgement and Ben did the same. Fantastic. Just what he needed.

"What can I get you?" The owner had come to stand in front of Kevin.

Kevin inclined his head toward Ben's plate. "One of those and a beer, please."

"On the way." He drew the beer, placed it in front of Kevin and headed for the kitchen.

Kevin took a long draw. He set the glass down with a thunk and half turned to Ben, who braced himself.

"So. What are your intentions toward my sister?"

Ben nearly choked on his burger. Kevin thumped him on the back. "It's probably a good idea to do that in front of a doctor," he observed dryly.

Ben shook his head and grabbed his beer. Was this a trick question? Did Kevin know he'd slept with her? He doubted it. Lainey would never kiss and tell to Kevin. Besides, big brothers weren't inclined to be friendly when you messed with their little sisters.

"Nothing. No intentions. She needed a date and invited me to the gala. That's all." His words were hollow but he hoped Kevin wouldn't pick up on it. He'd never intended anything to go as far as it had, physically or otherwise. She'd filled holes in him that had desperately needed filling, as hard as he'd tried to avoid it.

Kevin tapped his glass. "It doesn't look like *all*," he said. "You were looking at her pretty seriously. With her being pregnant, I need to know what your intentions are."

Ben picked up his beer and took a deliberate swallow. "Like I said—"

Kevin leaned in. "She deserves better than a guy with *no intentions*. A hell of a lot better. She's been through hell and back with that idiot of an ex-husband, not to mention our selfish, clueless parents."

Ben met the other man's serious gaze. "I completely agree. That's why I have no intention of getting tangled up in her life." *Anymore than I already am.* "She asked for a favor. I agreed. She's an amazing woman and I wish her all the best."

Kevin sat back with a frown. "She's got feelings for you."

"I hope not," he said quietly, but he knew Kevin was right. The hell of it was, he had powerful feelings for her, too. "Like I said, I can't give her what she needs." The truth was painful and he gripped the bottle tighter. "So. My intentions are to walk away and let her live her life." The words were like ash in his mouth.

Kevin nodded at the owner, who'd delivered his burger. "I'm not sure if you're smart or a coward."

Ben barked out a laugh. "Truthfully? Me either."

Actually, that wasn't true. He did know. He was keeping Lainey safe, and that wasn't a cowardly move.

Was it?

For all his not wanting to be part of a family, for not wanting home and hearth and kids and a wife, he knew underneath it all he was a sham. He wanted all of it. He wanted what Jason and Callie had had. He didn't know how to open himself up to have it. But if he could— Lainey was a good woman. She'd be a wonderful mother and wife to the right man.

Just not for him.

CHAPTER TEN

LAINEY HURRIED HOME after work on the day of the gala. Of course her mother *would* schedule this party on a Thursday. And, being only her and Beth at the shop, Lainey couldn't exactly take the afternoon off. So she was left with an hour to do all the primping required for a black tie affair.

Her nerves wouldn't settle. She hadn't seen Ben since he'd left that night. She took a deep breath and tried to focus on her hair and make-up, which were thankfully simple. Even with a redo of eyeliner due to her shaking hand. She got the dress on and tried to suck in her belly as she turned to study herself in the full-length mirror. Then she relaxed. The black fabric draped low over her breasts and gathered gently at her stomach, so the pregnancy wasn't obvious.

She eyed the black heels lying on the floor of her room. Sparkly and sexy, they absolutely killed her feet.

She'd make the sacrifice.

The doorbell rang and she scooped up the shoes and made a quick stop in the bathroom. She tried to examine her make-up in the mirror, but all she could see was flushed cheeks and sparkling eyes. She'd piled her hair on her head in an elaborate updo the likes of which she didn't have a reason for too often anymore.

For someone who'd insisted repeatedly this night meant nothing, she'd sure spent a lot of energy stressing over it.

Hearing the bell again, she took a deep breath and hurried over to open the door.

She simply lost her breath.

The tux emphasized Ben's broad shoulders and slim hips. His hair curled a little over the collar, and she took a step back so she didn't reach out to run her fingers through it.

His gaze swept over her in the way a man's did when he appreciated a woman he was interested in. Her nerve-endings sizzled, as if he'd actually caressed her. Heat ran down her spine and he gave her a rare, slow smile.

"You're gorgeous." The words were simple, heartfelt, and she felt her heart stutter at the raw edge in his tone. Daniel had never looked at her like that or said anything so simple—and meant it. Something inside her shifted.

"Thank you," she managed. "So are you."

She stepped aside to let him in. The butterflies in her stomach had grown into bats.

She cleared her throat. "I've just got to get my shoes on."

"All right." He studied her while she sat down and buckled them on her feet. When she stood he must have noticed her wince. "Why do you wear them if they hurt?"

No point in being cagey. "They look great." She lifted the hem of her dress over her ankle so he could see. "See?"

He lifted his gaze from her ankle to her face and she felt the heat of it. She was very glad she'd decided to paint her toenails a sexy red.

An answering sizzle ran through her as he cleared his throat. "Lovely." His voice was still a bit hoarse.

A visceral shudder ran through her at the memory of his hands on her the other night. How wonderful they'd been together. Until he'd left.

She swallowed and grabbed her clutch. "I'm ready."

He rested his hand on the small of her back as they went out her door. The touch was familiar and intimate. "What do women carry in those things anyway?"

"This?" Lainey held up the silver clutch. At his nod she continued. "Well, I've got keys, phone, lipstick, a couple of tissues. A couple of make-up things. The usual girl stuff, I guess." Other than things like tampons, of course. Pregnant girls didn't need those.

"Keys? In there?" He stepped aside so she could lock the door.

"Well, off the ring. Just for the door— Oh!" She turned around and stared at the black coupe, an exact replica of the one she'd owned a year ago. Daniel's gift to her. Recovering before he could notice her shock, she added, "Nice ride."

"Thanks." He opened the door for her and held it while she got in. The rich scent of the buttery leather and the new carpet hit her. A few seconds later he was sliding in the driver's seat. "I didn't think my usual ride was appropriate for tonight. I figured you'd be in a fancy dress and it might be hard to climb in and out of the truck."

Her heart caught. He'd done it for her. Even though she'd ambushed him with it less than two weeks ago, he'd come through. "Thank you," she said after she got her voice back. "It was very thoughtful of you."

"More what you're used to," he said, without looking at her.

Oh, so *that* was how it was. "Ben, you see what I drive now."

He said nothing and she sighed. "It's in my past. And I'm happier without it." The full truth there. That car had symbolized her ultimate failure and catalyzed her ability to do something about it. She gave the dashboard an affectionate little pat and heard Ben's low chuckle.

The full moon hung huge and silver in the obsidian sky as they drove to the Lakeside Country Club. As she looked at it, shining over the lake, she couldn't help but wonder if her mother had managed to call in a favor from somewhere to arrange for the moon.

The club, of course, was gorgeous. What had to be miles of twinkle lights outlined the building, luminaries lined the walkways, and through the wide glass doors she could see a roaring fire in the fireplace. Ben pulled up to the port-cochere and a valet glided forward to open the door. "Good evening, sir and madam," he said as Ben held his hand out and helped Lainey out of the car. She was perfectly capable of exiting on her own, but with Ben it didn't feel like a grand gesture for the sake of it but more as if he wanted to touch her any way he could.

So she let him.

The valet closed the door and took Ben's keys. He cocked his arm at her. "Shall we?"

She tucked her hand in the warm crook of his arm and enjoyed the little fizzy feeling touching him gave her. She took a deep breath and had to keep herself from turning into him to just breathe him in. "Yes. Let's."

After stepping inside and taking care of her wrap, Lainey proceeded with Ben to the hall where the gala was being held. It was early, so the room was little more than half full, and they perused the tables until they found theirs. With her parents, of course. And Kevin.

"Lot of people here already," Ben commented, looking around.

"Yes," Lainey agreed. "Mother does a wonderful job with this." Credit where it was due. Her mother knew how to throw a party.

Lainey spotted her mother heading toward them, a vision in designer gold. On anyone else the form-fitting gown would be tacky. On Jacqui it was perfect.

"Lainey." She offered her cheek and Lainey dutifully kissed her, then offered her own.

"Hi, Mother." She laid a hand on Ben's arm, felt the heat of him through his sleeve. "This is Ben Lawless. Ben, this is my mother—Jacqui Keeler."

Jacqui gave Ben an obvious once-over. He held out his hand with a smile and she took it.

"Nice to meet you," he said.

"Likewise," she said, and turned to Lainey. "Now, honey, you two mingle for a bit before you take your seats. And no leaving until ten o'clock." Someone must have signaled her mother, because Jacqui turned abruptly to leave before Lainey could say a word. "I'll see you at dinner." And she was gone.

"Sorry," Lainey said immediately. "My mom's a little intense. Don't take it personally." What Jacqui could find lacking in the smoking hot package that was Ben, Lainey couldn't fathom. Because he wasn't Daniel? Couldn't give her what her mother deemed most important—money?

"I see that," Ben said as he steered her toward a buffet table piled high with sinful goodies. "And I'm not offended. Let's get something to drink."

Along the way they got pulled into several conversations—people who knew Lainey, or thought they did. The whole process was as exhausting as it always had been to smile for her mother or stump for her father. Tonight was a bit of both.

"Here." Ben pushed a golden flute into her hand. "I know your…situation. But I think you need this. Just carry it if nothing else."

The champagne bubbled in the flute and Lainey took

a tiny sip. It fizzed in her mouth and slid down her throat. Ben was right. Just having it in her hand was enough. She didn't need anyone questioning why she refused to drink. "Thank you. It hits the spot."

Ben bent so his mouth was next to her ear. She could hear him over the band, which had just started up. "You're welcome."

Lainey hoped he didn't notice the little shiver that skittered down her spine at his warm breath on her skin. She was so, so lost to this man. And he didn't even know it.

He moved away slightly and she felt the immediate loss of contact. She chided herself for letting herself get caught up in this even for a moment. Despite her decision to enjoy tonight, it wasn't real. It didn't change anything.

"So, what's good here?" Ben asked her as they surveyed the table loaded with *hors d'oeuvres* of every persuasion. There were tiny *petit-fours*, as well as fancy little things that looked like shrimp, mushrooms, cheese. All high end. No mini hot dogs for this party.

"I'd say all of it," she said. "My mother doesn't skimp on this stuff."

He smiled and handed her a plate. "Not surprised."

Lainey took a few small things and put them on her plate, and Ben did the same. Her brother approached them and Lainey braced herself.

"Laine," Kevin greeted her. She noticed he was dateless, and frowned.

"Kev, where's your date? How did *you* get away with coming stag?" Realizing how her words sounded, she quickly turned to Ben.

He just nodded at Kevin and said, "I see someone I need to talk to. I'll catch up with you in a bit, okay?"

"Um, okay," Lainey said, feeling like a total heel.

"Nice job," Kevin commented, lifting a flute of champagne from a passing waiter. "You've got a way with men, sis."

Lainey sent him a sour look, even though he was right. "I didn't mean it how it sounded." Still, she'd hurt Ben with her thoughtless comment. And after he'd gone to such trouble for her tonight. She tracked him with her eyes and noticed he'd stopped next to a tall, gorgeous, slender blond. Who couldn't possibly have natural boobs. Lainey frowned.

"And you're not listening to anything I say," Kevin said, amusement in his tone. "You can't take your eyes off the guy, can you? Does Mother know?"

"Does Mother know what?" Jacqui materialized next to them and peered critically at Lainey's plate. "Be careful, dear. I know you're—" she glanced around and lowered her voice "—pregnant, but you don't want to gain a lot of weight."

Lainey looked at her and for the first time saw an unhappy, brittle woman whose need to control everything had nearly estranged her from her children and whose marriage had taken a serious toll on her self-worth. Instead of being insulted by her thoughtless words, Lainey felt only pity.

"No worries, Mother," she said smoothly, and selected a prosciutto something from her plate. She was eating for two, right? Might as well do it tonight. "Lovely party, by the way."

Effectively sidetracked, Jacqui glowed. "It is, isn't it? Almost time to get seated for dinner. Lainey, get your date. Kevin, thanks for coming. I know you have to get back later."

Lainey's gaze lasered to Ben as her mother hurried off. Now he was laughing with the blond, his dark head near her golden one. Something sour curled in her belly. Couldn't be jealousy, could it? Despite their night together, and all her feelings for him, she had no actual claim on him. None at all.

So it was silly and petty to be jealous.

As if he'd felt her watching him, he lifted his head and locked on her gaze. The sour feeling was replaced by something much, much sweeter.

Kevin stepped closer, into her line of sight, his gaze intense and knowing. Her stomach sank.

"Anything you want to tell me, sis?"

Lainey stared up at him. *Oh, no.* She swallowed hard. "No. Nothing."

He gave a little nod and stepped back. He looked as if he wanted to say something, then thought better of it and turned and walked away.

Ben made his way through the crowd to Lainey. Her gaze snapped to his and relief lit her big blue eyes just for a moment. Then it was gone.

"Sorry about that," Ben said, coming up next to her. She smelled so good. Like vanilla and something sinful. Sweet and sinful. That was Lainey, all wrapped up in one sexy package.

Sexy *pregnant* package, that was.

God, he was in trouble.

"It's okay." Her voice was a little remote. "Of course you know people here."

"Megan is an old friend, but not *that* kind of friend." Ben surprised himself by how important it was that she understand. "I was surprised to see her here."

She gave him a sideways look. "I get it."

He caught her hand and twined his fingers with hers. She looked down, clearly startled, then up to his face.

"Lainey. You are the only woman I can see." The words were rough in his throat, but true in every sense. There was no one but her. If things were different there would never be anyone but her. All he could give her was tonight. It had to be enough.

Her gaze stayed on his, her blue eyes wide and hopeful, fearful. He wanted to drown in them, in her. Instead he gave her fingers a squeeze and stepped back. "I take it we're supposed to sit down?"

A shadow passed over her face quickly, then she smiled. "Shall we?"

They made their way to the table. He noted she kept an eye on her parents, who were still mingling and mixing and chatting up the guests. The table was set for eight and Kevin was already there, his gaze firmly on Ben.

His words from the other night hit him hard. *No intentions.* Yeah, he was a liar. He wanted so much more than he could give her—wanted to give her what she deserved—and Kevin's hard stare said he knew it. Not only that, he knew Ben was going to walk. Ben met the other man's gaze squarely. They both knew she deserved better.

Dinner went fairly quickly. Prime rib, decadent desserts, rich sides all filled the plates. Ben hadn't eaten so well in ages. Lainey, he noted, only picked at her food.

"Not hungry?"

She looked up and flushed. "Not really. These things— it's not my cup of tea." She slid her plate toward him. "Here. Help yourself if you want."

He did fork up a couple of pieces of her prime rib, because it *was* prime rib and he was a guy. He caught Jacqui's fierce frown at her daughter as she got up and he wondered at it.

Jacqui walked to the microphone at the front of the room. After a little speech of welcome and thanks, she added, "Dancing will begin as soon as the last of the plates are cleared. Don't forget the silent auction—there's still time to place your bids."

"I'm going to hit the ladies' room," Lainey murmured to him. She stood and picked up her little silver purse. "Back in a few."

"So. Ben." Her father leaned forward across the table as soon as Lainey had left. "How do you know my daughter?"

Wow, was he sixteen again, or what? He kept his tone level. "Through my grandmother. Lainey's been helping her out at her place."

The man looked surprised. "Really?"

Ben nodded. "I think her visits are the highlight of Grandma's week." How could this guy not know the kind of person his daughter was?

"What do you do for a living?"

Ben tensed just slightly. This man could and would ferret out the truth, and Ben would bet he wanted to know. "I'm a firefighter."

Greg Keeler arched a brow. "Really? Where?"

"City of Grand Rapids." He hesitated for a beat as he met the other man's gaze. "I'm on medical leave right now." Better just to say it than have it found out and used against Lainey somehow.

The very fact he was even concerned was a problem.

The older man's gaze sharpened. It was no doubt only a matter of time before the man looked him up if he thought Ben was interested in his daughter. "I hope your recovery is going well."

Ben managed a smile. "Well enough." Actually, there was some truth to that. Being around Lainey had helped him. Better than any therapy.

Greg leaned across the table. "While being a firefighter is a very important job, you need to realize you're not what we have in mind for Lainey," he said, almost apologetically. "Her ex-husband is a partner in a very prestigious law firm. I understand they're considering reconciliation."

Ben's brow shot up, as did his pulse. He sure as hell hadn't seen any indication that Lainey was interested in her ex-husband. In fact, if memory served him, she was no fan of his. "Is that so? Then why isn't he here with her?"

"Because I didn't invite him." Lainey's voice was cold as she stood behind Ben and regarded her father with sharp eyes. "He's my ex-husband for a lot of very good reasons."

Her father sat back and shook his head. "Lainey—"

She shot him a hard look and turned to Ben as the band struck up. "Want to dance?"

"Of course." He pushed back from the table and inclined his head to Greg. The older man crossed his arms and frowned as he led Lainey away.

"How about a walk instead?" he asked. The band was playing, but it was too early to dance. They'd be the only ones on the floor, and possibly the center of attention. He doubted Lainey wanted that.

She nodded. "I'd like that."

He put his hand at the small of her back, because he couldn't not touch her, and they made their way to the glass doors at the other end of the room. They opened out to a sheltered patio that overlooked the water. It was chilly, but he figured he'd keep her warm.

As soon as they were outside she took an audible breath. Sympathy filled him. "Is that the first time you've breathed all evening?"

She gave him a rueful smile. "Seems like it. Old habits. I never wanted to do anything that might draw attention to myself. I always wanted to be anywhere but here."

"I can understand that." Seeing her interact with her family—except for her brother—was eye-opening.

"Can you?" She leaned on the railing and the position

allowed him a fantastic view of her breasts. He shifted position slightly so he could see better—if he chose to look—and so no one coming up next to them would get the same treat.

"You don't think I can?"

"I don't know. My childhood was so lonely. I didn't have a Rose. As you can see, I didn't even have normal parents." She didn't look at him. "What was yours like?"

He rested a hip on the railing. "Normal, I guess. Both parents—though they got divorced when I was twelve. My brother and sister. All of them live downstate, around Detroit. After the divorce things changed, but our parents took a lot of trouble to make sure we knew we were loved." Really, they'd been lucky. He could see that now, in Lainey's wistful expression.

She was quiet for a moment. "I'm sorry about my dad. I'm not sure what got into him."

"He wants what's best for you." The words caused an ache in his chest. It wasn't him. But part of him—a huge part—wished it was.

Her laugh was low and sad. "If that's true, they should know Daniel's not what's best. The man's a snake." She turned and looked up into his eyes. "There's no chance of reconciliation, by the way."

While he truly hadn't thought so, relief still trickled through him. "You definitely deserve better than a snake."

A smile tugged at the corners of her mouth. "Aw. That's so sweet."

He touched her chin. *You are the sweet one,* he wanted to say. Actually, he wanted to say much more than that, and it worried him. The band struck up a slower tune and he held out a hand. "Dance with me?"

She looked up, startled. "Out here?"

"We can go inside if you'd rather. But there are more eyes."

"Good point." She turned to face him and he pulled her into his arms, then steered her away from the railing into the deeper shadows caused by the overhang of the roof.

She felt so good in his arms. She fit so well. He tried not to think of the other night, when they'd moved together in perfect sync. He pulled her closer and felt her stiffen slightly. It shouldn't matter, but it did.

He lowered his head to her ear. "You can relax. I don't bite."

She gave a half-giggle, half-sigh, and he was pleased to feel her body relax a little. "I know. I'm sorry. Just trying to get through this…" Her voice trailed off as he tugged her a little closer, so her breasts touched his chest. Her breath hitched just a bit and she shivered.

"Cold?" His voice was low, and he pulled her in even closer. She'd be able to feel, now, just how affected he was by her. What he couldn't tell her was how right she felt in his arms, how much he felt as if he'd finally come home.

"Not at all," she breathed, and tipped her face up to his.

Unable to help himself, he pressed a kiss on her soft mouth. Two things crossed his mind.

He was in trouble.

And, after all she'd done for him, she deserved to know the truth.

CHAPTER ELEVEN

THE MOMENTS SPENT in Ben's arms were magical. Almost as magical as the other night. Lainey hadn't thought dancing could be so intimate, but somehow they were in their own little world of two. She didn't want it to end, and that was a first. But, since the band had taken a break for her mother to announce the winners of the silent auction, maybe it was time to take their own personal party elsewhere.

"Do you want to leave?"

Ben's arm was draped across the back of her chair and he brushed his fingers over her bare shoulder. "This is your shindig, Laine. You know the protocol better than I do."

She leaned forward to pick up her clutch from the table. "Then let's go. My feet are killing me."

His low chuckle warmed her. "Sacrifice over?"

"Something like that." She scanned the crowd. "I'll have to say goodnight to my mother. Give me a minute to track her down."

"I'll go with you." He unfolded himself from his chair and offered her his arm. She took it. All the vibes he gave off were those of a man who liked her, desired her—yet there was a layer underneath she couldn't quite get to…a place he kept away from her. It contrasted sharply with the intimacy of the evening. With how badly she wanted to open her heart to him.

How afraid she was, after tonight, that she already had.

Lainey found her mother near the auction exhibits. "We're heading out. It was a lovely party, Mother."

"You're leaving?" Jacqui's gaze darted from Lainey to Ben and back again. "So soon?"

Lainey kept her gaze steady on her mother's. "Yes. I'm tired and my feet hurt."

"Of course. I guess in your—" she lowered her voice "—condition that's to be expected." Someone called out to Jacqui then, and she offered her cheek to Lainey, who dropped the expected kiss. "Go straight home," she instructed, and hurried off.

Lainey sighed at the words and turned to Ben. "Shall we?"

"Absolutely." He put his hand on her back again—a gesture that Lainey was starting to love for its quiet possessiveness. It didn't take long for them to get the car and head toward home.

"Will you—will you come in?" she asked when he pulled in her driveway. The bold words startled her, especially in light of how their night together had ended before. Was she really willing to have him run away again?

He turned to her, and by the light of the dash she could see the pain in his eyes. "I'm not sure that's a good idea."

She sucked in a breath, the shininess of the evening tarnished. "Of course. Well. Thank you for everything." For the dances. For the kisses. For the feeling that this was actually going to be able to go somewhere when he must not feel the same. How could she have read it all so wrong?

He reached over the console and caught her hand as she fumbled for the door handle. "No. Lainey. Wait. I just don't want to hurt you."

She stared at him. They were in this far too deep for that. "We're adults. I know you're leaving, Ben. I know this isn't forever." But given the chance she'd take forever. The thought rocked her.

He rubbed his thumb over her lower lip and she closed her eyes.

"I can't stay the night."

The hesitation in his voice made her open them again. "All I was going to offer was coffee."

He laughed and rested his forehead on hers. "Lainey... God. I don't deserve you."

He got out of the car, and as he walked around to her door she whispered, "Yes, you do."

"Did you tell her yet?"

Ben put the leftover roast back in the fridge. For two people, they had enough to feed them for a week. Maybe two. "Tell who what?"

Rose wheeled around and he saw her frown. "Don't play games with me, Benjamin. When are you going to tell Lainey about Jason?"

He shut the fridge and stared at the sandwich he no longer had an appetite for. He was tired, he wanted to get out of the tux, and he had no idea why his grandmother had waited up for him. "I'm not, Grandma. She doesn't need to know." He didn't want her to think less of him.

Her gaze went to slits. "Oh, yes, she does. You are in love with that girl—"

Panic sliced through him. "She's hardly a girl—" *That* was what he protested? He'd meant to say no way was he in love with Lainey. Sure, she'd helped him open up in ways he hadn't thought were possible, but that didn't mean he was in love with her.

His grandma waved his words away impatiently. "Semantics. When you're my age a thirty-something woman is a girl. You love her—even if you aren't willing to admit it yet. She's got it equally bad for you. I would have thought going with her tonight would help you see that. You don't have forever, Ben. Ask Callie."

Her voice was quiet, and Ben sank down in a chair as if she'd taken an axe to his knees. "Geez, Grandma, how can you say that?"

She wheeled closer, her gaze intense. "Do you think Jason wasted one single minute when he first spotted that girl? No, he didn't. He had some good years with her, loved her fully. And he—he alone—was reckless and lost it all. How do you think Callie would feel, knowing you are throwing your own chance at love away because her husband is gone? Is that going to make her feel better? Bring Jason back?"

Her words pinged around in him, echoing in his head. "I— No, of course not."

She poked him in the chest. "Listen to me. I know a thing or two about love, having been married to your grandpa Harry for fifty-odd years. You've found a woman who'd give you everything. You're walking away because Jason isn't here. Ask yourself—would he divorce Callie if the roles were reversed?"

He shook his head and stood up. "Of course he wouldn't. But it's not that easy, Grandma. He went in that building after me. I shouldn't have been there to begin with. It was my job to keep him safe." *I failed him.*

"It was a miscommunication that was out of your control and not your personal responsibility," she said simply. "He made a choice. He knew the risks. You both did. It's part of the job. You weren't his babysitter. You need to go see Callie. But first you need to accept that it's time to move on."

He went cold. See Callie? See first hand the destruction he'd caused? He hadn't even been able to face returning her calls. He wasn't sure he'd be welcome, that she'd want to see him. He didn't want to make things worse for her, for her kids. For Jason's sake. For her own.

For his.

But this wasn't about him.

Rose laid a hand on his arm. "You need to accept that it's okay to move on," she said quietly. "You're a good man. You deserve Lainey, and Lord knows both of you deserve to be happy. Even beyond that, she needs you and you need her. Don't let it slip away."

Her words rang true. But he didn't know if he was capable of being the man Lainey and her baby deserved. The risk of failing them was far too great. He'd failed Jason, and by extension Callie.

When he closed his eyes all he saw was Lainey. All he heard was her laugh, her voice. He could still feel her in his arms. But he couldn't be in love with her. He'd shut that part of himself down for good.

Hadn't he?

It was time to sign the paperwork.

Lainey'd read over the pages from Jon and asked Beth's husband, who was a lawyer, to look over them as well. While technically she'd need to take him to court to finalize the custody transfer, it should be able to be handled with lawyers only. This was the necessary first step to being well and truly free of her baby's father. She signed them and put them away, both relieved and a little sad.

She went into the kitchen and had just started a pot of coffee—decaf, of course—when there was a knock on the front door. She padded over that way and took a look through the peephole.

Daniel stood on the front step.

Lainey inhaled sharply and leaned her head on the door.

She'd love to ignore him, but her car was in the driveway instead of the garage. And she knew he wouldn't go away.

She opened the door. "This is a bad time, Daniel. I'm really tired."

He looked her over, his gaze both hot and contemptuous, and she gripped the door tighter.

"I just want to talk."

He tried the old charming smile, but it did nothing but annoy her. She crossed her arms. "Try again. We've got nothing left to say to each other. Why are you really here, Daniel?"

He dropped all pretense. "You're pregnant." He nearly spat the words.

Her pulse picked up in warning. "Yes, I am."

"How are you going to raise it by yourself?" He stepped a little closer and she forced herself to hold her ground. "You'll be a single mother. Who's going to raise it with you?"

Ben. Oh, if only. "I'm going to be a single mother, yes. Did you need something? Because I've got things to do—"

He interrupted her. "You're making a mistake, Lainey. Your parents have opened their house to you. They're trying to help you. We all are. Don't you see? I can take care of the money problems you have. You won't have to do anything you don't want to do."

Anger spiked. "I won't have to do what? Work at a job I love? Something that has meaning to me? That I get up each morning and *want* to do? Why do you want to take that from me?"

He blinked at her. "No one's taking anything from you. We're offering solutions so you don't have to struggle anymore. Especially now that you are pregnant."

"What I need is to make my own solutions," she said simply. "Not have yours forced on me. And the fact you can't see that means you don't know me at all. You never did."

He frowned and put his hands in his pockets. "Of course I knew you. You were my wife for seven years."

And in all that time you never picked out one birthday gift. She shook her head. "I was a tool. I was the means to an end—which was my father." Funny how she couldn't muster up any fire. She truly didn't care. He was so far behind her now he'd never catch up.

His expression radiated sincerity, but she knew better than to believe it. "I'm sorry you felt that way, Lainey. I cleaned some things up before I came here. I've changed. I made a mistake or two. You of all people know what it's like to make mistakes."

The words hit home. Still. "Yes. I do. But my baby isn't one of them. Also, I never hurt anyone or deceived anyone like you did. You made a mockery of our marriage. Of me. And that's why, even if I'd ever loved you, I wouldn't get back with you. *That* would be the biggest mistake of my life." She stepped back. "Now, if you'll excuse me, my coffee is ready."

Daniel crowded closer and stepped inside the door. His tone was wheedling. "No, wait. It was good with us, Lainey. It's better for a baby to have a father. We can have some of our own."

"No." She'd never inflict a man like Daniel on a poor kid. No child deserved that. "You need to leave. Now."

Daniel grabbed her by the upper arms, and when she tried to pull away he dug in harder. She swallowed a yelp of pain. "Lainey. This is what works best for me. For both of us. You—"

The door banged open and Daniel let go of her in surprise. Ben stood there, and the smoldering anger on his face took Lainey's breath away.

"Get away from her." The words were a low growl.

Daniel reached for her again. "Lainey, listen—"

"Get out," she hissed. "Don't come back."

Ben took a menacing step toward Daniel and he took a step in the right direction. "She asked you to leave."

Daniel scowled, cursed, and slammed out the door.

She turned to Ben, willing her heart to return to normal, unsure if it was pumping so hard from the encounter with her idiot ex or Ben's very intoxicating nearness. "Why are you here?"

"I was in the neighborhood and saw him through the door." He shoved his hands in his pockets. "I thought you could use backup."

She pressed her hands to her face. "I wish everyone would stop trying to help me. I had it under control."

"Of course," he murmured. "I saw him handling you and jumped to conclusions."

She laid her hand on his arm as he turned to go. "No. Please. I'm sorry. I'm just so sick of my family interfering. You did me a favor by showing up here. It's not the first time he's handled me roughly."

His eyes went to slits. "He abused you?"

"No." She shook her head. "He'd grab me, like you saw tonight, but he almost never touched me. In any manner." Then she blushed as it hit her what she'd admitted.

Ben touched her face and the delicious roughness of his fingers on her skin caused a little shiver to run down her back. "Lainey. How could he be married to you and not see what he had?"

Her gaze pinged to his at his words and the rawness in his voice and she barely dared to breathe. The reverence she saw there made her want to cry. Daniel had never looked at her like that. Ever.

She clasped his wrist and turned into his touch. "I don't think he ever saw me, Ben. That's not what he wanted."

Ben didn't get that. He looked at her and wanted everything. Wanted the whole package. Wanted the baby, the chance to be a father. It was killing him. He didn't know how to reconcile things so he could have it. *Jason, dead. Lainey, pregnant. Baby, not his.* They all bothered him and worried him and he didn't know how to move forward. She looked at him with those big eyes and he wanted to take her in his arms, into his bed, and let her soothe away the pain. Only letting go of it all seemed like a betrayal to Jason. And dumping it on her was more than he could ask of her.

Would she think less of him? He couldn't deny it mattered, even though he wished it didn't.

"Ben?"

He looked into her worried face and couldn't help the question. He needed to know. "So he's not the father?"

Her head snapped up and she laughed—a sharp bark. "God, no." She stepped away and shut the door. "Can I get you something? A drink?"

He smelled coffee. "Coffee's fine."

He followed her to the kitchen, trying and failing to keep his gaze off her perfect ass in those clingy black pants. He leaned in the doorway while she opened cupboards and lifted slightly on her toes to get mugs. The movement pulled her shirt snug across her breasts and the slight swell of her belly. He wanted nothing more than to pull her against him, hold her tiny bump in his hands. The longing nearly brought him to his knees.

She poured the coffee with a slightly shaking hand, and he accepted his. She got out milk, sugar and spoons, and led him to the small table in the dining room. He sat opposite her and watched as she doctored her coffee.

"Let me tell you about my baby's father. This is not

a story I'm proud of," she said quietly, and took a deep breath. Then she poured out the whole thing, without meeting his gaze.

Ben cursed. "He didn't tell you he was married?"

She stirred her coffee without taking her eyes off the mug. "Nope. And I didn't figure it out. Pathetic, I know."

"He is. You're not." When her head came up and she opened her mouth he held up a hand. "Let me see if I've got this right. You were recovering from a marriage that was completely loveless and lacking in affection or respect of any kind. This guy showed up and took advantage of that. How is that *you* being pathetic?"

She stared into her mug. "I just should have known better."

"Oh, honey." The endearment startled him, but he meant it. "No. He took advantage of you. That's not on you."

"I could have said no." She shut her eyes. "It wasn't like I really wanted him. It was just the idea of someone actually wanting me."

"Yeah." He pulled her to her feet. "But if you had said no, you wouldn't have this." He laid his hand on her belly and her eyes went wide. She laid her hand on top of his. "Would you wish this away?"

"Never," she said quietly. She took a deep breath. "The only thing I'd wish for is a better father for him or her. Someone like you." The words were nearly a whisper, and her soft gaze caught his.

He froze as if ice had formed in his muscles. "No, Lainey, not like me. I'm no good for you, for a baby." He wasn't what she needed. Not anymore.

She saw the shields come down and all but heard the resounding clang as they locked into place. She forced herself to hold his gaze and pressed his trembling hand against her belly. He wanted this, wanted her. She knew it—could see it. Had been seeing it as they'd gone through the past couple weeks. She wanted him too, even knowing how impossible the situation was.

"Why not?"

He slid his hand out from under hers and stepped away. The coldness she felt was as much at the loss of contact as it was for his emotional shutdown. "I can't talk about it."

She gave a little laugh and fought against the burn of tears. "Oh? But it's okay for me to spill my shames to you? It's a one-way street?"

"It's not that simple." His voice was low.

She lifted her chin. "My problems aren't simple."

"No. No, they're not," he agreed. "I meant it's not—it's not something I can talk about."

That destroyed look was back, and her heart ached. She was falling in love with this man, and he would never let her close enough to help. To love him as he deserved. As he needed.

She thought of the nightmare but didn't bring it up. The fact he chose to shut her out hurt, but what claim did she have to him? They'd been physical, she was emotionally invested, but there was no actual commitment—nothing that would mean he should tell her what had happened.

Still. She had to try. "You don't have to carry this alone," she said quietly. "Whatever it is."

He stared at a spot on the wall, but she doubted he was seeing anything in the room. "Some things have to be," he said finally, and the pain in his voice burned in her heart. He shoved a hand through his hair. "I'm sorry, Lainey. It's just so damn hard to talk about."

She got out of her chair and moved to kneel next to him. He wouldn't look at her. "Why?" she asked, and held her breath.

His jaw worked. "I killed my best friend, okay?" At her

sharp whimper he looked her in the eye. "I made a stupid mistake and a great guy died. A family man. He left his wife and two little kids. Sons who will never know their daddy now because of a mistake *I* made."

Pain washed through her—for him, for the man's family. She wanted to climb in his lap and hold him, but settled for touching his face, feeling the roughness of stubble under her hand. "Oh, Ben. I'm so sorry."

His eyes glittered with unshed tears as he looked at her. "Not as sorry as I am. I'm not the man you want, Lainey."

"Don't you think I get to decide that?" she asked, and tugged him to his feet. He let her, and she slid her arms around him, rested her head on his chest and squeezed her eyes shut as she listened to the pounding of his heart beneath her cheek. The warmth of him seeped into her pores and pooled in her heart. He stood very still for a moment, then wrapped his arms around her, too. She hoped he would allow himself to take comfort from it, from her.

They stood that way for a few minutes, then Lainey heard her phone ring. Ben stepped back, the moment broken. "I'd better get going. You okay?"

She looked at him and saw the careful remoteness back in his gaze. Her heart ached as she nodded and followed him through the living room to the door. "Fine."

He turned around and lifted her chin, his fingers lingering. The look in his eyes was a strange mixture of regret and affection. He leaned down and planted a hard kiss on her mouth. "You're not any kind of damaged goods, Lainey. Don't let anyone make you feel otherwise. Ever. You're an incredible woman." Then he left.

Lainey pressed her fingertips to her tingling mouth, her heart heavy as the front door clicked shut behind him. The tears she'd been fighting finally broke loose, and as she sank back down at the table, head on her arms, she had another thought.

His parting words had sounded an awful lot like good-bye.

CHAPTER TWELVE

AT THE END of the next day Lainey went into the little office area in the back of the store and checked her books. The familiar feeling of dread pooled as she added up the numbers. Better, but not good enough. She could chart steady progress upward, though, so that was hopeful. But was it enough?

"What's the verdict?" Beth walked over.

Lainey leaned back so her friend could see the screen and rested her hands on her belly. "Better. Definitely better. But not there. Yet."

Beth hesitated. "Mark and I were talking. If you're interested, we can probably swing me buying in if you want a partner."

Stunned, Lainey stared at her friend. "I— Beth, I hadn't—"

Beth held up a hand. "I know you want to do this all on your own. But you can be a success even with a partner. It doesn't make it less because you have help." She smiled and touched Lainey's shoulder. "Think about it, okay?"

"I will," she promised.

After Beth left, she stared at the numbers on the screen. Beth buying in would mean a new cooler. Repairs on the van, which even today had given her fits about going into gear. Bigger payments to her parents and therefore being out from under their thumb earlier.

Excitement and hope flared.

It was tempting. But was it the right decision?

She stood and paced out into the shop. She took in the silk flowers, the cheery Halloween-themed window. Sure, the carpet was worn, and the cash register was old but completely reliable. The fresh scent of the flowers over-laid everything and made it feel almost homey. This place was more than just a business. She loved it—loved all of it. It suited her to a T. Because of that, she couldn't let it go under. What good was it to be determined to prove herself if ultimately it sank her? That would only prove her par-ents right and she'd be back where she started.

She'd gone too far to let it all go under now.

She took a deep breath and walked into the backroom. Beth was right. She just needed to make sure the numbers were stable enough for her friend to take the risk. And then she and Beth and Mark would look them over together. She wouldn't let them buy in if it turned out to be too risky. She wanted to succeed, but she was pragmatic enough to realize she wasn't out of the woods just yet.

A lightness she hadn't felt in a very long time crept into her heart. This was the right thing to do. Too bad she'd been so damn blind she hadn't been able to see it. Or maybe she hadn't been *ready* to see it. She owed Beth for putting it all into perspective.

After leaving work, Lainey pulled into Rose's driveway. She'd promised to take her friend to bingo. Ben's truck sat there, and she tried to quash the silly little spurt of an-ticipation. She'd stop in and say hello. Sort of face the el-ephant in the room head-on—see if his confession to her had done any good for him.

The light in the garage indicated he was in there, even though the big door was shut. She opened up the side door and stepped inside, almost holding her breath. How this went depended on how he looked at her when he saw her.

Her heart sank when he turned. His face was the polite mask he'd worn when she'd first met him. "Lainey."

"Hello, Ben." She kept her voice steady with effort. Two could play this game. He just looked at her and waited. "I just—wanted to see how you were. After last night." Darn it, she sounded tentative. But his impassive expression wasn't helping.

"How should I be?" He kept his gaze on her. Completely shuttered. "Nothing's changed, Lainey, if that's what you're asking."

Well, that was to the point. "Okay, then," she said stiffly. "See you around."

And she left the garage, slamming the door behind her. Not the most mature of moves, but the man frustrated her no end.

On the short walk to the house she took a couple of deep breaths, hoping Rose wouldn't notice her mood. She didn't want to be quizzed—just wanted to lick her wounds in peace.

No such luck. Rose took one look at her as soon as she entered the kitchen and frowned. "Okay. First Ben, now you. That boy's been in a serious funk all day. What happened? He won't tell me."

Lainey blanched but managed a small smile. "Nothing happened."

Rose shook her head. "Oh, no. I may be old, but I'm neither blind nor stupid. There's much more than that, isn't there?" She sat back and examined Lainey. "Did he tell you about Jason?"

She gave a little nod. "I don't know what to tell him, Rose."

Her friend gave a little sigh. "There's really not much to say. He's got a lot to work out. On top of that, nothing ties a man up in knots more than when a relationship that was supposed to be casual turns out not to be."

Lainey gave a little shrug that she hoped was casual, even though she felt anything but. "It's the wrong time."

Rose gave a decidedly unladylike snort. "It's always the wrong time. You don't get to pick when or who you'll fall in love with, child. I see how that boy looks at you. Does he know you're pregnant?"

Despite Rose's gentle tone, the words might as well have been a shout. Lainey winced. "Yes. How did *you* know?" Had Ben told Rose after she'd asked him not to?

"Not from him," Rose assured her. "I can just tell. You've changed physically. And the fact you told him should tell you something, honey."

Startled, Lainey met her friend's gaze. "Tell me what?"

"You told him before you told me," she said gently, and raised a hand when Lainey opened her mouth to protest. "No—no, wait. I'm not saying you should have told me first. But think about it. Why did you tell Ben?"

"I had to tell him why I couldn't go to the hospital for an X-ray," Lainey pointed out, but in retrospect she could see the holes in that theory. Why *had* she blurted it out?

Rose nodded. "But there were other reasons you could have given. Or, for that matter, no reason at all. He didn't need an explanation. A simple no thanks would have sufficed. He wouldn't have pushed. But you felt safe enough to tell him. Am I right?"

That was true. She hadn't needed to tell him. But feeling safe? With Ben? He made her feel anything *but* safe.

Well, that wasn't entirely true. He'd made her feel safe

and cherished the night they'd spent together. The danger from Ben wasn't that he'd take her for granted, or treat her like her ex had. It was that he made her want things she couldn't have, that he couldn't give. And she wasn't willing to open herself to any more emotional destruction.

"Lainey." Rose leaned forward. "I know you've been through an awful lot. You have very little reason to trust people. The fact you told him is significant. The fact he went to that party with you is significant. He hasn't done anything social in months."

"The timing is all wrong," Lainey said again, because it was true. "He's not in any place for a relationship, and I— Well, I really need to do this on my own." Actually, she was starting to rethink that statement. If Beth bought in to her shop what counted was making it a success. The same idea applied to her personal life. Having a partner in life would be wonderful—but only if it was the right man.

Was Ben that man?

Rose sat back. "I understand. I do. I just want to see both of you happy. And if the two of you could be happy together—well, that would do my heart good."

"I'll be fine," Lainey assured her. Fine wasn't the same as happy, of course, and she doubted very much the distinction would be wasted on Rose.

Rose studied her for a long moment, then nodded. "I'm glad to hear it," she said. "We should get going. Don't want to be late for bingo."

Grateful to be off the hook, Lainey stood up and gathered her purse and keys.

As she wheeled her friend down the ramp Ben came out of the garage. Her heart gave a little leap and she was glad she was behind Rose, so her sharp-eyed friend didn't read anything that might be on her face. He gave Lainey a nod and she managed to smile back. As he came closer she could see the stress lines bracketing his mouth. She wanted nothing more in that moment than to go to him and smooth them away, to hold him and be held.

She looked away instead.

Ben helped Rose into the car and took care of the chair while Lainey slid behind the wheel. As they backed out of the driveway Rose narrowed her gaze on Ben, who stood watching them, hands in pockets. She muttered something that sounded like, "Foolish boy."

No, Lainey wanted to tell her. He's smart enough to know his limits.

And so was she.

"So, we've got a Friday wedding this week," Lainey noted. The flowers were simple and seasonal, fitting for a second wedding for both the bride and groom. They were starting on the bouquets today. "And a big order for a baptism on Sunday."

"Isn't it great?" Beth asked as she cut open a flower box. "Word is getting out. We're doing good."

Lainey agreed. Part of her was a little sad, though, that her personal life seemed to be one-hundred-eighty degrees away from her growing professional life. But to dwell on it wouldn't do her any good.

"Speaking of weddings," Beth said casually, "how's Ben?"

Lainey sent her a warning look. "Beth—"

"What?" Her friend's innocent look didn't fool Lainey. She shook her head and Beth sighed. "Okay. I heard at the café that you and Ben were super cozy at the hospital gala." She plopped a box on the worktable and sent Lainey a mock glare. "Of course I didn't hear that from *you*. My supposed best friend and subject of such hot gossip."

Super-cozy. Well, she supposed they *had* been all

wrapped up in each other and the spell of the evening. Dancing and kissing in the shadows. His car in front of her house for hours.

"I— Well, yeah. I guess it would look that way." She winced. "Don't people have anything else to talk about? Surely there were more interesting couples than Ben and I?"

Beth gave her a pitying look. "Lainey, I think the interesting part was the chemistry the two of you have. I heard that you were so hot together people were concerned you'd combust. Or maybe get down right there," she added thoughtfully, earning a playful smack from Lainey.

"Well, it doesn't matter now," she said, thinking of last night and how he'd been completely shut down. Pain lanced through her. She'd give anything to have this work out, to make it so they could be a couple.

But that wasn't an option. It was silly even to think it was.

"How is that?" Beth asked. "The guy kissed you. At least that much. But from how red you just turned I'm guessing it's much more than that. He helped you move. He took you to a formal party on short notice. Guys don't just do that for women they aren't interested in."

"His grandma sent him to help me," Lainey muttered. Beth didn't know how far things had gone with them, but they must have been giving off some pretty serious vibes at the gala. "And that first kiss was a pity kiss."

"Pity kiss?" Beth raised her brow. "Oh, come on, Laine. Ben doesn't seem like that type. He's so reserved. He's not going to go around kissing women because he thinks it will make them feel better."

Beth had a point. Still… "I meant it was just the moment." They'd had a lot of wonderful moments that she held on to tightly. Privately.

"Moment or not—and I think you are withholding key information from me, but I'll let it go this time—there's clearly something between you. The question is, what are you going to do about it?"

A little shiver ran through Lainey. That was the question. What *was* she going to do? She knew what she wanted, but not what he wanted. She stuffed a 'mum in florist foam with a little more force than was necessary and nearly bent it. "I'm not going there, Beth."

Beth touched her arm. "All kidding aside, why not?"

She widened her eyes. "You know why, Beth. Look at my marriage. Look at how I got in this situation. I'm doing this alone. I'm barely hanging on. There's no way he and I could make it work, even if I wanted it to. I need to keep him at a distance." She wouldn't tell Beth about Jason. It wasn't her story to tell.

"So you'll shut him down?" Beth said quietly.

She winced. Actually, he'd shut *her* down. More or less.

Beth continued. "But you don't *have* to do this alone. That's the whole point. Okay, so maybe Ben's not the guy for you. I don't know one way or the other. Chemistry is wonderful, but definitely not the only thing to base a relationship on. But don't shut yourself off all the way. Single parenting is hard. You might want someone to share it with."

"I—" She'd love to share it with Ben. She didn't see another man coming into her life whom she'd want more. But it didn't look as if that was to be. Unable to finish her sentence, she cleared her throat and changed the subject. "Well, we've got a lot to do here. Let's get these done so the bride can relax."

Beth looked as if she wanted to say something, but simply shook her head instead.

Lainey knew she was a coward. But it seemed like the only way to protect herself.

That night, Lainey had just propped her feet on the coffee table and turned the TV on when a knock sounded at the door. She padded over and peeked through the peephole to see her parents standing there. It wasn't like them to drop by unannounced. She frowned as she opened the door.

"Is everything okay?"

"Of course. Do you have a minute?" Her father's voice was strangely formal. "We won't stay long."

"I—yes, I do." She stepped aside to let them in and tried to tamp down a little surge of nerves. There could be no good reason for this visit.

Jacqui looked around the room as she slipped off her shoes. Lainey looked too—she was proud of the home she had created. A fire crackled in the hearth, and the low light of the lamps cast a warm glow over the space. She took a seat on the slip-covered couch. Panda was draped across the back. The cat didn't even crack an eye open.

Her parents sat in the chairs while Lainey muted the TV. Frankly, *Survivor* was a great backdrop for her wranglings with her parents. She set the remote carefully on the end table, dismayed to note her hand shook slightly.

"Can I get you anything?" she asked, and they both shook their heads.

"This is certainly—cozy," Jacqui said carefully, and Lainey sighed. In this case, "cozy" wasn't a compliment.

"I think so," she said, choosing to ignore her mother's meaning. "I love it."

"Well." Always one to cut to the chase, her father leaned forward. "We've got some information you might find interesting."

Her heart kicked up a bit. "Information? About what?"

Her parents exchanged a look. "About Ben Lawless, dear," her mother said.

Lainey tensed. Oh, God. They'd dug into his past. She kept her voice level as she said, "Really?"

"Yes." Jacqui pulled some papers out of her monster bag and held them out. Lainey took them reluctantly. "I think you'll find it interesting reading."

Lainey laid the pages on the couch next to her. She couldn't bring herself to look too closely at them. *Local Firefighter Under Fire* was the heading on the first page. Poor Ben.

"Why are you doing this?" She tried to keep her voice steady but failed.

"So you can see once and for all why it's a bad idea to get mixed up with him. Lainey, he's directly responsible for the death of a fellow firefighter. Ben went in after being told not to. The other man went after him. As a result, a young family man is dead. Ben's been removed from the squad. He's had some mental health issues as well. He's not stable. It's in your best interests to stay away from him." She nodded at the papers. "It's all there."

Lainey sucked in a breath. "Oh, Mother. How could you? This is beneath you."

Jacqui recoiled and flushed slightly, and looked at her husband. Greg cleared his throat. "You don't want to get mixed up with an unstable man, honey. You deserve better."

Lainey stared. Surely they couldn't mean Daniel. "A lying, cheating man who threatens me is a better choice?"

Greg winced slightly. "No. Of course not. But if Ben isn't stable you could be hurt. And you've got a child to think about. You're going to be a mother. It's time you were responsible and made better choices."

Lainey's mouth fell open. She snapped it shut. "While

I appreciate you looking out for me, I'm perfectly capable of making decisions for myself. You don't know Ben. I do. He's a far better man than Daniel. Than most men. He's got honor, integrity and loyalty in spades. Not to mention he actually *listens* to what I say and doesn't make any attempt to manipulate me. He's a good man, and I never thought I'd find one like him. As for this—he's told me himself."

She stomped over to the fireplace and placed the papers on the flames. They went up with a *whoosh*. If only it were that easy to help Ben be free of his demons. When she spun back around she saw her parents staring at her and realized with a sinking feeling she'd said far, far too much.

"You're in love with him." Jacqui's tone was shocked. "What do you think he can possibly give you?"

Her mother's words stymied her. *In love with Ben?* She couldn't be. Could she? She'd been trying so hard not to be, teetering on the edge but holding her heart in reserve.

She swallowed and tried to focus. "He can't give me anything right now," she said, and heard the sorrow in her voice. "But then again he never said he could." *And I've never asked.* She'd been afraid of the answer. Just as she'd been afraid to admit she was flat-out in love with the man.

Jacqui simply stared at her, her throat working. Greg stood and pulled his wife to her feet. "Lainey, for your sake I hope this infatuation passes quickly. You've got a lot going on, trying to keep your shop going and getting ready for the baby. If you have a prayer of making this work you need to let Ben go. He's not the man for you."

"You're wrong," Lainey said, her voice quiet. She met her parents' gazes squarely. "He *is* the man for me." She knew it with all her heart. What she didn't know was how to make him understand it.

Greg herded a sputtering Jacqui out the door and Lainey sank back on the couch. In love with Ben.

She squeezed her eyes shut tightly. She'd been doing her best to ignore the truth, but there it was. She was in love with him—in all likelihood had been since they'd skipped stones at the lake. When he'd been so gentle with her. When he'd kissed her the first time.

Tears burned at the back of her throat. It was no good to love someone who had no idea how to accept it. Who was held up by the past, by something he couldn't let go.

She had to hope he loved her too, and would be willing to work through his past to give them a future. But what if he wasn't?

CHAPTER THIRTEEN

"LAINEY." HER MOTHER stood in the doorway of The Lily Pad, clearly agitated. "We need to talk. Can you take a break right now?"

Startled, Lainey took a few steps toward her mother. She hadn't thought she'd see her parents for a while after last night's little ambush had been thwarted. She'd never seen the older woman so distraught. "Mom? Are you all right?"

Jacqui shook her head. "I just—we really need to sit down and discuss this."

Beth hurried over to Lainey. "I can cover this right now. Why don't the two of you go ahead?"

Her eyes searched Lainey's face, and Lainey saw the concern there. If she disagreed, and opted to stay instead of talking to her mother, Beth would back her up. In light of last night's conversation with her parents, her mother's arrival this morning was a bit of a surprise.

She squeezed her friend's hand. To her mother she said, "Okay. How about Mel's?" It wasn't fully private, but this time of day—mid-morning—business at the café should be a little slower.

Jacqui nodded. "That's fine."

Surprised, Lainey grabbed her coat and followed her

mother out the door. She didn't think she'd ever seen Jacqui go to Mel's.

They walked in silence though the October chill. Halloween was only a couple days away, and November apparently had chosen to make an early appearance this year. Inside the warm café, Lainey led Jacqui to a corner table in the hopes they'd be undisturbed. They ordered hot drinks and sat in silence until the steaming mugs were delivered. Jacqui tapped her nails on the table relentlessly, a show of nerves Lainey didn't think she'd ever seen before.

Not wanting to wait any longer, Lainey reached over and touched her mother's hand. Jacqui looked more haggard, more tired, than Lainey could ever remember seeing her. "Mom, what's this about?"

Jacqui fussed with her coffee, then lifted her gaze to meet Lainey's. "I need you to explain how things got this way. How you could be so careless..." Her words trailed off.

"Careless as in getting pregnant? Or about Ben?" She hadn't been careless either way.

Jacqui nodded. "Either. Both. And you won't tell anyone who the father is!"

Lainey sat back. She had to choose her words carefully. "Mom, I wouldn't say I was careless. No, it wasn't planned. But it's not a mistake. As for the father..." She hesitated. She clearly had to say something, but what? She settled for an abridged version of the truth. "Well, he's not interested in being in our lives. He's got his reasons, and none of them are anything I want my child associated with." She hesitated just for a second before adding, "Why do you keep pushing Daniel on me?"

Jacqui looked her straight in the eye. "Because he can take care of you. And now the baby, too. It's going to be so hard for you to raise the child and run that shop. I'm sure he'd let you keep the store, and you can work when you want. But you wouldn't have to worry about money. Are you *sure* the baby's father is out of the picture?"

Lainey thought of the papers she'd signed with a little pang of sorrow mixed with relief. "Yes." She crossed her arms on the table and leaned forward. "Mom. I understand you want me to be taken care of. I do. And I appreciate your concern. But Daniel's not the way to do it. I'm managing—working things out. It won't be easy, but I'm going to make it work. You and Dad need to just let me do it."

Jacqui was silent for a long moment, fiddling with her untouched coffee mug. Then she said, "I just don't understand why you'd want to struggle when you don't have to. When there are people who can give you so much."

Lainey saw the puzzlement on her mother's face and knew she truly *didn't* understand. "It's not that I want to struggle. It's that I want to do something on my own. When you guys step in and try to take over you attach strings and conditions and you take the power away from me. It's not mine, then. Being a single mother isn't ideal. It will make everything a lot harder, to be sure. But that's how it's going to be, Mom. I can't change that." She took a deep breath and thought of Ben with a sharp pang. "If I ever get married it will be because I love the man, and because he loves and respects me for who I am—not who I come from or what I can do for him. Does that make sense?"

Jacqui clasped her hands tightly in front of her for a moment. Finally she lifted her chin. "Yes," she said quietly. "It does. Does Ben know how you feel?"

Lainey dropped her gaze to her mug of tea. Her heart squeezed. "I don't think so."

Her mother pushed her mug out of the way and leaned toward her. "Then you need to tell him. Sooner rather than later. Why would you let him walk away?"

Lainey's jaw actually dropped. "Mother..." she managed. "I— Whoa. I thought you were against Ben?"

Jacqui reached over and covered Lainey's hand with her own. "We don't want you to have to struggle when you have the opportunity to avoid it. But you need to be happy, too. It's been so long—" She stopped for a moment, then sighed. "I love your father, even with all his faults. When you talk about Ben you light up. The way you defended him last night—well, you should have the chance to see where that leads you. I'm sorry for making it so difficult for you."

It was quite possibly the first time her mother had ever really listened and actually heard what Lainey was saying. She got up and pulled her mother into an awkward hug, right there in Mel's. Her mother's quiet words were as good as Jacqui could do, and Lainey was willing to accept them as a start.

Her mother patted her awkwardly on the back. "Go get him," she said, and Lainey's eyes got damp. "And, please, if we can help let us know. I'll try not to shove myself where I've got no business being."

Lainey stepped back and laughed even as she swiped at her eyes. "Thank you." Jacqui wouldn't understand, but that was the nicest thing her mother had ever said to her.

"All right, then." Her mother gathered her bag and her coat. "I mean it. If we can help with the shop and the baby let us know."

"I will," Lainey murmured. She didn't want their help, if at all possible, but having it offered rather than rammed down her throat was a huge improvement. She tried and failed to picture her parents babysitting. The thought almost made her giggle. Maybe they'd come around.

She hurried back to work. Beth was ringing up a sale,

but by the time Lainey got her coat off and went back out front was already heading for her. "How did it go?"

Lainey reached for the watering can. "It was fine, actually. She made an effort to listen to me. I'm not sure she understands why I feel the way I do, but she seems willing to accept it. It's some small steps in the right direction." She'd take the olive branch and hope it held. To have her parents work with her rather than at cross-purposes would make everything so much easier.

That evening was pizza night with Rose. Lainey was half tempted to cancel. She was so tired, and the thought of seeing Ben and simply exchanging polite words, pretending there'd never been more between them, was just too hard.

But she picked up the usual pizza and headed out. She'd do her best to put on a happy face.

Ben was nowhere to be found when she pulled in, and relief tempered with a good dose of disappointment flooded through her. She tried to push it all away. She was here for Rose only, and had been long before he'd come back. She would be long after he'd left again.

"Come on in!" Rose called when Lainey knocked.

She pushed the door open and fixed a smile on her face which faltered when she spotted Ben's jacket draped over a chair. How far gone was she when the sight of a fleece could almost reduce her to tears? She busied herself putting the box on the counter and removing her own coat while making small talk. She thought she'd actually done pretty well until she sat across from Rose and looked at her sympathetic face.

"Oh, dear. You've got it that bad, huh?" Rose's question was gentle.

Lainey couldn't meet her friend's eyes so she looked down at the slice of pizza she had zero interest in eating.

Her answer stuck in her throat as if the words were glued there, and she was afraid if she tried to speak all her carefully rigged control would go right out the window.

The back door opened then, and Ben came in. Her gaze flew to his and Lainey would swear time stopped. Her breath caught at the pain and the longing she saw, which he quickly dropped behind the mask she was all-too familiar with. She looked away. She should have stayed home tonight. Rose would have understood.

"Pizza, Ben?" Rose's voice was overly bright, and it seemed to bounce off the tension that filled the room.

"No, thanks."

The deep rumble of his voice resonated deep in Lainey's soul. Oh, did she have it bad. Rose didn't know the half of it.

"I need this."

The jacket whooshed off the chair next to her and Lainey squeezed her eyes shut tight when she caught a bit of his scent mixed with the fresh air notes that came from spending a lot of time outside. She didn't dare look up until the door shut behind him.

Rose made a little noise of frustration in her throat. "Oh, my goodness, I'm not sure I've ever seen a couple so right for each other work so hard to avoid it! Talk to him, Lainey. Please. Don't let this get away. From either of you. You don't want to regret it later."

It wasn't quite that simple. "Rose—"

Her friend leveled her with a gentle look. "Do you love him?"

Lainey sucked in a breath. "Yes. Yes, I do." The answer was oh-so-easy, but not simple.

"He went back into the garage. Go to him. Please." Rose looked at her with shrewd eyes. "Don't waste anymore time. That little baby needs a daddy and Ben would be a wonderful one. Plus, not only does he need you—you need him."

He needs you. Lainey didn't know if that was true or not. If he needed her, how could he shut her out and hold her at arm's length? Still, she found her feet carrying her out the door to the garage. Her heartbeat picked up the closer she got to the building. Was she crazy to lay it all on the line? She hadn't come here intending to do so. Even though Rose was right. It *was* time. She couldn't go on in this half-life. She had to know.

Ben looked up when she came in, and she caught the longing in his eyes before he shuttered it. "Hi."

"Hey. How are you feeling?"

His voice was perfectly polite. She could almost see the force fields around him, trying to keep her at a safe distance. It hurt that after all they'd shared he could just lock her out.

"Okay." It wasn't a lie. Pregnancy-wise, she was. Otherwise, not so much.

He nodded, then met her gaze. "What do you need, Lainey?"

You. She took a deep breath and jumped in. "Can you tell me the rest of the story, Ben? About Jason?" Since everything seemed to hinge on his friend's death, she needed to know.

He set down the tool he'd been holding. His hands were shaking slightly. "I told you the gist of it."

"Yes, you did. But I don't know what actually happened." She moved a little closer. Her hands shook so badly she shoved them in the pockets of her coat. "I don't know exactly why you blame yourself, because from what I've seen you aren't so careless as to knowingly or intentionally lead another person into danger."

He winced, raked a hand through his hair. "Lainey—"

She kept her gaze on him steady. Kept her voice calm and didn't move any closer, so she wouldn't spook him. "Ben, please. Let me in. We've got the potential here for something wonderful, and I'd love the chance at a future with you. But with this between us we can't." She couldn't bring herself to ask if he wanted it, too. The very real chance of him saying no would destroy her.

"Don't make me a better man than I am." His words were harsh and he moved toward her, his gaze hard on hers.

She stood her ground as he stalked closer.

"I didn't get the order. Somehow there was a breakdown in the chain and I didn't get the order that the building was clear. As far as I knew there was one occupant left." He stopped, took a shuddering breath. "I went in. Jason came in after me because he recognized the signs that the situation was deteriorating rapidly. He'd gotten the order. He knew he wasn't supposed to go in." He shut his eyes. "He came in anyway. For me. When he had so much to lose. He had everything to lose. His wife—Callie. Those kids."

Lainey's eyes burned at the bleakness in his voice and she didn't even try to stop the tears. Now she got it. He blamed himself for living when his friend was dead. She came a little closer and rested her hand on his arm, feeling the tightness of the muscles beneath. He blinked at her, as if he'd forgotten she was there for a few moments, lost in his own private hell. "How can you blame yourself for Jason's choice? What does his wife say?"

He froze and then looked away, his jaw working.

Her heart sank. "Oh, no. Ben. How can she blame you?"

Misery was etched on his face. "I don't know if she does. I haven't seen her or talked to her since—since the funeral. She's called, but I haven't called her back."

Lainey inhaled sharply. "Ben, why not?"

He moved away from her, his movements agitated and

jerky. "I can't, okay? What if it's the wrong thing to do?" He paused and drew in a ragged breath. "You didn't see her at the funeral. She was so—lost. She's been through so much already. I can't make it worse for her. I can't take that chance."

She shook her head. "Okay, but who are you to decide what makes it worse for her? Ben, how can you possibly know? You're a living link to Jason for her, for her kids. That's so important. How can you leave them like that? Is that what he'd want?"

He turned around, propped his hands on his hips. "Lainey—"

She was too far in to back out now. "Go. Talk to her. See what she has to say so you can get some closure. If you can't do that we don't have a future. *You* don't have a future as a firefighter, much less as a husband. You can't punish yourself forever. You need to forgive yourself, and Jason as well. He didn't give up his life so you could spend yours all alone."

He opened his mouth, but snapped it shut when she steamrollered right over him.

"I love you. But if you can't choose me—choose a life with me over your past—then we've got nowhere to go."

She barely breathed as he stood in the middle of the garage and stared at her.

Finally he said in a low tone, "I can't risk it, Lainey."

Her heart shattered, the razor sharp edges of pain nearly bringing her to her knees. "Then you're not the man I thought you were."

It took everything she had to turn and walk away from the man she loved.

Ben stood frozen in the garage after Lainey had left. She had simply sailed out, her chin high, tear-tracks fresh on her beautiful face. He heard her car start, then the crunch of tires on the driveway.

The loss of her ripped through him. God, how could he be so damn stupid? He wanted nothing more than to go after her, tell her how much he loved her. But he couldn't.

Because he was an idiot. What kind of man let the woman he loved walk away?

One whose past held him firmly in its snare. He knew that. He'd allowed it because it meant he was able to hide, somehow thinking that would make up for the loss of his friend. Worse, he'd used it as an excuse to cement the belief he was better off alone. That was inexcusable. Even though over the past few weeks he'd been busy falling for Lainey. She'd burst right through his defenses, made him feel, made him want, and while he'd convinced himself those were the last things he wanted she'd gotten in his heart anyway.

But if you can't choose me—choose a life with me over your past—then we've got nowhere to go.

Her words echoed in his head. What kind of man chose to live in the past when the future hovered so brightly in front of him? Lainey wasn't wrong. It was past time he paid Callie a visit. Set some things right and got closure. Maybe Jason's widow needed it, too. And choosing to live his life and love Lainey seemed like a far better tribute to his friend's memory than staying in the shadows for the rest of his days.

Then he'd see if he could have a true future with Lainey. She deserved all of him—not some damaged shell. He'd prove he could move on. He pulled his phone out of his pocket, took a deep breath, and dialed a familiar number.

Beth came in and plunked down a small bakery bag. "Cheesecake muffin. Because I'm pretty sure you haven't eaten yet."

Lainey winced. "I'm trying, Beth. I'm just not very hungry."

Her friend nudged the bag closer. "I know, honey. But you've got to feed that baby."

Lainey managed a smile. "I know that. And I am." *Mostly.* Lainey opened the bag. Her appetite hadn't been stellar since her first conversation with Ben about Jason, and had virtually disappeared after their confrontation in the garage two days ago. He'd made his choice. It wasn't her.

So it was over before it really had a chance to begin.

The pain broke over her again. Every time the wave wore her down a little more. She took a shaky breath and took the bag from Beth.

"I know this is so hard for you. Can I do anything, Laine? I know I keep asking, but—" Beth broke off. "It's so awful to see you like this. Can you call him? See if you can work it out?"

Lainey managed a little smile. She knew she didn't need to pretend around Beth, but she was hoping to fool herself into thinking it wasn't as painful as she thought. "It didn't end in a way I can actually fix. He's got—he's got issues that only he can resolve. And he has to be ready to do that. I can't make him ready." And there was also the simple but excruciating fact she didn't actually know if he loved her.

Beth leaned forward. "I've seen him look at you, Laine. That man is in love with you."

"Maybe. But he never said the words, Beth." Her eyes burned with tears she did not want to shed in public. "I *think* he'd love me, if he could. But I don't really *know.* He knows how I feel." She took a shaky breath and tried to smile, even though it failed to actually form. "So I'm going to try to move on."

If only it was that easy.

"Oh, honey. I'm so sorry." Beth glanced back as the back doorbell buzzed. "Eat that. I'll get the delivery."

She left and Lainey opened the bag and removed the muffin, centering it on a napkin. She'd been through the whole thing over and over. No use going over it all for the umpteenth time. The story of a broken heart was as old as time. She'd manage to survive.

But it was a huge hole in her heart. She missed him. Missed what they'd never really had a chance to have. Missed what might have been.

That was almost as dangerous.

She broke off a small bite of muffin. Normally it was one of her favorite treats. It would take her all morning to eat it, because today she could probably eat the bag it came in and not notice any difference in taste. But Beth was right. She needed to feed the baby.

The front door chimed and Lainey's idiotically optimistic heart kicked, then crashed. It hadn't been Ben yet, and this time was no different. A smiling man approached the counter, wanting a dozen roses for his wife. Lainey put them together with a smile, but her heart ached.

"Thank you," he said as she handed him the roses wrapped in green and pink paper. "She's worth every rose you've got in your store. But I can only afford a dozen today."

Lainey gave a little laugh, but a little spear of sorrow pierced her heart. If things had been different would Ben have said the same about her? "She's a lucky woman."

He winked as he slid his wallet in his pocket. "Nah. I'm the lucky one."

Whistling, he walked out, and Lainey watched him go

with a heavy heart. People clearly could make love work. Some of them overcame crazy stuff to be together.

And some of them couldn't.

CHAPTER FOURTEEN

BEN STOOD IN front of the little white bungalow, with its cozy front porch and dormant rose bushes. A house not too different from the one Lainey lived in. Pumpkins on the front steps. Fake spiderweb on the porch. Like almost every other house on the block.

But this one belonged to Callie and Jason. Well, just Callie now. He swallowed hard at the thought.

He'd come to finally make amends—something he should have done months ago.

The front door flew open and Callie stood there, the baby—who wasn't really a baby anymore—on her hip. She looked at him steadily and his heart thumped in his chest as he started up the walk towards her.

"Callie." He swallowed, the words suddenly seeming inadequate. "I'm—"

"If you say you're sorry, Ben Lawless, you cannot take another step and come in this house." Eyes blazing, Callie stepped out on the porch.

Confusion stopped him in his tracks more than her threat. "What?"

"You heard me." She jerked her head toward the door and her coppery curls bounced on her shoulders. "Come in. We need to talk and it's cold out here."

He followed her into the house, the reminder of Jason

not as physical a punch as it would have been a few weeks ago. The oldest boy, Eli, who was three, looked at him out of his father's eyes and smiled his father's smile.

"Hey, buddy." Ben bent down and accepted the hug the little boy offered. His heart squeezed. He'd do better by Jason's kids if Callie would let him. He'd love to see them grow up—maybe play with Lainey's baby if she would forgive him.

"Have a seat." Callie nodded at the table which held a basket of crayons and a stack of coloring books. "Let me get them set up for a little while." To the kids she said, "How about *Bob the Builder*?" A chorus of yeses followed her words and soon cheery music wafted from the living room. She returned to stand across from him, her posture stiff.

"They'll be good for a bit now. Can I get you a drink?"

He shook his head. "Ah, no. Thanks. Callie—"

"No." She gave a sharp shake of her head, splayed her hands on the table and leaned forward. "You listen to me first—okay, Ben? I can't believe you stayed away for so long. It wasn't your fault. Jason did *not* die because of you."

Ben closed his eyes. While rationally he knew she was right that Jason had not died because of him—and a hard-won victory *that* was—being here, with Jason's young widow, he could still smell the smoke, hear the roar of the flames crackling in the back of his mind. It gave him a bad moment.

"I know that. It took me far too long to figure it out. I want to apologize for staying away so long. I never meant to. And I am terribly sorry for the loss of your husband and my friend."

"Thank you. That's an apology I will accept," Callie whispered. She threaded her fingers together. "While I know Jason for the most part followed the rules—he didn't want to be careless—he was at heart a risk-taker. Once he realized what had happened to you there was no stopping him." She took a shaky breath and Ben met her gaze, seeing the sadness in her green eyes. "He didn't think, Ben. That's the thing. He just acted. They told me—after—they told me they couldn't stop him. Nothing could have. He loved you like a brother."

"It was mutual." It was true. And he knew Callie was right about her husband. In a potential do-or-die situation there wasn't time to stand around and waffle about what action to take. He and Jason had both done the only thing they could do in the moment. If the situation had been reversed he would have done the same thing.

So many people said they'd walk through fire for their loved ones. Jason had actually done it.

The kids' laughter caused Callie to turn her head in their direction. She pulled out a chair and sank down into it. "I've been mad as hell," she said quietly. "But not at you. Or at least not about this. For staying away—that's something else entirely. Jason loved risk. I knew when I married him—well, I knew. I never thought it'd end like this, but it did." She tipped her head toward the living room. "And now they don't have a daddy. Jason didn't leave us on purpose. He wouldn't let you accept responsibility for his choices any more than you would have let him."

"I know that now," he said. "It took me a while to get there—longer than it should have. Callie—again, I am sorry. Sorrier than you know for your loss, for the boys' loss. Someone helped me see how blind I've been. It's been at your expense. I'm sorry." Lainey had been right when she'd said Jason hadn't given up his life so Ben could ignore his own.

Callie reached over and squeezed his hand, the sheen of tears in her green eyes. "Thank you for that. Please, don't be a stranger in our lives. You are such a valuable link to Jason, and I'd like the boys to know you. You can help them understand what their daddy was like as a fire-fighter."

"I will," he promised, relieved that the thought didn't fill him with the kind of pain he'd been accustomed to. The lightening of the load was an amazing thing, and while the apology he'd made had helped, it was Lainey who'd shown him the way.

He pulled Callie in for a hug. She hugged him back, then patted his chest.

"Who's the someone? She must be awfully special if you finally came to see me."

"Ah…" Uncomfortable, he looked into the living room, where the boys played with trucks and watched the movie. "She pointed out a few things to me that I'd been missing."

Callie gave a little laugh. "Well, I like her already. When can I meet her?"

He met her gaze. "Well, about that…"

Her eyes went to slits. "Oh, no. What did you do?"

Was he so transparent? He scrubbed his hand over his face, then gave her an abridged version of events and didn't cut himself any slack.

"Do you love her?"

"I do." There was no hesitation.

She gave him a small shove toward the door. "Then why are you still here? What you need to do is go back and see if she'll still have you." She gave him another little shove, her voice urgent. "Ben. You've got to go see if you can make it work. Don't waste any more time. You never know how much of it you have."

"I know. It's where I'm going next. Now I know—" He stopped, about to add, *what you and Jason had.* It seemed somehow cruel to bring it up.

But Callie nodded and smiled—a small smile, with tears in her eyes. "Yes. Now you know."

"I've got to go," he said. "I had to be sure you were okay."

"I'm hanging in there," she said softly. "It hasn't been easy, but I'm doing my best. I'll miss him every day for the rest of my life. But I knew my husband, Ben. I know how he was. I know *who* he was. And he's a hero."

"Yeah, he is." He drew her into another hug, rocked her back and forth. "Thanks, Callie."

She hugged him back tightly. "Go get her. Good luck."

"I will. And, God knows, I'll need it."

He left the house, with Callie standing on the porch, arms crossed against the cold, and drove away. He pointed the truck north, toward Holden's Crossing. Time to put the beginning of the rest of his life in motion. If Lainey would have him.

There was only one way to find out.

Lainey had shoved the last of the clothes in the dryer when she heard a knock on the kitchen door. It was seven-thirty on a rainy night. Who could possibly be stopping over this late? She trudged up the stairs and peeked out the peephole.

And gasped.

Ben stood there, rain glistening on his jacket. She blinked. Was it really him? Or was her mind playing tricks on her?

He knocked again and she jumped, her shaking hands making a fumbling hash of the lock and the knob. *Ben.* Why was he here? Could she take any more heartbreak? She was afraid the answer to that was no.

She swung the door open and simply drank him in. His intense gaze settled on her and she saw pain and longing there. Hope surged a little bit, but she tamped it down. He looked tired, and stress lines bracketed his mouth. Not for the first time she wanted to reach up and smooth them away.

"Lainey. Can I come in? I'll understand if you say no." His voice was a low rumble and she stepped to the side quickly, her heart hammering so hard she was afraid he'd hear it.

"Of course. I was just surprised." She shut the door behind him and turned to face him. As glad as she was to see him, a little anger flared. She welcomed it. She needed it to keep her distance from him until she knew why he was here. "Since you were pretty clear the other day that we weren't going to work out." She couldn't quite keep the bitterness out of her voice.

He let out a long exhale. The misery etched on his face echoed that in her heart. "I know. I'm sorry. I need to talk to you."

"I see. Well, come on in." Without waiting to see if he'd follow, she walked through the kitchen into the living room. She sat on a chair near the fireplace and wound her hands tightly together. The heat of the fire did nothing to soothe her nerves.

He didn't follow right away, but a thump from the kitchen area indicated he was probably removing his boots. A few seconds later he appeared and she had a hard time breathing. He seemed to fill the small space and absorb all the oxygen.

She gestured to the chair across from her. "Please sit."

He did, and she tried not to notice when he looked at her with a tenderness that nearly undid her. "Lainey. God, you're gorgeous."

She kept her gaze on his steady, even though she felt anything but steady inside. How could he say that? She'd barely slept and had no appetite. She was a mess, not to mention an emotional wreck. "Thank you." She didn't know what to say, what to ask. There was so much to say, really, she didn't know where to begin.

But, since he'd more or less rejected her, she'd let him talk first. He knew where she stood. She'd laid it out for him the other day in the garage. It was past time she could say the same about him.

He dropped his gaze, leaned forward and rested his forearms on his thighs. The awkwardness grew as he seemed to gather his thoughts. She watched the firelight dance on his dark hair. Finally, too tightly wound to wait, she gave in. She needed to know.

"Ben, why are you here?"

He looked up. "Should I be?"

The question threw her. "I don't know." Her voice dropped to a whisper. "You made it clear the other day you couldn't choose me." Despite her earlier flare of anger, she couldn't muster any heat in the words, only pain.

He took a deep breath and sat back. Her traitor cat came and wound around his ankles. She frowned at Panda, but of course the cat ignored her. Ben reached down to stroke his hand down Panda's back. "I was pretty screwed up, Lainey. In a lot of ways. I've still got work to do. I don't know when I'll be able to work again." He looked up and in his gaze she saw pain and something else. Her heart picked up. "You're going to be a mom. You need a guy who's stable. I can barely take care of myself. How could I take care of a family?"

"So you pushed me away," she said, unable to keep the hurt from her voice. She focused on the traitor cat at his feet.

He leaned forward and laid a hand on her arm, forcing her startled gaze to his. "I did. I thought it was better for you. I wanted to protect you," he admitted. "But you just kind of worked your way in and I started wanting more. A lot more. After you left the other day I realized how blind I'd been. I made an appointment with a counselor. And there was one last thing I needed to do."

"Callie?" she said softly.

He nodded. "I went and talked to Callie. Not for permission to move on, but because you were right. She was angry—but not for the reasons I thought. She was mad because she felt I'd abandoned her and the kids. She never blamed me. But even if I'd known that I'm not sure it would have made a difference."

His eyes were wet as he looked at Lainey and her heart broke for him.

"I blamed myself fully. But there were things that night that were out of my control, out of his control. I can't bring him back. But the way I've been living is no way to honor my best friend. Jason would kick my ass."

A surprised laugh bubbled out of her. "He sounds like a true friend."

Ben smiled. "He was. I wish you could have known him. He'd have liked you."

Tears stung her eyes. "I wish I could have, too. But—"

His smile turned sad. "But that's not how it is. I hope I can convince you to meet Callie, though. I think you'll like her. And the kids."

She circled back to the fact that had surprised her. "You saw a counselor?"

Ben nodded. "Well, not yet. The appointment is next week. Monday. One of the terms of coming off leave is I need to get a mental health exam, I guess you'd call it. I need to know—and my captain needs to know—I won't flashback and freeze the next time I go out on a call."

She swallowed hard. That didn't sound as if he was going to stay here. "Ah. Will it work?"

He gave her a crooked smile. "I don't know. I hope so. I'd like to be cleared in a month or so. I want to go back to work."

"That's great, Ben." She meant it. But, really, did the man have to drive all the way back here to tell her this? That he wouldn't be back, after all? A phone call would have given her a little more dignity. "Well, I'm sure they'll be thrilled to have you back."

Something in her tone must have given her away, because he looked at her quizzically. "They won't."

She stared at him for a moment, not comprehending. "But you just said—"

"I know," he interrupted her. "But you're jumping to conclusions. I won't be working in Grand Rapids. I'll be here. Or almost here. In Traverse City. Holden's Crossing is close enough I can live here. The job—it's time-consuming and there's always risk."

Her heart beat faster. Had he really just said what she thought she'd heard? "Oh," she said. "Here?"

Instead of answering right away, he came to his knees on the floor in front of her and cautiously laid his hand on her rounded belly. "I know it hasn't been that long," he murmured, "but I missed you. Both of you."

Lainey laid her hand on his and held her breath. She didn't trust herself to speak. She was afraid to ask the question, more afraid of the answer.

He slid a cold hand around the back of her neck and pulled her down toward him. "I love you," he whispered. "I love both of you. I missed you. So much." Then he kissed her, soft at first, then with more urgency.

"I love you, too," she whispered against his mouth. "Ben—"

He sat back and ran one hand down the side of her face. Her heart lifted at the reverence and love on his face. "So, to answer your question, yes. Here. In this house, if you want. I want to be your husband and a father to this baby. I know it's short notice, and I've been an idiot, and—damn it—I don't have a ring and you might not be ready—"

She laid her fingers on his lips, joy coursing through her. "I'm ready." Oh, was she ever? She'd been wrong about not needing a partner in her life—she needed Ben. She hadn't even known what she was missing until he'd come into her life. "There's no one I want to be with more than you."

His eyes widened and a slow smile spread across his face. "Are you sure?"

Her voice was strong and she was pretty sure she might burst with happiness. "Yes. I want forever. And I want it with you."

"Oh, thank God." He stood up and held out a hand, a wicked gleam in his eyes. "Then I say we go celebrate. Plus, I think we've got some making up to do." He gave her a little eyebrow-wiggle that made her laugh.

"Sounds good to me. We'd better get started." Lainey put her hand in his and smiled up at him, ready to embrace their future.

Ten months later

Lainey tugged at the bodice of her wedding dress for what had to be the fifteenth time in as many minutes. "Are you sure this looks secure?"

Beth, her matron of honor and business partner, laughed and pulled Lainey's hands down. "It looks great, Laine. No one can tell you've got nursing pads in the sexy bra under it. You are a gorgeous bride." She leaned over and plucked Lainey's bouquet from the box on the table, pressed it into Lainey's hands. "Here. Now, turn and look in the mirror."

Lainey did. The woman staring back at her barely resembled herself. Flushed cheeks, sparkling eyes, flowing off-white beaded simple strapless gown. The flowers, done by Lainey herself, were a perfect complement for a summer wedding in shades of pink and cream.

Beth touched the small veil that covered Lainey's head and shoulders. "See? Perfectly gorgeous. Are you ready?"

"Very." Lainey smiled at her friend. "I can't wait."

"Then let's go." Beth exited the small room, and with a deep breath Lainey followed.

As Beth took her place at the head of the aisle Lainey paused, out of sight of the guests in the sanctuary. A well of emotion threatened to break over her as her father and brother approached her. They were here to walk her down the aisle in this small church. Amazingly, her mother had exercised great restraint and hadn't interfered with the planning or the size of the wedding. Not too much, anyway. They'd made strides—especially after the birth of baby Lily.

Rose had her three-month-old great-granddaughter in the front pew. Lainey sincerely hoped she wouldn't have to take a break mid-ceremony and nurse her daughter.

Her heart was absolutely full.

"Honey, you look amazing," her father said, his voice rough with emotion, and Lainey blinked furiously.

"Don't make me cry," she managed on a laugh, and he squeezed her arm.

"No promises, there, my girl. It's your wedding. We may not have a choice."

She gave a little giggle as Kevin came to take his place at Lainey's side. He chucked her lightly under the chin. "Ready, little sis?"

She smiled up at him. Oh, was she ever? "Yes. Yes, I am."

The music swelled and Lainey moved to the head of the

aisle. She took the first few steps toward her future. Her gaze landed on Ben. Her steps nearly faltered as she took in how handsome he was in his tux and she couldn't take her eyes off him. He was hers.

Ben's gaze never left her, and she saw all the love, all the heat, all the joy in her own heart reflected on his face as she reached for his hands at the altar. Her heart swelled as she looked into his beautiful eyes.

"Hi," he whispered. "God, you're gorgeous."

She smiled back. "So are you."

Together they glanced at their daughter—the baby who was everything to Ben despite the fact she wasn't biologically his—then back at the minister, who now began the ceremony.

Somehow, despite everything, without even looking for it, they'd become a family.

Forever.

* * * * *

WAKING UP WITH
HIS RUNAWAY BRIDE

LOUISA GEORGE

To Sue MacKay and Iona Jones, writing pals, roomies and very dear friends. Thank you for your support, advice and laughs.

To my amazing editor, Flo Nicoll. Thank you for your patience, your wisdom and your belief in me!

This book is for my sister, Liz Skelton. I love you.

CHAPTER ONE

'NO WAY! I am *not* trying to impress him. Absolutely not! That would be cheap and tacky, and I don't do either. How could you think such a thing?'

Mim McCarthy peered down from the top of the wobbly stepladder perched precariously on the desk and laughed at her colleague's suggestion. Even though she'd hit the nail squarely on the head.

Then she daubed a second coat of paint over the stubborn Tasmania-shaped stain on the ceiling. 'I just thought it was time to say goodbye to Tassie.'

Skye, the practice nurse-manager, gripped the ladder in one hand and offered up the paint-pot in the other. 'So it's totally coincidental that you decided to tart up the admin office on the same day the Matrix Fund assessor arrives?'

'Okay, you got me.' Mim raised her brush in defeat as her grin widened. 'Lord knows why I employed someone almost as devious as me. You're right, I'll do anything to get this funding. We need the money to pay for the planned renovations and develop the practice, or…'

'It's…?' The practice nurse did a chopping motion across her throat. 'Goodbye to *Dana's Drop-In*? No, Mim. Never. Your patients wouldn't let that happen. They need you.'

'I wouldn't let it come to that. I'll sell my soul to the bank manager. Again.' Mim sucked in a fortifying breath. 'I'm afraid I'm running out of soul.'

No drop-in centre would mean hours of travel for her community to the closest medical centre and the end of a dream for her. The dream that locked in the promises she'd made to her mum. No way would she give that up.

Mim was anything but a quitter. Doing the hard yards as the quirky outsider at med school had taught her how to fight for everything she wanted. That, and the legacy of her unconventional childhood. She'd learnt pretty quickly to rely on no one but herself. Ever. 'A quick slick of paint will brighten the place up. And conceal the fact we have a mysterious leak. Pray it doesn't rain for the next week.'

'Forecast is good. Nothing but blue skies and late summer sun.' Skye wrinkled her pierced nose. 'Good job you bought low-odour paint—wouldn't want the assessor to be savvy to the ruse.'

'Well, if you can't win, cheat.'

Skye frowned. 'Another famous Dana saying?'

'Unfortunately. Not quite up there with inspirational go-get-'em quotes, but apt, and very Dana.'

There were plenty of them. In her infrequent sober moments Mim's mother had been adorable and well intentioned, always spouting wisecracks. Not always about cheating. Some were about love too, about keeping family close. *And your dealers closer.*

Mim winked at her partner in crime. 'I know the assessor from my intern days. Dr Singh is a sweetie. This assessment will be in the bag. We'll wow him with our refreshing approach to community medicine.'

Touchingly loyal, Skye smiled and nodded briskly. 'If anyone can wow him, Mim, you can. You've transformed this place already. You just need a lucky break.'

'I know. We were bursting at the seams at yesterday's

baby clinic. I think we're finally getting the message through. And the open-all-hours policy helps.' Even if her extended days were half killing her. Pride in her achievement of getting the locals to trust the McCarthy name again fuelled her determination.

She brushed her fringe from her forehead with the back of her wrist and stepped gingerly down the ladder. Standing on the desk, she strained up at the white paint patch. 'Shame everything in life isn't so easy to gloss over. Now the rest of the ceiling needs repainting.'

'And the rest of the clinic.' Pointing to the chipped window-panes and scuffed walls, Skye shrugged. 'We haven't time, he's due in thirty minutes. To be honest, paint is the least of our problems.'

Tell me about it. But she wasn't about to burden her best mate with the harsh reality of the clinic's financial problems. 'We've just got to get Dr Singh on side.'

'Ooh, I do love a challenge.' Skye placed Mim's proffered paintbrush on top of the paint-pot, then she rubbed her hands together. 'Okay. How shall we handle it? You take the bribery? I'll do the corruption?'

'No! I'd get struck off! But…on the other hand…' Mim giggled, then stuck one hand on her cocked hip. She raised the hem of her knee-length skirt to her thigh and wiggled her bum suggestively. A move she'd learnt from her salsa DVD— Spanish, sultry and super-sexy. 'If we want to influence a man, how about good old-fashioned women's wicked ways?'

'Ahem.'

At the sound of the man's purposeful cough Mim's breath stalled somewhere in her chest.

Excellent. Just dandy. Sexy salsa? On her desk?

With burning cheeks she dropped the hem, slicked on her most accommodating smile and swivelled slowly to face Dr

Singh. Trying desperately to cover her embarrassment. 'And then, Skye, you shimmy to the left… Ohmygod.'

As she caught a clear view of their visitor her heart stalled along with her lungs. Jolts of awareness and pain and excitement slammed through her veins. Heat and ice clashed in her gut. So not Dr Singh.

She gasped for oxygen and whispered his name on a jittery breath. 'Connor? Connor. What are you…?'

Framed in the doorway, filling the space, three years older, three years more distinguished in an expensive designer suit, and with three years' worth of questions simmering behind cool liquorice eyes, stood Connor Wiseman.

Here?

Why? Why today when she was up to her eyeballs in assessors? Why this millennium?

The years had been kind to him, he'd grown into those sharp cheekbones. Casual bed hair. And, *God*, those darkest grey eyes searching her face. No trace of the flecks of honey that had heated her and held her captive. Cold onyx.

He stepped into the tiny room. His presence, a stark study of monochrome against what now felt like the garish colours of her office, was commanding and alluring. Every part of him screamed of success. Just like she remembered.

His mouth curled into a sardonic smile as he spoke, 'Well, I guess the mystery of my runaway fiancée has finally been solved. I'll call off the search party.'

'Yeah, right. Wouldn't have taken Sherlock two minutes to find me.' *If anyone had bothered to look*.

Clearly she had hurt him.

That much had been obvious by his prolonged silence. But it was accentuated now by the anger glittering in those dark eyes, even after all these years. Uber-successful guys like Connor weren't used to rejection, so it would have cut deep to be thrown aside by someone very definitely not of his pedigree.

And now, on top of everything else, God only knew what he thought about her early morning silly burlesque performance. Judging by the fixed set of his close-shaven jaw, very little.

She sucked in her stomach, thrust her shoulders back and stepped down from the desk, wishing she'd chosen something more impressive to wear than her favourite jumper and skirt ensemble. Hoping against fading hope that *old and washed out* was the new demure.

'I was very clear, Connor. I called, but you refused to speak to me. And I said, in my goodbye note, that Atanga Bay is my home. This is where I will always choose to live.'

'And now finally I get a chance to see what was so much better than Auckland.' The top of his lip twitched then tightened back into a thin line. He glanced at the overstuffed cushions, the tumbling piles of paperwork, the brightly coloured, mismatched family-friendly atmosphere she'd tried to create in her beloved ramshackle clinic. 'Is this a heritage property? Or just plain old?'

'It might not be up to your swanky city standards, but it's mine. I'm updating it. Slowly. It's a work in progress.'

'Oh, so post-modern?' His lips tweaked to a one-cornered grin as he surveyed the white on a sea of fading yellow.

'Under construction,' she fired back as she straightened her spine even further. Damn him, Connor's ability to rile her clearly hadn't abated after all these years. She would not let him get the better of her. Where was her super-fast wit when she needed it? Playing hooky with her fabulous financial acumen and supermodel looks. 'And I love it here.'

'I'll leave you two to get reacquainted. Lots to do…' Skye scurried out of the room, taking the stepladder and paint-pot with her.

Mim watched her ally leave and ached to go with her. In the dark hours she'd imagined this reunion moment so many times. Planned what she'd say, how he'd react. But never had she imagined this intense pain in her chest. Or the mind-numbing paralysis of being in the same room as him again. She rubbed her hands down her skirt and looked up into his face. She knew it intimately, every curve, every plane. The face that stalked her dreams with alarming regularity even after three years.

And now he was here. What to say to the man you ran out on the night before your engagement party? Even if it was the most misguided, precipitous engagement in the universe.

'S-so, are you j-just passing through?' Hoping the blush on her cheeks and the irritatingly stammered words wouldn't give her away, Mim grabbed for nonchalance. 'A social call?'

'I'm here on business.'

'Oh, yes, business. Naturally.' For some reason her stomach knotted. So he wasn't here to see her. Of course not. Why would he? And why did it matter? Three years should have been been ample time to get over her all-consuming first, and last, love.

She breathed the knot away. 'There's a new development at Two Rivers, I guess? But there's nothing medical going in there. Just houses, I think.'

'I don't know. I've only just seen the place, but it's not a bad idea. Food for thought.' He looked out the window with a quizzical expression. Eyebrows peaked, clearly impressed at what he saw. Out there at least. How could he not be? The wide sweeping ocean and pristine white sands of Atanga Bay were breathtaking. 'Got potential.'

Understatement of the year. 'Pure Wiseman. Take a beautiful vista and reduce it to money. Your father would be proud.'

'Somehow I doubt that.' His hands curled round the handle of his briefcase, the knuckles showing white. She'd forgotten his relationship with his father was based on business rather than familial ties.

She forced a smile. 'I meant identifying *potential*. You always were good at that.'

'But not you, it seems.'

'I stand by my decisions.' Three years and a lot of dried-up tears ago they'd believed they'd had potential. A dynamic force in the face of his father's hostility. The regular rich guy and the kooky girl out to take on the world. If only for their very different dreams for the future, which she'd been unable to overcome.

But she'd never forgotten him. She wished her life had encompassed more of him, wished her mother—or rather, her mother's illness—hadn't bled away her ability to trust anyone. But there it was, a woman with a furious dependency had bred a child with fierce independence. Not to mention a deep suspicion of coercion, controlling men and hollow promises.

She pointed to the development over on the hill. 'Fifty houses going up, should bring in more patients. I hope. I could do with them.'

'Problems?'

'Nothing I can't deal with.'

'I'm sure you'll be fine. You always were. With or without me. You were never afraid of tackling things head on. Apart from when it mattered.'

'Like you'd have listened.'

'Like I had a chance.' He turned briefly to face her. Granite. Immovable. That steadfastness had been one of the things that had drawn her to him. And one of the reasons she'd left. Immovable might have bordered on criminally sexy, but not when it trampled over her dreams.

Brushing over the brutal loaded statement about their past, and the unanswered questions zipping in the air between them, Mim glanced at her watch. She didn't have time to tackle this, or a painful trip down memory lane. Or anywhere that involved Connor, her bleak past history of failed relationships or a distraction from her current path.

Where was Dr Singh? It didn't bode well that he was late. She stuck out her hand to wish Connor on his way. 'I'm not sure why you're here but, as you can see, I'm busy. I have a meeting right about now. So perhaps we could catch up another time?' *In another three decades? Millennia?*

'I have business here, at Dana's Drop-In. I'm from the health board. Matrix Fund.' He stuck a black and white business card into her outstretched hand. The interest in his eyes was replaced by something akin to amusement. No doubt at her flustering and her predicament. 'Seems we've come full circle, Mim. Only this time I'm in your space, ruffling feathers.'

'The health board? You followed your father and gave up medicine?'

'I just moved sideways.' He flicked his head as if a fly, or something extremely unimportant, was irritating him. 'No matter, I'm here.'

Her spine prickled. No way. Not only did she know his face intimately, but she knew every inch of his body, every divine part of it. And had just about managed to expel it from her memory. And now it would be here, taunting her. 'Seriously? *You're* here to assess me?'

She glanced around hopefully for secret TV cameras. Then realised, with a sorry thud, that it wasn't a set-up, someone's idea of a bad joke. It was real. Painfully, gut-wrenchingly real. Heat rushed back into her cheeks.

What an unholy mess. A jilted lover was here to decide her future. A jilted lover with radically different views about the provision of community medicine. She believed in flexibility and choice. He believed in routine and regimented processes.

A jilted lover she'd run out on with no real explanation—

no doubt deepening the rift between him and his domineering father. It had seemed logical back then when she'd thought she'd never encounter them again. Logical and rational and based on...fear.

All coming back to bite her. She threw his card onto the desk. 'I know who you are already, I don't need this.'

'I thought you might need reminding.' He glared at her.

As if I could ever forget. 'What about Dr Singh? What happened to your practice?'

'Dr Singh is sick. And I sold my share of the practice.' He ticked his answers off on his damned distinguished fingers. The last time she'd focused on them they'd been tiptoeing down her abdomen, promising hours of pleasure. Now they were tiptoeing through her worst nightmare.

'So now you work with Daddy? Thinking about taking over the board when he retires? Figures.'

'My future is not your concern. My secretary sent an email through to you last night, explaining. And for the record, I didn't know you'd be here. I didn't ask to come. I was sent.'

'Well, for the record, I expect you to give me a fair assessment, despite our past. I didn't get the email, I'm afraid. I've been busy.' Mim looked over to the dust-covered computer, a reject from the ark, and decided not to mention it took twenty minutes to warm up. Emails were patchy, internet more so out here in the sticks.

Connor glanced again at the shiny white blotch in the middle of the yellowing ceiling. 'Busy? Yes. Plotting ways to influence me? Bribery? Corruption? Not to mention...what was it, women's wicked ways? I seem to remember you were quite good at those.' Heat flared in his eyes.

God. He had heard. And enjoyed seeing her squirm now too, no doubt. That knot in her stomach tightened like a noose. 'It was a joke.'

'You couldn't afford me anyway.'

He quirked an eyebrow, the ghost of a daring smile on his lips. And he was right. She couldn't afford him. He'd always been way out of her league.

Forget bribery. Whacking him seemed a much more attractive alternative. Either that or killing him and stashing his body.

'Couldn't I just wait until Dr Singh gets better?'

'You might be waiting a long time. He's having emergency cardiac surgery. Don't worry, I excel at being impartial, Mim.'

'Don't I know it.' Sex with Connor might have been legendary, but she'd never really believed he'd trusted her enough to let her in. He certainly hadn't ever really listened to her.

'If I don't think you make the grade, I'll tell you. And remember, I'm assessing accounts, equipment, procedures. Not you.'

'So there's no way out.'

'You could withdraw your application.' He glanced round her admin office with sheer disdain. 'But I don't think you'd want to do that.'

Though she had grasped control and ended their relationship all those years ago, he held the trump cards now whichever way she turned. She had to make the best job of it and pray he'd see past their break-up and the paintwork. His gaze travelled the length of her, sending unbidden shocks of heat through her body. Nerves? Or something more dangerous?

Ridiculous. She'd submerged any feelings for him over the years. Downgraded their passionate affair to a casual fling, a summer of wild, heavenly madness—once she'd nursed her bruised heart back to health again.

So far all her experiences of unswerving love had ended in heartbreak. Getting over losing Connor Wiseman had been hard. But possible. Just. Getting over the death of her mother had taken a little longer. And she had no intention of inviting that kind of intensity of feeling again.

She shrugged. 'It looks like I'm stuck with you.'

'Guess so. Lucky you.' He rocked back on the heels of his leather brogues. Smug didn't come close. 'Lucky me.'

She swallowed the scream of frustration in her throat, and dropped her skirt hem, which she'd subconsciously wrung into a tight clutch of crumpled fabric. Possibly in lieu of his neck. 'How long will all this take?'

'Three months.'

'That's ridiculous. It doesn't say that in the information pack.' Three minutes had been long enough for all the mixed-up feelings to come lurching back.

But, on the other hand… A glimmer of hope in her soul blew into life. If she did pass the assessment…three months was shaping up to be a lifeline and a life sentence all rolled into one. Her stomach felt like it was in a food processor, choppy and whirring at full speed. 'I assume we get time off at weekends for good behaviour?'

'Truly, I couldn't think of a better way to spend my weekends. Out here, in Nowheresville, with an ex who thought so little of me she couldn't run away fast enough. That takes masochism to a whole new level.'

He sat down at the desk, opened his briefcase and pulled out a thick questionnaire.

Thank God he didn't look up to see the rage shivering through her. She would not explain. She was not embarrassed. She had done them both a favour.

So why had regret eaten away at her ever since?

He scanned the pages in front of him. 'Hopefully, it'll all be over quickly and painlessly. It'll be part time. Odd days here and there. I assess specific areas of healthcare delivery, then give you time to review and make changes. I have other things to do as well as this.'

'Like?' She wondered briefly why she wanted to know.

'Assessing other practices, advising the government.'

No mention of family. A wife. A life outside work. But, then, why would he tell her anything about his private life? She'd given up any claims to that when she'd vanished from his family home in the middle of the night.

He retrieved a smartphone from his jacket pocket. Mim noticed the lush cobalt blue silk lining of his suit. His clothing alone could probably fund another month of Skye's wages. Then he looked gingerly up at the Tassie-free spot.

'Let's get down to business. The sooner we start, the sooner I can leave—and I get the feeling that's what we both want. First question: Why *Dana's Drop-In*? It's an unconventional name for a medical centre.'

I'm so not ready for this. Hauling in a deep breath, Mim resigned herself to the first of what she knew would be thousands of questions about her work, her strategy, business plan and practice. But the first simple question burned into her heart. Hopefully the others wouldn't be so difficult to answer. 'It's named after my mother, Dana.'

'Yes.'

She tried to look over his elbow to see what he was scribbling. 'Do you have to write all this down?'

'No. But I assume you'd want to give an explanation? It might help your case. Just outline your decision.'

'Come on, Connor, you knew about her past. She had an illness for a long time. One that prevented her accessing healthcare on any kind of regular basis. She was an addict.'

'I'm sorry, I know this must be painful.'

'It happened. And we all have to move on.' She saw her pain briefly mirrored in his eyes. Then the shutters came down, eradicating any emotion in his gaze. Moving on from tragedy was clearly something they'd both had to do.

She knew Connor's sister had died a long time ago as a child—she'd seen a picture of a pretty blonde kid. But when she'd asked about it she'd been met with a wall of silence. And she'd never found the courage to enquire again.

For Mim, talking about her mother brought out a fierce love and protective instinct in her. The same, she imagined, that Connor felt about his sister. The same instinct she felt for her burgeoning clinic.

'The drugs didn't just destroy her, they destroyed any kind of family life. She was scared to go to the doctor in case she was judged. And she would have been. Dana was judged her whole life for winning and losing and everything in between. For what she could have been. What she wasn't. Sad when a town pins their hopes on you, and you fail.'

Mim shrugged, fired now to continue. 'She hated the sterility of the doctor's surgery, the smell. I thought if I made this place accessible and non-judgemental, open and caring, then more people like her would come.'

He put his pen down and finally looked up at her, rested his chin on his fist. Like he was really seeing her for the first time since he'd walked back into her life. 'You never talked about it like this. I didn't realise... I'm surprised you got out whole.'

You don't know the half of it. 'Who said I was?'

'From what I remember, you're more whole than most.' He smiled. It seemed genuine enough. Warm honey flecks flashed in his eyes.

Ah, there they are. She relaxed a little. It had taken time, but they were back. At least for now. At least he remembered some of their time together with fondness, then. Maybe he'd be gentle after all.

'Dana's dramas were a long time ago, and I had a great role model in my nan. My focus now is on family medicine. Keeping families healthy and safe. Besides...'

She forced a smile, trying to lighten the mood she'd sunk into. No point in dwelling on what had happened. She had a future ahead of her and she was going to make it work. *Three months*… 'It fits well. Dana's Drop-In. Imagine if she'd been called something like Janice or Patty. Janice's Joint. Very inappropriate. Or Patty's Place. Sounds like a pole-dancing club.'

He laughed. A deep rumble that teased the dark corners of her soul. Another thing she remembered about Connor. His laughter was infectious and rich. And she'd missed it. The granite softened. 'Calling it Atanga Bay Medical Centre would have been just fine.'

'Sure, but where's the fun in that? I want to remind people of how Dana was before she got sick. How proud they were of her when she left to represent their country. Darling Dana. Not druggie Dana who came home in disgrace, who stole and lied and became an embarrassment.' She dragged in a breath. 'You've got to admit it's unique. It's open house, there's free tea and coffee. A place to sit and chat. A small free library. Community resources. It works. Until I opened there was nothing in the way of medical services at all. Just look at the increasing patient list.'

'Yes, I can see. It's a surprising place to have a practice. The middle of nowhere. Albeit pretty spectacular. And you have a very unusual approach. But, then, you always were… unpredictable.'

His mouth curled into a reluctant half-smile. As if remembering something sweet, a past innocence. He reached out to her arm—a gentle gesture that five minutes ago she wouldn't have believed he was capable of making. Hidden in the folds of that expensive suit, behind the cool exterior, was the determined and passionate man she'd fallen hopelessly in love with. There'd been a glimmer of him just now. But he'd gone again as he'd withdrawn his hand. 'Now, on to question two.'

'So? How's it going?' Two hours into the assessment Mim leaned against the doorway of the smallest admin room Connor had ever seen and nibbled the corner of her lip. A nervous habit he remembered of old.

In fact, lots of things had him spinning back three years. The scent of her mango body butter smell lingering in every space. The hesitant smile that was slow to blossom but that lit up her face. That pale, creamy thigh he'd glimpsed earlier. The way she looked at him as if she knew exactly what he was thinking.

The one who'd disappeared without trace and left him reeling.

Walking in and seeing her laughing and dancing on the desk—acting pure *Mim*—had been a body blow. Hard and low.

He'd thought he'd hammered his heart back together with armour plating. He had vowed never to let himself be so vulnerable again. Loving hurt. Losing hurt more.

His latest ex described him as closed. Cold. Clearly his approach had worked well with her. It had always worked for his father too. He was only doing what he'd learnt by parental example. Don't let anyone in, and you won't run a risk of being destroyed in the fallout.

But being here with Mim had the plating cracking already. Despite the million promises he'd made to himself. Take a leaf out of Father's book. Focus on work. Work was easy. Structured, rigid, predictable. With outcomes he could control. Unlike relationships.

And still she hovered. Could she not see how distracting she was being? 'Early days, Mim. I'm busy here.'

'Sorry. If you need anything…'

'I'll call. This place is so small you'd hear me if I whispered.' Uncertainty tainted her chocolate-fudge eyes but she didn't move. He exhaled and tried to keep the exasperation hidden. 'How desperate are you to pass this assessment, Mim?'

'I'm not *desperate*. Not at all.' Her shoulders went ramrod straight. He remembered her pride and ingrained independence. He'd been on the whipping end of that before. And it stung.

Her pupils dilated. 'But getting the accreditation will help. I have plans to expand, and I need more rooms, a visiting physio, counsellor, nutritionists.'

'Okay, we'll start with the financial reports. I'll read through them now. Then have a quick chat about budgets and audit.'

'Ooh, I can't wait. You really know how to impress a girl.' She laughed, then edged back a little as if she'd overstepped the mark. Her voice quieted. 'Sorry. Must be nerves.'

'You cut your hair.'

Why the hell had he even noticed that? Let alone said it?

She ran a hand over her short bob absent-mindedly. 'Not that it matters but, yes. A while ago now.'

'It suits you.' It was probably a good thing that the long dark curls he'd loved to rake his hands through were gone. No temptation there.

The style made her look older, more mature. And she was thinner. Her watch hung from her wrist. Her misshapen green jumper draped off her frame.

'You're looking good yourself. Very executive. A big change from…before.' She looked away, heat burning her cheeks. Not for the first time today. She was either embarrassed as hell—as she should be—or just plain nervous. *Desperate*.

She ran a slow finger across her clavicle. Not a sexual gesture, again it was more absent-minded than anything else. He'd swear on it. But his gaze followed the line her finger traced and a video of kissing a path along that dip played in his head.

Damn. He clamped his teeth together to take his mind off

her throat. He didn't want memories burning a hole in his skull. Memories and emotions were pointless and skewered his thought processes. They couldn't fix a problem or bring someone back. And they hurt too much.

He wasn't going to hurt any more.

No, he just needed to get the job done, then out. Unscathed and unburdened. And having her right here in his space was not going to work.

He scraped his chair across the faded pink carpet. 'Okay, scoot. Get out of my hair. I need to concentrate. There's a lot of paperwork to get through. I'll call you when I need you.'

She nodded, her finger darting from her neck to her mouth. 'One quick question.'

'You are insufferable.' But, then, he'd always known that, and it hadn't made a difference to loving her. He held up two fingers. 'Two seconds then you have to leave. Okay?'

'Okay, boss. I just wondered—first impressions?' She looked at him through a thick fringe. Her eyes accentuated by the matching chocolate hair colour. Rich and thick. Frustration melted into something more dangerous.

Maybe running his fingers through couldn't hurt…

First impressions? Sexy as hell.

'That's going to take a heck of a lot longer than two seconds. And you might not like it.' He pulled his gaze away. Tried to find something positive to say before he hit her with the unassailable truth. Kiss-kick-kiss. Perhaps then she'd leave. When he'd broken her heart with his first impression. 'I've scanned through the Imms register and I'm surprised.'

She looked expectantly at him. 'Good surprised?'

'Come on, Mim, I'm just starting. I've hardly had a chance to get my head around things. There's a lot of work to be done yet, but your immunisation rates are outstanding. Big tick for that.'

Pride swelled her voice. 'Every time I see a patient I remind them about imms. So important.'

'Admirable.'

She was trying so hard to impress he almost felt sorry for her. But for their history. He ran a hand over the windowsill and showed her the peeling flecks of yellow paint. Now for the kick.

'But the structure and organisational processes leave a lot to be desired. Your intentions are good, but from where I'm standing it's a shabby practice in the middle of a rundown township. I'm hoping I'm going to find some better news in your business plans and policies.'

'Of course, policies, your hobby horse. Don't hold your breath. Not really my strong suit. But...'

'I know, it's a work in progress. That might not be good enough. Perhaps we should do this in a year or so, once you've had time to prepare in accordance with the guidelines.'

She visibly flinched and he briefly wished he could take it back.

But he wasn't there to protect her. He was there to do an objective assessment as a representative of a local authority. 'Routines and regulations make things run smoothly. Save lives in the long run. Without them people get lost. Accidents happen. People die.'

Janey. The armour round his heart quivered then clenched tight at the thought of his sister. No point trying to explain to Mim. What would she care? He wasn't inclined to share his motives with an untrustworthy ex-girlfriend. However sinfully sexy. 'I said I'd be honest.'

She turned back to him, eyes now firing with determination. The old Mim shone through. She may have been subdued, but she was there simmering in the background.

'Okay, so, Dana's Drop-In might not be conventional, it's not standardised and faceless like your fancy chrome

Auckland offices. I admit I need processes. But it will work, Connor. What did you say about potential?'

'I was talking about Atanga Bay in general, not this place.' Grateful for the clash of swords and not sentiment, he began to relax. 'Bowling it and starting again would fix a lot. But you always were…how did my father put it? Odd.'

'I might be odd by your father's standards, but my style works out here. You love a challenge, Connor. Dig deeper, and see what I can see.'

'Er…? Sorry to interrupt, Mim...' The goth with the pierced nose arrived in the room. Perhaps she was all Mim had been able to get out here.

'There's been an accident up at Two Rivers. Details are sketchy, but it seems there's been an explosion and a fire. Tony's bringing the walking wounded here. Four or five so far, I think.'

Mim nodded. The fire in her eyes was replaced with a calm, steely precision. Professional and businesslike. 'Thanks, Skye. I'll be right there.'

Connor jumped up, adrenalin kicking deep. 'I'll help. Sounds like it could be busy.'

'That's kind of you.' Mim smiled softly, gazed the length of his body. Heat swept through him on a tidal wave, prickling his veins and firing dormant cells to full alert, taking him by surprise. He'd expected a vague flicker of awareness, but not full fireworks sparking through his body.

'But we'll be fine here at the coalface. Why don't you go back to your paperwork? We don't want to get that lovely suit dirty, do we?'

CHAPTER TWO

To Mim's infinite irritation, Connor appeared unfazed by her barbed comment. He stared her down, then shook out of his jacket and rolled his Italian cotton shirtsleeves up. Sparks flew from his onyx eyes.

'Mim, you never worried about getting down and dirty before. What's changed? Frightened you might get burnt?' He threw the jacket onto the desk. 'I'm not going to sit back while there's a major incident unfolding. I'll go up there and see if I can help.'

'What are you going to do? Waft the fire out with your questionnaire?'

He visibly bristled but the sensual flare in his eyes spelled trouble. Connor had always loved sparring with her. Said she was the most fiery woman he'd ever met. That it was the biggest turn-on ever. Some things hadn't changed. He smiled confidently, inviting more. Seemed they couldn't help firing incendiary shots back and forth even after three years. 'It would work better than all that hot air you're generating.'

'You haven't changed a jot, Connor Wiseman. Still as bloody-minded as ever. But right now I'm sure the firefighters don't need a do-gooder city slicker hindering their work.'

She walked up the corridor, sucked in a breath and tried to concentrate on one disaster at a time. Priority: bush fire. Lives at risk. And he followed, clearly undeterred.

She stopped in Reception and explained to him, 'There's a campsite not far from Two Rivers. It's been a long, dry summer and the bush is brittle. A fire could get out of hand pretty quickly. As I'm community warden, and the only med centre for miles, protocol states they bring the injured here. It's safer and out of the line of fire.'

Protocol. He'd like that.

'So we stay here for now. You'll need all the help you can get.'

'We need to be ready. Dressing packs and oxygen cylinders are in the treatment rooms, there's labels on the drawers and shelves. It should be self-explanatory.' She paused as sirens screeched past the surgery towards the new development.

Time hadn't diminished his bombastic streak. Connor still went hell for leather along his own path without taking much notice of what anyone else had to say. But he was right, she didn't have the luxury of turning away another pair of skilled hands in an emergency.

'We also have a walk-in clinic running at the moment, which is always busy Monday mornings. Sure you can handle this, city boy? Things could get messy.'

To her surprise, his smile widened. Irritating and frustratingly appealing all at the same time. He stepped closer, his breath grazing her neck. Making the hairs on her neck prickle to attention.

'Is that a threat, Mim? Or a promise?'

'I don't make promises I can't keep.' The words tumbled out before she could stop herself. He'd got her hackles up. Just having him there threw her way off balance.

He arched an eyebrow. All the raw, potent tension, zinging between them like electricity, coming to a head. 'Oh, really? Tell that to my parents and the caterers and the party guests.'

'I didn't ask for an engagement party. Once your mum got a whiff of the idea she ran with it.'

'Okay. Let's clear the air, then we can focus on what's important.' He breathed out deeply, put his palms flat on the desk. 'My mum was trying to help. Then you ditched. It was a long time ago and I'm over it. No second chances, like you always said. Never look back. Great philosophy. You missed the boat, princess. Don't blame me if you didn't know a good thing when you saw it.'

'I knew it wasn't for me.'

But it *had* been a very good thing. Until she'd had to make impossible choices. Atanga Bay or Auckland. Break the promises she'd made to her mother or to Connor? 'And I made the right decision. You're doing well. And I'm happy here.'

'But obviously you're still bothered about it. Embarrassed perhaps? Regretful? Don't they say that the first form of defence is attack?'

The smell of his aftershave washed around her. The same as he'd worn back then. Leather and spice and earthy man. Throwing her back to their long, lazy afternoons in bed. When they'd believed their dreams were possible. Before she'd been bamboozled into a life she hadn't wanted.

Her hackles stood to attention again. At the same time her stomach somersaulted at the memory of kissing his lips and the way he had tasted. Ozone and chardonnay, cinnamon whirls and coffee. *Connor.* And how once she'd started to kiss him she'd never wanted to stop. She shook her head in despair. Memories were not helpful.

'Our relationship ran its course. I'm not sore or embarrassed, and I'm not trying to attack you. I'm sorry if it came over that way.'

'Want a little advice? Seems you need me more than I need you right now. You have an assessment hanging over your head and an emergency. And I could walk out that door and *never look back*. But I don't think you need that, right? So maybe if you want my help, you could try being civil.'

She turned away and swallowed hard. He was right. In a cruel twist of fate, he was her only hope. Civil it had to be.

Mercifully the door swung open before she could answer, and four men limped in. Their faces were streaked with black and their clothes singed. Hard hats and heavy work boots were left at the door.

'Okay, gentlemen. Take a breath.' Mim sat them down in Reception, gave them all a fleeting assessment. Triaging four injured construction workers was way more in her comfort zone than needling an old flame.

'What's the story, Tony?' She nodded at the foreman, a local and friend, knowing he'd have the details covered.

'A gas cylinder blew, hit a couple of the lads square in the face—they've been airlifted to Auckland General. There's a fire burning out of control on the site.' He coughed long and hard, then pointed to his pals. 'This motley crew are mainly smoke inhalation, a few cuts and bruises, and I reckon Boy here's got a broken finger from falling over. Daft coot. Never seen anyone away run so fast. Or fall so hard.'

Connor stepped into the fray. 'Okay. Tony? You come with me, sounds like you could do with some oxygen to help clear those lungs. Boy, you go with Mim. Skye, take the other two through to Treatment Room Two.'

'And you are?' Tony stood and faced Connor, his face grim beneath the soot.

Just great. Mim's heart plummeted. For the last few months Tony had been playing suitor, quietly. Little gestures, the odd interested phrase. Dinner for two at the pub. She'd let him down gently as soon as she'd realised his intentions were more than just friendly.

It wasn't just that she didn't fancy him, but she'd sworn off men. Men wanted her to need them. To rely on them. She couldn't. She hated the thought of losing control over any-thing—particularly her emotions.

She stepped in, tried to infuse her voice with a quiet plea for calm. Tony was hot-headed at the best of times and obviously stressed. 'Tony, this is Connor Wiseman. He's that assessor I told you about. He's going to be here for a while, on and off. He's also a doctor and is keen to help out.'

'Okay. Connor. A word of warning, mate.' Tony stuck his hand out. 'Our Mim doesn't take too kindly to being told what to do.'

'Believe me, I know. I've still got the scars.' *Our Mim.* Connor squared his shoulders and gripped the man's hand. Clearly Tony and Mim were more than well acquainted. The man had possession written all over his sooty face. And the way Mim looked at Tony, in such a conciliatory way, those full lips curling into a gentle smile for another man, sent jolts of jealousy and anger spasming through him. She'd thrown him over for this? This nowheresville town and this hulk of a man?

Well, good luck to them. Traces of fading arousal from their early spat cemented into a clarity of focus. He wasn't here to woo her back. Not a chance. He'd lost her once. What kind of idiot would invite that kind of grief again?

Letting him go, Connor nodded. *But for the record...* 'Mim and I go way back.'

'Yeah, me too.' Tony put a hand on Mim's shoulder. His voice threw down a gauntlet. 'Primary school? High school? Pretty much all her life.'

Mim tried to stand casually between them. 'Right, then. Let's not waste time trawling through my life, shall we?'

She almost laughed. The scenario made her seem like some kind of diva. Little Mim, who hadn't had so much as a kiss for three years, trying to keep two men from taunting each other. Surreal. 'Second thoughts, Tony, you come with me. Boy, go with Connor.'

She bundled Tony into Treatment Room One and applied

an oxygen mask, measured his sats and vitals. She decided not to mention his possessiveness. That would only draw attention to something she wanted to ignore. 'Take a few deep breaths. You hurt anywhere else?'

'Nah. All good, Mim. Scary, though. Those guys were hurt badly. Nasty business.'

'Anyone I know?' A likely prospect, as she knew every single inhabitant of Atanga Bay.

'Macca Wilson and Toby Josiah.'

'Oh, no.' Her stomach knotted. Two of their finest. 'I'll phone the hospital later and see how they're doing. Shelly's going to need a hand with those little kiddies while Macca's in hospital. And Toby's mum'll be worried sick. Any others injured?'

'No one else got the blast. Just us, and we were a little way back. But the wind whipped up a blaze in no time. Civil Defence is up there, assessing with the fire department. No real danger, but they're evacuating the campsite as a precaution.'

'I'll grab the key to the community hall and go open up. That's the designated assembly point. Besides, there's nowhere else to put a campsite full of people.' Measuring Tony's sats again, Mim smiled. 'No major problems here. But I'll leave you with the oxygen on for a couple of minutes while I go start the phone tree. We're going to need bedding, food and water for the evacuees.'

After opening up the hall next door, starting the cascade of calls firing the locals into action and discharging Tony, Mim found Connor suturing a deep gash on one of the construction worker's legs. Connor looked up as she entered, those dark eyes boring into her. Energy emanated from him, as electric as ever. Plug him in and her power-bill woes would be over.

Seeing him there, in her space, so incongruously smart and chic in her tired treatment room, and so very Connor, threw her off centre again. She gripped the doorhandle as she inhaled, deeply, to steady herself. Leather and spice and earthly man again. Her body hummed in automatic response. Inhaling was a big mistake.

He smiled, adding an urgent charge to the humming. She squeezed the handle harder and calmed her body's reaction to him.

For goodness' sake, she'd purged her grief at their split years ago, when it had become so obvious she couldn't give him what he wanted. What they both wanted. Clearly her brain had reconciled that, but her body was living in a time warp. If only she could fast-forward to the end of the review, hopefully some cash. Getting her practice to its full *potential*. Connor leaving.

He waved gloved hands towards her. 'Mim? Pass that gauze, will you? Just closing up. Tommo here's had a tetanus and we're starting antibiotics as a precaution. I was just telling him, gravel wounds are a haven for bacteria.' He nodded at his patient. 'Finish the whole course of tablets, okay?'

'Yes, Doc.' Tommo grinned. 'And keep off the grog too, eh?'

'Just cut down, mate. A couple of stubbies a night, that's all. That liver's got to last you a lifetime.' He smiled as Tommo headed out the door. 'And don't forget about that well-man appointment. You won't regret it.'

'Sure. Cheers, Doc.'

To her irritation, Mim couldn't fault Connor's bedside manner, suturing skills or efficiency. He was assertive, professional and fast. But as Tommo left she couldn't help but satisfy her curiosity. 'Well-man Clinic? Good luck with that. I've been trying to get one up and running for a while. No one came.'

'Here? Wrong venue. Try the pub.'

'I've put adverts up in there. But you can't do a clinic in the pub.'

'It worked fine in the some of the low-decile areas out West. We took mini-health checks out to some bars. But now we've educated the clients to go to the clinics, where there are better facilities. Still, a pub is a good starting place.' Connor whipped off his gloves and threw them into the bin. Direct hit. Of course. He was precise and perfect and professional. And poles away from the reality of rural medicine.

'You don't know these people. There's not a metrosexual among them. We're lucky if we get a blast of deodorant, and no one uses hair gel.' She tried to keep the knowing smile out of her voice as she surveyed Connor's carefully dishevelled hair. It must have taken hours to perfect that morning. It looked good enough to run her fingers through.

Check that. No finger running. 'Anything else is considered just plain girly. They're stoic blokes and think being sick is a weakness.'

'What about just before a game? Tried a clinic then?'

'On a Saturday night?' Okay, he had a point. The pub was always heaving at that time. But she wasn't going to admit that. 'Preventive medicine like that is a pipe dream. I tell you, the only way to get these men to see a doctor is if their head's falling off or their heart's given out.' Remembering the four that had just pitched up to her surgery, she smiled, smugly. Case in point. 'Or if there's a drama. By the way, what happened to Boy? Have you finished with him already?'

'Yep, but X-ray facilities would help.'

'I agree. But two years ago there wasn't even a clinic here, until I set this one up. Facilities take funding when you live in the real world.' He never had—and that had been part of their problem. He still didn't get it. She sighed. 'Get your daddy to wave his magic wand. While he's at it I'd like an MRI scanner, a decent coffee shop and lots and lots of shoes. In the meantime, we'll make do with what we've got. Anything that needs more investigation goes into the city.'

'An hour and a half's drive away. No fun if you're in pain.' He shrugged, obviously choosing to ignore her barbed comment. Again. She bristled at his self-control. Maybe he wasn't as riled by her as he used to be. That was good. Wasn't it? She didn't want to have any effect on him at all. Except a positive impression for the fund assessment. Really. Honestly. Then she could move on with her life, without giving a backward glance to Connor Wiseman.

'Luckily for Boy, his finger wasn't broken. I'm pretty sure it's just a bad sprain so I've buddy-strapped it. Told him to come back in a couple of days so we can double-check.' Having replenished the dressing trolley, Connor cracked his knuckles as he stretched his arms out in front of him. 'Man, that felt good. It's been a while since I did hands-on.'

'I let you loose on my patients when you're out of practice?' She glowered at him. Had she allowed him to bulldoze her into something she had doubts about again? One word from him and she was almost rolling over, asking him to scruff her tummy. When would she learn? She would not let him badger her into anything any more. 'Please tell me you have a valid practising certificate.'

'Of course. Simmer down.' He laughed. 'And I thought we'd agreed to be civil. Don't worry, I do a few hours consulting a month to keep my hand in.'

'But why bother do all those years at med school just for a few hours a month? The internships? The GP training? What a waste.'

'Why? I know my way around a clinic. I've lived and breathed medical practice.' For the first time since his arrival he looked uncomfortable. His lips formed a tight line and a frown sat edgily over his eyes. 'But systems management is important too. Someone needs to make sure everyone's reached a certain standard.'

He closed his eyes briefly and Mim noticed his fist

clenched against the desk. He looked like he was trying to gain control. And unbelievably sad.

'Connor?' Her heart stammered as she bit her lip. 'Are you okay?'

When he opened his eyes again they resonated a steel calm. Devoid of any kind of emotion. 'You have your demons, Mim, I have mine. And we're both trying to work the system to fit them.'

Demons? His sister perhaps. Who knew? No point in asking. Clamming up was Connor's forte. She'd never managed to break through that hard exterior before.

But they needed to get on to move on. She touched his fingers in a meek attempt at a handshake. 'So how about we start over? Let's go for civil. Who knows? We might even like it.'

Connor inhaled sharply. Mim had always been right about one thing: moving forward was the only way to go. He couldn't change what had happened to Janey. Or that Mim had thrashed his heart. He just had to make sure that nothing like either tragedy ever happened again.

She looked up at him through thick lashes, held his gaze, her lips parted slightly. Her pale complexion was punctuated with two red circles of anger, the passion for her work flaring deeply in dark irises. Her belief and pride in her good intentions was clear in the way she held that pert body erect and taut.

As if answering her clarion call, his blood stirred in a sudden wild frenzy.

He let her hand drop and forced himself to remember all the reasons their affair had failed before. Passion and lust had never been a problem. But their clash of backgrounds and vision of their futures had pulled them in opposing directions. Walking away had been her chosen option. Three years had made no difference to her naive idealism. But this time he could do the walking.

Connor eased out the irritation rippling through his shoulders. He'd work this on his terms. Keep a professional distance.

'Okay. Let's start again. Hi. I'm Dr Connor Wiseman, here to assess your practice.'

'How-de-do, Dr Wiseman. I'm Mim. Welcome to beautiful Atanga Bay, where we have sunshine and smiles in abundance. Oh, and the odd bush fire…but only once in a blue moon.' The corner of her lips tweaked upwards as she folded her arms over her tiny frame. She was extremes and opposites. Combative and defensive. And yet he knew she enjoyed a good spat as much as he did. No one had ever riled him so much, hit the spot every time. And got a rise out of him. Figuratively and, very often, literally. Their fights had been legendary, but their make-up sex had been stellar.

He sneaked another glance down her body. She was thinner, sure, but there were still curves there, hidden under her shapeless jumper. She was every bit the woman he remembered. And then some.

And he had to endure being with her for the next three months. More if he kept being delayed by fires and regular cat fights. But he refused to be baited by her. Had to remain controlled and calm. And *focused.* 'So, give me a clue. How to write notes in a computer that refuses to start?'

She picked up a pen from the desk and waved it at him, her intensity and passion transformed now to a flutter of lightness. 'Can't function without your gadgetry? Try using a pen.'

'You are joking? This is twenty-first-century New Zealand, not the *Pickwick Papers.*'

'If we're busy, or the computer's playing up, like today, I write them down on cards, and type them up later. They're always up to date by the end of the day.' She cringed, and had the decency to look apologetic. 'But you're right, the computers do need updating. I'm looking into buying wireless laptops. Chicken and egg thing—I need the money to buy computers, need the computers to get the money. But it's high on my priority list. Is that something you can put a big tick next to?'

'Sure. When you get them you'll have a tick. Not before.'

Then he walked back to Reception, torn between helping her patients and completing his brief. In the end, professional compassion won out over fiscal duty. But as he directed his next patient into Treatment Room Two, he swallowed his frustration. The day he walked away from Mim and Atanga Bay couldn't come soon enough.

CHAPTER THREE

THE sound of more sirens had Connor striding to the surgery door. Again.

He should be used to it by now—after three hours the shrieking wails had become a regular distraction.

He watched as a fire-service helicopter hovered in the distance out over the sea. A dangling monsoon bucket scooped its gallons then was swung off in the direction of the fire. Smoke billowed from the bush in the distance, an acrid burning smell filled the air and tiny fragments of ash periodically fluttered onto him like confetti.

Further up the road a steady stream of camper vans and overloaded cars zoomed towards him as the campsite decamped into Atanga Bay.

Mim joined him on the step outside and wrapped her arms around her chest. Worry and concern tightened her fragile features. She jerked her head in the direction of the fire. 'What d'you reckon? Does it seem to be coming under control?'

'Don't know. Does this happen a lot out here?'

'No. First time. Normally it's a peaceful seaside community.' She smiled. 'Sure, we have fire bans in the summer, who doesn't? But gas explosions on construction sites can happen anywhere. Why? Worried about your papers catching fire?'

'I was more concerned that *you* lived in a dangerous place.' The surprise on her face told him he'd said too much. But he wouldn't sleep at night if he thought she was at risk. Just a guy's natural protective instinct kicking in. Right? 'How far away is Two Rivers?'

'Five kilometres or so.' Another rural fire service truck sped by.

Duty tugged at him. This tiny community was at risk, and he couldn't sit idly by and watch the emergency services rattle past. 'It's on the main road, right? Far end of the peninsula?'

'You're not thinking of going to help?'

He dragged his car keys from his pocket and pointed them at his car parked at the kerb out front. 'We have an empty surgery. I can't just hang around. I've got to do something.'

'No. It's better if they bring the injured here out of the fire zone. They'll let us know when to evacuate if we need to. In the meantime, we wait.' She shook her head and put her hand on his chest. Her smile was the same one she'd given to that hulk, Tony. Conciliatory. Close. So tempting. So bad for him.

'You'll like this, Connor, this is *our* protocol. We managed to work it out all by ourselves, me and the fire chief. It's going to kill me to say it, but I need you to stay here with me.'

He forced a smile. 'Honey, if I thought you meant that I'd give it a second's thought.'

The pads of her fingertips pressed into his skin and heat from her touch spread across his torso like a fast incoming tide. A sudden need to kiss that smug smile away overwhelmed him.

He edged back from her palm, put air between them. It had been three years since Mim had dictated terms, and he wouldn't slip back into that after a few hours. He wouldn't let her stop him doing something he believed in. 'Great that you have a system for *you* to work with, but I'm going.'

'So it's just your own protocols you like to follow? Forget anyone else's?' Her hands slid to her hips as her jaw jutted towards him. Her body hummed with muted frustration, almost tangible. Her eyes sparked fury, melting fudge and fireworks. Full lips pouted under sheer lipgloss. Damn it, if his body didn't stir at her reaction. 'These are the rules, Connor. Stay here where it's safe.'

'Your rules, your problem. If you have to sit here and bide your time, that's fine by me. But I'm going to *do* something.' Then he jumped into his car and gunned the engine. Out of sight, out of mind, right? Out of arm's reach. And while he was up at the development he'd ask the fire guys to douse him with cold water too.

Mim rapped hard on the car window. *Stupid, rash, insane.* 'Wait.'

The tinted glass gave way to his mock impatient face. 'I'm going. Don't argue.'

She laughed despite herself. 'And I'm coming with you. Skye can manage in the surgery for a couple of hours. The action plan is up and running. There's nothing to say I can't help a dumb doctor with a death wish.'

'Maybe you should write that in the plan for next time.' A flicker of something she couldn't quite place flashed across his face. Excitement? Confusion. Yes, probably confusion. He rolled his eyes and tutted. 'You can't trust anyone to stick to protocols these days. I'm going to have to have a word.'

'Haven't you heard, Connor? Rules are made for breaking.'

And she was doing just that, God help her, trashing her own hard and fast rules. There was a danger to getting into cars with strange men.

Connor mightn't be a stranger. But he was dangerous.

And seemed hell bent on helping her friends so, heck, she had to go with him. She swallowed hard, for some reason seeing him so fired up had her dry-mouthed and aching to touch him. 'There are houses up there near the fire. Might be some casualties. You'll need some help.'

'I think I'll be fine.' He leaned closer and grazed her cheek with his breath. 'I know exactly what to do when things get hot.'

No. Five hours. That's all it had taken for the innuendo to start. Resisting his cheek was too hard. Next thing they'd know, it'd be hot talk, hot kisses, then hot sex. Then…making and breaking promises again.

Taking her time to calm down her flushed reaction to his words, she walked round to the passenger side. Then hopped into the leather seat, brushed her palm along the curve of the cherrywood dash. 'Gosh, there's a year's worth of my clinic's operating expenses just in this car.'

'Top of the range.' His chin tilted in pride. 'You could have had fancy cars, you know. And more…lots more, Mim.'

She chose not to dignify his comment with a reply. He obviously still didn't understand why she left him. Her need to be in control of her own life. Why she didn't believe in the picket-fence dream. Not for herself anyway. Those childish dreams had faded as she'd watched her mother slide from one crappy relationship to another lost in her search for her next fix of love. And dope. But she never got her fill, and died trying.

No, she managed her own life. She would never let need and dependency rule her heart. After all, that was why she'd walked away from Connor in the first place.

At the entrance to the campsite they were met by a police officer and Tony, who indicated for them to go back to town.

Connor braked with no intention of turning round. 'Great, a welcoming committee. I've driven straight into Deliverance.'

Punching the electric window button, he nodded out to them, scanning for stetsons and firearms. Luckily neither was obvious. 'Need any help?'

'I'll handle this.' Tony held his palm up to the police officer and swaggered towards the car, his chest puffed out.

He nodded towards Mim in a brief salutation, then back to Connor. The look on his face was ill-disguised distaste. 'Fire Chief's downgraded the threat. They've contained the fire at the edge of the development. No need for you, Doc. Thought you'd play hero?'

'Thought you might need one. Shouldn't you be taking it easy after the explosion?'

'No.'

Beside him Mim bristled. She leaned forward and put a hand on Connor's shoulder. 'Let me talk to him.'

'No.' That fast incoming tide washed over him again. He pulled away before he drowned. 'Give me a chance.'

Hauling in a breath of smoke-tinged air, Connor slammed down his irritation. He was on their territory, he understood that, understood Tony's need to protect, his alpha rivalry. And his distrust of an outsider, ill-dressed to help. But that wasn't going to stop him. *Step back and bad things happened.* 'I don't want to tread on anyone's toes. But I wondered if there's anything I could do to help?'

'Sure. Go back to Atanga Bay. The road's blocked from here up. No traffic allowed. No one. Not Mim. Not you. Orders.'

'Has everywhere been evacuated? Anyone injured? Anyone need help up there?' He knew Tony would never allow himself to be told what to do, but a few questions wouldn't go amiss. 'I only want to do the right thing here. And I have skills you could use.'

The police officer stepped forward and placed a hand on Tony's shoulder. 'Listen, mate, maybe they could help with Steph? Get her down to town? Out of harm's way, eh? We're still on standby. The wind direction could change and the fire could sweep back around here.'

Tony looked at the officer, his hard face unreadable. But

eventually he nodded. 'Stubborn old boot. She's refusing to leave.'

'Why?'

'Because she can. Maybe Mim can talk sense into her.'

Mim blanched. She looked uncertain as she spoke, like she was trying to convince herself as much as anyone else. 'I'll give it a go, but she probably won't take any notice of me either.'

Connor got the sense that there was some kind of history between the two women. But he couldn't focus on that. He had a potential emergency to deal with. History would have to wait.

They walked up the steep hill to the leafy campsite.

Trailing a thick black hosepipe, a heavily pregnant woman in a floaty dress and gumboots walked round the outside of the neat welcoming office. Her breath was ragged and her cheeks puce. She raised her eyebrows at the entourage advancing towards her. 'Mim. Tony. Bruce. I've told you, I'm not going anywhere. Stop badgering.'

Making a quick assessment of the situation, Connor stepped forward and held out his hand. 'Hey, Steph. I'm Connor, a doctor friend of Mim's. In town for a few days.' He watched recognition register. But he chose not to look at Mim. *Friend? Not likely.*

'Hi.' Steph wrapped her large hot hand into his, shook briefly and eyed him suspiciously. Her palms were sweaty, perspiration dripped from her forehead. Two bright red spots shone from her cheeks. She looked bewildered and breathless and not pleased to see him. He'd have put money on a threatening pre-eclampsia. And on her refusing to do anything about it.

He feigned vague disinterest rather than acknowledge the growing urgency. Didn't want to spook or stress her further. 'This your place?'

'Sure.' She dug the heel of her palm into her flank and winced. 'What of it?'

'Nice. You obviously look after it well. Lucky escape. You must have been worried.'

'All good. Just doing my job.' Her shoulders straightened. Then she waved the thick hose at him. He had to admire her strength and capability in her condition. 'I've finished damping down the outside. Managed to get all the punters out, though.'

'Who knows if it'll sweep down here? Nasty business, fires.' Connor looked down at her swollen belly. 'How long to go?'

'Six weeks. Kicking like a good 'un.' She ran a hand across the small of her back and through the thin fabric he saw tight ripples across her belly. He needed to measure her blood pressure. Check her ankles for swelling, her urine for protein. Feel the babe's position. 'Little blighter's going to be the best first five the All Blacks ever had.'

Tony checked his watch. Connor took it as a signal to hurry. For once they were in agreement on something. 'Braxton-Hicks?'

'Yeah. Catches your breath sometimes.' Doubling over, she grabbed her stomach.

Mim closed the gap and took the woman's arm. 'You okay? You need a hand? You really should get out of the danger zone.'

'I said I'm not leaving here.' Steph straightened. 'Not if you ask me, Mim McCarthy. Nor any of them.'

Connor watched hurt flash across Mim's eyes. Was that the kind of response she generally got? Was Steph's mistrust directed at Mim or at them all? Hard to tell.

But if Mim was up against this kind of antagonism she'd need a lot more than a positive Matrix assessment to build her practice. He knew more than anyone else that once Mim put her mind to something she achieved it. But she'd need support. Belief. Faith in her abilities. A chance.

And he wasn't the guy for that job. Was he?

No. He was here to help Steph, do the assessment, then leave. Easy.

He stepped forward. 'You did your job well, Steph. Now let me do mine. I can see you're uncomfortable. How about Mim and I take you down to town and check you over?'

'I heard about a bush fire once where they evacuated the town and it was wrecked by looters. I can't afford for anyone to nick my stuff.'

So it wasn't about Mim after all. But the idea of supporting her lingered—rather more than he wanted it to. For an ex-girlfriend who had dumped him she was lingering in his head too long altogether.

'I can't afford for you to put yourself and your baby at risk.' He regarded Steph's puffy fingers and breathlessness. She winced again and he fought back a need to carry her out of the bush himself.

He didn't have local knowledge or *mana*, the respect from Atanga Bay residents. But he had one thing he could use as leverage. One thing most women wouldn't turn down. 'I've got a de luxe room booked at the pub in town. King-size bed. Fresh linen. It's yours for the night if you want. Have a rest, bubble bath. Take a load off. Tony can stay here and look after the place for you. Can't you, Tony?'

He glanced at his audience. Mim's eyes popped. The foreman's face was agape with anger as he spat out, 'I have other things to—'

'Fresh linen? Room service?' That suspicion bit deeper but Steph chewed her lip. Tempted.

Mim's huge eyes got larger, her mouth opened and her tongue tip ran round her lips. She looked entranced and shocked.

But impressed. God forgive him, but impressing Mim sure felt good.

Which was downright absurd when he thought about it. She'd made her feelings very clear all those years ago, and again now. So he tried to convince himself he was offering this to a sick woman out of the goodness of his heart. 'Okay. Yes, room service.' He turned to Mim. 'Are all you country women so difficult to please?'

'You betcha, city boy.'

Then he focused back on Steph. 'If you promise we can check you over. Make sure that smoke's not got into your lungs, what d'you say?'

'Okay, I suppose. Just one night.' She smiled towards Tony and nodded like she was doing them all a huge favour. 'Anything to get that lazy good-for-nothin' fella to do something useful, eh?'

Great, now he had Steph on side, he just had to work on the rest of the hillbillies.

'Just got off the phone to the fire chief. The danger's over. For now at least.' Mim placed a plate of *kai* and a cup of hot malted drink on the desk in front of Connor. He nodded his thanks and smiled, momentarily whipping her breath away.

The danger outside was over, but it was steaming hot in the office.

A shower in the community hall amenities and a change of clothes had transformed Connor from executive to beach bum. But even in shorts and a black T-shirt he oozed authority and X-rated sex appeal.

She watched him swallow the drink, his Adam's apple moving mesmerisingly up and down. Then she dragged her eyes away and made for the door. 'Bring your dinner outside, it's a warm evening and a lovely onshore breeze. Lots of fresh air, no smoke.'

He scrubbed a hand through his wavy hair and looked up

from the pile of files. Tiny lines crinkled round his temples as he squeezed his eyes shut, then opened them and focused on her. Pierced her with his dark gaze. 'No. You go. I've got a day's work to catch up on.'

'Given any thought to where you're going to sleep tonight?'

When they'd got back to town and handed over Connor's room to Steph they'd discovered the pub was fully booked with campers. Guilt ate at her soul. He'd rushed off to help her friends. Given up his bed for a pregnant woman. Broken protocol, which would have been hard for him.

Made her break protocol, or at least bend it a little.

And now he had no bed for the night. She'd hesitated to offer her couch—it was all she had in the small apartment at the back of the surgery. Way too cosy. And judging by her frisky hormones, the safest distance she could keep between them was a whole block, not a flimsy wall.

'There's not a lot of choice. It's *marae-style* communal sleeping in the hall, on hard mattresses with a load of people I don't know. Or my car. Oddly, neither option appeals.' He shrugged and pointed to the paperwork. 'Think I'll do an all-nighter.'

Good. The sooner he was finished with her accounts, the better. Then he would go and normal service would be resumed.

'Then eat. You can't work on an empty stomach.' She pushed the food towards him. 'This is from Steph's mum, by way of a thank-you. She's grateful you saved her daughter from the ravages of the fire. You're quite the hero. And Boy said to say hi. And Tommo told me he's having a night off booze. Seems you've made quite an impression on the community already.'

'Good.' Was it her imagination, or did his hard-muscled chest swell just a little under that tight T? Surely not? Pride from helping such a small community in *the middle of nowhere*?

'Don't people thank you at the health board?'

'Sure they do.' He frowned and scrubbed a hand under his chin, thinking for a moment. 'No, not really. Praise more than thanks. Paperwork doesn't usually bring forth a whole heap of gushing. Anyway, I was just doing my job.'

'Oh, yes, and Steph said to say thanks to that *new doctor fella.* I think you impressed her with your one over on Tony. Her BP's a tad high but nothing to worry about. I'll keep an eye on it. The ankle swelling went down after a couple of hours' bed rest and a soothing bath. For a farmer she sure likes her townie comforts. If I'd known winning the Atanga Bay residents over was as easy as providing fresh cotton sheets I'd have opened a linen shop instead of a surgery.'

'Dana's Drapery has a certain ring to it.'

'Touché. You're not as daft as you look.' Another Dana saying. And, as always, slightly off the mark. He *looked* breathtaking. But that was all she could do—look. His comment about no second chances rang true and was definitely the right course of action. But it didn't stop her looking. 'I'm afraid your room service bill's going to be huge.'

'It's no biggie. I can't imagine it'll break the bank. And think of the karma.' His mouth curved into a smile. A genuine, warm-hearted, tired smile that reached down into her soul and tugged.

She perched on the edge of the desk, a whisper away from him, remembering what it was like to be wrapped in his gaze. Remembering how his arms had felt tight around her.

No matter. *No second chances.* No looking back. She'd lived with her decisions just fine. And having him here wasn't going to change that. 'Well, that's raised you from, what? Slug to cockroach in your next life. Yip-de-doo. You've still got a long way to go.'

She felt her eyes widen as she spoke to him. Her voice came in thready whispers. Her hip pressed against the desk in an involuntarily seductive move. *No.* Flirting? Although quite when slugs became flirting fodder she didn't know.

'Ouch. I was thinking something a bit more macho—horse fly or beetle. Slug? Really?' He grimaced. 'That bad, eh?'

'Well, Tony would think so. You dumped him in it. I imagine slug is the nicest of the things he'd like to call you.'

'Ah. Tony. Incredible.' He laughed. That deep rumble that transformed his face, softened the edges, spun her back three years to passionate, joyful sex on carefree days off. 'I hope he'll forgive me, but I couldn't resist.'

'Tony's not the kind to forgive and forget.'

'Not with someone stamping on his territory, eh? At least, working in close proximity with delectable Dr McCarthy.'

His gaze travelled down her washed-out jumper, then back to her face where it stayed, for a lot longer than it should. Something deep inside her wriggled and fought for freedom after three long years' dormancy. She tried to swallow it away, stood up from the desk. 'We're just friends.'

'He looked the jealous type.'

'No, seriously. He's not my boyfriend.'

'Then more fool him.'

She needed to take hold of her long-lost senses and leave. His smile and proximity and leathery smell jumped on her frayed nerves and made her tongue loose. And an impulse to touch him again, to feel the beat of his heart under her fingers, was sudden and unwanted. *Don't be a fool. Once bitten...* Dana's Drop-In took all her energy and living out her promise left no space for a relationship. Especially not with someone who lived hundreds of miles away and who had shared such intense passion with her. She wasn't going there again. Three years and a lot of water had passed under that bridge. She wasn't tempted to dip her toe back in.

'I have to go check on the hall. Make sure everyone's okay. Catch you later. If you need anything…'

'I won't.'

'And thanks.' It was the least she could say. He deserved her gratitude for helping her, and her friends. 'You were a big help and raised the profile of Dana's Drop-In no end.'

'Ah, shucks. What's a guy to do?'

She turned to leave, but his voice dragged her back to his side. That, and his hand on her wrist. And a need that zapped between them like an invisible thread. Pulling them closer and closer.

Within a heartbeat he was in front of her. His hard body fingertips away from her. Strength from God knew where stopped her from touching him.

His scent filled the air, his breathing came heavy and fast. Hot. Hungry. His breath whispered along her neck like a summer breeze, making her turn to his mouth. Heat pooled in her belly. She didn't know how long her strength could hold out. But it had to.

'Sweet dreams, Mim. I'll see you nice and early for another exciting instalment.' His voice, loaded with desire, was thick and dark. 'And for the record, I have no doubt Dr Singh would have passed you with flying colours. One glimpse of you on that desk and the poor guy would have been like putty in your hands. Shame I'm not him, eh? I'll take a lot more convincing.'

CHAPTER FOUR

'Do you ever sleep?'

Connor's deep voice startled Mim as she stirred the large pot of porridge in the community hall kitchen. She took a long, slow breath before turning round to look at him.

'Sure I do. I take a power-nap between the hours of four and five in the morning. You? How did it go? You don't look like you've been awake all night.'

Dressed again in his suit and another crisp shirt, this time in palest baby blue, he looked completely out of place in the Formica kitchen, but he didn't seem to notice. He looked as comfortable in his skin as ever. Shame she couldn't say the same about herself. Having him there brought such a tsunami of emotions she could barely breathe, and her equilibrium seemed to have got lost somewhere in the folds of her duvet.

Thanks to spending most of the night tossing and turning, trying to forget about the way his words had made her feel as she'd edged away from his desk, she looked like she'd done ten rounds with a heavyweight boxer. Puffy eyes, blotchy skin and creases in her cheeks where creases shouldn't have been.

He leaned towards her and smiled, his hand brushing against hers as he gently took the wooden spoon out of her hand. 'I managed to catch up. I'm now on track to be out of your hair in the allocated time.'

'Great. Excellent. That's good. The sooner, the better.' Did skin have a memory? A thousand shockwaves thrilled up her arm at his touch. Seemed her skin had forgotten his authoritarian ways. How she'd promised never to let a man convince her that her dreams were less worthy than his.

She snatched her arm away, cursing her treacherous body, but couldn't resist a glance into his face.

He'd felt the static too. She knew just from the heated onyx gaze. And he'd enjoyed it. Damn him.

But so had she. It frightened her to realise it, but the one thing she'd felt since seeing Connor yesterday was *alive*.

She gave herself a good mental shake. She needed to put that energy into her work and community, not into an ex-lover with a penchant for rules and regulations.'I'm starving.' He tested a little of the porridge, then held the spoon to her mouth. 'Taste test. Come on. Needs something more…'

'Thanks.' She licked a small morsel and swallowed quickly, the fiery heat of it burning her mouth. She struggled for a breath, wafted her hand over her mouth and tried desperately to maintain her cool. No chance. Her eyes watered and a wheezy cough caught in her throat.

In an instant he was rubbing the space between her shoulders and cooing gently in her ear. His words were thick with amusement and concern. 'I'm sorry. Do you need some water? Didn't mean to choke you.'

Jumping back from him, she forced herself not to blush. Forced herself. *Forced.*

Damn it, in the middle of choking to death she was worried about how she looked in front of Connor. What was he doing to her head? 'I'm fine. Thanks. It's okay.'

'Are you sure?' He ran his thumb down her cheek, stopped at her mouth and smiled kindly. 'Good job I didn't have to do the Heimlich, eh?'

'Yes. Now. Please. Stop.'

He looked at his thumb, at her lips.

Then he abruptly turned and added three heaped table-spoons of sugar into the pot. Putting space and a good deal of untamed static between them. Her cheek hummed with the last trace of his touch. She wiped the back of her hand across it to extinguish the heat there. Luckily he didn't notice.

He tasted the porridge again. 'Needed more sweetness. That's better. Okay, I'll finish phase one this morning and leave you with some ideas to mull over. Back on Friday for phase two.'

'Phase two already. We are doing well. Great.' At least she thought it was. Would she ever get used to having him in her space again? Unlikely. And not when his presence had such catastrophic effects on her hormones. But she'd started today renewed and determined to focus on the assessment. And to co-operate fully. If it had been any other doctor doing the as-sessment she'd have co-operated fully already. 'I'll be happy to look at any suggestions you might have.'

He eyed her with mock suspicion. 'Really?'

'Of course. You're the expert. I did some thinking and you're right, we do need better processes.' Perhaps conced-ing to his higher knowledge would also win some Brownie points. 'Now, let's go serve.'

He hoisted the pot from the stove and edged backwards through the door into the main hall. A riot of noise greeted them. Babies screeched, pyjama-clad campers yelled and waved from their sleeping bags, and a succession of small children skidded on their knees across the lino towards the food tables.

Connor stopped, his face a picture of bewilderment. 'Hell, what a racket. I bet you'll be glad to get back to normal to-morrow.'

'Not likely.' Mim stifled a laugh at his discomfort and nod-ded towards the front door, where a snaking line of school children paraded through. 'The Walking School Bus is here for the breakfast club. Right on time. The campers are just extra padding.'

'This happens every day?' Horror etched his features.

'Except for high days and holidays, obviously.'

Connor shuddered, wondering what fresh hell he'd found himself in. Bad enough to be stuck in close quarters with Mim and unleashed testosterone whizzing round his body. But throw in children, mayhem and noise and he was living his worst nightmare. 'But there's so many of them. And they're so loud.'

'That's kids for you.'

'Yeah, well, they bring me out in a rash.' He scratched his cheek with his raised shoulder to prove a point.

'So you're not thinking of parenthood as an option any time soon?'

He put the pot on the table and shivered. Kids? He'd had enough of pouring every scrap of emotion into his little sister then having his heart shattered into tiny unfixable pieces. Never going there again. 'Not in this lifetime. I'm allergic.'

'You can't be allergic to kids in general practice. You get a hefty dose of saturation therapy. Here's your chance.' She laughed and ruffled a young boy's hair. The kid coughed then his face broke out in a gappy grin as he stared up at Mim. She might have had trouble winning over the adults of Atanga Bay, but this child certainly adored her. And she clearly adored him back.

Funny, he'd never thought of her as parent material before. She'd never mentioned any desire to have children. Another thing they hadn't got round to discussing before she'd hightailed it northwards. But she had the same natural ease around everyone, young and old.

She pointed to the bowls of chopped kiwifruit and bananas. 'Make sure you get some fruit, Oakley. Then we'll check that cough, okay?'

''Kay, Mim.' The boy sank his gums round a piece of toast then stared up at Connor. Suspicious dark eyes fixed him to the spot. 'Hey, mister. You the mayor or something?'

'No.' Connor looked down at his suit. 'Why?'

'You rich, then?'

He laughed and bent to level with the boy. 'Bright spark. I'm just visiting Mim.'

Oakley's face screwed into a frown. 'You her boyfriend, then?'

Did every male in town have his eye on her? 'Why, d'you want to fight me for her?'

Oakley scowled as if he'd trodden in something nasty. 'Ugh. No way, I hate girls.' And then he was gone, scuffing knees into a crowd of onlookers.

Lucky kid. Being seven and hating girls was something Connor remembered with affection. A time when life had been uncomplicated and predictable. Before he'd met Mim.

The scent of her mango body butter alerted him to her proximity. All his nerve endings fired on full cylinders whenever she was close. It was exhausting.

Call it self-protection, but he needed to get away from the woman as soon as possible. He knew only too well what spending time with her meant. And it wasn't pretty.

She stacked slices of toast into a pile. 'Kids ask the most difficult questions, eh?'

'I'm just not used to them.' Hadn't ever planned on getting used to them.

Her voice twinkled with laughter. 'Don't get to mix with the real world often?'

He laughed along with her, not sure what to make of Mim's world of chaos and colour. Made him feel just a little bit staid. But solid. And safe. 'The board has dedicated quiet time every day. Just for thinking.'

'Lucky you. I call that sleep. Or death.'

Or keeping a low profile and not opening up to a chance for fresh hurt.

'Where does all the food come from?' He shouted over the noise as the queue helped itself to the toast and fruit and large helpings of the thick porridge.

'The mini-market donates the bread and Vegemite, orchardists from round and about give us the fruit. The other stuff comes from government schemes and...donations.' She shrugged, as if she'd said too much. 'The kids love it and they have a healthy start to the day. You must know about the link between learning and breakfast?'

'Sure, but this is taking it to another level. I saw some state houses on the way in, but there's some top-dollar properties around here, too.' He looked at the range of clothing worn by the kids. Designer stuff mixed with obvious hand-me-downs. A regular neighbourhood. 'Surely all these kids aren't from impoverished homes?'

'No. It's equal opportunities here. The more affluent families have jobs, but those parents have to travel to work, so that means an early start and sometimes the kids miss out on breakfast.' She picked up a pile of dirty plates. 'The poorer families simply can't afford three meals a day.'

She paused briefly with a strange sad look on her face.

His heart thundered against his ribcage. Had Mim been one of the kids who'd had to start the day without breakfast? She'd always glossed over the subject of her childhood. *Never look back.*

But he'd bet any money she was doing this because she'd been at the harsh end of neglect and poverty herself. He knew from his own clientele that addict parents had little space in their heads to cater for their kids' needs.

Her life had been so very different from his privileged upbringing. Had she ever hinted? Or had he been so hellbent on his own mission that he hadn't heard what she'd said? Having put their foolhardy engagement behind him, he now found himself wanting to learn more about her, to work out where they'd gone wrong. But now wasn't the time to ask. He just tried to fill in the gaps.

He remembered she'd said she wanted different things, that a six-month stint in Auckland had made her realise the need to go back home, but he'd tried to convince her otherwise. He'd tried to show her a different life, believing his hotshot urban practice was the template for every practice in New Zealand. But now he wasn't so sure. Three years and experience visiting many practices had matured his outlook.

Okay. Maybe seeing her in her own space was colouring his judgement.

'Ah, Mim. There you are. Hello, Connor.' There was the goth again. She looked at him with a mixture of awe and distrust. A response he was getting used to out here. 'I've opened up the surgery. Tanisha needs a new prescription for her inhaler. Jordan's got sores on his legs. And Shelley Wilson's been on the phone—Emily's started wetting the bed again.'

Connor watched as Mim processed all this. He'd always known she was a dedicated doctor, but had lived under the misconception that she was blinkered and idealistic. *Wrong.* She was idealism in action. He hadn't expected that. Not at all.

She took a deep breath. 'Okay, thanks, Skye. Put Jordan in Treatment Room One and get the dressing trolley ready. I'll start him on antibiotics too. There's a script for Tanisha in her file. And I'll call Shelley back as soon as I can. I think it's time to start Emily on Minirin. This bedwetting's going to take time, especially now her dad's in hospital—she'll miss him terribly. I'll be there in two minutes. Oh, and Oakley's coughing again. Collect him on your way through?'

'Quite a double act, you two.' Connor took the now empty porridge pot and followed Mim across the room towards the kitchen. 'What do you do in your spare time—assuming you have any?' *Hot dates?*

Not that it mattered.

Skye called across the emptying room, 'Salsa. But, then, you know that already.' She winked and then disappeared next door.

'Mexican food? You cook too?'

Mim laughed to distract from her flushed face. Was he winding her up? If only Skye could keep out of it. She didn't want to share her life with him. Especially not the things she did in her precious spare time. Especially not the things that were loaded with memories of her mother.

'No, you fool. Salsa, the dance.'

'I didn't know you liked dancing.'

'It's been three years, there's lots of things you don't know about me. I love dancing. I take after my mother in some things. Thankfully not others.'

'You fancy showing me some time?'

His slow, sexy smile tugged at her mood and melted it into something more relaxed. Typical, it had been years since she'd allowed herself to relax with a man. Just irritating that it happened to be this one. The one she'd compared all the others to, and none had come close. The one who'd let her go without a backward glance. 'No. Absolutely not.'

'Okay. No.' He looked like he suddenly thought it was a very bad idea. 'Yep. That's fine.'

'Good.'

'But...' Then a wicked glint heated his black pupils. 'It could be fun, though. Might help me endure those long evenings of paperwork. In my lonely room. At the pub. You work all hours too, Mim. When was the last time you let loose?'

A very long time ago. Letting loose wasn't something that came naturally to her. 'I don't know...'

'Come on, it's a great idea. Have a laugh. For old times'

sake.' His eyebrows peaked and she could have sworn his pupils flared with lust. 'If you show me yours, I'll show you mine.'

'Connor!'

'Dance steps, you depraved woman. See, you're laughing at the thought of it. But be warned, I am rubbish.'

She felt like she hadn't laughed for ages. Spent too much time working. Appealing though it was, laughing with Connor could be dangerous. Exciting. Possibly a little wild. And foolish.

A better idea formed in her head. 'Okay, Dr tick-boxes Wiseman. Put your money where your mouth is. If you can get a well-man's clinic up and running on Saturday night in the pub, I'll give you one hour's dedicated salsa.'

'Too easy. The pub will be heaving, there's a game on.'

'Easy? With Tommo? Boy? Easy with those guys, who think doctors are for sissies? You have got to be joking. And you have to get Tony in too. Or the deal is off.'

'Tony?' His Adam's apple ducked up and down as he swallowed.

'Tony.'

Connor's hesitation was fleeting—he oozed with confidence. 'Okay. Deal.'

She was safe. It would never happen. She shook his hand, trying to ignore the thrill of his touch. This was a business matter, pure and simple.

He would lose, no doubt, and she'd have the moral upper ground.

And if he won the wager, he'd have worked a miracle in preventive healthcare, more boxes would be ticked and she'd be closer to her goal. The small matter of the dance lesson was just one small sacrifice in support of a much mightier cause. And she'd deal with it if she had to. One dance would

be fine. At arm's length. The old-fashioned way. Fingertips
to fingertips, no grinding or gyrating.

Dancing with Connor—the thought excited her. Scared
her too. But her fear was quickly extinguished. He'd never
convince the men to have a health check. 'Like there is any
way on this earth you can achieve that. Give it all you can,
city boy. The deal is on!'

'No way. You didn't. How did you…?'

Mim stared in disbelief at the blood-pressure cuff wrapped
around Tony's tattooed arm and actually enjoyed the anger
ripping through her. It felt so much better than pointless frustration, and dampened down some of the wayward lustful
thoughts she'd had in the last twenty-four hours since Connor
had been back in Atanga Bay. She'd had five days' reprieve
but, Lordy, the lust was back with a vengeance.

The thought of him failing had fuelled her thoughts as
she'd got dressed that evening. In a very sexy salsa wrap-dress
and sky-high dancing shoes. Just so she could make her point.

And now. Her heart thumped. In the tiny makeshift waiting area a small huddle of men perused brochures about pros-
tate cancer and compared their blood-pressure numbers like
rugby scores.

Unbelievable.

Not only had he succeeded but, standing in this very male
pub, she looked like she was a lost hooker on the pull.

This was such a bad idea.

Connor nodded, pride curving the corners of his tantalis-
ingly aloof mouth. His broad shoulders relaxed under another
black T-shirt, this one with the insignia of the national team.
Spot on for winning the respect of the locals. Never mind the
fact it outlined his finely toned biceps and clung to his powerful body like a sheath.

'Ah, Mim. You underestimated us. Atanga Bay men are

serious about their health. You just need to know how to appeal to their higher logic.' He winked. Annoyingly. 'Now, if you could just wait behind the screen, Mim. Tony and I need to have a chat.'

She threw a scowl at Tony. *Traitor*. But he was intently watching the cuff inflate and listening to Connor's spiel about cerebrovascular disease. He even looked interested. Damn him.

'Behind the screen…' Connor's smug grin pushed her back round the dusty flowery screen he'd hauled out of one of the cupboards in the back of the surgery.

'Sorry.' She edged into the waiting area, threw the huddle a wobbly smile and leaned against the window-sill to rub her aching feet. Tried to make sense of the mumbled voices behind the screen.

Eventually doctor and patient appeared. Connor handed Tony two sheets of paper. His voice was assertive and professional. 'I can't stress enough. Make sure you come back first thing Monday.'

'I will. Cheers, mate.' Tony shook Connor's hand. Actually shook it. And smiled cautiously.

Cheers, mate?

Was she dreaming? She rubbed her eyes, careful not to smudge her mascara. No. Tony was shaking hands with Connor, and the whole darned male population of Atanga Bay was sitting in line for a check-up.

She should be grateful, she knew it—she'd had to call the ambulance for too many, too late. But his success irked her. Impressed her too, but irked came out winner.

Connor gently pulled her to one side. His gaze meandered slowly down her figure-hugging silk dress then back up, and lingered for a moment on her mouth.

Damn. The lipgloss. A last-minute addition that she was regretting now.

But the way he looked at her with such blatant interest and anticipation sent tingles of heat skitting across her abdomen. She'd tried to ignore it, but the way he made her feel with just one glance hadn't abated in three years.

She couldn't dance with him. She just couldn't. She didn't have enough willpower to keep him at arm's length. And salsa was never about keeping a distance.

'You look stunning.' His voice was soft and thick, like chocolate sauce over hot sticky toffee pudding. 'Your eyes are amazing. You got contacts?'

'No. I just prefer seeing things through a blurry haze. Especially you.'

'Especially me winning, you mean? Don't like seeing that in full focus? Keen to settle your half of the bargain?'

'There's no hurry.'

'I'll see you in half an hour. Your place?'

Her legs almost gave way. She dug her fingers into her palms and tried to summon as much failing courage as she could find. It was a dance lesson. Nothing more. Could never be anything more. One hour where they could forget about figures and policies and kick back and laugh. And dance. *Just dancing.*

Where's the harm? Her mother's haunting words rattled round her head. *Just one more hit. No harm in that.*

But she wasn't her mother. She was Mim, calm and totally in control. She wouldn't spin out. She knew what level to take things. And when to stop. *It was just dancing.*

He smiled slowly, the glint in his eyes flaring, waiting for her response. 'Mim? You owe me.'

She did. For a million reasons. Not least the guilt at running out on him, but he'd got the clinic up and running. Now she needed to honour her side of the bargain. 'Okay. Thirty minutes.'

'I'm looking forward to it already.' He turned back to the

waiting huddle, humming something vaguely resembling a salsa tune. 'Next.'

She tottered through the pub, staring straight ahead, trying to avoid eye contact with anyone. Trying to regulate her breathing. Who was she kidding? It was just dancing, sure. But it was salsa. The most sexy dancing of all.

'Hey, Mim!' Tommo stopped her, pint in hand. He nodded towards the flowery screen with a kind of hero-worship glint in his eyes. 'Good man, that new doc. Wish he was staying.'

'Oh. Well, he can't. He's far too important for that. He has to go back to Auckland.' *Not soon enough.*

'Shame. Could do with a few more free pints.'

'I thought you were off the beer?' *Irked* kicked into suspicion. Something was amiss here. There were never free pints on offer, the landlord was far too tight. Plus, the number of men suddenly interested in their health didn't seem natural. 'Wait… What do you mean? Free pints?'

'N-n-nothing,' he stammered, and turned away. 'Sorry.'

'Nothing? Tommo Hayes, you tell me the truth. Now.'

Tommo shrugged, his face a picture of discomfort and embarrassment. She actually felt sorry for him. It took guts to dob in your hero. But she knew enough dirt on Tommo Hayes to keep him on side for the rest of her life. 'Just…he sent out a message to all the blokes. Get down to the pub for six, have a quick blood-pressure thingy and there'll be free beer till eight.'

The muscles between her shoulders froze into a hard plane of tension. Her head hummed with a dull ache. So much for helping her. So much for her extra ticks. How could she get extra ticks if he'd bribed everyone into coming for a check? 'I'll kill him.'

She kicked off her stupid shoes, picked them up, and stormed across the road to the safety of her flat. 'That is, until I can think of something worse to do to him.'

CHAPTER FIVE

'HEY, honey, I'm home!' Connor rang Mim's doorbell and spoke to the closed door. He hadn't felt this cock-a-hoop in weeks. Months. Success sure felt good. He'd probably prolonged a few lives because of that clinic. If not saved at least one. And now there was an hour of fun to celebrate.

Of dancing. With Mim.

His stomach suddenly hardened like a colossal lump of lead. Never in a zillion light years did he think he'd be knocking at her door, looking for fun.

Mim McCarthy. The one that hadn't just got away, but had run hard and fast. Confirmed what he already knew—loving someone wasn't liberating, or joyful. It hurt. Like hell.

And yet for some reason he'd agreed to this silly wager. He leaned his fist against the doorframe. Now he was starting to lose his bravado.

Dancing with Mim. Really dumb idea.

He looked back across the road at the twinkling lights of the pub. Better idea.

Mim peered through the spy hole, watched Connor falter. *Good. He's going.*

Although if he went she wouldn't be able to rage at him about the beer deal. Wouldn't be able to give him a piece of her mind, which was screaming to let loose.

Anger shook through her. Fury laced with a raging desire

that she couldn't seem to shake. Half of her wanted to shout at him, but the other—rash and foolish—part of her wanted to haul him in and smack a kiss on that irritating smile.

She didn't know where to put the anger; it seemed way out of proportion to what he'd done. And was so mixed up with need and sheer fear at having to dance with him. But where Connor was concerned, every emotion she had was magnified a million times.

Her hand hovered over the doorhandle.

He turned to leave.

The ache of him leaving was much greater than the fear of him staying.

Before she knew what she was doing, before she could stop herself, she'd twisted the handle. 'This is not your home.' She flung the door wide before he had a chance to walk away. And before she lost her nerve. 'So cut it out.'

'Shoot, you spooked me. You weren't supposed to hear. It's a figure of speech.'

Connor might have been on the verge of leaving, but he couldn't help noticing she was clothed neck to floor in navy cotton pyjamas. What a shame. Those curves had looked interesting sheathed in scarlet silk.

A sultry frown hung over her forehead and she had her glasses back on. *Bad sign.* Sparks flashed in her eyes. And they didn't say, *Take me.*

So why did every single part of him strain for her? This was getting way too dangerous. His body and head were at total odds with each other. But she was cross and he got the feeling it was because of him.

'What's wrong, Mim? Forgotten the dance lesson? Salsa? Don't like losing a bet?' With the last vestige of his good humour he shimmied on the doorstep, trying to raise a smile from her. But the way she glared at him had unease shimmying down his spine instead. 'Are you feeling okay? Are you sick?'

'Of you, yes. Go back to your mates in the pub. Or go find some other hapless GP to annoy.'

Whoa. Cross? Understatement of the year. 'But—'

'I'll see you when you come back next month. I've got a lot of work to do between now and then. Because you know what? You can never rely on anyone else to help you out.'

Her frown cemented into something he could only describe as abject sadness. This was serious. And he suddenly needed to fix it. She went to close the door, but he stuck his foot in the way and touched her hand. 'Hey. What's wrong?'

She looked at his hand as if it belonged to the devil. But she didn't pull hers away. 'You're what's wrong, Connor. For a few mad minutes I thought we were a team. I thought you were helping me change the way people thought. Introducing positive wellness. But you bribed those men to come and see you tonight. They're not interested in their health. They just wanted free beer.'

'Ah, is that it? The wager. I won and you don't like to be beaten.' Relief trickled through him. Rather more than he liked. He could fix this. For some daft reason he wanted to put a smile back on those heavenly lips.

A group of men from the pub bowled past, stopped and waved. 'Hey, Doc! Great pint! Thanks. Oh, hey, Mim!'

'You know, sometimes this cosy community can be a little claustrophobic. Let's get some privacy.' He took hold of her hand, stepped into the apartment and closed the door. Unwittingly trapping her in the tiny hall. Her mango scent washed over him. All his senses magnified and hit full alert. *Explain. Then leave.* 'Anything it takes, right? One pint of beer isn't going to harm anyone, especially if it got them to see a doctor.'

'It was cheating, Connor. And I hate that.'

She dropped her hand from his grip. Her mouth formed a pout that was half cross, all sex. And damn him if he didn't want to kiss it.

She pushed past him into the kitchen.

He found himself following her, for no rhyme or reason. The opposite direction from where he should be going. But the only path that made any sense right now.

More mango scent in here, mixed with coffee. A bottle of wine and one half-drunk glass of red stood on the table. He downed it in one go. Anything to distract his mouth from hers. The wine tasted earthy and fruity and warmed his stomach. The quick shot of Dutch courage loosened his taut nerves.

Somehow he managed to dredge up a voice, albeit hoarse and dry. He cleared his throat and spoke doctor-speak to take his mind off those lips that were driving him mad. 'Anyway, the clinic worked. You're going to be busy next week with follow-ups. Of the fifteen men I saw, eight have mildly concerning blood pressure. One has gout. And, strictly confidentially, Tony has glycosuria.'

She filled two glasses with the wine. As she handed him one her anger morphed into concern. 'You think he might be diabetic?'

'Can't think of many other reasons an overweight man has sugar in his wee. But there are a few, so obviously I told him to come in for more tests. Non-fasting glucose of thirteen. Type two, I reckon.'

'Maybe it's all the alcohol you're bribing him with skewing the result?' She managed a smile. Albeit sarcastic. Then she flicked a hand over her fringe and the pyjama top stretched across her breasts. A tiny gap between buttons allowed a glimpse of creamy flesh. She was braless.

Did he need to know that in the middle of a conversation about diabetes? He tried to focus on his consultation. 'I didn't let him have any beer tonight. That would have been stupid.

You know me, above all, I don't do stupid. He's coming in
on Monday, so please be co-operative.'

'I'm always co-operative, especially with my friends.'

'Ha.' The sharp sting of jealousy twisted in his chest.
'Tony's not your friend. He wants you.'

Like me. The reality hit him full on in the groin.

He hated to admit it. Hated to even think it. It broke every
rule.

He didn't want to just dance with her. He didn't want to
stop her being cross. He liked her cross. He liked her the way
she looked right now. Flustered and indignant, feeling something. Believing in something so much she'd fight for it with
everything she had. He wanted her.

And had done since the second he'd seen her on that desk
with her skirt round her hips.

More fool him. That would be diving headlong into disaster. Without a safety net. *I don't do stupid.*

But she looked like she'd been slapped. Her cheeks went
pink and her eyes flared. 'There is nothing between me and
Tony. He's a nice guy. Straightforward. And he wouldn't fool
me into wearing a fancy dress to the pub. I don't like being
swindled. Or controlled. Don't you remember? That was why
I left.'

'Really?' God, he'd missed this. Her fiery temper and sultry passion. He stepped closer as if some weird magnetic
force was pulling him to her. A force so strong he couldn't
pull out of its grip. He touched her cheek, pulled her to face
him, full on. Her mouth was mere inches away from his, her
lips moist with wine. Her breathing full and fast. Her chest
heaving with effort. Filled with life, vibrant. Vivid.

'I thought it was because you were too chicken to stay.
Your head was so full of ideals you thought everything around
you was wrong. Including me.'

'God, no. Connor. You're not wrong. You have a dream. A great, honourable dream. It just isn't mine.'

Common sense told her to walk away. That being so close to him was foolish. Any dealings with Connor needed to be based on work, not on a silly wager and definitely not a dance lesson where she'd have his hot skin under her fingertips.

He'd made her cross, although she realised now that was just a jumble of emotions all caught up in being with him. A smokescreen for desire. She tried to cling to the anger, to formulate a resistance to him based on that.

She put her hand on the hard wall of his chest to push away from him. Felt the raging thunder of his heart. The full force of his heat burnt her fingers but she couldn't draw them away. Not now. This was too real. Too raw.

Blatant need zipped between them. Pressure throbbed through her body to fever pitch. She reached up to touch his mouth. Couldn't stop. No matter what. She had to run her fingers over those lips.

He grabbed her wrist and his gaze fixed on her. Held her captive.

'I want to kiss you, Mim.' It was more groan than words, a deep, low sound that tugged at her abdomen and sent rivers of desire skittering through her.

She drew in a breath to fight against the heat swelling through her. 'No.'

'Why not?'

She couldn't think of a rational reason. Her brain was filled with him, his closeness.

Kissing him was inevitable. Had been since he'd walked back into her life. Whatever would happen after that she didn't know. Right now she didn't care. She just wanted to touch him, feel him, taste him again. 'Do you have a procedure manual for that?'

'Thought I'd go with you on this. Gut feeling.'

'Tut-tut,' she breathed. 'Breaking rules again.'

His mouth grazed hers, slowly at first, tracing a line across her bottom lip. His hand cupped her neck as he pulled her to him, pressing his hard body against her.

Resistance was futile. No man had ever had this effect on her. It was all or nothing with Connor, no middle ground. And she wanted it all. Right now. Nothing mattered except tasting him again. She opened her mouth to his, felt a surge of pleasure ripple through her as his tongue licked against hers.

Yes, this was foolish. It was deliciously losing control. For the first time in too many years she felt really alive, in his arms.

Desire made her bolder. She pulled him closer, ran her hands down his back, ripped the T-shirt from his jeans. Pressed her breasts against his chest, grazed her nipples against the thick cotton. Shafts of need arced through her as he kissed a trail from her mouth to her neck.

Lilting salsa music filtered through from the lounge, cementing her focus. The dance lesson. The bet. She dragged her neck away from his delicious nibbles. 'You are so not off the hook. I am still cross.'

'So I see.' He rocked against her, his hardness skimming her thigh. 'Let's go through to the lounge. Is that salsa music I hear?'

'Aha.'

'Then let's dance.'

'You can't get round me that easily.' Kissing was one thing, but *dancing?* The only salsa moves she knew involved close hips and writhing groins. She'd never get out unscathed.

'Are you sure?' He licked her collar bone. Pure lust shivered through her. 'Come on, Mim. Settle the bet. Let me have my prize.'

She looked down at her PJs, her bare feet. The deep red nail varnish she'd added as a final flourish. The only thing now that looked vaguely sexy. 'I'm not really dressed for dancing.'

'More for bed?' He followed her gaze, undid three of her pyjama buttons and slipped his hand over her breast. 'Is that an invitation? Nice toes. You want to know what I'd like to do to them?' He took her hand, and licked the length of her finger.

Something akin to fear loaded with sexual heat, a shudder of wicked excitement, skipped down her back. She wanted him, but she wanted to savour the moment. There would be no more after this. Could be no more. 'Okay, let's dance.'

In the lounge he wrapped an arm around her waist and took her hand in his. Classic old-time dance style. He wiggled his hips, cupped her backside and ground against her. 'Now what?'

'Connor, that is sex, not dancing. Watch.' She laughed, enjoying the feeling of lightness of just being in his arms. Like the world had suddenly lifted, like she was floating. Her heart thundered in anticipation of more kisses. Her breath became staccato.

She let go his hand, kept his arm firmly round her waist and stood next to him, shoulder to shoulder. 'It's easier if I teach you side on.'

'But I like the bit where I get to hold you.' He squeezed her side. 'And the grinding. Obviously.'

She shook her head, laughing up into his dark eyes. She could see fire sparking in those onyx pupils in response to her words. 'Grinding is advanced salsa.'

'I'm a quick learner.'

'Let's see, shall we?' Playing with him was too easy. She'd fallen straight back into it. Three years gone in a second. Three years, all that heartache. All that pain. And there'd be more to come if she didn't stop. But she couldn't stop. How could she? Besides, where was the harm in just one dance?

'Okay, watch. And follow. On one. Forward on the left, one, two, three, and...'

She stepped forward on her left foot, showed him the move. Then stepped back. 'Back with the right. Five, six seven.'

'Whoa, too many moves, too many feet. Er? Back with the...?'

'Back with the right.'

'Oh, you mean the other right.' He tripped and laughed. 'Told you I was rubbish.'

Whether it was a dupe or whether it was an accident she didn't know, but he swung her round and somehow she ended up facing him again. Smack bang slammed against him, against his hardness.

She ran one hand down his arm to his wrist, wound her other hand round his neck and swayed. 'Just feel the rhythm. One, two, three, four. In time with the music helps.'

'Sure does.' He swayed with her. His fingers slid over her back as she shimmied to the left. He followed. To the right. To the left again. The music changed from salsa to slow. His hands smoothed down over her PJ bottoms, then up to the sensitive small dip in her back. A steady rhythmical caress in time to the music that filled her head. And there was nothing left in her world, in her mind, except being there in his arms. With his earthy scent, his fingers brushing her side, her ribs, underneath her breast.

As she tipped her head to look at him, he smothered her mouth with his. Hot and hungry, and just like she remembered. He cradled her head in his hands, ran his fingers through her hair. Kissed her like he was feeding his hunger. Like he'd die without more. Just like she remembered.

It was the same Connor. The same wonderful, powerful Connor. But he was different somehow. More sensitive. More crazy with desire. More perfect and wrong all at the same time.

Being wrong didn't stop her. There was no stopping, no

going back. Only forward, headlong into the unknown. To the familiar. To the different.

And probably all the way to hell.

When she pulled away he was looking at her with such force she felt dizzy. A million questions darted between them. All came down to the same thing.

'Bedroom?' His breath became erratic as he waited for her answer. 'Sofa?'

Desire and a desperate need to gain control warred inside her. She wanted him. To assuage this burning craziness that had taken over her thoughts, her body.

If she didn't do something soon, she'd explode. His hard body pressed against her. So good. So right. Swaying to the left. To the right.

The only option she had was to take control. The only thing that would rid her of this need would be to have him. Exorcise all thoughts and wants. Get him out of her system. For the last time. Then she could let him go. Then she would be free to follow her dream again. 'Sofa's closest.'

Mim woke, her neck twisted into the crook of Connor's arm, legs entwined in a velvet throw, up against the arm of the sofa. How long had she slept? Eight hours? Surely not? She never slept for eight hours. She checked her watch again. Crikey.

They hadn't even made it to her bed.

Bright sunlight filled the lounge, illuminating Connor's face. His features were soft and carefree. His breathing slow and rhythmical. He looked perfect. He was perfect. The evening had been a blur of kisses and stroking. Of three years' worth of need. Of the most fabulous sex she'd ever had. And each time she'd thought she'd gained control.

All control had gone with their first kiss. All rational thought, all reasoning. Once started she had been addicted to his kisses, to his touch. Couldn't have enough. *Just one more. Where's the harm?*

She was no different from her mum after all.

Never again. She remembered her mother's next-day promises. The remorse. The tears. *I'm so sorry, baby. I won't do it again. Mummy loves you.*

Not enough. Always the addiction had driven her for more. Driven her away from her daughter and her responsibilities.

In the cold light of day Mim shivered, knowing the only means of control was to keep away from him. Cold turkey. There'd be too much damage otherwise, to her heart. To her dreams and promises.

She lifted his arm and squeezed to the edge of the sofa.

'Hey, Mim, come back.' His warm hand gripped her thigh, held her on the sofa. He grinned, a smudgy smile filled with sleep and sexual satisfaction. 'We always were good at make-up sex, eh?'

'This wasn't make-up sex.' *This was getting-you-out-of-my-system sex.* Big fat fail. The only way for him to be out of her system was for him to leave. And never come back. Certainly, for him never to be naked on her sofa again.

She edged from his grip, dragged on her PJs and made it to the door. 'I'm going to make coffee.'

'Mim?'

'No, Connor.'

In the kitchen, away from the heat of the lounge, from the scent of their lovemaking, she searched for words. Couldn't find any that didn't sound trite or cruel or weren't a rerun of three years ago. But she had to say them if she wanted to stay sane.

She waited for the kettle to boil, watched the steam rise to the ceiling. It clicked off.

She clicked it on again. And again. Killing time, passing

time, wasting time, before she had to go to him and say the inevitable.

'I think it's boiled already.' He stood in the doorway, his jeans unzipped and hanging loosely from his hips. Unsculpted bed-hair curled in cute tufts. His bare chest rose and fell quickly. Brief unfettered memories of that chest rising in time with her filled her head. Did he have to be so damned gorgeous? Did this have to be so hard?

But he didn't need to tell her how much he regretted what they'd done. It was written all over his face. 'We need to talk.'

She jumped in. Seized control. Properly this time. Even though she had no regrets. Not one. Making love with him had been divine. Extremely misguided. Not being able to share anything else with him would be a regret for the future. 'It's okay, Connor. You don't have to say anything. I know. It was a huge mistake. We won't mention it again. No second chances, right? We live too far apart, have too much to lose and not enough to gain. We can't keep going round in circles.'

He opened those delicious lips to say something, but she careered along her own path. 'Besides, you're my assessor. Don't want the powers that be to think I coerced you? How much is sex worth these days? Extra-big ticks in all the right boxes?' Answering the dark look that shadowed his face, she forced a smile. Dragged one from the depths of her splintering heart. 'I'm just joking. You know I didn't sleep with you just so I'd get special treatment, don't you? I was only joking about women's ways, you know.'

'I know, Mim. Even you wouldn't stoop so low.'

Even you. He really did regret it.

And every word she uttered dug her deeper. Change the subject. 'Perhaps you should go. Haven't you got meetings in Auckland tomorrow?'

He took the kettle out of her hand, filled two mugs and steered her to the table. 'Well, at least you're still talking to me. Blathering and incoherent, but that's got to be one step better than finding you gone in the morning. I think.'

He winced inside. She looked intoxicatingly sexy, pitifully hurt and everything in between. Damn and blast. Could anything be worse? So much for *I don't do stupid.*

Whichever way he looked at it, he was up to his neck in disaster. Something he'd promised he'd never do again. He needed to tell her straight. 'Sit down. Listen, will you? I need to tell you something.'

At the tone of his voice she sat immediately. Pierced him with wary eyes. 'What? What is it? You're scaring me.'

He cleared his throat. Tried to soften his voice. Tried to take the sting out of the ugly reality. 'One of the condoms broke.'

Mim's heart slammed against her ribcage. She was slap bang in the middle of her cycle. The most fertile time. Nightmare on top of nightmare. 'But we were so careful. When? Which one broke? Why didn't you tell me before?'

'I didn't want to spoil it, we were having such a good time and it was so...' His words faded on his lips as he leaned his elbows on the kitchen benchtop with his head in his hands.

Mim stared at him. It was so...*what*? Beautiful? Intense? Foolish. *All of the above.*

Then he seemed to shake himself. He smiled. At least his mouth did. His eyes, however, were guarded. He was trying to make light of it. For her sake, she guessed. 'It was magical, Mim, and I was a bit distracted. I don't know which one broke, I didn't name them.' He scratched his head as he thought. 'It was the third time. Yes, pretty sure. Man, we were good. I think that was my favourite.'

'Connor!' A smile grew from the knot in her chest. An odd feeling, laughing in the face of panic. But it helped settle her nerves. 'We shouldn't joke at a time like this. We're not reminiscing, we're establishing facts.'

'Ever the doctor.'

'Someone's got to be.' Although he was right. Third time had been the best. Slow and exquisitely tender, he'd taken her to places she'd never even dreamed of.

She stopped her hand from reaching out to him as a full-body blush seeped through her skin at the memory.

'Okay, well, let's not panic.' He closed the gap between them, sat opposite her at the table. 'Now would be a good time to tell me you're on the Pill. Depo? IUD?'

Hope died from his eyes as she shook her head. 'Why would I be? My periods are regular as clockwork and I haven't had sex in three years.' Last night's passion had been enough to keep her stocked up for another three.

'Okay. Well, we'd have to be very unlucky if anything came of it.'

'Unlucky. Yes.' He was allergic to kids after all. Never mind the fact that neither of them were in a position to bring up a child.

The trashed condom was just a loud wake-up call confirming what she already knew—their make-up, break-up sex had been founded on lust rather than anything pertaining to a solid relationship.

With her health professional hat on she also knew the only sensible course of action. 'Morning-after pill works up to five days.'

'Its effectiveness diminishes over time. The sooner you take it...' He scraped his chair back, the hollow sound slicing across the silence. The distance between them stretched like a thousand miles, not a few inches.

She stumbled across the yard and opened up the surgery. He followed closely behind, coffee in hand. Naked chest. Bare feet. The most dishevelled she'd ever seen him. And the most sexy. Shame that there was no way she'd ever get to touch him again. Regret and the threat of pregnancy sure put a downer on libido.

'Luckily it's a Sunday, no one comes in to town much.' She peered out the blinds into Main Street, the raw ache of remorse eating her. 'I feel like a thief breaking into my own practice.'

He frowned. 'Why? Don't be silly. You're entitled to the morning-after pill. It's free to all. I can write you a script if you like, to make it above board.'

'Ugh, that makes me feel worse somehow. It's okay. I just hate all this sneaking around.'

Was this how her mother had felt? When she'd opened her friends' purses and stolen their money for dope? When she'd driven through the night with her seven-year-old daughter to find a dealer? Then, when guilt hit, sneaking around trying to fix her mistakes?

In some ways now she could understand her mother's desperation. And the shame of reneging on promises and having to deal with the fallout.

'In here.' She opened the drug cupboard and grabbed a packet.

'Great.' He was running a glass under the store cupboard tap. The look of relief on his face told her what she already knew.

'It's okay, Connor. You don't have to watch me take the damn thing. I will. You've made it clear you don't want to take any chances. I know how you feel about kids.'

'Yeah. Sorry.' Connor shrugged. 'I'm not exactly parent material. One thing I've learned from my dad is that men in our family don't carry the doting-father gene. We can do aloof and distant, but I wouldn't want to inflict that on anyone. Least of all a child.'

Damn. Connor turned away and tried to calm down. He was rattled. By the ace sex and Mim's frank assertion that it had been a huge mistake, by being with her when he'd made all those promises not to go near her again. And now by this. A broken condom.

If ever there was an omen screaming at him that being with Mim was a bad idea, this was it.

He followed her back to the apartment. A difficult silence reverberated between them. Weird that they'd shared so much last night and couldn't even share a decent conversation now. He gathered his clothes from the floor of the lounge. She'd already opened the windows and late summer heat breezed through, whipping away the last vestiges of her smell. He wished clearing out memories could be so easy.

She was right, sex had been a bad idea. Mim had already left him high and dry once, he couldn't trust her not to do it again. But last night his body had seemed hellbent on self-destruction. He must have left his brain in the pub.

He needed out. And fast. 'So, I should be going, then.'

'Yeah. It's probably for the best.' She nodded as she leaned against the doorframe, clutching a folded velvet throw tight to her chest in one hand and a pink furry cushion in the other. He got the impression she couldn't get rid of him quick enough before she could restore order into her life.

'I'll be back in a few weeks. I'll email to confirm.'

'Sure thing.' She stepped closer, dropped the cushion onto the sofa and looked up at him. A trace of wistful desire in her eyes, mixed with frustration and a little panic.

His chest hurt with the weight of leaving, but staying wouldn't do any good. It was clear she too regretted what they'd done. Seemed they spent most of their time together finding ways to cut lose.

At least this time they were parting on speaking terms. Just. At least neither of them had sneaked out. And they could both muster a smile. Albeit a painful one dredged from a deep corner of his gut. Damn it. Why were they always saying goodbye? 'Best we don't do this again, eh?'

'Back to being friends.' Her eyes glistened.

'Ring me if anything…you know. Changes.'

She nodded. Her smile wavered. 'You got it.'

'It's for the best. Really. We can't do this again.' Well, he couldn't. Not do this and stay sane. He'd been too close to losing himself in her, in an idea of *us*. Lucky break that she'd called a halt. He wouldn't risk his heart over her again. Put himself on the line. No way.

He planted a coy kiss on her cheek and grabbed his keys. 'Friends. Sure. We can do that.'

CHAPTER SIX

Four weeks later...

'SHE'S absolutely gorgeous.' Mim handed the screeching tiny pink bundle back to a grinning Steph with a mixture of excitement and relief. Holding such a new baby was amazing. Seeing the potential in those tiny fingers and toes, the fresh start. A whole new beginning. The idea was growing on her. Kind of.

She'd gone from *Never really thought about it* to *What the heck would I do?* To *downright panic.* In a month. Holding newborns didn't really help. And there seemed to have been so many in her clinic recently. They melted her to absolute goo and threw her into a state of flux.

The crying was bouncing off her clinic-room walls. It had started just as she'd taken hold of the wee thing. The new mother hadn't seemed to notice the wailing and had continued to coo as if the baby was asleep. Mim only hoped she'd be so one-eyed about her own kids. One day.

Her heart squeezed at the sight of the puce, screwed-up face slowly uncreasing to relaxed quiet.

'Peace at last. She is truly gorgeous. I'm glad the breast-feeding's working out, Steph. It's the best thing for baby if you can manage it. Here's the prescription for your eye infection. Try to keep your hands clean and away from little Bella's eyes.'

She passed the paper to Steph and couldn't help grinning. If she had decided to come to the clinic, then this was a new start indeed. 'If you need anything else, call in or phone. And the midwife's here, as you know, on Tuesdays and Thursdays now. Thanks for coming in.'

'No worries. You're not Dana. Can't be blamed for what she did.' Steph shrugged and flashed her a reluctant smile. 'Word is you're actually okay.'

'Thanks. I try my best.' Mim remembered that playful smile from the playground. From the youth group. From being best friends, then enemies. Having a mother who made a fool of herself had made short shrift of Mim's friendships. Some had stuck by her, but many others, like Steph, had walked in the opposite direction.

But things were changing. They were all growing up. Babies were coming. And maybe, just maybe, people were starting to forget.

'Now, go home and rest. Sleep when Bella sleeps and try not to get stressed about getting everything done.'

'No chance.' Steph stood, strapped her baby into a bright striped pushchair and pulled the raincover over. Happy exhaustion etched dark circles underneath her eyes. 'Luckily we're moving into low season, so we won't have many punters. But this is the time when I get all my planning and paperwork done. And the renovations sorted for next year. My business needs me just as much now as it ever did. Can't stop just 'cos I have a little one.'

'You have help up there at the campsite, don't you?'

'Sure, but you know what it's like, if you want a job done, do it yourself.' She closed the door as she left.

'Oh, yes, I know all about that.' Mim stared at the space where Steph had been standing, milky baby smell addling her brain. As a single mother and business owner Steph had a hard road ahead. She had no one to rely on, no one to help her out. But she seemed perfectly resigned to it.

Earlier that morning, as Mim had sat on her bathroom floor and contemplated her future she'd determined to focus on the positives. She was turning both the McCarthy reputation and her practice around. Phase three of the Matrix assessment was completed.

If a little one came along, she'd cope. She would. She could do this.

Mim dragged on a smile. Focusing on the positives was going to take a gargantuan effort today.

Connor was due in five minutes. She might be putting on a brave face but she was scared as all heck. Not just about his reaction and how they would forge a future between them now. What had also kept her awake last night had been worrying over what kind of mother she would make. A happy relaxed one like Steph? Or disinterested like Dana?

A little voice whispered in her head—a childlike one that craved a mother's love. *'Dana was a good mother when she was sober.'*

But those moments had become fewer. Dana had relied too heavily on uppers and downers and the wrong sort of men to get by. Controlling ones who had held all the power.

She hauled in a couple of breaths and tried to settle her spiralling thoughts, fixed her mind firmly on the things she could control. She would not be like her mother. She would cope. She would put this child first, before her own needs, before Connor's.

All she had to do now was tell him.

'Hi. Finished?' Skye peered round the door. 'Two things. Firstly, Tassie's started to make a reappearance on the ceiling in the admin room. I'll try keep Connor out of there. And, secondly, Oakley's not well. Have a look, will you? I'm very worried.'

At her friend's concerned face Mim's professional core solidified. Skye was an experienced nurse and nothing flapped her. Ever. 'Sure, I'll sort the admin room later. Is Oakley here?'

'Yes, we've just collected him from school. They rang. I've tried to get hold of his mum, but no luck.'

'Bring him in.'

'Thought you might need some help.' Connor's thick, deep voice rumbled into the room. He strode in with a red-faced Oakley in his arms. Rain spots pocked their clothes, their hair bedraggled from the biting south-westerly. God knew how far he'd carried him in the gale and lashing rain, but it didn't look like his muscles were being tested by the weight of a seven-year-old boy.

Connor looked the same as he had that fated morning after. Sexy, ruffled and yet totally in control. A slow thrill snaked down her back, pooling in her thighs, making her legs wobble slightly. Her face blushed to match their patient's. She pressed her palms to her cheeks and hoped the chill in her hands would cool them. She had so much to say to Connor. But it would all have to wait.

She found some long-lost self-control and stood. 'Hey, stranger.'

'Hey, yourself. Sorry I haven't been in touch.' His face was serious as he walked in, looked around for the couch. 'Busy, you know.'

'Too many allergies these days?'

'Huh?'

'Allergic to kids. Allergic to phones?' She was sniping him, but she'd been glad of the reprieve. Hadn't thought about him or their chances of pregnancy at all. Save for a few minutes… okay, hours, every day. 'We'll talk later?'

'Great.' He seemed to relax a little, gave her a concerned smile that asked her a million questions. None of which she felt able to answer. Then he placed Oakley on the examination couch. 'Right, mate. In safe hands now. Mim's here.'

The fact Connor admired her professional skills reddened her face even more. Safe hands? She hoped so. She hoped she hadn't missed anything when she'd checked the boy over a few weeks ago. He'd had very minor symptoms then, a cough and sore throat. Nothing serious. 'Hey, there, big fella. What's the story?'

'He's got a fever,' Connor explained. 'Complaining of pain in his joints.' He looked at Oakley kindly and patted the boy's head. His voice was smoother, softer as he spoke to the lad. Genuine concern lit his eyes. 'Your knees hurt, eh? And your hands.'

Something in Connor seemed to melt when he was around Oakley. A mischevious glint appeared in his eyes, a connection. Mim bet he would never admit to it, though. He prided himself on keeping aloof and distant, and spurned closeness. That much had been evident when they'd been together.

It seemed he had no space in his head for love. He'd thought he had. He had fervently believed in what they could achieve. But passion and love weren't the same thing.

She pressed a hand to her belly and prayed he'd at least acknowledge his mistake, even if he refused to love it. Or her.

'Hi, Mim.' The boy was weak, lethargic, but managed a small smile. Perspiration trickled down his face, his mouth dipped into a sad frown. A far cry from the zooming, tumbling boy they'd laughed with in the breakfast club. He'd gone seriously downhill.

'Feel yuck? Looks like you've got a temperature. We'll try to get you a bit cooler.' Even from this distance Mim could feel the heat emanating from Oakley. His body shook. She edged next to Connor to get closer to the boy. Ignored the brush of Connor's arm, the tingling in her skin. Refused to look into his face in case the swirling emotions in her head gave her away.

She focused instead purely on Oakley. 'You're shivering? That's okay, mate. Don't be scared. It's normal. Your body's trying to cool itself and kill those nasty bugs that are making you sick. Don't worry, we'll fix it.'

She loosened his shirt buttons, dampened a hand towel and placed it on his forehead. Then she attached an automatic blood-pressure cuff to his arm. 'Just going to give a little squeeze on your arm.'

Skye stepped forward and filled them in on details. 'Apparently he's been out of sorts for a couple of weeks, grumpy, tired and irritable. His teacher said they'd been doing handwriting exercises at school today and he couldn't seem to grip a pencil. She tried him with some fine-motor stuff, picking up building bricks, but he couldn't do it. Very unusual for him. That, coupled with the fever, had her straight on the phone to me. Talking of which, I'll go and try his mum again.'

She disappeared down the corridor.

Mim nodded, trying to piece together the jigsaw of symptoms. 'Oakley? Can you tell us where it hurts now?'

The boy tried to peer over at them, but his neck jerked a little. It took him a moment to focus. 'H-here. L-egs...and... h-h-hand.'

'Okay, sweetie, we'll have a look.'

Connor watched Mim fuss around their patient, her demeanour slightly frazzled yet focused. It had been four weeks since he'd even heard her voice. For real. But her image and her words ate at him every night. And in the quiet moments at work. And the busy ones. Yeah, pretty much all the damned time.

But he'd done what they'd agreed was the best thing. Certainly the best thing to escape yet another foray into disaster.

Created distance and space. Making love with her had been a massive mistake, but coming back for more would border on insanity.

Clearly nothing had come of their…indiscretion. If she'd been pregnant she'd have told him. One thing he knew about Mim, she was always honest. Too honest sometimes. But at least they could progress as planned, and he could get out of there as quickly as physically possible. Then work on getting her out of his head.

He started processing Oakley's signs and symptoms. He needed more information to form a diagnosis. 'He seems to be having trouble getting his tongue round words. All very strange. It doesn't add up. Anything we're missing? Past history?'

'Nil of note, really. He had a cough and sore throat a few weeks ago. It's autumn, there's a lot of minor infections about.'

'Yes, I remember.' Connor had recognised the boy immediately. His gappy smile, tufty hair. The innocent yet sage cinnamon eyes. 'He had a cough at the breakfast club. This is the lad who thought I was the mayor.'

'In that suit you look more like the mafia.' She laughed, her eyes lighting up for the first time since he'd walked in the room. 'The mayor? You?'

Or Mim's boyfriend. She'd sure as hell laugh at that. He kept his mouth shut.

Oakley was the cute kid who'd brought back happy memories of being carefree.

His hands fisted at his sides. Carefree didn't mean lying on a doctor's bed with a raging temp and weird symptoms. Or being scared to death and wondering where the hell your mother was.

Since Janey had died Connor had shunned anything but a passing connection with his patients, especially children. It was so much easier when they were nameless and faceless. But this kid's huge scared eyes stared at him, pinned him to the bedside, held him accountable.

He'd spoken to this boy, had laughed with him. Knew him. On the short journey from school to the surgery he'd learnt that Oakley's first love, after Mim, was rugby league. That his favourite colour was *red and black*, like his favourite team's strip. That he hated cauliflower.

He'd learnt that Oakley was funny and clever and brave. This was a sick boy who needed him. He couldn't hide behind a flimsy mask of paperwork and regulations here.

He watched Mim take the aural thermometer out of Oakley's ear and stroke the boy's forehead. An absent-minded action but loaded with affection. She truly cared for each and every one of her patients and friends. Surrounded herself with chaos and colour.

Whereas he preferred the safety of black and white. What had happened to him? He used to care. Used to sit and chat and get to know his patients.

He'd scraped through med school and GP training in a haze of dispassionate distance. Had treated symptoms, not patients.

Maybe he'd avoided meaningful contact for too long.

'Connor? Are you okay?' Mim's hand on his arm dragged him back. He controlled his raging heartbeat as he looked into her face, which was soft and her smile reassuring.

'Sure. I'm fine. Hey, Oakley, I'd like to have a quick listen to your chest.' Connor warmed the bell of his stethoscope in the palm of his hand, lifted the boy's school shirt and gasped. Beside him he heard Mim's sharp intake of breath. 'Snake-like rash.'

'Erythema marginatum.' She pointed to the raised edges of the lesions that covered Oakley's torso. 'Look at the red borders. Rheumatic fever.'

He was impressed with her knowledge. 'But rheumatic fever's pretty rare in developed countries, which makes it unlikely. What's his temp?'

'Thirty-eight point three. Too high.' She blinked up at him through dark lashes, her focus now steely and determined. 'I've certainly never seen it before, but it's getting more common in rural and poorer areas. Particularly in indigenous communities. Oakley already fulfils two of the Jones criteria. Joint pain and skin rash. Now for the heart sounds.'

She prompted him to auscultate Oakley's chest.

He moved the stethoscope over the boy's ribs, front and back, listening intently for the tell-tale flow sounds. 'He has a slight murmur. Has he always had one?'

Mim frowned as rain hammered on the windows, making her raise her voice to compensate. 'I'd have to check his notes. But off the top of my head, I'd say no.'

'Okay, then we need further tests. Definitely an echocardiogram to see if there's any changes or inflammation. Finally, let's do a grip test.' He held out both his index fingers towards the boy. 'Okay, Oakley, I want you to grip my fingers and squeeze as hard as you can.'

Oakley gripped hard with his left hand, held on strong and tight.

But the right squeezed and relaxed, squeezed and relaxed in a milking motion. He just couldn't seem to control its movement. This didn't bode well. 'I…c-can't.'

'Milkmaid's squeeze, too. Evidence of Sydenham's chorea. Jerky, uncontrollable movements. Usually a late-onset effect of the disease.' And more often than not patients with the chorea had heart complications too. Connor was convinced. Against the odds, Oakley had rheumatic fever. Indeed, had probably had it for some time.

Connor already had the action plan in his head, dredged up from his memory of guidelines he'd reviewed recently. 'Okay, a bolus of intramuscular penicillin now will start to fight the infection, paracetamol will bring down that temp, nice and slowly, and he needs an urgent admission.'

'But his mum's not here yet.' Mim motioned for them to move out of Oakley's earshot. 'We can't send him off to hospital on his own. I have a queue of people waiting, and Skye's got a dressing clinic.'

'What about his dad? Grandma?'

Mim shook her head.

He followed her to the desk and whispered, trying to keep the urgency out of his voice. And failing. 'You want me to wait for his mum? For how long? We haven't got time. We need to check his C-reactive protein, ESR, he needs an echocardiogram and a hospital bed.'

She frowned. 'I know, but we haven't got parental consent. We can't just whisk him miles away.'

'Taking a child without his mother's permission is nothing compared to waiting around for him to get worse. Acute rheumatic fever has a host of complications.'

'Nothing that can't wait a bit longer.'

No way would he stand by and watch Oakley deteriorate. Standing by did nothing except invite tragedy. He knew that to his cost. 'I'm not prepared to take a chance. He's sick, Mim. If we don't act soon he could get worse. Spending the next ten years injecting antibiotics won't be fun for him, and neither will being limited by an irreparably damaged heart. But that's what he's looking at if we don't take him in.' He dragged some oxygen into his lungs. 'Phone her again. Get her to meet the ambulance here. Or at the hospital. And, yes, I know it's ninety minutes away.'

She bit her bottom lip and nodded. 'Okay, I'll get Skye to phone.'

'Wh-what's th-that?' Oakley's wide eyes stared up at Mim's hand. She was holding the intramuscular dose of antibiotic. A needle and syringe.

'That's special medicine to fight those bugs.' Connor scruffed the boy's tufty hair and squeezed his hand. 'It'll be a quick scratch and then all done. You'll be fine, buddy.'

'Okay.' Oakley's bottom lip protruded as he glared at the needle. It was the first time he'd shown any sign of being scared.

Connor found himself wanting to ease the boy's nerves. To protect him.

Hell, first he'd wanted to save him. Now to protect him. Whatever next, adopt the damned child? His proximity radar was flashing red alert. Too close. Hold back. He need some air. Perspective. A different life. But he wanted the kid to smile again. 'Seriously, Oaks, you are taking all this like a pro. I mean, league legends have this too when they're sick. And I bet none of them are as brave as you.'

Oakley finally gave him a small smile. Even through his spiking temperature and fear Connor could see pride in the boy's face. It kicked in his gut too. Hell, okay. He liked the kid. No big deal. 'Yeah.'

'Yeah.' He knocked his fist against Oakley's and nodded.

'C-can I have a C-Coke instead?' Oakley's bottom lip slipped into a cheeky grin that reminded Connor of his sister. She'd always had him wrapped round his finger. One smile from her and he'd been putty.

Her smile. He'd forgotten about that, her earthy giggle, her sweet smell of vanilla and fresh air. The memories of his sister had always been tinged with guilt. Until now.

A minuscule ray of light chinked the plating round his heart. He'd been too scared to remember the good things in case his heart broke too much. Had locked away his memories and his feelings. But being with Oakley kind of helped. A bit.

Saturation therapy. Not avoidance. Maybe Mim had been right. Damn. Did she always have to be right?

Had she been right when she'd called quits on their relationship? Had she been right to walk away? He hadn't thought so at the time. Had taken a lot of getting over.

So was she right now? Would spending time with Oakley be one step in healing his heart or was he opening himself up to a thousand kinds of hurt all over again?

The practice nurse returned with bad news. 'The storm's getting worse. There's been a multiple pile-up on State Highway One so there won't be an ambulance for a while. Possibly thirty, forty minutes.'

'Then I'll take him myself.' He winked at the boy. 'Some guy time, eh? A road trip, away from all these girls.'

'Are you sure?' Mim frowned and looked at him, her gaze questioning, scrutinising him. 'Guy time?'

And she probably guessed what he already knew. What his kicking heart rate was beating into him. He didn't want to spend hours on his own with a sick boy who played havoc with his heartstrings. But there was no other way. 'Why can't you live within range of decent services? Or somewhere where phone coverage isn't shoddy? Or where people have the decency to stay in reasonable contacting distance?'

'Because life might not be perfect, Connor, but Atanga Bay is. Generally.' Mim paused from sponging Oakley's forehead. 'Seriously? You'll take him in your car? In this weather?'

'Yes, in my car. There is no choice.' He glanced at Oakley. 'Convertible. Goes like the wind.'

'Cool.' The boy's eyes widened. 'G-go now?'

Mim's stance softened as she looked over at Connor's equally bright eyes and fixed jaw. He looked scared half to death but determined as hell. There was no way she'd be able to stop him. 'Do you want me to come with you?'

'No, stay here, finish your clinic.' He slid his palm onto her shoulder and squeezed. His mouth fixed into a straight line. 'Looks like things are going to be delayed again. If we don't get onto phase four we'll never get your assessment done. I'll come back soon as I can to make a start. In the meantime, get a message to Oakley's mum.'

'Forget the assessment. It can wait one more day.' Or was he so determined to get it finished and out of her life?

She drew away from the faux security his arm offered. Too tempting to sneak right under and snuggle in. Tempting. And way too foolhardy. She couldn't get used to having him around. Not when he was impatient to leave. Not when she had so much to tell him her throat was almost too full of words. And what she had to say would have him running back to Auckland, she was sure of it. Too much to say and too much to lose already. 'Be careful, Connor.'

'Sure thing. Got to go.'

She knew that, for Connor, action was the only thing that would assuage his urgency. And that he had to remain in control at all times.

But she'd never seen him so committed.

Except maybe once, years ago, when they'd discussed marriage. When his eyes had burnt as fervently as now and she'd been drawn in to his passion, his plans and ideas. And her heart had melted then too.

Could she be falling for him all over again? It was folly and all kinds of foolishness. And a step away from madness. Especially when she knew the future held nothing for them but problems and hurdles they would never surmount.

She couldn't, wouldn't, fall for him again. The guy didn't care one iota for her dreams. He lived a million miles away in another world. Didn't share her vision. Didn't want kids. Had been clear about that to the point of being hurtful. Had taken every step possible to prevent pregnancy.

She watched him drive down the road, his car lights glittering in the sheet rain. Idiocy to be driving in this weather.

A cluster of tears threatened to close her throat. He'd put his life on the line for Oakley, for somebody else's child. Would he even give a second glance to his own?

CHAPTER SEVEN

THICK darkness greeted Connor as he turned off the highway intersection towards Atanga Bay. His shoulders dropped back a little and his stomach unclenched for the first time since he'd left the hospital and seen Oakley in safe hands with a sound prognosis. Breathing seemed easier here somehow. Must be the sea air after hospital disinfectant had clogged his lungs. Surely.

He hummed along to a salsa CD. Hadn't been able to get the rhythm out of his head since their dance. He grinned. What he'd give to dive right back there and sway with Mim's tight body pressed against him again. Rewind the clock.

As if she'd let him. As if he'd let himself. And with good reason. She'd stepped on his heart before, he wouldn't let her do it again. All well and good to admire from a distance.

But no second chances.

Almost there. 'Goddamned middle of nowhere, no street-lights.'

He flicked onto full beam. But he knew the place blind-folded now. The sharp twist to the left as he drove past the superette, the bump in the road at the pelican crossing. The rows of palm trees lining Main Street. The impressive colonial villas.

And across the road from the ever-full pub, Dana's Drop-

In stood proudly in the middle, a bright yellow beacon beckoning one and all. Beckoning him.

Not right now.

He pulled up outside the pub, ran a hand quickly through his hair, peered grimly at his reflection in his car mirror. He could have done with a shave. A wash. A sleep, but that would have to wait.

Saturday night and he was back here to run a well-man clinic, instead of cruising Auckland nightlife looking for an empty-headed bimbo for no-strings-attached sex. What was happening to him?

For a committed city dweller, middle-of-nowhere living seemed to have crawled under his skin when he wasn't looking.

Voices greeted him as he entered the pub. 'Hey, Doc!'

'Yo! Fancy a pint, mate?'

'You're late.'

The lone female voice grated above the rest, but that was the one he instinctively turned to. The one, he realised, he'd been listening out for. The one that gave him a rush of something he didn't want to admit to through his veins. He waved, trying not to look too pleased to see her. Trying not to feel too pleased to see her. Damn it, don't say she'd crawled under his skin too?

No way.

He made his way over to get the clinic moving. To the shocked look of everyone at the bar, he didn't even get a drink first. 'Lovely to see you, too, Mim. Missed me?'

'Like a hole in the head, Wiseman. How's Oakley?' She regarded him over her glasses. Sometimes, when she wasn't concentrating on rebuffing him, he glimpsed the young woman of three years ago, in the sparks of gold in her eyes, in the impish turn of her perfect lips. The familiar innocent sweetness of what they'd had.

And then, at times like this, the hard set of her jaw, the steel cold of her glare reminded him of how far apart they were, and how they had nothing in common but a shared fling. In typical Mim fashion, she'd put up barriers again. He knew. Understood it even. But it didn't stop the intense and unbidden tug of desire coated with hurt.

Although he should talk. He wavered from wanting her to shunning her. And fresh from an emotional trip with a sick child, he should be putting the locks down and shutters firmly in place until he could find some equilibrium.

She was sitting at the makeshift consultation suite. *Suite.* Ha! A dusty and tatty screen with bizarre nineteen-seventies flowery swirls. But it fitted right in with the pub decor. And the workworn men sitting in the queue. They nodded in greeting as he passed them.

'Oakley's doing okay. I'll give you the lowdown later.' It had been a wrench to leave the kid, but he didn't want to discuss his case with an audience. And he was glad to be here, right now, with Mim and his…mates. That felt weird, but it was true. Over the last few trips here some of these guys had become more than passing acquaintances. 'The game's on in thirty minutes and we have patients to get through first.'

'Sure. Let's get a wriggle on. And at least I didn't have to bribe them to come this time. Word spreads fast.' She smiled, but looked torn. Unease flitted across her eyes. A frown formed in the 'V' of her forehead. The pen in her hand shook. That beautiful mouth formed a tight line that told him she was anxious, distracted, but her dark, shadowed eyes pleaded about something he didn't understand. And as always his body hungered to touch her. 'You look awful, Con. Long day?'

And she was making small talk. Which was about as far from Mim's usual forthrightness as it could get. Something wasn't right in her world. Something that niggled in his gut. Perhaps she was worried about Oakley.

'You say the nicest things, Dr McCarthy. Yes, I probably look strung out. Sleepless nights tend to have that effect on people.'

'Sorry.' Seemed everything she said came out wrong. She was both glad and frustrated to see him. He had the same shirt on as yesterday, had obviously not showered, and somehow his cocky demeanour seemed softer, yet more masculine. He fitted right in with the locals, at ease joking with them, and was here, in her well-man clinic, instead of being in bed. Looking after her friends even though he'd been up all night.

Obviously neither of them had got much sleep. She'd lain awake worrying. About Oakley. About Connor. About their baby. The only thing she could think of was that they were in deep, deep trouble. Trouble he wouldn't want any part of. Trouble that would drive a wedge further between them.

As if they needed any more.

But he was the father. He deserved to know—then he could do what he wanted with that information. She had to tell him, but she didn't know how. What words to use? Indecision grabbed Mim's throat like a vice. And when? Not now, obviously. Later? Tomorrow, in the cold light of day? Next week? After the scan? Crikey, she'd only known about it herself for twenty-four hours. And was still getting used to the idea.

Still trying to make plans. How to fit maternity leave around Dana's Drop-In. Her dreams seemed to be slipping through her fingers. No thanks to Connor. Again. 'It must have been a hell of a day. If you're as tired as you look, maybe we should call it quits after this clinic and talk tomorrow? Meet for brunch?' *Some time, never?*

'Brunch?' His eyebrows peaked in surprise. He didn't look pleased. 'Okay. If that's what you want. I guess.'

'Yes. It is.' Then she could spend the night going round and round and round what she was going to say again. Great.

'Er...Doc? Mim? How about you two stop arranging cosy dates and do your job?' Eric Bailey's candid tones interrupted her thoughts. *If only you knew.*

The old farmer smiled beatifically at her and then Connor in turn. He shuffled off one of his grimy work boots. A strong, ugly odour mingled with the stench of stale beer as he waggled his foot towards them. 'The Blues are on soon and I need you to look at my toe. It's infected.'

'Oh, the joys of general practice,' she muttered to Connor, holding back the dry heave lurching through her stomach. 'At what point can we shift this clinic over to the surgery?'

One covert vomit, a few hours and a spectacular Blues victory later Mim found herself in her kitchen, talking with Connor at the old rimu table. She couldn't remember the walk from the pub. Had they talked? She remembered fidgeting a lot, trying to avoid eye contact. What the heck had happened to the brunch plan she didn't know.

Pregnancy brain already?

The prospect of solo parenthood glared at her. A huge mountain to scale, but one she was happy to do. Apart from the vomiting, which she'd always believed started at around six weeks, not four. So unfair. Typical that Connor's baby had to rewrite the rule book.

She could do it. Had to. But didn't want the fight she knew would be inevitable when she told Connor. She didn't want him to walk away. She wanted him to be involved, to love his child. To open his heart. To give his love without conditions, rules or regulations. To let go.

'You look a bit off colour. You okay?' he asked as he fixed them a hot drink, moving lithely round her small kitchen as if it were his own. Knew where the cups were kept. And the sugar. He sat beside her at the table oblivious to the bomb-shell she was about to drop.

'Probably Eric's toe, turned my stomach a bit. Yes, I'm fine, thanks.' Apart from the need to vomit. The painful breasts. The missed period. She just had to find the words to say it…and they seemed woefully absent right now.

She almost felt sorry for him as he started to chat. 'Now we've got them engaged in the well-man's clinic we need to get them to bring their problems to the surgery. The pub was a good jumping-off point…but, well, pseudomonas and real ale don't mix.'

'Not to mention the infection risk. I'll put up a sign that from now on the clinic is here. No free pints, but a free BP check. How's Oakley?'

'He's in good spirits, actually. His mum arrived a couple of hours after we got to the hospital. But I hung around, just to make sure he was okay. He's had more antibiotics, is on a drip. His echo shows some valve damage, but not extensive.'

'Thanks so much for taking him. I know it was a big ask.'

'It was nothing. Honestly.' And yet it was everything. Connor shrugged. Spending time with that kid had hammered fiercely against his armour-plated heart. Left a few dents, too. But hadn't cracked the darned thing open. 'I watched the interns like a hawk. Couldn't fault them. They even refused to give me any details because I wasn't next of kin. Did everything right by the book.'

At that point he'd realised how foolish he was being, not trusting them.

'I hope it wasn't because of something I missed. I'm always so fastidious.' Running her hand across her chin, Mim blinked up at him. Her shoulders were hunched, her eyes blurred with tears. She looked about as small and vulnerable as Oakley.

And he had a strong urge to protect her too.

He wrapped his fist over her hand. No doctor ever wanted

to feel they had made a mistake, but at some point in their career they wondered what they could have done differently. And this sentiment coming from the guy whose family sued for malpractice? Mistakes couldn't happen. Ever. But this was about judgement and misplaced guilt. And he'd had a guts full of that. 'Don't be silly. How were you to know he had Strep A? Most sore throats are viral and come to nothing.'

'I should have swabbed.'

'If we swabbed every single child that came into our surgeries we'd be too busy to do anything else.' He shook his head. 'Don't worry about this. He hasn't complained of a sore throat for the last few weeks. His mother hasn't brought him to see you, she wasn't concerned. He's had no obvious symptoms that anyone could see.'

Her chest heaved in staccato jerks as she hauled in a breath. Connor watched the tears brim in her velvet eyes. And the way she wiped them away with the back of her hand as if crying was a weakness she wouldn't allow. His heart snagged. 'What's all this? Hey. Don't worry. Oakley's fine.'

'It's not that…it's…'

'Is it the Matrix assessment, then?' In an impetuous movement he was pulling her to sit on his knee, in his arms. He held her tight, kissed the top of her head. Breathed in the so-familiar mango smell that made him feel like he'd come home. And wondered for the hundredth time where the heck they'd gone wrong. He could have saved her from all this financial worry. Offered her a settled future away from the haunting memories of her mother.

How could they have been so close and yet worlds apart?

If only they'd talked more. If only she'd let him look after her, like he'd wanted. If only he'd listened. Maybe they'd have made it.

Well, he was listening now.

She needed to pass this assessment. And he needed to

help her. 'Seriously, don't worry. You're not that far off,' he lied. She was about as far as feasibly possible from securing the Matrix funding. 'I can work you out a step-by-step plan.'

'Connor…it's not that.'

'Is it the—?'

'No. No.' Mim jumped out of his embrace, suddenly realising she was there, in the safety of his arms. Being lulled into his comfort. She couldn't allow herself to be taken in by his heat. She had to do this on her own. Her way.

She tapped her fingertips against her collarbone, paced up and down. Searching for the right words. 'You have to stop trying to fix everything, Connor. You can't. You can't fix my practice, you can't fix Oakley, or a medical system that's so huge and full of people who sometimes make mistakes. We're all human, not robots. You can't fix me. And you sure as hell can't fix this.'

She held her palm over the bump she couldn't feel or see but which she knew was there. A tiny bud of life growing inside her. Like a miracle. And now, she realised, like a blessing. Knew it, loved it already. And was ready to defend it with every last ounce of strength she had. 'I'm pregnant.'

'Pregnant?' How could a word be so difficult to say? It hit Connor like a bullet in the chest. Breath blasted out of him.

He watched Mim's face contort as she scrutinised his reaction. More tears spilled down her face and a silent sob racked her chest. But she brushed the tears away. Wrenched her shoulders back, too far than looked comfortable.

Typical Mim, defiant and determined as ever. Sucked in a deep breath and pierced him with her dark chocolate eyes. She almost looked proud. A fighter, for sure. Lucky kid to have someone like Mim to fight for it. 'Yes, pregnant. With your child. Your baby. Our baby.'

'*God.*' He didn't have space in his heart or his life for a child. Someone to love. Someone to rely on him. Somebody else for him to let down. He couldn't have a child.

The armour-plating quivered again. Then froze into place. Locked tightly, solid as a rock. No damned emotion would penetrate it. Nothing. Not Oakley. Not Mim. Definitely not a baby. 'What about the morning-after pill? You did take it, didn't you?'

For a brief moment he wondered whether this had been her plan all along. Get the hapless assessor into bed. To hell with the consequences. She was desperate for the cash after all.

Then he cast that idea aside. They'd had sex. The condom had broken. He'd seen her with the tablets, as convinced as he was that pregnancy was not an option. He was to blame as much as she was. Truth was, his reactions were all kinds of confused, and trust seemed to be an ugly issue for him right now.

Mim nodded. Took another step away from him. Well out of touching distance. Which didn't matter. He didn't want to touch her either. Just wanted to go back to Auckland to his empty apartment. To his ordered life, away from this chaos of emotions.

'Yes, I did take it, and I was sick as a dog. But as of six o'clock this morning. And six-thirty. And seven. And eight, and eight-thirty, I'm pregnant.' She shrugged coyly and smiled. 'I did a few tests just to make sure. Five, to be exact. All with a pretty pink line.'

'All positive?'

'Positively positive. Like me, I'm trying to be positive. I'm trying to thank my lucky stars. I didn't plan this. I didn't want this.'

'And you're keeping it?'

Mim understood the implication loaded in that question. It had to be asked, she supposed. 'I've thought long and hard about my options. Termination doesn't come into them. This pregnancy is here despite every attempt to the contrary. And I want it, even if you don't. And you obviously don't.'

Please convince me otherwise. She examined his face in the half-light. Tried to get an inkling of what he was feeling, thinking. He was pale, sure. Sheet white. His jaw was fixed, doing that twitchy thing it did when he got angry. His left leg jagged up and down. Fast.

But his face was devoid of any emotion. His black eyes were flat, dull. Cold. Shut down. The silence stretched between them and darkened.

He looked at her bleakly, then turned away, appeared to gather some control, took a few shaky breaths.

'Okay. Then we'll deal with it. I'll provide for you both. Of course. Financially.' His voice was too loud, too authoritarian. Connor was doing what he did best, taking control. 'My child won't want for anything. And there's your job to consider, Dana's Drop-In… Where are you going to live? Here's too small.'

'Stop. Stop. Stop.' She paced the room, her heart hammering, wanting to get rid of the excess adrenalin racing through her arteries. Wanting to rid herself of the pain that tore through her. Wanting to run. Into his arms. As far away from him as possible. None of it made sense.

She wanted to throw up all over again. 'Damn you, Connor Wiseman. I don't want you to *deal* with it. Or to provide for it. I want to know what you think about it. How you feel about it.'

I want you to love it. She ran a protective hand across her stomach, as if cradling it would stop the hurt. The bond she'd forged with their child was so strong already it almost left her breathless. She longed for him to feel the same.

He stalked into the lounge. 'How am I meant to feel? I don't know. There are so many things to consider. Being a dad was the last thing I ever wanted. Hell, look at my father.

Great template there for an absent, noncommittal, useless dad. I don't know how to raise a kid, not in a decent, loving way.'

'Right back at you, Connor. My upbringing was a fairy-tale. You're just hiding behind that excuse. You'd make a great dad. You're fine with Oakley when you let your guard down.'

He shook his head vehemently. 'That's different. He's a patient. I'm not responsible for him.'

'He's a little boy who likes you and it's not a crime to like him back. It's not a crime to have a heart,' she fired at him. 'Neither of us did well in the parenting stakes. But I'm not hiding. I have to face it. This wasn't exactly what I envis-aged either. This isn't the right time. Or the right…person.'

Those words hovered around them. He was totally the right person, for another life. For another time when things weren't so mixed up. Totally the right person for someone else who could love him unconditionally, who would happily give up everything to share his life.

'I have the review. I have my work,' she continued. 'And I was trying damned hard to be a success to give a child a proper upbringing, some time in the future. I didn't plan it to be now. And I didn't plan to be a single parent like my mother.'

Connor was taken aback by the vehemence of her words. Her hand wobbled over her mouth. Strong, capable and in-control Mim looked on the verge of tears again. Despite her fighting spirit she looked scared and vulnerable.

He wanted to make her feel better, to tell her everything would be okay. That he'd look after her, and any one else that came along.

But he couldn't say those words. Not right now. He knew she'd throw his sentiment back at him. She'd done it before. And walked away leaving him wounded.

He ignored the churning in his gut. The taut pull of his

heart at the mention of a baby. Tried to obliterate the images in his head of a child. His child growing inside her.

At the thought of a baby his thoughts swung to his sister's face. Her first smile. The way her tiny just-born twitching hand had grasped his finger, and squeezed his heart with such a force he'd barely been able to breathe with the love flowing out of him.

But when he'd buried her all that love had poured into the grave with her. He was empty. All out of love. He didn't have anything left for another child, did he?

Or its mother?

Mim would never let him love her anyway. She hadn't before. She'd thrown everything he'd offered her back in his face.

Just because there was a child in the picture, it didn't mean anything had changed between its parents.

He sat down and rubbed his temples, trying to rid himself of the stinging headache. Sat opposite her on the sofa where they'd shared so much loving. Where their baby had been made.

She glared at him. 'Tell me, Connor. What do you truly feel? Are you in? Or out?'

'I don't know. I'm in, I guess.'

'I guess? What a great start to the poor kid's life.'

'It's hardly a lucky blessing. We don't even live in the same district. And don't get me started on our rocky past.'

Mim loomed above him, hands fixed on her hips, a fervent, almost passionate, look smudged across her features. There was no way he'd ever be able to fight her on this. The love she already had for this baby was evident in every taut muscle in her body. 'Well, Connor, you've made yourself very clear. Thanks for the ringing endorsement, but me and the baby will get on just fine. This is about as low as we can get. *I guess* the only way from here is up.'

CHAPTER EIGHT

Chat message: 17:03: From Mim McCarthy
I am not Steph. I will not be bribed. You can't buy me.
Take them back. I don't want them.

Chat message: 17:05: From Connor Wiseman
I will not take them back. They were a gift. You need
them. You might not want them, but look—you are
using them! I suspect double standards :-)

MIM smiled despite herself, and despite the overwhelming
gut-wrenching anger she still felt for him. For herself. They
had both handled everything so badly. And got nowhere.

Apart from two very disjointed phone calls that had led to
nothing but grim silence for the last couple of days, this was
the first time she'd had any meaningful contact with Connor.
And the first time she'd felt anything like a smile cut through
the stark, tight line of her ever-pressed-together lips.

An hour ago three shiny silver laptops tied up with pink
and blue ribbons had arrived by courier. With a message:
'I'm sorry.'

From a self-righteous prig like Connor, that was a big
apology.

She glanced around the dishevelled admin room, at the
laptop taking pride of place on the desk, up at Tassie, who

seemed to be getting bigger by the day. Autumn was here, bringing dark nights and dark thoughts, and today the rain just hadn't stopped. She really did need to fix that damp spot before he got back.

When would that be? He'd only been here a handful of times and yet the place seemed empty without him. Her bottom lip began to quiver, as it had developed a habit of doing in the last few days. Her head hurt, too. Acid bit into her stomach. Her joints hummed with an overwhelming fatigue. Pregnancy was playing dipsy with her body.

She bit down hard and tried to gain control.

But the mind-blowing, devastating truth was that she missed him. Missed sparking off with him about his darned rules. Missed laughing with him. Missed his smell. Which was madness, really. Stark, raving madness. She couldn't miss him—couldn't have any feelings for him at all. What had happened to independent Mim? Self-reliant Mim?

She'd worked too hard to start needing someone now. And God knew, she didn't want a rerun of her own life, being dragged up by someone who didn't want to give centre stage to their child. She didn't want a rerun of her mother's life either. Always relying on someone else. And always being let down.

Chat message: 17:20: From Mim McCarthy
Take your %%#@% laptops and stick them where the sun doesn't shine. And do not smiley face me
Chat message: 17:30: From Connor Wiseman
:-) :-) :-) :-) :-) :-) :-) :-)
Miriam, sadly I suspect this is the only way I can smile at you without getting glared at. Or my head bitten off. We need to talk.

Chat message: 18:00: From Mim McCarthy
I'm ignoring your smiley faces. Your puerile humour doesn't amuse me.
Only my Nan ever called me Miriam. Last time I looked you weren't my Nan.

Chat message: 18:01: From Connor Wiseman
Just looked ;-) I am definitely not your Nan. Unless your Nan was devastatingly good looking, with an enormous ##@@!
(You have such a dirty mind: appetite. Enormous appetite.)
I don't suppose you'd like to tell me what you're wearing? Panties...?

Chat message: 18:03: From Mim McCarthy
Nearly choked on my noodles! Of course I'm wearing underwear, I'm at work. But more than that you'll have to guess. BTW, this is talking. Or rather, chatting. On a new laptop. That I don't want.

Chat message: 18:05: From Connor Wiseman
Talk, for real. In the same room. Where we can see each other and work out what we're going to do about, you know...the pregnancy.

Connor was running scared, she knew that. He was feeling his way...badly, of course. But she liked it that he was trying.

His sister's death had devastated him and destroyed his attempts to allow others in. At least, she assumed that was what had created his barriers. He'd refused to talk about it, so she just had to guess.

One of the reasons she'd left him before had been because he'd thought that loving someone meant taking over their dreams, not allowing them to grow. That making decisions and formulating plans showed he cared. And his single-mindedness had jarred heavily with her tough independent streak.

But in the midst of all the pregnancy news daze, he'd offered to support her. Which, although she wouldn't accept it, had been all she'd expected, really. Because she knew he couldn't offer anything more, however much he wanted to.

A tight fist twisted her heart. Their baby needed a loving father—deserved to be wanted and loved. She massaged her temples and closed her eyes briefly.

When she opened them again his name was still flashing on the screen.

Connor. A few weeks ago she'd never have thought seeing him again could be possible. Never mind having these deep feelings that she couldn't exorcise.

She wrinkled her nose at his name and smiled again. The smile curling the corners of her heart. All those years ago he'd tried so hard to love her, had been potent and passionate. But the time hadn't been right, his grief too raw. And now it was too late to even try. Too late for them to work as a couple. Too much had happened.

But he'd been capable of loving his sister once. Maybe, over time, he'd learn to love his child.

Maybe she should ease off and cut him some slack.

She reread his chat message.

No chance.

Chat message: 18:17: From Mim McCarthy
< the pregnancy.> Sounds like you're running a stud farm. Which I sincerely hope you're not. Are you? Connor, it's YOUR BABY.

Chat message: 18.20: From Connor Wiseman
Trying to get my head around it all. Need to talk to
you. Let me know when. I can get there late tonight.

Chat message: 18.47: From Connor Wiseman
Mim? You there?

Chat message: 19:00: From Connor Wiseman
Mim? I said I was sorry. Msg me now.

Chat message: 19.30: From Connor Wiseman
Mim? I'm setting off now. Answer your damn phone.

'What the…?' Mim lay on the floor of her pitch-black office
surrounded by dust and debris as her chest heaved under the
weight of something sharp and metal. A biting sting at the
back of her head stabbed and jabbed. She lay still for a moment. Dredged her memory for what the hell had happened.
Her heart slammed against her sore ribcage. The baby!

She ran a mental check over her body. No. No abdominal pain.

Relief flooded through her. She'd been hit on the head, not
her abdomen. That was fine. The baby would be fine.

The ceiling had fallen in. Had it? What had happened?
Yes, the ceiling.

'Ha.' The irony of her world crumbling around her wasn't
lost on her. 'Of course. Why not?'

Lifting her grime-covered head, she shouted through the
roof to whichever god she'd upset today. 'Perfect. Thanks.
Bring it on.'

Literally shouted through the roof. She twisted her neck.
From this angle she could see right through the hole to the
stars mocking her. Winking as if to say, Ha, got ya!

'Is that all you've got?' She raised a fist skywards. 'Try harder next time.'

'Mim? You okay? Where the hell are you?' The sharp, deep voice made her jump; a Connor-shaped silhouette appeared in the doorway. Her heart skittered, doubling her frustration.

'Dandy. Just dandy.' She slumped back onto the crusty floorboards. The vice round her head tightened. Could things get any worse? Her business was collapsing, her body was ganging up on her, and the father of the child she was carrying would now think she was a complete nut-job. 'I'm fine, thanks.'

'What's going on? Why are you shouting? In the dark?'

'I'm okay.' She lifted her hand from the floor to try to keep him away. She didn't want him to find her like this. She wanted him to think she was competent and in control. Didn't want him to be here to confuse her even more. Her head felt woozy, weirdly empty, confused enough.

But for some reason everything seemed much better now he was there. 'The lights all went out.'

'You don't say?'

'And the roof fell in. Yes. Yes.'

Everything was a blur. She couldn't remember. Like a thick fog floating in and out of her head misting her memory. Had the roof fallen in? There was a hole there now. 'I think. On top of me and my new laptop.' Which she appeared to be cradling like a baby. 'Aw, I think the screen thingy's smashed.'

'No torches? Stay there, I'll come and get you. Whatever you do, don't move.' The shape moved towards her. 'Ouch. Damn desk…. What's all this…wet?'

Exact details were hazy. She'd been sitting looking at his emails. It had been raining. 'The roof had a leak in it. We called it Tassie.'

'Just typical. Most people fix a leak, but you give it a name and treat it like a pet.' A light flickered between them. His face loomed above her, in a weird haze of white. 'I have a flashlight app on my phone.'

'Of course. You would. Everyone else has those things…' She clicked her fingers to help her remember. Odd. She couldn't remember the name. She knew it. But she couldn't remember…weird. 'For birthdays. You know…little fires.'

'Candles. Mim…you're not making sense…are you sure you're okay? What about the baby?' His voice softened further. But there was concern buried deep in it, too. He sounded like he cared. Like he was truly worried about her. She didn't want him to care, to speak in those rich, sympathetic tones that made her want to crumble, just like her roof. So long as he didn't touch her she'd be able to hold it together. 'Stop being so damned crazy. I want to help you.'

Connor stumbled across the floor towards her, his heart beating wildly in his chest, adrenalin rushing through his veins. She was talking, so that was a good thing.

But what about the baby? Ice flowed through him. He'd come here to talk about making an action plan, a contract for paternity rights. To forge a way forward. He had allowed himself to think about being a father and what that would mean. He hadn't figured that one out yet. And now what if…? He couldn't go there. Didn't want to crack open that armour and let emotion in. Wouldn't. He had to stay strong, make them all safe.

He didn't want to upset Mim so he kept his voice light. 'Trust you to get into trouble.'

'I want to get up.' He felt her arm flailing around, focused the light on her. Broken roof tiles lay around her head. Dust covered her hair, her clothes. She looked like a pile of rags. His heart contracted. Damned heart—no use in an emergency. He needed to be focused here. Get her out.

'What happened? Why is it dark?' She sounded scared.

'Whoa. Wait. You just told me. The roof fell in. Don't you

remember?' Concussion? Fluctuating memory loss. Bad sign. He prayed there was nothing more serious going on. Locked his heart. Activated doctor mode.

'Any pain in your neck? Back? Legs? Arms? Pins and needles?'

'No. Hush. I want to stand up.'

'Okay, easy does it.' He was next to her now, shoving his hands under her armpits, picking her up in one swift action. Dust fell from her hair onto her shoulders. He took the broken laptop out of her hands then ran his fingers down her face. All the time resisting the urge to haul her into his arms and squeeze her against him, safe in his arms for ever. But no matter how right she felt there, he couldn't have her again. He'd blown it. They'd both blown it too many times for it to work.

He banished all thoughts of her curves and delicious body and focused on which part of her might be broken.

He checked her cheekbones then patted her shoulders, ribs. She flinched. 'Does it hurt here?'

'A little.' Her voice wavered. Shock?

Onto her stomach. Where his hand stilled. He forced the question in his mind. His child.

Was it hurt? Damaged? Now his throat constricted. No. It was not going to happen again. He was not going to lose anyone else. He forced all emotion to the darkest part of his soul. He needed to check. He was a doctor after all. 'Now, listen to me. Do you have any pain here? Mim? Anything at all?'

'Not there. Just my head.' Mim shrugged away, fighting the urge to close her eyes and lean against him. Just for a minute. To stop the room spinning. To feel warm. But somewhere far away in the back of her brain was her own voice whispering to her to stand strong. *Don't lean on him.* 'I'm fine.'

'Did you hit your head when you fell or did something actually fall on top of you?' He leaned back as the beam of light swung down her front.

'Watch it…' The world tipped. She reached out to grab hold of his tie and swayed on the end of it. 'Hey. Big boy.'

'Big boy? Now I'm seriously worried. Drop the tie, honey. You're choking me.' His palm cupped her cheek. She'd missed him. He smelled good. He made her feel good. Connor was there. Everything would be fine.

Oops. Too close. *Don't…don't do something.* She couldn't remember what she wasn't supposed to do.

Too tired to move, she slumped forward a little, held onto Connor's shoulders to stay upright.

He touched her forehead with the back of his hand. 'You're hot.'

'Hot? Cheeky, sexy baby.' Surely he didn't want sex right now? Getting her mouth round words was practically impossible. She'd never manage sex. She raised her eyebrows and looked into his blurry, ghoulish face. 'I don't feel good.'

'I mean temperature hot. You're burning up.' He took her by the shoulders and pulled her to face him. 'You need to go to hospital.'

Now he sounded cross. 'Don't be cross, Connor. I want you to be nice to me.' She wanted him to hold her and get rid of this headache. Really, that's what she wanted. She wanted him to hold her and love her.

It was a nice thought.

Was it? He was big and strong and there. And maybe she could love him too?

Yes, it was a really nice thought. Easy. And perfect. 'I love you, Connor Wiseman.'

'No, you don't. Behave.' He still sounded cross. 'Mim. Focus. Look at me.'

'Yes, sir.' She saluted with a hand that didn't seem to want to salute. Tried to shake away the foggy feeling in her head. But her vision seemed to narrow onto him. Strange spots and stars glittered over his face.

'Lack of impulse control, poor concentration. Confusion.' His words were a long way away. Echoing in and out. And he was shaking her shoulders. 'Try and think, Mim. How long ago did this happen? Did you get knocked out?'

She shrugged, barely finding the strength to raise her shoulders. 'Dunno.'

His beautiful sparkly face was lit in a halo but his eyes were gooey. His hands ran over the back of her head and he pulled a serious face. 'You've got a bad gash on your head. Can't you remember hitting it?'

'Not…really.' Absolute exhaustion crawled through her veins. 'I think I'd like to go to sleep now.'

'No way. Look at me.' He flashed his light into her eyes. Back and forth.

'Stop.' It was too bright. All she could see was big white circles making her feel dizzy. 'Stop.'

'Okay. Come on.' His hand squeezed into hers and he towed her to the surgery back door. 'Let's get out of here so I can get a better look at you without risking both our necks.'

'Wait.' She slipped out of his grip and aimed for the door-mat, which looked nice and soft. 'This looks fine. A scratchy pillowy thing.' Surging in and out of focus.

In and out.

Closer. Further away. Closer. Her head spun. The door-mat loomed up. And back. Her stomach churned. Heaved. Her head pounded. 'Can you stop that thing moving? It's making me feel…'

In one big convulsive moment she lost her dinner down her front and onto the surgery floor. 'Oops.'

'Wow. Mim. That was…epic.' His hand rubbed her back as her stomach heaved until it hurt. Heaved every last drop of strength she had left.

'Feel better?'

'No, I feel bad.' Her arms and legs were shaking. Her head

was being crushed by a huge weight. Pressing down. Harder and harder. 'I want to sit down.'

'Here we go, missy.' He helped her onto the floor, sat her against the wall. He sounded cross again. 'Hello? Emergency. Can I have an ambulance, please? Yes. Yes. Pregnant female with a head injury.'

'I'm closing Dana's Drop-In and you're coming to my place where I can look after you.' Connor's voice was affirmative and authoritarian—it bounced off the pale green hospital walls, pounding into Mim's swollen brain. 'This is final. I'm not going to have a discussion with you about this.'

She kept her raging heart rate in check, understood he was trying to help. Smiled sweetly into his liquorice eyes as he leaned forward in the chair next to her bed. Where he'd been glued for the last few days. And she'd been so relieved to find him there, a constant presence, stroking her hair, feeding her sips of iced water.

Through various stages of semi-consciousness she'd heard him in deep whispers with the staff, checking and rechecking her pills and obs. He had conducted his work by smartphone, fielding increasingly fraught calls from his father, and had left only to get food and the odd shower in the doctors' mess. She couldn't fault him on his dedication and steadfastness.

Today he was wearing dark green scrubs he'd borrowed from the hospital laundry. All serious and doctor-like.

Even though he looked delicious with his tousled hair, perfect mouth and frown, she preferred the quiet, caring, *holding-hands-in-the-middle-of-the-night* version. The one that didn't jump in and dictate terms, regardless of his good intentions. But that was the Connor package, serious, passionate. Commanding.

He smiled in that inimitable Connor way. A quick, boyish, flick of his upper lip showing his almost perfect teeth.

Which was irritating and beguiling at the same time. A prickling of awareness tiptoed up her spine. His dedication to her had been sweet, but the pooling of heat in her abdomen was far from that. It was needy and desperate and simmered at his every touch.

Even with a head ache the size of Australia she found him irresistible. *Really?* She battened down her defences. He was pompous and annoying.

With a cute, heart-melting smile.

And not going to take control of my life.

'You know, it's a real shame my head's getting clearer. Life was so much better in a concussive haze, when you were nice to me because you thought I was going to die.'

'Quit the exaggeration, lady. I never thought you were going to die. You have more lives than a moggy. And more cunning and guile. You had a minor tap on the head. Anyway…it's too late.' He looked down, straightened the blanket and had the decency to look shame-faced. 'I've phoned Skye. And I don't want any arguments.'

'You are damned well going to get arguments until you take me straight back to my own apartment.' If only the world didn't curve her sideways every time she stood up, she'd head off there right now. 'Did you think I would be fluttering my eyelashes and saying thank you? You had no right to do that. Butt out of my business.'

'Ten out of ten on the stroppy scale: obviously you're almost back to normal. We won't be needing a second opinion on that.' He flicked through the charts that hung on the end of her bed. The V-neck of his scrubs allowed a glimpse of sun-kissed skin and a smattering of fine hair. Fleeting memories of lying against that chest washed through her mind.

His smell had been faded out by the overpowering scent of lilies and hospital soap, and she found herself straining to get the full Connor aroma every time he plumped her pillow or gave her a drink. And every time she caught a faint whiff of him her world seemed right again.

Why was it that with Connor she could feel both excited and irritated at the same time? Must be the head injury. Definitely.

He frowned, scanned. Nodded. 'Your blood pressure's okay. Neuro obs are fine. If we can get on top of your temp and chest infection you'll be discharged in the next couple of days. But you still need looking after and three weeks off, Mim. You know the protocol for concussion.'

'Come on, all I have now is a bit of pain. Which is manageable with paracetamol. Just.' She rubbed the dressing on the back of her head, running her fingers over the stubble where the ER doctors had shaved a small patch for suturing her scalp back together. 'Skye can take the clips out and do a dressing change.'

He fiddled with her IV line and drip. Probably putting arsenic in. Or something to shut her up.

'Sure, Mim. Give it all to Skye. Skye, who is run off her feet covering for you with nurse-led clinics, trying to keep your business ticking over. Skye, who spends her after-work hours going through the Matrix review documents. Skye, who has an elderly sick mother to look after in her very rare spare time. That Skye? And now you'd like her to nurse you too?'

'I don't need nursing. I just want to go home. I'll be okay in my own space. I'm strong, and young. Pretty please. Nice Dr Wiseman.'

She threw him a smile just to make sure he was getting her *I'm all right* act.

Clearly he wasn't taken in. He huffed out a breath, the corners of his mouth curling upwards, this time sarcastically. 'Don't even start. Cheeky, sexy baby.'

'What?'

His grin widened. Sparks flew from his eyes as he enjoyed his, obviously private, joke. 'Never mind. Some things are best forgotten. You can't sweet-talk me. Rules are rules.'

'Stuff the rules.'

He ran his fingers through his hair and little tufts stood on end. Desire rushed through her. She swallowed it away and reminded herself that he was back to the old Connor, dictating terms. She didn't need his kind of help.

He shrugged. 'This is all the thanks I get for taking some control of the chaos I found you in?'

'I don't need anyone to take control, Connor. I know all about what happens when you let someone else take control.'

She scrunched her fingers into her fist and squeezed down hard. Trying not to scream. Screaming would be bad for her head, aside from the fact her lungs were too full of gunk to allow more than a squeak out.

Twice in her life she'd lost control—once when she'd agreed to marry him, and everything she'd worked for had threatened to go down the gurgler. The second time, she'd got pregnant by him.

She wasn't willing to try third time lucky. 'It usually ends in a big fat let-down, right?'

'Damn woman.' Connor kicked up the IV infusion rate to stop her getting dehydrated. Did she not realise how sick she'd been? Concussion and morning sickness made for more vomit than he'd ever imagined possible for a woman her size.

Her skin was unnaturally pale, her eyes sunk into their sockets. The hospital gown hung off her shoulders like a shroud. A few days ago she'd been unable to walk. And she wanted to go home. On her own.

Frustration surged through his belly. Frustration, powerlessness and a deep, almost feral need to protect her. From herself. 'You are so damned independent. Let me look after you. You need to be somewhere warm and dry and safe. Where you're not tempted to run a breakfast service for the whole of the neighbourhood or sit in a derelict admin room. Do you hear?'

'Not listening. Not listening.' She coughed, held her ribs as she inhaled. Her gorgeous frail face screwed up in pain. Just like he had a million times over the last few days, he wanted to wipe away the pain for her, take it himself. But she forced a smile through her thin lips. 'Where did the chest infection come from?'

'Maybe it had something to do with lying on a wet, dirty floor, inhaling the carcasses of a zillion dead ants and who knows what other monstrous decaying exoskeletons were in your antiquated ceiling space.'

A loud siren dragged his attention away. A blur of coloured scrubs rushed through the corridor to an accompaniment of bleeping phones and shuffling feet. He shuddered, itching to go and help but knowing he'd probably get in the way of a slick operation. He turned back to Mim, simultaneously hating the fact someone was in distress and enjoying the thrill of adrenalin he used to get from saving lives. 'Arrest?'

'Yeah, sounds like it. I always hated it when we got to that.'

'Me too. Let's hope it's successful.' He would never forget those sounds. The rush of the crash team. The rhythmic squeak of the hospital bed during chest compressions. And the dull, low monotone drone that said his sister wasn't coming back.

The cold chill of remorse snaked up his spine. That memory had dogged him through med school and beyond. Had given him bitter-sweet successes and devastating losses.

Mim seemed unperturbed by the scene unfolding in the side ward. She leaned back on the pillow, closed her eyes, rested her hand near his on the blanket. Despite the aggravation she instilled in him, he couldn't help but pick her hand up, trace the long lines on her palm. Just having her squeeze his hand sent a relaxing balm over his nerves.

He felt the roughened skin from hours of clinical hand-washing, the calluses around the edges of her fingernails. The nub where a pen had rubbed from countless hours of study. Although she'd rarely mentioned her past, he knew she'd fought hard to be a doctor. To do what she could to save her mother's reputation and to prevent anyone else having a childhood like hers. She'd survived so much and with such fortitude. And fought like hell for everything she wanted.

He could certainly learn a lot from that. From her, with her positive, forward-looking attitude. *Never look back.*

A few days ago she'd said she loved him. In a concussive fog, she'd said those words. But he didn't believe her. Couldn't. She'd said it before and it was hollow and meaningless in the end.

And yet…their summer of fun had been intense, amazing. And even now he couldn't get her out of his head. All he knew was that he enjoyed being with her; she made him laugh. Made him ache for something deeper in his life.

Whoa. Stop. His internal proximity radar alarm went off again. He was getting too attached. It was just because he'd spent so much time with her recently. It was coming to an end. Just a few more weeks. Then he'd sever emotional ties with her. That was something he could do well. He'd had enough practice over the years.

Right now, he had to make sure she was safe and that their baby was healthy. He had to provide for them. Make plans.

Then he'd send her back to Atanga Bay. He would complete the Matrix assessment online, now that she had two decent working laptops. He would keep in email contact, and at arm's length until the baby was born.

Monthly paternity visits would be fine. He'd be a more hands-on dad with that than his own father had been. The only thing he'd been hands-on with since Janey had died was his work. And a couple of secretaries.

Connor had no blueprint for being a good father—a distant one, yes, in every sense of the word. An angry and disappointed one, definitely. But even if he couldn't be everything he believed a father should be—which meant love and proximity and fun…

His thought processes stalled. The kinds of things he did with Oakley. Joking around, watching over him, teaching him important stuff. Like how to build a toy castle and the names of the best prop forwards over the last ten years.

It was easy with Oakley, there was no investment there. It was just fun. Wasn't it? But could he do that with his own child, on a once-a-month basis?

He swallowed hard. He didn't know. He wanted to. Oakley had taught him a lot. But, damn it, he was still scared. His child. Another Wiseman. He didn't know how to be anything other than a Wiseman father.

He'd be faultless in his provision, though. He'd write it all into the contract.

In the meantime, he had to get Mim to agree.

'So, how about it? Rest up at my place. I've booked a full pre-natal scan here for next week. We can get your roof fixed in the meantime. And we can work out what we're going to do long term about the baby. Like grown-ups.'

'Grown-ups? Us? Fat chance.' Mim smiled and relaxed back into her pillow. It was nice just to be. To be here, holding Connor's hand. To be in bed. To be looked after. Without spending every waking minute obsessing about her business, her future…the baby.

The scan he'd ordered would be reassuring. 'Tell me again about the ultrasound I had when I came in. I wish I could remember it.'

'Stop hedging. I won't tell you anything until you agree to come with me. Be sensible. My place is five minutes away. Unlike yours. Separate rooms. I promise.'

'You drive a hard bargain, Dr Wiseman.'

Relief and disappointment bit at her. Something in his eyes told her he'd keep his promise—and his distance, too. Not that she was remotely worried. Although he'd been kind and generous and attentive, she knew they had no future together as anything other than co-parents.

But he was right. The pain in her head and ribs was debilitating, no matter how much she pretended it wasn't. Her clinic needed urgent renovations and she couldn't work until they were done. Plus, she needed to rest. If not for her sake, then for her baby's.

She ran her palms over the flat plane of her stomach. She'd do anything to make sure this baby didn't get hurt. She had to do what her mother had never done, and put her child's needs first. Love it unconditionally. Without blaming it, like Dana had, for what might have been. For snatching away her future.

This baby was her future. How had it happened that in barely a month her whole life revolved around something so small, so cherished, so magical? A lump lodged in her throat. Somehow she bet Dana had never thought her baby was magical.

Enough. She refused to dwell on her past or the feelings of loneliness that ate away at her in her vulnerable moments. The only sensible thing was to look forward. To make things work for them all. If not as a family then a unit of people bound by a shared love. She could cope with not having Connor in her life so long as he promised to be in their child's. Recuperating at his apartment was one way to forge ties with him. 'Okay. I'll come. For a few days only. No more. Then I have to get back to my business before there's nothing left of it.'

'It won't come to that after a few days.'

He smiled his killer smile again. And she tried not be sucked right in, needing to set some boundaries.

'This is purely because I'm thinking about what the baby

needs. Okay? Nothing else. No funny business. I don't want to find you half-naked on some sofa.' *Or fully naked in my bed.*

'Yes ma'am.' His pupils flared. 'Cheeky sexy baby.'

She ignored his inane comment. God knew why he kept saying it. 'And don't go telling anyone I'm pregnant until I'm back in Atanga Bay, okay? I want to get to twelve weeks before I tell anyone.' *And I need to work out what the heck I'm going to say about the father.* 'I don't want gossip spreading.'

'Okay. Deal. I haven't mentioned it to anyone. Not even Skye.'

'And one more thing…'

'Another condition? Okay, anything for an easy life.'

'I'll come to your flat, but I don't really want to see your folks…not yet. Call me a coward, but we've got a lot to work out before we spread our *happy* news.'

'Coward. Imagine their surprise.' He grinned, but he didn't look remotely like he was looking forward to that adventure. 'They'll have the kindergarten booked and his name down for the best prep school in New Zealand.'

'No, they won't. I'm doing this my way.' It looked like she'd have plenty more big fights to come. A few days' extra rest seemed like a good idea, she needed to amass all her strength. 'Don't even go there.'

Connor pulled out an already dog-eared scan of a grainy tiny blob, and her heart skittered at the sight of it. His parents might not be pleased at the thought of her having Connor's baby, but she couldn't get enough of looking at it.

'Now, here's another look.' He ran his fingers over the black and white image as if it was fragile. 'There wasn't a lot to see, just a flicker of a heartbeat. And he's perfectly formed for dates.'

His eyes glittered with pride and his voice dipped in a reverent tone. He was trying so hard not to care. And failing. If only he could see that and let the love in. Her chest ached with the sadness of it all. Here was a guy who desperately needed to love and be loved, and the only thing holding him back was himself.

But he was certainly putting on a show. The smile he threw her was half-hearted at best. 'Poor kid, spending the rest of his life with a crazy mother.'

And a father who was…where? Hundreds of kilometres away.

She handed the picture back but he propped it on the bedside table facing her. 'You can look at him all you want.'

'Him? He? They can't tell the sex on a six week scan.'

'I know.' His mouth lifted at one corner. 'I just don't like calling our baby *it*. Maybe we should call it Junior or something.'

'But it could be a girl.'

'Yeah. I guess.' Something flickered across his eyes, the pride she'd seen earlier mixed with fear. The guy was scared and couldn't admit it. Where they were headed she didn't dare to think, but they were talking about their child now. That was at least a step in the right direction.

CHAPTER NINE

'M-Mim! M-Mim! W-watch this!'

Mim watched with a sharp ache in her chest as Oakley's face fashioned a lopsided grin. Poor kid. With his chorea, his facial muscles refused to contort into a full smile. But having a body he couldn't control didn't hamper his sense of fun. At his nod Connor spun him a full three-sixty in his wheelchair. The boy finished the turn with a dramatic flourish of his hands. 'Ta-da! Cool, eh?'

'Yeehah!' Mim reached over and high-fived the little boy, whose daily visits to her hospital ward had brightened up the slow days of her recovery. 'Hey, guess what, Oaks?'

'What?' He climbed up onto the bed next to her, staccato movements making a usually simple task quite slow. But she could see a slight improvement. It could take months for the jerky actions to disappear altogether.

She knew he'd be disappointed at her news so she broke it to him as gently as she could. 'The doctors say my head's almost better now.'

'That's a matter of opinion,' Connor whispered, sotto voce, in Oakley's ear. 'I don't think her head's ever going to be right.'

She scowled at him playfully, then flashed Oakley a smile. He'd be more upset at losing Connor's attention than anything else, she guessed.

When Connor hadn't been at her bedside he'd been in Paeds, checking up on his new pal. He'd said he was doing it for her, but she knew he'd become quite fond of the boy.

He might hide behind a steel exterior, but she could see the softening in his eyes, the relaxing of his shoulders, the goofy grin he saved just for Oakley. He'd make a great father, if only he would believe in himself, relax a bit. But always there was that little bit of him that held back.

She lowered her voice, made it more of an apology than a statement. 'Look, Oakley, I'm being discharged today.'

'Going home?' Oakley's smile slipped. 'Lucky, I...I've got to stay a bit l-longer.'

'Actually, I'm going to stay with Connor in town, just for a few days.' She fastened her fingers around the little boy's wrist. 'Maybe you'll be discharged by the time I get back to Atanga Bay.'

'Dunno.' He shrugged, his little shoulders heaving with ennui. In Mim's experience hospitals and seven-year-olds tended not to mix too well. Even though the paediatric department was the best in the country, kids still wanted to be in their own space.

'I know, let's have a race.' Mim felt his hand shake under her grip. 'We both have to work hard at getting better and who ever gets home last buys the ice cream. Biggest ones they have at Mr B's General Store.'

'Okay. I g-guess.' She could see his attention was taken by something out of the corner of his eye. He pointed at her bedside cupboard. 'What's that?'

Mim's stomach plummeted. The baby scan. The last thing to pack. The last thing she wanted anyone but the hospital staff to see. She grabbed it, put it in the top of her handbag. And zippered it away. 'It's...it's...nothing much.'

She threw a confused look at Connor, begging for help. His eyes flashed in mini-panic and his eyebrows rose. His back stiffened, but he leaned in to the boy and explained, 'It's a picture of a tiny baby in someone's tummy. Six weeks old.'

Connor squirmed. He'd opened a can of worms now. He grimaced towards Mim, her eyes bulged back at him. Then she smiled sarcastically as if to say, *Get out of that one, Wiseman.* Did the boy even know that babies came from women's tummies? At what age did you tell them that kind of stuff? He suddenly felt as if he was tiptoeing across a minefield.

Discussing league legends was one thing, but the birds and the bees was another thing altogether. It wasn't his job to tell Oakley.

But it would be his job to tell Junior one day. He was not prepared for man-to-man talks with a seven-year-old. Would he ever be? There was so much he wasn't ready for. First scans, then the birth. Did Mim want him to be there? Did he want to be there? Sure as hell he did. That was one thing he wouldn't want to miss.

Then changing nappies, schooling, puberty. Falling in love with his child. That idea scared the hell out of him.

His future lay before him, uncharted and in enemy territory.

Everything in him was screaming, *Stop!* But he couldn't. He had responsibilities now. And he wouldn't shirk them. Everyone would be expecting him to cope. A doctor, for goodness' sake. And he felt woefully unprepared for each step.

But Connor needn't have been worried. Oakley didn't seem remotely fazed. He stuck out his tongue. 'Yuk. Babies. C'mon, Connor. Do another wh-wh-wheelie.'

'Okay, one more, buddy.' He exhaled. Close call. Thank goodness for a short attention span. And good old seven-year-old male disinterest in anything remotely girly.

So maybe dealing with children wasn't quite as tough as he'd believed. Maybe it was a case of just easing into it. Not analysing it so much. *Saturation therapy?* It had worked a treat with Oakley. Maybe spending time with his own kid would be just as easy.

He could only hope, but with his track record of relationships he wasn't convinced.

He grabbed the wheelchair and spun it round. 'Then back to the ward for your antibiotics, my man. Say goodbye to Mim.'

He turned to look at her, feeling the connection that always pulled him to her, like a force field. Glad she'd agreed to the only sensible option of coming to recuperate at his place, but scared as hell at how he'd cope with her in his space again.

'Bye, Mim. See ya.'

'Sure. Hurry up and get better soon.' Mim waved them away with a lump in her throat. Damn these hormones, making her weepy at the slightest thing. An unlikely pair, the new BFFs. The smart and trendy city doctor and the country waif.

But gone was Oakley, her buffer, back to the paediatric ward. He'd unwittingly been a diversion for Connor and herself that had stopped them getting too intimate, too intense.

But soon Connor would be back with her meds, then whisking her off to his apartment. How the hell she'd ever agreed to that she didn't know. It was folly and stupid and would open a thousand wants and wounds she would never be able to close.

She drew in a deep breath, filling her lungs with the soothing scent of the fading lilies. Trying to draw strength from this moment of serenity. Trying to work out how she was going to act, to survive the next few days with Connor, with so much they needed to discuss. And so much zinging between them that could never be fulfilled. Before she was discharged into enforced proximity with the one person she knew she should be avoiding at all costs.

* * *

The shower was utter bliss. Hot water cascaded down Mim's back as she relished the uninterrupted flow through her hair. Just to have the privacy of a locked door and no time limit was healing in itself.

Connor's bathroom was divine in his masculine minimalistic way. Not what she'd have chosen, but she could appreciate the quality of the high-end fixtures. Dark mahogany and chrome that shone so pristinely she could see her reflection. His new Albert Street apartment, with floor-to-ceiling windows and breathtaking views of the business district and glittering Hauraki Gulf, must have cost three times her surgery mortgage. It had an expensive designer edge and a luxurious feel. But it wasn't home.

It wasn't her cosy apartment where people popped by without an invitation. Where she knew every face, breathed in fresh, unpolluted air, where there was birdsong and peace. The sound of waves crashing onto the shore. The sound of nothing, of silence and peace. Not traffic hum and car horns.

'Mim? You okay in there? I got your peanut butter and gherkins. Are you sure you want to eat something so gross?'

'Thanks.' *Not at all.* But it had been the only way to get him out of her space for a few minutes. She'd needed time to breathe, where his body wasn't in full view. Where she didn't have to fight against the urge to lean into him. It was bad enough being enveloped in his smell, which pervaded every corner of his apartment, without spending every waking moment fighting temptation.

So she'd given him a dubious shopping list and sent him out.

She rinsed off the conditioner, flicked off the tap and smiled away her frustration. Now she just had to put on a brave face and eat the darned stuff without throwing up. And somehow survive the next few days without reaching for him. 'I won't be a minute. Just getting out of the shower.'

'That chair work okay for you?'

His voice from the other side of the door was loaded with touching concern. For some lucky woman he'd make a wonderful husband. Just not her.

She shivered as water trickled down her back. 'Sure, great idea putting something in the shower for me to sit on. Although I do feel a bit like my Nan.'

'No way, princess. Just being safe. Are you decent? I think I left my phone in there.'

'Princess? Since when was I your princess?'

'Slip of the tongue.' He sounded suitably chastised.

She wrapped a thick fluffy stone-coloured towel round her body and opened the door to him, handing him his phone, which beeped every three seconds. Reminding her of how very important he was and what a busy life he had. Here.

He'd had a shave and changed out of his scrubs. Another snug-fitting black T clung to his sculpted muscles and left little to her imagination. Strong, capable arms that could pull her to him in an instant. Tiny blond hairs running down his forearms that demanded to be stroked. Grey designer jeans slicked over his thighs.

Thighs she wanted to touch, to press against her again like the night they'd danced together. But that had got her into this difficult situation in the first place. It would be very unwise to go down that path again.

Being here was such a bad idea.

He held out two huge jars. 'I didn't know how much you wanted so I got man-sized stuff.'

'Maybe I'll eat later. Suddenly I'm not hungry.' Her mouth dried. She diverted her gaze. Staring at him only made her wish for what she couldn't have. 'I'll go and dry my hair.'

'Okay. This whole pregnancy and food thing has me really confused. Let me know when you're hungry again, and I'll make you something.' He smiled and she could feel his gaze wander down her towel-clad body. 'Good look you have there.'

'Sure beats those hospital nighties. And it was great to be able to clean my teeth properly.' She'd made him stop en route and buy an electric toothbrush and essentials. 'Even if the buzzing hammers into my head. I do not like furry teeth.'

'Oh, yes.' He grinned and shook his head. Playful streaks flashed from his eyes. 'That was an interesting escapade. Trying to clean your teeth. Luckily I got out of the way before you chundered on my feet, that time at least. You are a very messy vomiter.'

'Gosh, I'm sorry.' Vague memories of throwing up on him a couple of times in the hospital flitted through her head. She looked down at her towel. 'And you must have undressed me, or was it the nurses?'

'Er…me.' His mouth kinked up at one side in his boyish grin. 'Three or four times over two days. That has to be a record, even for me. Would have been more fun if you'd been even semi-conscious but, hey. Who's complaining?'

'Connor!' She tightened the towel around the ever-growing cleavage that she hadn't quite got used to yet. Would she ever? He seemed rather distracted by it too. Her cheeks burned. 'Wipe all memory of my naked body from your mind. Now.'

'After that much vomit, believe me, I was not thinking about sex.'

The air around them stilled the second he mentioned sex. An electrical charge zipped between their eyes. She tried to look away, but couldn't drag her gaze from his face. His features softened, his mouth opened a fraction as his breathing quickened.

Then he was over the threshold, closing in. Her brain made a token effort at moving away, but her feet refused to budge.

He wiped a drip of water snaking down the side of her cheek, then tiptoed his fingers down her shoulder in feathery strokes. Her ragged breathing matched his as his fingers stepped along her clavicle towards her breast, and teased at the edge of her towel. 'But I can now if you want. Pregnancy suits you.'

'Connor.' She kept her voice level, with a warning tone, reality finally hitting home. They'd agreed on a plan of action and keeping her distance from him was the only way to get through the next few days. 'I don't think that would be a good idea.'

'Oh, I've had worse ideas.' His mouth was inches from hers. All she had to do was reach up and cover it with hers. Easy. His lips seemed to fill her vision as he spoke. 'Much much worse. You sure you still want to sleep in the spare room? Plenty of space in mine.'

'No. We promised. You promised.' No naked romps in his fabulous king-sized wrought-iron bed.

She held his gaze as her nipples reacted to the feather touches at the top of her breast. Her stomach contracted in a savage need for him to touch her lower, and lower. To kiss her, take her and fill her. She clutched the towel tighter, keeping her eyes fixed on his. The onyx burned, captivating her, mirroring the raw desire that engulfed her.

This wasn't a flirty fling, this was real and intense. And dangerous. Every minute she spent with him, every second, confused her, addled her brain. Pressed her for answers she didn't have. All she knew was the tangible loss she felt when he wasn't around, and the relief at his closeness. How being in his arms felt like coming home.

But being in his apartment didn't. 'Connor. We can't. Please don't do this.'

Connor closed his eyes just to get rid of the vision in front of him. A Herculean effort. After seeing her so vulnerable in the hospital something inside him had clicked into place. He'd seen her at her most weak, cleared up the detritus of her spent body, but nothing had dampened down the ache he had to be inside her. But it was more than that. He wanted to protect her and the baby. And he wanted so much more. Things he knew he couldn't have. She was right. They couldn't take this to another level.

He took a step right back out of the bathroom. 'I know, sorry. It's just you look so damned kissable standing there. Can't blame a guy for asking.'

'This isn't for real, Connor. I have a perfectly good apartment of my own, ninety minutes away in a different world. This is make-believe and temporary. Very temporary.'

'Got you.' He gave his head a minuscule nod then turned and headed off to the kitchen, giving them both all the space they needed.

Mim stalked to her bedroom on wobbly legs and closed the door, willing the burning on her cheeks to subside. She didn't know if she could do this. Be in the same confined space as him for a few days, with her body thrumming and responding to him in such a way. Everything about him infuriated her. But drove her wild with need too.

A loud knocking had her gasping in a shuddering breath. She leant against the door, ran her fingers over the wood. No veneer here, not like her home. This was the real deal. And so was Connor. She pressed her ear against the cooling frame and called to him, 'I'm busy, Connor.'

'Okay. I know. Don't worry I won't ravish you, I get the message loud and clear. And I wholeheartedly agree. But I got you a surprise. Hope you feel up to it. It's in two days.' He pushed a white envelope under the door. 'The Russian Ballet is doing *Cinderella* at The Civic. I know it's not salsa, but I thought you'd like to go.'

Yes! Connor and the ballet? In the same place, at the same time?

She gathered her composure. 'You don't give up, do you? Us? A date? I thought we'd just agreed...?'

'Not a date.' His voice was firm on that. 'But you are sharing my flat, my food and my water, so I didn't think you'd mind sharing a night out. I've never been to a ballet and I might need some help with translation.'

'What about your work? I don't want you to get behind because of me. Don't you have a lot of catching up to do?'

'It can wait one more night...' She could hear his ragged breathing as he paused. A difficult silence hovered between them. He knocked again, this time more lightly. 'Mim? We can't be at loggerheads for ever. It's not good for us or the baby. Besides, I thought you liked dance.'

'I do.'

'I could ask the theatre to seat us in separate rows if you like.'

'Okay, okay.'

'Okay, you'll come?' His words were tinged with laughter and relief. She liked it that he was so easy to please at times. 'Or okay to the separate rows?'

She laughed along with him. Looking after a vomiting pregnant head case must have been hard on him, as would having the same pregnant woman as a house guest. She determined to be more easygoing on him.

And he was right, they needed some fun, pure non-sexual fun, a new level on which to base their future. She couldn't remember the last time she'd been to the theatre or to see a ballet. Or out in a vibrant city with a single man. 'Either. Although it might be hard to translate if we're at opposite ends of the theatre. And I'll pay for my ticket. No arguments.'

'But it's a gift.'

'Connor, I can't take any more from you. You've done enough.' She ran her hand across her stomach. *Way too much. And I don't have the strength to keep fighting.*

CHAPTER TEN

CONNOR scanned the spreadsheets in front of him, did more maths. Shook his head.

He looked at the proposed fifth phase of the Dana's Drop-In assessment and felt the thud of his heart, as slow as a dirge. Mim's practice was going to fail the assessment. Which would mean no extra funding, no development.

Whichever way he looked at it, there was no salvaging this.

He thought of Oakley, and Tommo. Of the goth and Tony. And the rest of the community. Where would they be without Dana's Drop-In? Most of all he thought about Mim, and how her dream was crumbling.

He'd analysed and shuffled the numbers, tried ticking boxes that were on the cusp of passing, but in his heart of hearts he couldn't pass a practice that wasn't up to the mark. Not even Mim's.

Dammit. This was one side of his job he hated but there was no way he could sugar-coat the news.

He'd tell her soon. Tonight. After the ballet. The thud of his heart resonated against his chest. She'd be here in ten minutes. Ten minutes to work out how to soften the blow.

It was his job, after all, and sometimes, as his father said, it had to be dirty.

Mim's face floated in front of Connor. Distracting him again from his work. He'd only been away from her for a few hours. Lunch, to be precise. And yet the mango smell and the image of her slick naked body wrapped in his towel lingered with him wherever he went. Damned woman. Got him wrapped around her twirly finger and then some. And now, due to their future offspring, they'd be inextricably in contact for ever.

Although their relationship would be tinged with the fact that it was he who had stalled her business plans. Stalled? Squashed.

'Am I interrupting anything?' Mim stood in front of him, her eyes glowing in curiosity.

'Er…no. Just finishing up.' *Just working out the gentlest way to break your heart.* He scraped a hand over his hair. Waited for his raging heart rate to slow. It didn't. He tried not to stare at the amazing vision in front of him. 'Wow.'

'You like it?'

'You bet.' She'd pulled her hair into some kind of side parting thing, covering up her shaved patch. Her eyes glittered with shimmery make-up and her lips shone with gloss. Kissable. He wanted to lick it off her mouth.

Her cheeks glowed, fresh and plump. Her cleavage was thick and creamy. She was starting to blossom, like all the maternity books talked about. She looked ripe and ready for… being a friend.

He concentrated on dampening down his body's visceral reaction. But he doubted it was humanly possible not to be turned on by her.

She twirled in her kitten heels and soft silk dress that skimmed her knees, and was the colour of a hazy summer sky. 'I went shopping. Guilty pleasure, I know. I have so little cash, but the shops have so many nice things here compared to Atanga Bay Fashions.'

'Yeah, I've seen Atanga Bay Fashions' window display. They still have Crimplene and flares.' Suddenly he wanted to whip out his credit card and buy her every damned dress in the city. And the shoes, and anything else she wanted. But she couldn't be bought. Any man had to earn her trust. He'd learnt that to his cost.

She was incredible—what woman wouldn't let a man buy her things?

But she was nursing a legacy of a mother who'd let men dictate her life. And he knew she wouldn't allow that. Whatever happened to compromise? He was walking on slippery ice. One false move and she'd be gone. One failed assessment and she'd be gone. Either way he lost. 'How's your head? Chest? Baby?'

'Better. Okay. Great.' She ticked off on her fingers and flashed a smile that warmed his heart. 'Especially the baby bit.'

The internal phone buzzed, dragging his attention away. 'Connor Wiseman.'

'Ah. The wanderer finally returns.'

Connor's fingers curled tightly around the handset. His father's clear, clipped tones irritated him even down the phone line. He turned his back to Mim and lowered his voice. This was private and not something she needed to witness. He prayed his dad wouldn't bring up the subject of the Dana's Drop-In report. 'Father.'

'The three-year business plan. I've been waiting for it for two weeks.'

'I've been busy.' Busy impregnating a *no-hope do-goody misfit*. That's what his father had called her way back when. How would Wiseman Senior react if he knew his son was spending time with her again? That she was carrying the next generation of Wisemans? It was unexplainable. And almost laughable. 'I'll get onto it as soon as I can.'

'What's all this nonsense about you putting a coffee machine in Reception? For clients? Ridiculous. Caffeine makes them jumpy and demanding. It's going to cost us a fortune.'

'Simmer down, Father. You'll have a coronary. It's good business practice to make people feel at home.' He swallowed his irritated laugh, imagining his father serving coffee in the slick reception area. Trying not to think too hard about Mim's cosy, ramshackle clinic in stark contrast to their cold intimidating monochrome one. 'It makes it look more homely.'

He glanced over at Mim, whose eyebrows peaked in question. He winked at her and imagined sinking his mouth onto that shimmery pout.

Instead he had to endure his father's monotone. 'We don't need homely. We need efficient. Homely won't make you a better administrator. Now, tell me what was suddenly so important that you had to dip under the radar for a week?'

'Nothing to worry about. I'm back now.'

Why bother even explaining? His father wouldn't understand. He hadn't missed a day's work in fifty years, had barely managed a half-day off for his daughter's funeral. And since that day he had poured all his grief and sorrow into work, ignoring his remaining family in the process.

And that had left Connor's mum to endure her grief stoically, watching the relationship between her husband and her son disintegrate and acting as mediator between the two people she loved. She deserved so much more. They all did.

And yet all his life Connor had striven to be like his father. Successful. Steadfast. *Forgiven.*

He breathed that thought away. His father would never forgive him.

'Next time book it in advance. I don't like to be kept waiting.' His father's deep, rumbling voice rose slightly and Connor could feel the anger rippling through the wires. 'Get that plan on my desk by tomorrow morning, Connor.'

Which would mean pulling another all-nighter and letting

Mim go to the ballet on her own. He couldn't do that to her. Frustration wormed into his gut. He was damned if he was going to end up like his father, with no meaningful relationships. *Like hell*. One thing he knew, he wanted to be involved in his child's life. And Mim's—somehow. He wanted to have a life. The whole package. The ups and downs, the tragedy and the glory, the highs and the lows.

He just hadn't worked out how. 'I have plans for tonight. I'm going out. It's important.'

Mim watched as Connor spoke to his father, his cheek muscle twitching. Clearly something serious was unfolding. Her heart jackhammered. From what he'd said, he'd always had a sticky relationship with his dad.

She felt the sting of regret burning into her heart. If only she'd stayed all those years ago. Or at least talked to him. Explained. Maybe she could have smoothed things over with them. For the first time she realised her actions hadn't just been about self-protection, they'd been selfish.

At some point, too, he'd have to tell his parents about the baby, and face the embarrassment of getting his ex pregnant. The girl they had been relieved to see the back of—now here, with a baby, to haunt them for the rest of their days. She wondered how badly her disappearance had reflected on Connor.

'Don't disappoint you?' Connor turned his back to her again, his shoulders tightened against his cotton shirt. 'What, again? I'm trying to strike a balance here. You and I are way off kilter. We're both trained doctors who spend every waking hour shuffling bits of paper. We could be out there saving lives. Making a difference. Living a good life. But we're not. We live in the past, chasing ghosts. The only person I'm disappointing is me.'

Mim's stomach churned. She bit her lip to keep her retort in. How could Connor disappoint anyone? He was dedicated, determined and successful. Anyone would be proud to have him in their lives. Only his father couldn't see it.

This was a battle she couldn't win, but it didn't stop anger shivering through her. A new kind of pain, this one. Taking Connor's hurt to somewhere deep inside her.

Connor's voice was even and assured. 'I'm going to the ballet with Mim McCarthy. Yes.' The pause filled the room like a pressure valve waiting to explode. '*That* Mim.'

To hell with this. He was sick of his father's attitude, his unwillingness to bend, to reach out. He didn't want to be like that, he wanted to care, not to be afraid. To be a father his child would be proud of.

'Mim and I are having a baby. We have things to work out. It's a lot to take in, I know. Now, go home. Talk to Mum. Kiss her, Dad. Look after her. She needs you. Then think of the future, how you're going to be a grandfather and how that might work out for you.'

He put the phone back in its cradle and turned to find Mim staring at him, her eyes brimming with tears and her hands shaking. 'Connor...are you okay?'

'Sure. I should have done that years ago.' But he had lacked the strength. He'd found it now, in his unborn child and the woman who carried it.

For the first time in years he could breathe. Deeply. It was time to look forward.

Mim's glossy lips formed words and he tried to focus on what she was saying rather than watch her mouth move and ache to touch it. 'You didn't need to tell him about the baby. It could have waited.'

'Yes, I did, Mim. I'm proud of what's happened, not embarrassed. You're having my child and that's okay. More than okay. I don't know what we're going to do, it's crazy as hell. But we'll work it out. Come on, let's get out of here.'

When they reached the city street and cool air slammed

into them, he pulled her to him, feeling her soft body against his, inhaled her scent and focused again on her mouth. He plunged his hands into her hair, knowing that all the promises they'd made were lost. As lost as he was under the gaze of those intoxicating eyes.

He'd cut ties with his father, blown the spell of his guilt into the ether, and was floating rudderless against a storm of desire. Yet never had he felt so alive. 'I've been needing to do this too.'

He pressed his mouth on hers, felt the slight tensing of her back, then the relaxation as she opened her mouth and let him in. Her tongue licked against his, sending shots of heat through him.

She tasted of strawberry gloss and honey ice cream.

He licked the corner of her mouth, her cheek, in small tiny circles, back to her lips, her tongue, her teeth. She tasted of freedom and chaos. Of an uncontrollable desire that raged through him. She tasted of vanilla and fresh air, of the bustling city night and her beloved Atanga Bay. And always, always mango.

He pulled her into a dark alleyway next to his building, pushed her up against the hard wall. All his senses were heightened, the taste of her, the taut arch of her body as she fitted herself perfectly into his arms, the cold clash of chrome cladding against his skin.

His hands ran over the silk of her dress, sliding easily up her thigh. Then up her hard stomach to feel the full swell of her breast, the tightness of her nipple.

God knew what the hell they were doing. But it felt so right. They had so much to thrash out, so much chaos to tame, and the only rational thing to do was to kiss her in the dark until he'd had his fill.

But somewhere a clock struck the hour. He managed to drag himself away from her perfect mouth. The gloss gone, leaving only a trace of their combined taste and a heated smudge across her lips.

He ran a thumb along her bottom lip. 'Should we skip *Cinderella*? Or do you fancy a quickie?'

'Your charm needs serious work.' She bit down on his thumb, wriggling her hips against his hardness. 'But it's very tempting.'

Then she tiptoed her fingers down from his collar to his waistband, where she played with his belt, sending more arrows of need shooting through him.

He grabbed her wrist and held it over his zipper. 'Just a bit lower?'

'Hmm. Now, that might be illegal in such a public place.'

'Can't think of a better reason to get arrested, can you?'

'I'll ignore that.' She pushed him away, gently. 'It's such a lovely ballet, shame to miss it. So romantic and dramatic. Imagine how we'll be after seeing all that unleashed passion.'

He let her hand drop and rested his forehead against hers, felt every breath shudder through her as she too struggled for control. 'Okay, we should go, I suppose. Besides, the tickets did cost a bomb.'

'Please, please stop with the charm offensive.' Her laughter was like tiny snowflakes over heat. A soft balm, cooling and delicious as she slipped her hand into his. 'Come on. Let's have some fun.'

CHAPTER ELEVEN

'IT's exactly like I remember.' Mim sat in the theatre stalls, clutching her empty vanilla ice-cream tub, and watched the theatregoers file in wearing evening gowns and finery. As she looked up at the ceiling, a childish sparkle bubbled in her stomach.

A thousand shimmering stars lit up the roof. Every now and again a shooting star skidded across the painted inky blue sky. Someone had brought the night sky inside against a backdrop of minarets and turrets. The auditorium had been designed around a Moorish theme. A fairy-tale setting for a fairy-tale ballet.

'So you've been here before?' Connor wrapped his arm around her shoulders, pulling her closer into his heat.

Her first response was to pull away, to put up the barriers between them again. The kiss had been a mistake. A heavenly, sexy mistake; when she was with Connor she made such bad choices.

But she let her head rest on his shoulder, for once allowing herself to relax. This was indeed a fairy-tale and, like all stories, it would come to an end very soon. Just for tonight she could pretend. Soon enough she'd be back to fixing roofs and completing her Matrix assessment.

'My mum brought me once to see Swan Lake. She liked the sad ones best, loved the drama, the futile martyrdom, and she always cried at the swan who died of a broken heart. It was a big deal to come down from the country for the matinee.'

It had been a big deal, full stop. Coming into the city had been a thrill. Her mother had been sober for a few weeks and Mim had basked in her attention, believing her fairy-tale childhood was just beginning, albeit off to a late start. 'When we got home we stayed up late, put on her Great Ballet Favourites record and danced all the parts. She let me stand on her feet and she swirled around. She loved the ballet, the stories of love conquering all. She was an incurable romantic.'

'And you?'

'Oh, yes, sure. Look at me, knocked up by an ex, with a collapsing building complete with sunroof.' She twisted to look at him and pointed to her belly, which still showed no trace of their baby. Flashed him a smile that she hoped would tell him she wasn't being overly serious. 'Living the dream.'

'Hey, I have queues of women wanting to be knocked up by me.'

'The only women in queues around here are the purple-rinse brigade.'

'I attract all types. Just wait. We'll be mobbed outside.'

'And I'm meant to be thankful?' She laughed. 'In your dreams, mate.'

'One day.' He squeezed her against him and she curled into the thick heat of him in his fancy suit. 'So then what happened? After the dancing? Did you get to come down here again?'

'Oh, no. It was just one night. One lovely night. Then life was just back to same old Atanga Bay normality.'

Her lungs heaved against her healing chest. After that one night of joy her mother had found her way back to the bottle, then to the drugs that had stolen her happiness and soured Mim's life.

Reality with her mother had knocked the corners off her

dreams. 'But at least I'll be back there soon. And by all accounts, Skye's been working like a demon on phase five, so we're not far away from securing the funding, and things will look much better for me and the baby.'

'Mim…I need to talk to you about—'

She placed a finger against his lips. His frown made him look sad. Maybe she'd shared too much with him already. She didn't want her sordid past to ruin their night out. This was off-limits stuff that she shared with no one. For the first time ever, she'd opened up. But was regretting it already. Too much pain, too much hurt, too much to remember. And she wanted to forget.

She didn't want his sympathy or pity—she wanted to live the fairy-tale. In a spectacular theatre with the sexiest man alive, listening to fabulous music and watching perfect body forms. Anything else could wait. 'Hush, it's starting.'

The curtain rose and the music began, whisking her away to a fantasy land she could believe in for a few hours.

All too soon the interval came round and they shuffled out into the crowded foyer. Clusters of theatregoers pressed into the bar, and Connor went to buy drinks.

'Lucky I know the story or I wouldn't have a clue. It's complicated when you add dancing in.' Connor handed her a glass of lemonade. 'And what's with the tights?'

She glowered at him. 'Typical guy. I guess it makes the dancing easier.'

He shrugged. 'I just thought he was showing off. I'd wear tights too if I was that well endowed.'

'You mean you're not? How disappointing.'

'Hush. Don't ruin my reputation.' He laughed, leaned in close and whispered in her ear. His breath skimmed her neck like a soft breeze. 'Anyway, you weren't disappointed a few weeks ago. How about we try it again soon, just to make sure?'

'I'll be very disappointed if I find out it's all just codpiece, like the male lead.'

'I won't disappoint you, Mim. Ever. I promise. Not at all.' He kissed a trail up the curve of her neck, sending shivers of desire through her. She couldn't deny it any longer. She wanted him more and more.

Seeing him argue with his father had activated some dark force in her. She loved that passion in him, that determination, the virile, urgent need for action. His protection and declaration of their pregnancy. She loved the way he'd looked after her. Had brought her food, given her this gift tonight. She loved the way he tasted, how he felt when he filled her.

She loved… She loved him.

No. No. No. Blood rushed to her face. The revelation shocked her. Frightened her. She wasn't supposed to fall in love with him. She couldn't let him worm his way back into her heart. Couldn't let him squash everything she'd worked so hard for.

Would he?

Right now he was treating her like the princess he called her. Carefully, with grace and delicacy.

But that was because she was carrying his child. He'd made no attempt to compromise, to work out any solutions or even talked about a future. They'd failed before, so why would now be any different? They still had separate careers in separate places, different ideals.

And he damn well hadn't mentioned love either.

So where did that leave her? Spiralling out of control faster than a hurricane. And with no way out.

Suddenly the theatre seemed claustrophobic. Being here with him seemed too cosy, too picture perfect. She needed fresh air. Space. 'My headache's coming back. I think I'll go home… Oh!'

Out of the corner of her eye Mim caught a quick movement, but Connor raced across the room like a shot. She caught up with him kneeling beside an elderly man who had collapsed on the floor.

'Keep back. Give us some room, please.' Mim cleared a space as front-of-house staff rang the bell to return to the auditorium. For a split second she watched the audience return to their seats and wished she could go back to the fairytale. But duty tugged at her. Connor needed her too. 'Is he breathing? A pulse?'

'Hello? Can you hear me?' Connor watched the erratic rise and fall of the man's chest, felt for a pulse along his floppy right wrist. 'Disordered. I'd say he's in atrial fibrillation. We need an ambulance, quick.'

The man's eyes flickered open and he stared up at them with a glazed expression. He seemed awake but not present. He thrashed around with his left hand, felt his forehead and tapped at blood on his cheek. His lips moved, but he managed only strange noises.

'You fell over, mate. Easy does it, Best to stay lying down for a minute. You cut your cheek too but it's not too bad. I'll mop it up. Don't worry.' Mim spoke as gently as she could, wiping the blood away with a tissue. The man's watery eyes screamed of panic. 'Please don't worry. We're both doctors. We'll get you sorted.'

'Is there anyone here with him? A wife? A friend?' Connor asked the stragglers, who looked on with sympathy at the old man in the saggy brown overcoat and bird's-nest hair. They all shrugged. Connor removed his jacket and put it under the man's head. 'Don't move him.'

'What's your name?' Mim knelt and asked their patient again. 'I'm going to check your pockets to see if there's anything with your name on.'

The man just kept on staring up at her, his pale eyes boring into her.

'Can you tell me your name?' She fished in his pocket, found a wallet. 'John Wilkinson? Are you called John? And, oh, a prescription for…an ACE inhibitor. John, have you got high blood pressure?'

He didn't respond. But his left hand closed around her wrist. He was trying to communicate, but couldn't. She couldn't imagine the hell of being in a prison of silence, not being able to speak or be heard.

'I know it's frustrating and scary, but we're here to help you.'

'Looks like he's had a CVA. He's confused, in AF, and has a right hemiparesis. He's using his left hand, but his right is flaccid.' Connor completed his assessment then turned to a staff member. 'I think he's having a stroke.'

He watched as Mim touched the man's cheek, held his hand and muttered soft words to him to try to calm him down while they waited for the ambulance. Strokes were often caused by escalating and dangerously high blood pressure so letting him get more worked up wouldn't help.

Frustration ripped through him. 'Wish I had my stethoscope, I could at least monitor his BP.' Their patient's pulse was all over the place and a theatre was no place for an emergency.

The man's long, bony fingers trembled as he clung to Mim's wrist. Connor thought he looked about the same age as his father. Shockingly similar build. And with no one.

Connor felt despair mingle with frustration. Why was this old man on his own? Cruel to be alone during such a loss of control.

The paramedic crew arrived and assisted John onto a stretcher. Connor vacillated on the step of the ambulance. He felt torn. This lonely old guy was going to hospital on his own. Who knew where or who his next of kin were?

And Mim stood looking up at him, shivering in the cool

night air. Shadows edged her eyes and she'd been eerily quiet since John's collapse. He needed to get her home. And brave the subject of the failed Matrix assessment when she was feeling better.

'I should go with him, but I want to get you home. You look worn out.'

'I can manage. I'll be fine on my own. Please, go with him.'

One of the AOs stepped in. 'Just found a mobile in his coat pocket. We've contacted his son, he's meeting us at the ER. We'll take it from here. Thanks for your help.'

'No worries.' Connor took Mim's hand and walked her slowly towards home. 'Poor guy. He reminded me of my dad.'

Mim leaned against him as they walked. Still shaken from her realisation. She loved him. For all the good it would do her. In her head she was packing already, but her heart wanted to fix itself firmly to Connor. Especially after an emergency that seemed to have affected him so much. His shoulders hunched slightly forward and his profile, in the streetlight, was stretched and tight. 'He did look a bit like him, I guess. From what I remember.'

'But he looked so scared. Only once have I seen eyes so terrified.' His voice cracked. 'And that was the day we buried Janey. I watched my father crumble, knowing I'd done that to him.'

'You didn't do that.' She inhaled sharply. Connor had never spoken about this before, no matter how hard she'd pushed him to open up. 'Connor...did you?'

Connor cursed inwardly. He'd already said too much. She stared up at him as if needing to understand. And he needed to explain. Needed to tell her. But he didn't know how to find the words. The hurt seemed to block his thought processes.

'I did, Mim. At least I thought it was my fault. For a long time.'

She cupped his cheek with a gentle hand and pulled him to

sit on the steps outside his apartment. 'Tell me about Janey. Whatever it is that's haunting you. Trust me, please. I want to help.'

'And then what?' Could he trust her? He thought so. Maybe now after everything they'd shared he could trust her enough with his hurt.

'Then we work through it.' She took his hand in both of hers. A streetlight shimmered above them, illuminating her. She looked the most fervent, the most concerned, the most beautiful thing he'd ever seen.

And every part of him ached to unburden itself. To tell his side. To share with her what he'd been carrying around and had closed off from everyone. The reason he'd nailed armour plating to his heart. Maybe then she'd understand his reluctance to give anything out.

'I was there when Janey died. At the hospital.'

'That must have been so hard for you.'

Memories swung him back to the ER room where he'd watched them work on his precious little sister. 'We were on holiday. She fell from her horse. Broke her arm. That's all it had been. Nothing more than a silly fall.'

'An easy fix that went wrong somehow?' She nodded softly and slipped her small hand into his fist, and he forced his words out through a throat thick with tears. He'd never told anyone this before. Apart from at the inquest. He'd thought he'd dealt with it. But in reality he'd been too scared to live through it again. In case he was too weak to survive it a second time. But with Mim here anything felt possible. 'I'm sorry I didn't tell you before.'

'It's okay. Better late than never. You're doing it now.'

His throat ached with the pressure of the words. His chest stuttered as he forced them out. But he couldn't look at her. He had to get through this without seeing the pity in her eyes.

He fixed his focus on a piece of old gum on the pavement.

'It was a busy Saturday evening in a back-of-beyond hospital. An overworked, harassed intern and a brand-new nurse, just out of training school. Janey was in pain and I begged them for some meds. The doctor drew up the drug and I waited for them to cross-check.'

He hauled in oxygen. 'Janey started crying again, and I hurried them along. All I wanted was for the pain to go. But they still didn't cross-check. Why not? Why didn't they cross-check? That's what everyone does. It's protocol instilled in every hospital.'

The sooner it was all out, the sooner he'd be able to steady his composure. He fisted his hands, his nails drawing blood. 'And I didn't ask them to. But I was only a first-year medical student. He was a senior doctor. I just didn't have the guts to say anything. I stood there, gutless and stupid, and instead of speaking up for my sister I watched them inject ten times the prescribed dose of painkiller into her arm.'

As his sister's life had drained away, so had his belief in the very system he'd been working in. His belief in love. His belief in himself. It had taken ten years to see even a flicker of hope.

He dropped Mim's hand. He couldn't handle any kind of physical connection. He gulped air but felt like he was choking.

'Connor. It's okay. I understand now. The protocols, the routines. All your rules. The reason you hold everyone at a distance. I understand. I do.'

'Good job you do. My father still holds me responsible. He's never actually said it, but I can see it in his eyes.' He needed to be on his own. That's what he always did. It was safer that way. No one to hurt but himself. He headed up the steps.

'Connor. Stop.' Her voice was sharp now. 'Connor. Come back to me. I said stop!'

He stopped in his tracks. Pivoted back. Saw her with her arms stretched out to him. Something fundamental had changed between them. She understood his pain. Hadn't judged. If he went to her now, there'd be no turning back.

He faltered only for a second, then nothing could stop him going into her arms.

She reached around his neck and pressed close. 'It wasn't your fault.'

He huffed out a breath. It felt good to be in her heat. To say the words that had choked him for so long. 'I know now. But it felt like it at the time.'

Mim's heart was breaking for the man she loved. For as long as she'd known him she'd had the impression he was holding something back. But now, finally, he'd let her in. Let her glimpse the tragedy he'd endured. She imagined the young man bound by hierarchy, losing someone he loved so much. Tears pricked her eyes.

As he swiped the keycard in the apartment-block door she pulled him closer, right there on the pavement. Tried to infuse all the love she had into him. She ached to wipe away his sadness.

He reached round her waist and hugged her close, rested his chin on her head and held onto her like she was his salvation.

She didn't speak, because there were no words to compensate for the loss of a loved one. She knew that well enough. How long they stood in silence on the dark city street she didn't know. Many times she heard his raspy intake of breath. Many times she felt him shift as he nuzzled her hair, the solid beat of his heart as it normalised.

And then suddenly it quickened again. Like the crackle of static, the swift metallic tang in the air a moment before a storm, the tender hug became more. His hands moved up her back, heating her skin. Prickles of awareness fired deep into her belly. Every part of her came alive and sensitised, and desperate for his touch. In a feral reaction she pulsed against him, relishing his hardness pushing between them.

He pulled her closer, molded himself to her, and she didn't argue, didn't move away, even though she knew she should. Even though she knew that she would be lost again with him. But better that than lost without him.

She wanted to feel unburdened skin on skin. To free her body of the clothes that constrained her, and free her mind of the barriers she'd built. One more time she'd surrender control to this need that burnt deep inside her. One more time.

Tomorrow she would go back to Atanga Bay, to her people, to her life. It was the only possible option she had. But tonight was theirs. The whole darned fairy-tale.

When he lifted his chin from her hair she tilted her head a fraction toward him. His breathing was ragged as he gazed down at her with burning desire in his eyes. Then his mouth was on hers, the graze of his stubble a brand she wanted to wear for ever.

And she tasted him, exploring his mouth, so familiar. So Connor. So utterly dangerous.

He pulled at the opening of her dress, slipped his hand onto her bra, running feather-light touches across her hardened nipples.

When he took his mouth from hers and slicked a trail across her neck she managed to find her voice. 'I think we'd better go inside.' Had it been hers? It hadn't sounded like her. It had sounded like a wanton hussy craving hot sex.

'Why? Don't fancy getting arrested?' He pressed against her again, and she ached to feel him deep inside her. She couldn't wait. Couldn't imagine anything but Connor. Couldn't see or hear anything but Connor and his kisses and his touch.

He cupped the back of her neck and planted hard kisses on

her lips until they burnt and ached for more. Then he breathed into her ear, 'Because right now, I wouldn't care.'

From somewhere along the street she heard a woman laugh, the crunch of stiletto on gravel. 'No. There's that queue forming. And I need to see your codpiece.' She giggled, took his hand and pulled him into the lift.

'Up?'

'All the way.' He jabbed the penthouse button and leaned her against the mirrored wall. Writhed against her as he ripped the top of her dress open and palmed her breasts. Felt the silky-smooth skin under his hardened skin. He'd laid his soul bare and she hadn't shunned him. The world hadn't ended. Instead, she'd offered herself to him, and he was going to take her.

'Connor. Oh, Connor.' She could barely speak, but each word sent him into a vortex of desire.

'Yes. Mim. God, you drive me crazy.' His teeth tweaked her nipple, then he sucked it, the hard bud peaking under his tongue, firing sensation after sensation through him.

'Connor, you don't live in the penthouse.'

'Hell, woman. Stop talking. I just wanted to take my time. The fun's all in the anticipation.' He sucked in a breath, his abdominal muscles twitching under her caress. He wanted to plunge into her, to possess her. Again and again.

'Then you're not doing it right.'

'Oh, but I am.' His fingers were on her thighs now, stepping closer and closer to her panties. She squirmed as he edged the lace to one side and slid a finger deep into her wetness, ripping his breath away as she tightened and bucked around him. 'Slowly, Mim.'

'Slowly? Like hell. We're on a time limit here.' She rubbed her hand against the swell of his erection, pulled down his zipper and stroked the length of him. 'Lift sex?'

'If you insist, cheeky sexy baby.'

Through gasps and between kisses she panted, 'Why do you keep saying that?'

'Because you said it to me. That night the roof fell in.'

And that you loved me. And he'd held that knowledge close to his heart ever since.

And, God knew, he was just about as lost. Loved the touch of her, the smell of her. Loved her ardour and her passion. Loved it that she'd listened and understood, and hadn't judged him. Loved it that she'd instilled courage in him to share his story. Finally.

But loved? Wholly? Totally? He didn't know. Didn't want to think. Wanted only to fill her, to bury himself deep inside her, to kiss her again.

His tongue slicked tiny circles over her swollen breasts, up her neck, and once again he savoured her mouth.

'Clearly I was delusional.'

'Oh, yeah? Doesn't seem that way now.' The lift pinged and jerked to a stop. He pulled away. The door opened to dark emptiness. He laughed into her hair, relieved that no one had caught them. Fired up by the risk. 'Lower car park? Down again?'

'All the way, city boy. And fast.'

'You got it.'

His jet eyes sparked with intense desire, a fervour like Mim had never seen before. It reached to her innermost parts and stroked them, fired her with a longing that she'd never known.

She wiggled her bum onto the handrail, wrapped her legs around his waist and then he was sliding into her, thrusting deep and hard. Every part of her gripped him as he rocked against her. Never to let go. Only Connor had ever made her feel this sensual. This worthy. Only Connor had taken her to the heights of such frenzied pleasure. Only Connor.

And then, as he shuddered inside her, she was lost in ripples of sublime oblivion.

CHAPTER TWELVE

CONNOR found Mim in the lounge the next morning, staring out at dawn across the central business district. The room was flooded with a hazy autumnal light, catching her silhouetted frame through the flimsy dress she wore.

God, she took his breath away. Every time he looked at her his heart jumped. And was it his imagination, or did she have the tiniest bump there now? The urge to hold and protect her curled deep in his gut.

She turned and smiled at him, her mouth curled upwards, but her eyes dulled. Despite her blissfully swollen lips and ruffled hair and the fact they'd had the best sex ever—twice—a frown creased her forehead. His heart thudded. Whatever words she was going to say, she was choosing them very carefully. 'Hey, there.'

'Finally, we managed to get to the bed,' he ventured, unsure of her agenda.

'Yeah.' She ran her fingers over the window-frame.

His heart pounded now. She was almost monosyllabic. The tension zinged across from her and she had put up an invisible barrier he didn't know if he could break through.

He tried for lightness. 'Why don't you come back to bed? Make good use of it now we know how.'

'No. I'm fine.'

Her words were razor sharp. She obviously wasn't fine.

But this was double-meaning woman-speak and he didn't understand it. 'How's that headache?'

'Better, I guess.' She gave him a half-hearted smile. 'That was foolish, Connor.'

'I know. Next time we won't be so public.' He took a chance and crossed the distance between them—at least physically anyway—slipped his hands round her waist. Pressed palms against her belly. Against the life that was growing there. His child. Their child.

She shrugged away. 'There won't be a next time.'

He was suddenly cold. 'What do you mean? I thought—'

'What did you think? That we'd work it all out? That this…' she pointed to the lounge and then out to the sprawling jungle of high-rises that stretched to the ocean '…would be our home? That you'd take care of me and we'd do the cosy family thing?'

'I…don't know. I hadn't got that far. I thought we'd try.'

'I can imagine, you had it all worked out.' She walked over to his laptop. Clicked onto his server. Then glared at him as if he was the royal executioner. Guilty as charged. 'When were you going to tell me?'

'About?'

'The Matrix assessment. I came to check my emails. Imagine my surprise when I saw your completed report.' She slammed the lid shut. The crash reverberated around the room, like the lid shutting on their relationship. Again. 'Sent yesterday to the board. Failed. Reapply in two years.'

'I was going to tell you.'

'When? After we'd made love? When you'd convinced me to stay here? After the scan?'

He turned her to face him. 'Today. I was going to tell you today. Honestly. I didn't want to ruin what we had last night.'

'You couldn't give us more time? You didn't give us a chance. You didn't even finish all the phases.'

'You haven't got a roof. Section One point three states you need a building fit for purpose.'

Her chin lifted. 'I'm hoping the insurance will pay out. I'll hear any day.'

'For wear and tear? Doubtful. You've been covering over that leak for too long. You need a schedule of planned renovations. You can't leave things to chance.'

Mim's stomach tightened into a knot. He was right. Damn it. But she wasn't going to give him the satisfaction of admitting it. 'And you couldn't have waited a few more weeks?'

'You know as well as I do that there's a time limit on these things. You need—'

She threw her hands up in frustration. 'I know...processes. I'm working on it all. I'm a damned fine doctor.'

'You are.'

'Then believe in me.'

'I do. More than you could imagine.'

'Then it's not enough. Nowhere near.'

His hands ran down her shoulders as his gaze softened over her. Mim had no doubt that he did believe in her to some extent. What man would spend his days and nights at her bedside? What man would send her laptops? Take her to the ballet, if he didn't believe in her? But, by God, she wanted to shake him.

The man who had gone through so much and fought the system so hard was now fixing it, and failing her. The man who she wanted to love unconditionally with all her heart was exercising more control over her future than anyone ever had. It was a joke.

She picked up her shoes from the rug where she'd dropped them yesterday in a daze of heated frenzy, grabbed her handbag from the coffee table. Her body ached with the unfamiliar exercise of last night, her lips were bruised from kissing him so hard and so long. She still had the smell of him on her breasts, on her mouth.

She fought back the tears that threatened. She wouldn't cry for him. Not again. Although she wanted to cry for their baby, who would miss out on having a father around every day. 'I'm going home. I need some time to work out what I'm going to do.'

'I'll pay for an administrator. I'll get the roof fixed. I'll talk to the board and see if we can grant an extension to the assessment due to unforeseen circumstances.'

'This isn't about the assessment, Connor. It's not even about the fact you didn't tell me you'd failed Dana's Drop-In.' Her stomach knotted and again she wrapped her fist against her belly. Every part of her wanted to protect their child from hearing this argument. 'You think that everything can be solved with money and rules. That order means love. But it doesn't. Love is messy and disordered. It's chaotic and fragile. And it needs to be treasured.'

She waved a hand at him. 'I don't need your money. I don't need you to fix this. I need more than that. We all need more.' I need you.

But she couldn't have him. So the only thing she could do was to walk away. Again. But this time she would do it with her head held high, not sneaking out in the darkness.

She reached into her handbag and touched the tattered, dog-eared scan picture, so often held and now so creased she could barely make out her baby's shape any more. She would love her child no matter what, would put it first. Would give it the kind of upbringing she'd always dreamt of. She would let her child believe in the fairy-tale. She would work her hardest to make damned sure. And she'd do it all on her own.

She was aware that he'd followed her into the spare rom and was watching her as she threw things into a holdall.

Then he stood in front of the wardrobe. 'Come and live

in the city. We can get a place somewhere more suitable for a family. You can choose. You can give up work for a while. I'll support you. I want to support you.'

She ducked under his arm and grabbed the few paltry items she'd bought from the swanky shops. She didn't need them any more. They wouldn't fit into Atanga Bay life. They were all part of the desperately sad fantasy she'd allowed herself to live for a day, until harsh reality had bitten her. 'And fit into the nice round hole you have all planned out? I'm a square peg, Connor.'

'You don't even want to try.'

She snapped the bag closed and glared up at him. Into his face, which was a picture of incomprehension. 'You never listen to me. I feel like poor John yesterday. I'm saying things but you don't appear to understand them. I need to work, I need to keep my practice going.'

'I'm trying, goddammit.'

She squeezed her eyes shut as pain flowed into her heart. 'This is heading exactly where I didn't want it to go. Exactly the same place as last time, and I don't want that. I never did.'

'I want to understand. I haven't dared ask in case it sent you scurrying back to Atanga Bay. But seeing as you're all revved up to do that anyway, I might as well hear the full story. Why did you leave?'

He pulled her to sit on the bed. Somehow, for that last question he'd managed to control his temper. His voice wavered, but was soft despite their disagreement. Once he would have flared up at her, but now when he looked at her she could see the hurt flaming in his eyes. Not anger.

He wasn't arguing. He was giving her the opportunity to explain. He'd changed. He would never have done that before. He'd have jumped in and tried to make her stay. Would have tried to bring her round with his impassioned arguments. But he was controlling that. He was trying to listen. He truly cared for her.

But she had to grasp her independence and walk out with her pride intact. 'I don't want to talk about it.'

'Why not, Mim? Don't give me your famous never-look-back speech. For someone who refuses to look back, you sure have a huge chip spoiling the view of the future.' He grabbed her hand, turned it palm up and ran his thumb across the lined skin. 'Why won't you even remember the good times? What makes you so certain that moving away from the past is the only thing you can do? And why do you have to do it on your own?'

She dragged in as much oxygen as she could. Breathed out deeply and found some self-control. He'd asked and she owed him an explanation. She'd hurt him once before and was hurting him now. Seemed he'd moved forward but she hadn't. Maybe she couldn't.

'Because looking back hurts like hell, and I'm not a masochist. My mum lived in the past, Connor. To the point that she couldn't see anything else apart from how wonderful she'd been, and how much I'd ruined everything for her. She went to an international dance contest and came back having lost, and pregnant, with no support and no hope of getting a job. She couldn't retrain because she had a baby and lacked the strength to fight for anything. She ended up dependent on men who controlled her life. By dictating how much dope she could have, and when. Who kept her in just enough debt that she'd do anything they asked. Who threatened her if she didn't do what they demanded.'

He shook his head, but didn't speak, just held her hand and listened.

'So, no, I don't look back. I don't want to get eaten up by remorse. I want to look forward. And I never want to be controlled. Ever. That's why I left you. Because the second I agreed to marry you your family took over. I was told what to do, how to act. Who to be. Mrs Connor Wiseman. Not Mim McCarthy. You and your father snatched away my dreams, and wanted to take away my independence. Just like now.'

Because, although you said the words 'I love you', you didn't know what they meant.

At least Dana never did that.

'I didn't realise that my mother's enthusiasm for a wedding and my offering you a future had been so stifling for you.' He shrugged. 'Mum guessed what I'd been going through and wanted to show me some solidarity. To make up for my father's disinterest. And everything I suggested to you just made sense to me then—there are plenty of surgeries here in the city you could work in. You could do as much good here as anywhere. There's nothing for me in Atanga Bay.'

Except me. And now our child. A rock formed in her throat, too hard to swallow round. But she forced it away. He meant well. He just didn't understand.

And he was trying to salve her hurt with pretty words. 'You should never have been made to feel like that when you were a child. You should have been loved. Cherished. You must have hated it.'

'No. I loved my mum. And—like you—I wanted to save the person I loved. And failed so many times I lost count. I jollied her along, tried to point out the good things in our lives. I hid the booze, hid the dope money, burnt the dope stash in the barbecue, let the car tyres down so she couldn't drive to get her fix. But have you ever tried living with an addict?'

'No. But my father's close. Addicted to his work, his sorrow, and almost to the bottle.'

She understood. What little time she'd spent with Max had highlighted his compulsion. Both she and Connor were products of their parents' addictions. Taught from an early age that they were insignificant time-wasters. Unimportant. Not worthy of their love, affection, attention.

Sadness clutched her heart and squeezed. It was too late for them all. 'Max hasn't moved on from losing Janey. Dana never moved on from losing her future. And we got caught in the fallout. It's so sad. So many lives tarnished. I remember seeing pure joy on Mum's face maybe once or twice in her whole life. Once or twice, Connor. Not at me, her precious daughter, but at the little package she had in her hand. Was she only happy when she was high?'

'Did no one help?' Connor tried to make sense of what it must have been like to crave attention and get none in return. Worse, to be blamed and abandoned.

He knew what hopelessness there was in blame. He'd been living under its shadow for long enough. No wonder Mim was so fiercely independent—no wonder she ran from any kind of security. She was frightened that it wouldn't last, that she'd be abandoned all over again. That any control over her life would be wielded by self-serving men. Experience told her it would.

What hell she'd been in. And he'd only made it worse. His heart squeezed. Twisted.

And now he'd lost her all over again.

She gazed up at him, determination and drive written across her face. 'That's why I need my clinic. So I can listen. So I can work with my families and prevent them from becoming as dysfunctional as Dana and me. "Don't let anyone steal your dreams, babe", she used to say.'

Mim sighed, stood up and straightened her shoulders. Tilted her head back a little and smiled. The fight in her had been renewed and the shutters were firmly in place. 'So I'll go to the bank, arrange another loan and I'll move along just fine. Once that new development's up, I'll double my clientele.'

'And us?' He reached out and touched her elbow but she shrugged away as if she'd been stung.

There was no way Mim could stop her eyes brimming, so she allowed herself one tear. One tiny tear. She felt it trickle down her cheek, and refused to wipe it away. She deserved one. Then there'd be no more.

No more wanting things she could never have. No more dreaming of the fairy-tale. No more heartbreak.

'No, Connor. You live here and believe so much in what you do. And it all hurts too much. I can't do this again. I'm sorry. I want you, Con. I want you so much. I even think I love you. No. I don't think so. I know I do. I love you, and that's what makes this so hard.'

And now the secrets of her heart were all out there, fluttering in the wind, with nothing to cling to, nothing sturdy to ground them. Just words, ether, dust. Nothing, really. When it came down to it.

She'd loved him before, never stopped loving him. Just like with her mum, it was a hopeless, pointless, futile love that wasn't returned or celebrated. A love that hurt. A love that should have fuelled togetherness and yet had forced them apart.

'Love…?' His hand was over hers as confusion and desire and pain transformed his face. He spoke to her gently, as he might speak to a child. To Janey. 'Then stay a while. Let's talk some more.'

She brushed her hand over her face, tried to wipe the tears away. His questioning eyes tugged at her. The easiest thing would be to stay and talk. It was tempting to just grasp a few more minutes with him. To pretend they could fix it, but that would prolong the inevitable. A deep ache spread across her chest, numbed her throat. 'No. I'm all out of talking. It doesn't get us anywhere. I need to go.'

'Running back to Atanga Bay. Again. Don't you ever want to face up to reality?'

'That we can't live together, can't live apart? That every time we do this we just hurt each other more?'

As if that was possible. Okay, so another tear followed. She couldn't stop them. She didn't have the energy, the fight or the will. Her heart was breaking and there was no way she could stop that either. 'Look at us. We can't compromise, we can't take a risk and both of us are too darned scared to try.'

CHAPTER THIRTEEN

'THERE he is.' The sonographer pointed out the pumpkin-headed shape floating on the screen. 'All his organs are formed now and seem to be working fine. In the next few weeks he...or she...will develop genitalia. So soon we'll be able to tell if it's a boy or girl.'

'I don't care which. Either would be fine.' Mim stared up at the shape, barely able to contain her excitement. Her baby was swimming around her womb, she couldn't feel it, but seeing it on a monitor felt surreal. 'He looks like a monkey nut.'

'A what?' Connor, beside her, shook his head and squinted at the shape moving slowly on the screen. His eyes glittered and he looked about as smitten as she felt.

How would he bear not being able to see his child every day? To watch him grow. How could he be satisfied with occasional visits?

Because she'd forced that on him. For all the right reasons. But it didn't feel right. None of it felt right.

She struggled with a need to hold his hand, but dug her nails into her palms to stop herself from reaching to him. She'd been apart from him for three days. And every hour, every minute away had been torture.

She'd found herself wanting to tell him things, to hold him. Smell him. Taste him. So many times she'd picked up the phone and dialled, but had hung up before he'd answered.

She loved him, she missed him. Missed his humour and his strength, his steadfastness, his damned determination and passion.

But the fresh sea air had cleared her head and she was determined to make the best of her life as a single parent. With the monkey nut. 'You know, one of those long papery-looking nuts.'

Connor squinted again. 'No way.'

'Or a jelly bean. With a big head. And with legs. And arms. Obviously.'

'So not like a monkey nut at all, then?'

'No. I guess not. Like a foetus, really,' she conceded. Reluctantly. Why did he have to make her laugh? And be so damned hot? Why couldn't he be serious and dull?

But then she wouldn't be having his baby. Her chest felt as if it had a huge weight pressing down on it.

He laughed. 'Can't say I've missed your weirdness.'

'Or your charm.' She nudged him and shook her head, trying to speak through the lump in her throat. She'd missed so much more. 'He has your stubborn streak. Look. He's hitting against the same part of my womb. Over and over. And I can't even feel it.' She spoke to the image. 'I'm not letting you out, mate.'

'Would you like a picture?' The sonographer smiled over at them, oblivious to the turmoil in Mim's heart.

'Yes, please,' they answered in unison, then laughed again. To everyone in the clinic they must have appeared as a happy couple.

They had been once, hadn't they?

A couple?

If laughing together, loving together, being happy just to be in the same room meant being a couple, then they had been.

If sharing their most intimate fears, their dreams and desires meant being a couple, then they had been. If seeing his image first thing in the morning and last thing at night and a million times during the day meant she had been part of something special, a once-in-a-lifetime, life-affirming heart-breaking affair, then they had been.

Had they ever given themselves a chance?

Too late for any more chances.

With a heavy heart she went to the loo and met Connor outside. A cruel autumn wind whipped around them. Traffic and people buzzed by, time ticked along but she wanted to freeze-frame him, right here. His hair caught up in the wind in little tufts, the kindness in his eyes. His leather smell. Just being with him brought her comfort, a little peace. A lot of other annoying fluctuating emotions, but peace too, as if he finally understood her. But it was too late.

Connor watched as she placed the picture into her hand-bag with such care it melted his heart. She looked beautiful. Thriving, with clear, glowing skin. The armour plating on his heart had completely shattered, blown into tiny pieces.

He'd freed himself from his guilt, but instead of feeling the weight lift he was burdened with loss. He wanted to tell Mim how much he missed her, that he didn't want her to go. Again. That every time she left it tore him apart. That his cold apartment now felt like his heart—empty, barren and worthless. But what use would it do? He didn't want to invite an argument. Didn't want her to say that these precious moments together were too painful. Didn't want to jeopardise the next meeting. Or the time after that. Or their whole future, which hung between them on a frail thread. 'Has the morning sickness stopped?'

'Just about. I'm ravenous now, though. And piling on the weight.'

'You look fine to me. Spectacular.' He nodded towards a café on the street corner, trying to grab just a few more minutes. 'Coffee? Something to eat?'

She checked her watch. 'I'm really sorry, but Tony will be here in a minute. He's giving me a ride back.'

'Tony.' The sting of jealousy jabbed at him.

'He brought me down because he had to go to the timber suppliers. He said he'd swing past at three o'clock so he'll be here any time. Look, there he is, other side of the lights.' She waved at the scruffy blue ute, whose lights flashed in reply.

'Tony?' Just the thought of her with another man made his blood run cold, even though he considered Tony to be a friend now, not a threat.

The ute drew up into the pick-up zone. Tony waved, but thankfully stayed in the car.

'Yes.' She smiled and waved back at her friend. Held her fingers up to indicate five minutes. Tony nodded, cut the engine, flicked open a paper and tactfully started to read. 'Now, don't get the wrong idea, Connor. There's nothing going on. He's just a friend, giving me a lift.'

'So you told everyone about the baby?'

'No. He thinks I'm here about my head injury. He's been very kind.' She gathered her bag close and smiled. 'Actually, he's hit it off with Steph. Getting quite cosy. She's been asking Skye for diabetic recipes. Seems he's always had a thing for her.'

There she was with that conciliatory smile again. The one she used all the time, trying to get people to come round to her thinking, to like her. To not reject her. She didn't even realise she did it. How desperately she tried to make up for all the rejection she'd had in the past.

There he'd been, three years ago, rejecting her again. In a veiled attempt at doing the right thing by his sister he'd rejected Mim's ideas, her hopes, her plans. Had been blinkered by his own issues rather than taking hers into account.

He had been just as bad as the rest of them. Worse. He was

supposed to have loved her. He'd told her so. But he hadn't shown her, not with his actions.

All he'd done was confirm what she believed. That she was worthless, that her dreams didn't matter. That she didn't matter. That men were controlling and manipulative.

He squeezed the envelope in his pocket. The one he'd been carrying with him and had not had the heart to give her yet. Another time. Maybe once things were on a firmer footing. He'd rewrite it all.

For now, he'd have to be content just to look at her and the tiny bump, and bite back the almost overwhelming primal need to wrap her into his coat. 'Okay, so I'll meet you here again in a few weeks for the nuchal scan?'

'Fine.' She looked like she wanted to say more, but then decided not to. She made a study of the pavement. But made no move to get into the ute.

'Tony's waiting.'

'Yes.' She tipped her head and held his gaze. Her dark brown eyes pulled him in. There was so much to say to her. So much he wanted to do. He ached to tell her how much he wanted to be a father. How she had taught him to open his heart. How Oakley had bashed against his armour plating with a tight fist. Taught him that being with a child was as much about fun as it was about protection. And how he knew he could do it now. They had given him the courage to try.

But she didn't want to hear it. And, dammit, he didn't want her to throw it back in his face.

She raised her eyebrows, ignorant of the turmoil in his heart. 'How's your father?'

'Are we at small-talk again now? Tony's waiting.'

She looked hurt. 'I want to know. I'm not making small-talk. Has he forgiven you?'

He didn't want to talk about his father. 'I don't think so. Not yet. Mum says he's calmer somehow. They're planning a cruise. So maybe he heard me. I don't know. Maybe he's just getting old.' Like me.

Older and alone.

He plunged his hands into his pockets to prevent them from holding her. The pressure in his chest was almost unbearable.

It was like a piece of him was missing. The hole in his heart had grown exponentially every day he was apart from her and the only thing that filled it was a giant sense of loss.

He missed her, missed the surgery with its dilapidated walls, the mismatched paint and the cushions. He even missed the goth. They were a tangible part of him that had gone. 'And next time you can fill me in on Atanga Bay. And Oakley. How's Tommo?'

'They're all fine. Atanga Bay's just the same.' She hugged her arms around her waist, bit down on her lip. 'I guess this is goodbye.'

'I guess so.' He dragged his hand out of his pocket, reached out to kiss her cheek.

She leant towards him, a breath away, then pulled back. 'Oh, you just dropped something.'

She bent to pick it up. Turned the envelope over as his heart crashed.

'It's nothing.'

'It's got my name on.' She eyed him suspiciously. 'A solicitor?'

Fool. Stupid, misguided, damned fool. 'Yes.'

'What is it?'

'A contract. For access.' Dumb. Only now could he see the pointlessness of what he'd done, arranged this without discussing it with her. Why did he always act first and think later? But she was staring up at him with an incredulous look in her eyes and he was condemned to continue, 'Some provision for the baby. I've set up a trust fund. And help for maternity leave.'

'A contract? On your terms, I presume?' She handed it back to him, her hand trembling, like her lip. If it were possible, she looked even more sad, angry. In despair. 'I don't want it. I'd never deny you access to your child.'

'Even when you're married, and have other kids? Another man? Things could get messy.'

'How could you even think…?'

'These things happen. You're beautiful and fun, you'll meet someone one day. I just thought it was better if we were clear.'

'Oh, yes, Connor. It's all very clear. Black and white. You don't believe in me. You don't trust me.' She thrust the paper into his open palm and glared at him. 'Can't you see that you can't always fix things with regulations and rules and bits of paper? I don't want this. Goodbye.'

Don't go. Every cell in his body screamed after her. Anger clutched at his stomach. Anger with his stupid, foolish, clumsy self. Anger that she was leaving. That they couldn't work it out. Anger as he watched her climb into Tony's ute. The second time he'd watched her leave in a matter of days, when he was so full of love for her.

Yes. Despite everything. Her rejection. His fear. He wanted to love her. He wanted to believe she wanted him. That she'd stick with him. He wanted to convince her that what they had was worth fighting for. But he had no idea how.

'Hey, you want to buy me a drink?'

The cloying, alcohol-laced voice jumped on Connor's nerves, as did the proximity of the barely clothed woman. She leaned towards him in the dimly lit bar and smiled with come-on eyes.

He took a step away from her dense perfume and over-rouged face. Another time he might have taken her up on the offer, knowing it could lead to mindless sex, getting wasted. No strings attached.

None of it appealed. This was his life now? It repulsed him. He turned away. 'No, thanks. Just leaving.'

'You only just got here. You could stay awhile.' The music up-tempoed to a salsa beat. Irony of ironies. She smiled through glossy lips and gyrated her hips against his. 'Dance with me?'

'I said no.' Connor glared at the woman and she shrugged, turned away.

The bar bumped and throbbed with the music. Everywhere he looked couples linked up, smiling, dancing, kissing. Somehow their pleasure in togetherness made his loneliness worse.

He slammed his drink on the bar and left, seeking fresh air, some peace outside, anything to get rid of the pain in his head. In his heart.

Saturday night and he was cruising the bars, looking for… what? A pretty bimbo to lose himself in? No. Temporary relief from the ache in his soul. Oblivion? Hell, yes. But what good would that be in the end?

Saturday night and the only place he wanted to be was in Atanga Bay. With Mim.

Yes. As he allowed himself to think of her, to remember her beautiful face, the pain intensified. A hollow, dull ache that pervaded every cell, backlit with a shimmering love.

Mim.

He missed her. There weren't enough words to describe the way he felt. Like life had been sucked out of him.

He stalked down the hill to the Viaduct district, dodging the crowds of partygoers. Walked to Queens Wharf and beyond, stopping occasionally to watch the cruise ships, anything to prevent him going back to his apartment. Sterile. Cold. Empty. Just like him. Like his life.

The only thing that made any sense was to be by her side.

To hold her and their child. Being there every day, watching her belly grow, feeling her soft body change. Feeling his child kick and move. To wallow in the love he had for her. That she'd professed to have for him.

The only thing that made any sense was to be with her.

But she'd gone. Left him with a shattered heart, again. He didn't have the strength to even try to piece it back together. The only thing that could do that would be a life with Mim.

An impossible dream. A dream of colours, emotions and heat. Lots and lots of heat.

He drew his leather jacket around him as the sea breeze lifted strands of his wayward hair, curled around his collar and shivered down his spine. He felt like he'd never be warm again.

Neither of them had the courage, she'd said. They were both too scared. Well, hell, he didn't have the courage to face a life without her.

His hands tightened around the railing as he stared out to sea. He'd had courage in his conviction once, had asked her to marry him. Had rejoiced when she'd said yes. Had rejoiced last week when she'd admitted she loved him.

But she also loved her people and her practice. Loved Atanga Bay too much.

And he...well, he loved her. Loved her passion, her intensity. Her weird sense of humour. Loved her changing body.

He loved Mim. Plain and simple. It was a relief to admit it. To relish it.

And the bump. Junior. He could barely think of his child without a catch in his throat. He had a family. A long-distance family. A family he was going to miss out on. Because of what? His failure to listen. An inability to let in love. Too much focus on the past.

He'd given up his medical career to assuage his guilt, a mighty, grand gesture, but now he didn't enjoy the work.

Mim had opened his eyes to another life, a way to connect. With her. With people he was getting know, to understand. People he wanted to know more. Way up north, away from this city, away from his stark desk, his cold life. In Atanga Bay.

His heart stuttered, and then his answer was blindingly obvious. Simple. Perfect.

He shoved his hands in his pockets as he picked up his pace. His mind was suddenly a whirl of possibilities.

'Okay, come back in about eight days and we'll take the stitches out.' Mim smiled at her patient as she finished suturing his lacerated thigh. She had to shout over the hammering to make herself heard. Getting the builders in and running a clinic at the same time was nigh on impossible. 'And don't dare do wheelies down Main Street again, d'you hear?'

'Yeah. Sweet.' Young Danny Parker grinned at her as if she was bonkers.

'I mean it. If I see you out there I'll phone your mum. And don't think I won't.'

She wrote up her notes on the swanky laptop that reminded her of Connor every time she used it. Of his chat messages that made her smile. Of…everything. Of the last two weeks that had been empty and cold. Of the decisions she'd made and whether she'd done the right thing after all.

'Quick! Quick!' Skye hammered on the front window, sending her heart into spasms of tachycardia. 'Come now. Quick!'

'What?' Mim dashed outside with the emergency trolley, and oxygen cylinder. 'Wha—?'

What she saw made her heart soar and tears prickle her eyes. 'You absolute superstar! Come here and give me a hug.'

Oakley was standing up from his wheelchair and walking towards her. His movements were jerky, but he fixed his gaze on her and made it without veering, without stalling, almost fluid. Ten metres. 'Hey, Mim! I've come to buy you an ice cream. A big one.'

No stammer. She wrapped him in her arms. Ruffled the kid's hair and wondered whether seven was too old to be ruffled. There was so much she didn't know about child rearing, but she had a lifetime to find out the rules of engagement of ages and stages. And she was so looking forward to it. 'Hey, Oaks. I'm so pleased to see you. My shout on the ice cream. No worries. You worked hard, eh?'

He nodded. 'Yeah. How's your baby? You're not fat yet.'

The hammering stopped. The chattering and whoops of delight ceased. It felt like all eyes were on her. A weird, embarrassing silence hovered around the little crowd outside her building.

Her secret was out. Pressing a hand to her stomach, she shouted to Tony, somewhere on her roof, to Skye whose eyes just about bounced out of their sockets, to Oakley's mum. And anyone else who happened to be walking past. 'Yes, I'm pregnant! I'm going to have a baby. Get the gossip over and done with.'

After a round of applause and group hugs Skye sidled over. She grinned. 'Thank goodness for that.'

'Why?'

'I thought you had some sort of residual brain damage. You've been so moody. Unpredictable. I was all out of ideas. Didn't expect this, though.'

Mim laughed, relief that she could share her news with someone washing through her. 'It has been a bit of a shock.'

All of it. The intense love, the longing, the wanting to make things right with Connor. The endless ache in her chest whenever she thought of him standing outside the hospital after the scan. The look of desolation on his face as he'd handed her the contract. And the guilt at how she'd handled things so badly. Again.

'So what about the father?' Skye nudged Mim in the ribs. 'I presume it's the suit?'

'Why, oh, why did I employ someone as perceptive as me?' Mim nudged her friend back and wished she could give Skye a happy ending. She hugged her growing belly. 'Yes, it is. Connor Wiseman.'

'And he's where? In Auckland? Does he know?'

'Yes, and he's happy about the baby. He'll be involved.' Not as much as I want. She gave her friend a wobbly smile, dragging up every bit of self-control. She was happy about the baby. She was. But she missed Connor too much.

Skye frowned. 'So, you're going to be here and he's staying in Auckland?' She tugged Mim to a quieter corner and whispered, 'Your heart is breaking, I can see. Doesn't he want you? Did he tell you that?'

Mim's eyes blurred with tears. 'We had a fight. He gave me a contract for access.'

'Did he tell you he didn't want you?'

Had he? Had she been too blinded by her anger and need to keep control to hear him? Had he said he didn't want her? No. Not exactly. 'I don't know.'

'But you want him?'

A fist tightened in her solar plexus. This was something she knew with every fibre in her body. 'Yes. Yes, I do want him. More than anything. But I can't.'

'You could ask him.' The frown deepened. 'I don't see what's holding you back. If he says no then at least you'll know where you stand.'

'And this place?' Mim pointed to her beloved surgery. The roof was almost fixed, the freshly painted sign about to go up. The official reopening lunch laid out in the new admin room. Her baby, this clinic. One she'd nurtured, fought for and poured hours of long hard labour into. For her mother, for her people. For herself. 'I couldn't leave this behind. I've worked too hard.'

'It's a building, Mim. Bricks and mortar. In a small town. There are plenty of small towns just like this. It's beautiful, sure. We have lots of lovely memories, fantastic people, but don't let them hold you back. I wouldn't. If I wasn't looking after Mum, I'd be out there, chasing my dreams.'

'This is…was my baby, my dream. I did this for my mum too.'

'And she'd be very proud.'

Mim's throat stung with pain. 'I don't know about that. Would she be proud? Would she even have cared?'

She didn't know the answer. The trouble with Dana had been that no one had ever really known what she'd felt. She had been closed and bitter. And was gone for ever.

Mim's chest heaved as she gulped air. She sighed, realising a harsh truth. 'I was trying to create a bond between me and Dana, but that never really existed and it can't now she's not here.' I just wanted someone to love. Someone to love me back.

'You have another baby to care about now. A real one. Who needs a father.' Skye wrapped an arm around Mim's shoulders and steered her to the surgery door. 'There are plenty of practices in Auckland that need dedicated doctors. And a good man, who might need you more.'

All through lunch Mim's mind worked overtime. Had Connor ever rejected her? Had he ever said he didn't want her?

She picked at the salad. Left her drink half-finished. Couldn't sit. Didn't want to stand. Small-talk stuck in her throat. Something niggled her. Didn't feel right. She was restless. Irritated.

Damn right. She'd been irritated for weeks. Ever since he'd walked through that admin door.

Had she done exactly what she'd accused him of and not listened?

Not listened to him or to her heart, which was now calling, no screaming, for her to take some action?

Other people moved continents for love. Gave up a lot more than a building. Bricks and mortar. Some gave up freedom, cultures. They all learned to relinquish absolute control—for love. They compromised.

Connor had cut ties with his father because of her, which must have made his working life hell. She imagined him coming home to that faceless empty apartment every night, surrounded by nothing but cold chrome and dark buildings.

Connor was a man who deserved to be surrounded by love, to be close to his family, to his child. She couldn't deprive him of that.

And above all else she loved him wholeheartedly and wanted to be part of his life, to make a home with him.

Maybe it was time to try to compromise. She could have a conversation with him. Explain how she felt. What she wanted. If she could work that out.

She found Skye outside, looking at the new sign that hung slightly to the left from its chains outside the surgery.

'Skye, I think I'll go and see Connor at the weekend. Talk to him. See if we could work something out. Something more than being alone. Take a risk. What do you think?'

'He'd be mad to turn you down. And Atanga Bay?'

'I don't know. I truly don't. And I'm scared to death, but whatever it takes... Holidays? A weekend cottage perhaps? I'll miss the place, but sometimes you have to compromise on your dreams to make better ones. Maybe I'll win him over with my irritating positivity and quirkiness.'

Yes. She'd go and see Connor. The thought of never seeing him again, never holding him, was too raw to contemplate. A dream with him in it was far more appealing than a dream without.

She looked up at the crooked sign again. 'That's annoying me. Pass me the stepladder.'

She climbed up three steps and straightened the bottom of the sign, leaned back a little to admire her handiwork. Just a little more to the right.

'Get the hell down from that ladder, woman.'

Her hand froze in mid-action, then it began to shake uncontrollably. She gripped the sides of the ladder and held on for grim life. That voice. Double chocolate devil's cake. Tugged at her. Broke her heart all over and reassembled it again. Stronger, whole.

He'd come here to Atanga Bay. Connor had come to see her.

'I said, get the hell down. Or I'll come and get you.'

She twisted to look over her shoulder. Her heart stuttered and stammered. He was striding towards her, wearing a checked shirt, dusty jeans and work boots. 'Well, aren't you just the sweetest thing I've ever seen? You look like an extra from a DIY advert. Come and get me, city boy.'

'Yeah well, I've got a power tool and I'm not afraid to use it.' Within seconds his hands were round her waist pulling her from the stepladder. 'Looks like your place could do with some work.'

Why was he there?

She didn't care why he was there. He was, and she could breathe again. He placed her on the ground, stuck his hands in his pockets. 'What the hell are you doing up there in your condition? What is it with you and stepladders?'

'Finishing touches. I'm tarting it up. Thinking of renting or selling.'

He glanced scornfully at her beloved building. 'Oh, yeah? Who'd buy a ramshackle place like this?'

Indignation ran down her spine. He still didn't damn well get it.

'It has potential, Connor.' She peaked her eyebrows at him.

He waved his wallet at her. His sneaky smug grin fired sparks of irritation, mixed with heat and love and desire, through her body. 'Oh, no, you don't Connor. You can't buy me. I don't want that. Don't you dare.'

'God, it's good to see you. You are so easy to tease.' He cupped her cheeks, pressed his fingers into her skin and planted a rough kiss on her lips. Hard.

She tried to wriggle free but he pulled her closer, deepened the kiss, filled her mouth with his taste and his tongue, clashed his teeth against hers.

Every cell in her body relaxed at his touch, craved him, ached for him. And for a moment she was lost, lost in his arms, lost in the way he made her feel. She wrapped her arms round his neck and kissed him back hard. Thinking of all the things she should say and letting them fade away to nothing. To this moment. To this kiss.

When he pulled back he was breathing heavily. 'I'm not remotely interested in buying you, but I would like to make an offer. Equal partnership.'

'And you're going to be what? A silent partner, running things from Auckland?' She daren't hope for more.

'Actually, no. I've resigned. I realised I was working with my father because I wanted to impress him as much as save the system. I need a change, back to medicine, doing something I love, with the people I love. It's not healthcare I need to save, Mim, it's me. I can do that here, with you and our child.'

He'd said, 'people I love'. Her heart fluttered, flexed a little, grew a little more.

'Here?'

'Yeah. Here.' He shrugged. 'In the middle of nowhere. God help me. I must be mad, but I kind of like the place. Although I do have one condition.'

'I couldn't imagine you doing anything without a darned condition. Hit me with it.'

'I know you'll fight me for this, but at least listen.' He was serious now, the ardent, passionate look in his eyes pulling her in deeper until she thought she might drown right there. 'We need to consider changing the name of the clinic. Atanga Bay Medical Centre has a good ring to it.'

'Come here.' She turned him back to the sign. 'Read it and weep, city boy.'

'"Atanga Bay Family Healthcare".' His mouth opened in shock, but it soon curled into a grin. 'Fabulous, but why the change of heart?'

'You were right, I need to move on from the past.'

'Well done. I know that would have been hard.'

'Besides, one of my clients said it sounded like a hippy joint and I got to wondering if it might have been putting people off after all.'

Connor held onto her, breathing in her mango scent and relishing the feeling of coming home. He'd been afraid she'd changed towards him, that she'd keep him at a distance after everything they'd gone through. She hadn't changed.

She was still as obtuse and quirky and beautiful as ever. And she loved him. He could believe that now. She had considered giving all this up for him and their child.

He wrapped his hands around her waist, cradled mother and baby. And wondered if he would ever feel this lucky again. 'Promise me you'll never change. I love you, Mim.'

'You really do, don't you?' She snuggled in close and the armour around his heart fell away to nothing. All the bits floated away and were replaced by an intense love for this woman. She smiled up at him and his whole world felt complete. 'I love you too, city boy.'

'How could you ever doubt me?' He pressed his mouth on that delicious pout. 'Now, kiss me some more, cheeky sexy baby.'

Seven months later

'How's my new granddaughter?' Connor's mum bustled through the door of the nursery and wrapped him in a motherly hug. A familiar lavender scent followed in her wake. Connor relaxed a little. Having her there would help the get-together run more smoothly. 'Good to see you, my boy.'

'Hi, Mum. You look great.' Connor glanced over her shoulder, steeling himself for the arrival of his father. 'Is Dad…?'

'Just parking the car. Give him time.' She patted his arm. 'Oh. My. She's truly gorgeous.' And then she was lost to him as she fixated on his daughter, fast asleep in her crib.

All too soon Max peered at the door, knocking gently. His body stooped slightly as he tiptoed into the room. 'Er…hello. Nice house. Good views across the estuary.'

'And close to the surgery.' Connor stepped away from the picture window overlooking Atanga Bay and shook his father's hand. He was surprised to be drawn into a hesitant half-embrace. The first physical contact he'd had with his dad in ten years.

He drew away and looked at the old man. Gone were the shadows and the sorrow that had haunted his eyes for so long. He'd filled out, had a decent tan from spending time outside in his part-retirement hours. 'You look well too, Dad. That cruise has done you good.'

'A lot of old people trying to relive their youth.' His father smiled and Connor glimpsed a warmth he hadn't seen for a long time.

He offered his dad a genuine smile in return. His heart squeezed a little. Perhaps the wounds were slowly healing. Although Connor suspected it would take a lot more time to get his relationship with his father back onto an even keel. He hoped his beautiful daughter would help heal the breach.

A fresh start for them all. They deserved a new beginning.

'A girl, eh? Well done.' Max nodded, then leaned into the crib and stroked the baby's head. 'And how's Mim?'

'I'm fine, thanks, Max.' Mim followed behind him, wearing her dressing gown, fresh from a shower, her hair curled up into a towel. Connor's heart jumped to see her. Every time he looked at her it kicked a little, pumped a spurt of adrenalin and desire round his veins. Every single time, and nothing would ever stop that.

She kissed Max's cheek. Connor was so glad she found it within her to make an effort with his old man. 'Good to see you.'

'And you.' Max turned to look at the sleeping baby in her cot. 'Do we have a name?'

Connor edged round to look at his father, to measure his reaction, to see if their decision would cause more anguish.

Then he glanced at his mother. Connor had already told her their baby's proposed name. She'd given her blessing and been sworn to secrecy. Now she nodded. As did Mim. Gave Connor a shot of courage. 'We thought about Janey. Janey Dana Wiseman to be exact.'

Max nodded, steepled his fingers and looked lost in thought for a moment. His wife went to his side and held his hand.

His mother's devotion, after all they'd been through, caught Connor in his chest and he realised now where he had got his steadfastness from. Not from his father after all.

When Max looked into Connor's face again his eyes were

blurred with tears, but he was smiling. 'Janey. Yes. That would be perfect.'

'I'm so glad you're happy about it.' Mim wrapped her hand over Max's, hugged her husband close, washed a watchful gaze over her peacefully sleeping daughter. Who'd have thought they'd have managed this? All her dreams rolled into one. The whole damned fairy-tale and the promise of so much happiness to come. 'We thought so too. Just perfect.'

* * * * *

WEEKEND WITH THE BEST MAN

LEAH MARTYN

For BRISROM—Brisbane Romance Writers—
where it all began.

I hope you're all still out there. And still writing.

CHAPTER ONE

FRIDAY MORNING IN Casualty was the last place Senior Registrar Dan Rossi wanted to be.

And not with this patient—a seventeen-year-old drug-addicted youth. He'd arrested. And now the fight had begun to save his life. A life this skinny kid had valued so cheaply. How dared he?

Dan's thoughts turned dark. 'Start CPR!' He bit the words out as the team began the familiar routine, working in concert around the senior doctor, responding to his clipped orders.

Expectations rose and fell as they treated the patient. Rose and fell again. Dan glanced at the clock. They'd done all they could but he didn't want to call it. Not yet. Not today of all days. And not with this patient. What a waste of a young life. 'Ramp it up!'

He felt the sweat crawl down his back, his heart like a jackhammer against his ribs. He shouldn't be here. He'd lost his mental filter. Lost it.

Lost it. Lost it…

'OK, he's back.'

Thank God. Immediately, Dan's chest felt lighter as if a valve had just released the pressure building inside him. He woke as if from a nightmare.

'Pulse rate sixty,' Nurse Manager Lindsey Stewart relayed evenly. 'He's waking up.'

Yanking off his gloves, Dan aimed them at the bin, missing by a mile. 'Do what you have to do,' he said, his voice flat.

And walked out. Fast.

Lindsey's eyebrows hitched, her green gaze puzzled as she watched his exit.

'That was a bit odd back there,' Vanessa Cole, Lindsey's colleague, said, as they watched their patient being wheeled out to ICU. 'What's biting Rossi?'

'Something's certainly got him upset,' Lindsey agreed. 'Dan's usually very cool under pressure.'

'He hasn't been here long.' Vanessa shrugged. 'And we don't know much about him yet. Perhaps it's personal—girlfriend trouble?'

'Does he have a girlfriend?'

'Please!' Vanessa, who seemed to be at the sharp end of all the hospital gossip, gave an exaggerated eye-roll. 'With that dark, smouldering thing happening?'

'That's a bit simplistic,' Lindsey refuted. 'Dan Rossi is a senior doctor. He wouldn't bring that kind of stuff to work with him. I'd better try to speak to him. If it's a work-related matter, it'll need sorting.'

'Oh, Lins.' Vanessa's voice held exasperation as she pushed the privacy screen open. 'Don't start taking the flak for Rossi's dummy spit. We run—that is, *you* run an extremely efficient casualty department. It's my guess he'll take a long lunch and snap out of whatever's bugging him.'

Lindsey's instincts were not quite buying that scenario. She recognised mental stress when she saw it, and Dan Rossi had been far from his usual self since the beginning of the shift. She frowned a bit, wondering just where he'd fled to.

'Dan's usually pretty good to work with.'

* * *

Dan knew he'd been discourteous to the team but today, for very personal reasons, he'd had to get out.

Had to.

In a secluded part of the grounds he sank into a garden seat, taking a deep breath and letting it go. Every sensible cell in his brain told him he shouldn't have brought his personal problems to work today. In fact, he shouldn't have come to work at all. If he'd thought it through, he'd have taken a mental health day available to all staff. Instead, he'd come to work in an environment where emotions went from high to low in seconds.

He made a dismissive sound in his throat. Having to treat that last patient had been the trigger that had shot his ability to be objective all to hell.

Addiction. And a foolish boy, abusing his body with no conception of the amazing gift of life. A gift Dan's own babies had never had. No chance to draw one tiny life-saving breath. Two perfect little girls.

It was two years ago today since he'd lost them.

At the memory, something inside him rose up then flattened out again, like a lone wave on the sea. The grief he felt was still all too real. Grief with nowhere to go.

A shiver went right through him and he realised he'd rushed outside without a jacket. Lifting his hands, he linked them at the back of his neck. He needed to get a grip. Once he'd got through today, he'd regroup again.

Flipping his mobile out of his pocket, he checked for messages and found one from his colleague and closest friend, Nathan Lyons. The text simply said: Grub?

In seconds, Dan had texted back.

Leo's in ten.

* * *

With things in Casualty more or less under control, Lindsey decided to take the early lunch. She needed to get her head together. In the staffroom she collected the minestrone she'd brought from home and reheated it in the microwave. Ignoring the chat going on around her, she took her soup to a table near the window and buried her head in a magazine.

Halfway through her meal she stopped and raised her head to look out of the window. She'd have to say something to Dan. She couldn't just pretend nothing had happened. But how to handle it?

It wasn't as though they had any kind of relationship outside the hospital. What did she really know about him anyway? She knew he'd worked in New York and, more recently, he'd left one of the big teaching hospitals in Sydney to come on staff here in this rural city of Hopeton. But beyond that? Except for the fact that Dan Rossi kept very much to himself—and *that* alone was an achievement in an environment where you were thrown together all the time—she knew next to nothing about his personal life. But she remembered his first day vividly.

She'd sneaked a quick peek at him as the team had assembled for the start of the shift. Her quick inventory had noted his hair was dark, very dark and cut short, his eyes holding a moody blueness, the shadows beneath so deep they might have been painted on. His shoulders under his pinstriped shirt were broad. She had taken a deep breath and let it go, realising as she'd done so that she'd been close enough to smell he'd been shower-fresh. In the close confines where they worked *that* mattered to Lindsey.

Then he'd caught her looking. And it was as if they'd shared a moment of honesty, a heartbeat of intimacy. His mouth had pulled tight then relaxed. He'd almost smiled. Almost but not quite.

And for what it was worth the vibe was still there between them. But it seemed to Lindsey that for every tiny
bit of headway she made with Dan Rossi on a personal
level, he took off like a world-class sprinter in the opposite direction.

She blew out a long breath of frustration, slamming her
magazine shut as she got to her feet. Why was she even
bothering to try to find out what made Dan Rossi tick?
After her last boyfriend had cheated on her so spectacularly, she'd questioned her judgement about men. How
did you work out which of them to trust and recognise
those who were into game-playing? And right now, after
the rotten morning they'd had, it was all too heavy to
think about.

Leo's was five minutes away from the hospital, the unpre-
tentious little café drawing the hospital staff like bees to
puffy blossoms. Chef Leo Carroll kept his menu simple.
And he'd done his market research, opening at six in the
morning to accommodate the early shift who just wanted
a coffee and a bacon roll. Lunch began at noon and lasted
until three. Then Leo closed his doors, cleaned up and
went to play guitar at a blues bar in town.

Dan settled into one of the comfortable side booths
and stretched out his legs. Already he could feel the tension draining from him. Nathan's continued support had
steadied him in ways that were incalculable. Dan recalled
the day he'd flown into Sydney from the States. He'd been
standing feeling a bit bemused in the passenger lounge,
getting his bearings, when he'd heard his name called.
He'd spun round and found himself looking into a familiar craggy face lit with a lopsided grin.

'Nate!'

Before Dan could react further, he'd been thumped
across the back and enveloped in a bone-crunching hug

that had almost undone him. 'Glad you made it back in one piece, dude,' Nathan had said gruffly.

Dan had swallowed. 'How did you know I'd be on this flight?'

'I have my ways.' Nathan had tapped the side of his nose. 'Now, come on, let's move it. I'm short-term parked and it's costing me a fortune.'

Dan had booked into a boutique hotel near the harbour, intending to stay there until he could find an apartment. As they'd driven, Nathan had asked, 'Do you have some work lined up?'

'Starting at St Vincent's in a week.'

'Still in Casualty?'

'It's what I do best. You still in Medical?'

'It's what *I* do best.' Nathan had shot him a glance. 'Uh—not going to see your folks, then?'

'Not yet.' His family lived in Melbourne and while he loved and respected them, he just wasn't up for receiving their sympathy all over again.

A beat of silence.

'I've met a girl.' Nathan's embarrassed laugh eased the fraught atmosphere.

Dan spun his friend an amused look. 'Serious?'

'Could be. Think so. She's a flight attendant. Samantha Kelly—Sami.'

'Get out of here!' Dan leaned across and fist-bumped his friend's upper arm. 'Tell me about her.'

'She's blonde.'

'Yeah?'

'Funny, sweet, smart…you know…'

'Yeah. And she's got you wrapped around her little finger. Nice one, mate. I hope it works out for you and Sami.'

'Uh—if it doesn't pan out for you in Sydney,' Nathan said carefully, 'you could come across the mountain to us at Hopeton District. Get some rural medicine under your belt. We're always looking for decently qualified MOs.'

'Mmm—maybe.' Dan gave a dry smile. Nathan went on to enthuse about the vibrant country city a couple of hours from Sydney across the Blue Mountains.

'And would you believe you can still fossick for gold around Hopeton?' Nathan concluded his sales pitch emphatically.

And six months later Dan had taken everything on board and made the move and now here they were, with Nathan's and Sami's wedding just a week away and *he* was Nathan's best man.

Dan looked at his watch just at the moment Nathan burst through the door.

'Sorry I'm a bit late,' he apologised, sliding his big frame onto the bench seat opposite. 'Would you believe I've just had to cannulate three old coots on the trot—no veins to speak of, dehydrated as hell. Why don't old people drink water, for God's sake?'

'Because it's a generational thing,' Dan said patiently. 'They drink tea. Probably have done so since they could hold a cup.' Dan turned his attention to the short menu. 'We need to get a wriggle on. What are you having?'

'If there's pasta of some description, I'm your man.'

'There is,' Dan said. 'And I'll have the steak pie.'

Leo was there in a flash to take their orders. 'Won't be long, Docs,' he promised, batting his way back through the swing doors to his kitchen.

Nathan sent a narrowed look at his friend. He was well aware of the significance of the day in Dan's life. 'How's it going?' he asked quietly.

Dan's mouth bunched into a tight moue. 'Getting there, as they say.'

Nathan wasn't so sure and he knew his friend well

enough to ask, 'It's got to be hard for Caroline as well. Have you tried contacting her again?'

'What would be the point? She couldn't wait to dump me and our marriage—such as it was.'

'Yeah—well.' Nathan decided it was time for some straight talking. 'I don't want to be brutal, but it was never going to work after the babies died, was it?'

'Probably not.' Dan frowned. 'But she wasn't even willing to try!'

Nathan shook his head. They'd had this conversation before—or one similar. 'Listen, Dan, I've known you for a thousand years. It's in your DNA to be decent and, to use a very old-fashioned word, honourable. But you and Caroline weren't in love and, believe me, that's the only reason you should get married. And stay married. For your own sanity, you can't keep second-guessing all the what-ifs.'

Dan knew what Nathan said made sense and, God knew, he'd tried to let it go. His mouth gave a wry twist. 'The last time I spoke to Caroline, she said she'd *moved on.*'

'Then maybe it's time you did as well,' Nathan said frankly. 'Hey!' He injected an air of enthusiasm around them and beat a little drum roll on the table. 'It's Friday and Sami's decided we need a night out. There's a new club in town. Why don't you join us?'

Dan's insides curled. He could think of nothing worse than tagging along with a completely loved-up pair like Nathan and Sami. 'Thanks, mate, but I'll be fine. You and your bride-to-be have better things to do—or you should have.'

'Speaking of brides…' Nathan picked up the pepper mill and spun it between his hands. 'Sami wants us to wear cummerbunds.'

Dan snorted. 'I'd rather shove my head in a bucket of prawns.' He took a mouthful of water, very carefully replacing the glass on its coaster. 'I'd probably walk through fire to save your butt, Nathan, but I am *not* wearing a cummerbund at your wedding.'

Nathan gave a bark of laughter and confided, 'Sami reckons it's *modern vintage*.'

Dan looked unimpressed. 'Tell her the menswear shop in Hopeton have never heard of cummerbunds, let alone stocked them.'

'She said she'd order them online—but don't panic.' Nathan held up a hand in a staying motion, deciding to let his friend off the hook. 'I've talked her out of it.'

'How?' Dan's interest picked up. From what he'd seen, Sami was one determined lady. In the nicest possible way, of course.

'I had a mental picture of us with bulging satin waistlines and fell about laughing. Sami wasn't amused. She wrestled me to the sofa and belted me with her slipper. Then she saw the funny side and laughed too.'

And then they'd probably gone to bed, Dan thought. It was great Nathan was so happy, so…loved. He deserved to be. Dan wondered how long it would be before he had someone special to call his own. Someone to love and who loved him back the same way. Unconditionally. *And that was what had been missing with Caroline.*

'So it's sorted, then?'

'It is. When are you coming up?'

'The day before, on the Friday, if that's OK?' The couple were being married in Sami's home village of Milldale, some thirty miles north of Hopeton. The wedding reception was to be held at Rosemount, one of the historic homes in the district that had been revamped into a functions venue.

'Friday's fine,' Nathan said. 'Sami's booked us into the local pub. My folks are staying there as well.'

'Your meals, gentlemen.' Leo slid plates the size of cartwheels down in front of them. 'Enjoy.'

'This looks good.' Nathan rubbed his hands in anticipation. 'Dig in.'

Halfway through their meal, Dan said, 'When is Sami leaving her job?'

'She has already. She's going to start up her own business here, a travel agency cum tourist thing. She's had mega hits on her website already.'

'That's fantastic. You're going to settle here in Hopeton, then?'

'Yep.' Nathan twirled a length of spaghetti around his fork. 'It's a good fit for us at the moment. And my job's safe—well, as far as any job can be these days.'

Dan's throat closed for a moment. Nathan's future seemed secure and...*good*. If only his own future had a semblance of the same simple expectations attached to it. He shook his head. God, he'd better lighten up, or he'd be like a wet blanket at his friend's wedding.

As if he'd tuned into Dan's thoughts, Nathan said, 'Have you written your best man's speech yet?'

'Not yet.'

'Don't say anything too incriminating that'll get me hanged, will you?'

Dan's mouth twitched. 'Like the after-rugby parties when we were at uni?'

'You were there too, matey,' Nathan reminded him. 'Let's not forget that.'

A swirl of emotions juxtaposed in Dan's head. They had been good times. Uncomplicated. Until *life* had happened. He swore inwardly. He had to release this choking collar of useless introspection. But it was the day, he justified. The date. The memories. 'I suppose I could talk about your peculiar eating habits.'

'Like what?' Nathan gave an offended snort.

'In all my travels, I've never seen anyone consume food as quickly as you.'

'It's a gift.' Nathan gave a Gallic shrug. 'What can I do?'

Dan chuckled. 'Ratbag.'

'So,' Nathan asked, suddenly serious, 'how was it this morning in A and E?'

'I wish you hadn't asked me that.'

'You didn't kill anyone, did you?'

Dan shook his head. 'Probably worse. I dumped all over the team in Resus and walked out.'

'Crikey. I'll bet Lindsey Stewart was impressed—not!'

Dan grimaced.

'Did you apologise?'

'Not yet.'

'Lins has the respect of the whole hospital.' Nathan looked serious. 'You'd better do a real grovel. Ask her for a drink after work and do it then. Properly.'

Dan felt worse and worse. He'd apologise, of course. But ask her for a drink? She'd probably turn him down flat. And he wouldn't blame her. In the short time he'd been at Hopeton he'd hardly put himself out to get to know her or anyone else. Out of nowhere, Lindsey Stewart's flashing green eyes seemed to challenge him. And he realised on some basic level that he *wanted* to get to know her. To break away from the past. He had to turn things around. 'I shouldn't have come to work today.'

'Possibly not,' Nathan agreed. 'Just fix it, mate. Hopeton's not so big that bad behaviour goes unnoticed.'

CHAPTER TWO

BACK AT THE STATION, Lindsey glanced at the clock and sighed. She couldn't wait for the shift to end. And thank heaven she had some leave coming up. And where was Dan? She scanned the precincts with a practised eye. Probably, as Vanessa had supposed, enjoying a long lunch. Except he wasn't late back, she admitted fairly. It was her own fault she'd taken only the briefest lunch break. But she'd got sick of her own company and her mixed-up thoughts had been driving her nuts. She needed to be busy.

Dan made his way slowly towards the station. There she was, sitting with her back towards him, her dark head with its subtle streaks of auburn bent over some paperwork. He silently thanked all the gods she was on her own. He couldn't do this in front of an audience. His breathing faltered, his stomach churned and he went forward. 'Lindsey…'

She spun round and looked up. 'Dan…'

Dan rubbed at the back of his neck, feeling his muscles bunch but not release.

For a few seconds there was an awkward silence as they both took stock.

'I owe you an apology,' Dan said eventually.

Lindsey stood up. She'd feel better able to sort this standing eye to eye. She sent him a cool look. 'Do you have a problem with the nursing back-up in the department? Or a problem with me?'

'Of course I don't.' Dan felt a spark of anger. Where had she got that idea? He gave a tight shrug. 'I was out of line earlier. I'm sorry. It won't happen again.'

Lindsey felt her whole bearing soften. His ownership of his lapse was more, much more than she'd expected. She lifted her chin and met his gaze, suddenly aware they were close, too close for comfort. What was he thinking? She couldn't tell. His eyes were clouded with uncertainty. Out of nowhere, Lindsey felt a twist of uncertainty herself. She hated being out of sync with any of her colleagues. Hated it. 'Stuff happens in Casualty.' She gave an open-handed shrug. 'Don't beat yourself up.'

'Thank you.' Dan felt the ton weight lift from him. He gave a tight smile. 'Put it down to an off day. We all have them, don't you agree?'

'I guess we do,' Lindsey said carefully. And if she was any judge of the human condition, he was still having an off day. He seemed a bit…*desperate*, for want of a better word. Edgy. And there were shadows beneath his eyes. Again. If anyone needed a hug, it was Dan Rossi. But that would be totally out of order. Unprofessional. And embarrass the socks off him. She looked away quickly. In seconds, the tenor of her day had changed completely. What was going on here had no rhyme nor reason. It was just… happening. And she felt she was jumping fences ten feet high and couldn't stop. It was an extraordinary sensation.

Dan swallowed through a very dry throat. She had her hair twisted into a topknot and flyaway strands were coming loose. He wondered what it would look like if she were to let it tumble down, releasing the scent of the flowery shampoo she used. It wasn't going to happen. In an almost reflex action she reached up, pushing the wayward strands back in. Dan fisted his hands, resisting the urge to do it for her. 'So, what's on the agenda?'

Lindsey put her nurse's head on quickly. 'We have a little kid waiting for sutures. Michelle and Andrew are presently treating a youth with burns, the result of walking barefoot on coals after a bush barbecue. If you'd rather take over there and have one of them see the child...?'

'No, no.' Dan frowned a bit. 'Our junior doctors need to gather experience. I'll see the child. Point me in the right direction.'

'I'll come with you,' she said, as Vanessa took over the station.

'Fill me in,' he said, as they walked towards the cubicles.

'Preschooler, Michael Woods. He was chasing a ball out of bounds, tripped and hit his chin on the edge of a brick garden bed. Fair bit of blood. Panic stations and the school rang mum. She's with him.'

'Good. She'll be a calming influence.'

Lindsey chuckled. 'You hope.'

'Are you saying it's the mothers we have to be afraid of, Lindsey?'

Lindsey turned her head and caught his gaze. She blinked a bit. Unless she was mistaken, there was actually a curve happening to one corner of his mouth. On impulse, she sent him a full-blown smile in return, urged on by a feeling of oneness with him she couldn't explain. 'I've met a few.'

Five-year-old Michael was sitting on the edge of the treatment couch, his small legs swinging rhythmically back and forth. He didn't look overly upset, Lindsey noted thankfully, although the blotches of dried blood on his T-shirt indicated it had been a heavy bump to his chin.

Dan smiled at the mother. 'Mrs Woods? I'm Dan Rossi. I'll be the doctor looking after Michael.'

'I'm Stephanie.' Michael's mother kept her arm protectively around her little boy's shoulders. She gave a wry smile. 'He's a bit of a tornado in the playground.'

'So, you like playing footy, Michael?' Dan asked.

'I can kick the ball as high as the house,' Michael declared, aiming upwards with one small arm.

'Fantastic.' Dan looked impressed.

Lindsey gave him a tick of approval for keeping things light and thereby gaining their small patient's trust. Unobtrusively, she gloved and said quietly, 'I'll pop that sticking plaster off Michael's chin, shall I, Dr Dan?'

'Let's do that.' Almost casually, Dan hooked over a mobile stool and snapped on gloves. He sat in front of Michael. His eyes narrowed slightly. The removal of the plaster had revealed a gaping hole underneath. The mother's gasp was audible. 'Easily fixed.' Dan's tone was gently reassuring. Tilting Michael's chin, he examined the damage more closely. The edges of the wound were uniform. They would align nicely. It would be a neat scar.

'Is he OK?' Stephanie asked anxiously.

'His bite seems even,' Dan responded. 'And his baby teeth all seem in place. I'll put a stitch or two in his chin and he should be as right as rain.'

Gently, Lindsey positioned Michael for the suturing procedure, laying him back with his head at the end of the bed.

Dan rolled across the trolley containing the instruments he'd need and switched on an overhead light. 'Now, Michael, this is where you have to be as brave as the best footy player in the world,' Dan said, flicking up the syringe of local anaesthetic.

Michael's blue eyes lit up. 'Like David Beckham.'

Dan huffed a laugh. 'That's the guy. Now, if you lie very still for me while I make your chin better, I'm sure

I can find an amazing sticker you can wear on your shirt tomorrow and show the kids at preschool.'

'My shirt's all dirty,' Michael said with childish logic.

'Honey, we'll find you a clean one to wear.' Stephanie smiled at her son and held his hand tightly.

Dan looked up. 'Lindsey, if you would, please?'

She nodded. The injection of the lignocaine would sting and be a shock to the little one. 'Squeeze Mummy's hand hard, Michael,' she said, placing herself gently across the child's body in case he tried to wriggle free.

In a few seconds the local had been injected and they waited a couple of minutes for it to take effect. Dan prodded the wound gently in several places. 'Can you feel anything hurting, Michael?'

Eyes squeezed shut, Michael said, 'No...'

'Good boy. Keep holding Mummy's hand and we'll be finished in no time.'

In a short time Lindsey watched Dan snip the last suture close to the skin. 'There you are, sweetheart.' She gave the little shoulder a gentle pat. 'All finished.'

'Can I get my sticker now?'

Dan looked a question. He'd promised one to his small patient. He just hoped they had some in the department.

'They're in a box at the station,' Lindsey said right on cue. 'Won't be a tick.'

'Gorgeous little boy, wasn't he?' Lindsey remarked lightly as she went about tidying the treatment room.

Dan was parked at the mobile tray, writing up his notes. He lifted his head in query. 'Sorry?'

'Michael,' Lindsey said. 'He'll probably be a real heartbreaker.'

'Yes, probably...' Dan went back to his notes, finishing them swiftly.

'Thanks.' He gave the ghost of a smile and left quietly.

Lindsey bundled the soiled linen into a bin with a vengeance. What was with this guy? Would it kill him to indulge in a bit of normal conversation?

Dan was amazed how quickly the rest of the shift passed. The ache in his shoulders had disappeared. Cautiously, he began to feel, as a result of the sudden turnaround with Lindsey, he might have a chance at some kind of normal life here at Hopeton. A chance he couldn't afford to ignore.

Deep in thought, he began collating paperwork at the station. There were some end-of-shift letters he needed to write to several GPs. In Dan's opinion, their respective patients would need referral—

'Still at it?' Lindsey stopped at the station, her brows raised in query.

Dan's mouth tipped into a rueful smile. 'Still a bit of tidying up to do. You're off, then?' His fingers curled round his pen. Idiot. It was the end of her shift. Of course she was *off.* Gone were the hospital scrubs; instead, she was wearing soft jeans that clung to her legs and a long-sleeved silver-grey top, a silky scarf in a swirl of multi-colours around her throat.

And knee-high boots.

Dan felt his heart walk a few flights of stairs. He couldn't think of a single thing to say to the beautiful woman standing in front of him. And how pathetic was that?

'It's Friday, you should give yourself an early mark.' Lindsey looked more keenly at him. The lines of strain were still there around his eyes. He needed to relax. But whether or not he'd allow her to help him do that was another matter entirely.

But for some reason she couldn't fathom, she had to try.

'Most of us are going to the pub. Few drinks, a game

of snooker, a pizza or five later. You're very welcome to join us.'

Dan's heart suddenly came to a halt. *Thank you, God.* 'Sounds good. Uh—which pub?'

'The Peach Tree. Ancient red-brick place at the top of the main street. See you there, then?'

'You bet.' He nodded enthusiastically. 'Thanks for the invite.'

'Welcome.' Lindsey hitched up her shoulder bag and turned, moving off quickly to catch up with Vanessa.

A fleeting frown touched Dan's eyes as he watched the two women make their way towards the exit. He took a long controlling breath and let it go. Thanks to Lindsey's invitation, he'd taken the first steps towards his new life.

With the thought still humming in his head, he went back to his office to type up his referrals.

Letters completed, Dan swung up from his desk, looking up in question when Martin Lorimer, the senior doctor on take, poked his head in. 'Ah—Dan. You're still here. MVA coming in. Pile-up on the highway, two vehicles, all teenagers. Can you hang about?'

Dan felt his gut contract. Did he have a choice? *Hell.* Lindsey would think he'd bottled out or just been plain rude. And he didn't need that kind of misunderstanding after today's debacle. He'd text her if he could but he had no idea of her mobile number. He swore under his breath. If the injuries to the kids were not too serious, maybe he'd still make it to the pub. Holding that thought, he made his way towards the ambulance bay.

'I got you another OJ.' Vanessa placed the glass of juice in front of Lindsey. 'And what's with you tonight, Lins? We could have won the snooker if you hadn't been so not into it. Now I owe Andrew ten bucks.' Vanessa pleated a

strand of her blunt-cut blonde hair behind her ear. 'Um…
do you think Andrew might be a bit keen?'

'On you?' Lindsey took a mouthful of her drink.
'Maybe. Every time he needs a hand with a patient, he
makes a beeline for you.'

'So, do you think he's ever going to get off his butt and
do something about it?'

'Why wait for him? Van, you live in the same building.
Surely you run into him about the place. Just ask him in
for a coffee or something.'

'But if he said no, I'd feel stupid,' Vanessa moaned.
'And I have to work with him.' She ran her finger around
the rim of her glass. 'Did he seem to miss me while I was
on leave?'

'Not that I noticed,' Lindsey said drily. 'But he's coming over now. Perhaps you're about to find out.'

'You bet I will.' Full of resolve, Vanessa whirled to her
feet. 'Are you off home?' She gave Andrew a pert look
and a very warm smile.

'Think I'd better. I'm back on a late tomorrow.'

'Oh, me too.' Vanessa grabbed her bag. 'Let's share
a cab. I'll put the ten bucks I owe you towards the fare.
Deal?'

'Deal.' Andrew's white smile gleamed. The two took a
few steps away then turned and chorused, ''Night, Lins.'

Lindsey dredged up a smile and fluttered a wave. Ten
minutes later her eyes did another tour of the lounge. Still
no Dan. Inwardly, she gave a philosophic little shrug. She'd
invited him and he hadn't shown. And yet he'd seemed
keen enough. Perhaps he'd thought better of it. Her mouth
turned down. And perhaps she'd come across as being too
pushy. Well, whatever, she wasn't going to hang about,
wondering.

Outside, the night was clear and crisp. Lindsey looked

up. The moon looked so pretty, hanging there like…a silvery seahorse…

'Lindsey!'

She spun round. She'd know that voice anywhere. Her heart jagged into overdrive. 'Dan?'

Dan emerged out of the shadows and into the filtered lighting at the pub's perimeter. 'You waited,' he said, and looked at her. 'I got caught up.' Briefly he filled her in.

'When will kids realise speed can be a potential killer?' Lindsey shook her head. 'They'll all be OK, though?'

'Should be, in time,' Dan replied, fisting his hands into the side pockets of his bomber jacket. 'I'm whacked,' he admitted frankly. 'Are they still serving meals here?'

'Long finished,' Lindsey said. 'The club scene's taken over now.'

'Uh, OK. Thanks for hanging about,' he said, hunching his shoulders in a shrug. 'I thought my not turning up might have ticked you off. I didn't want that.'

'I guessed you'd had an emergency,' Lindsey said, forgiving herself the small untruth. 'It's a bummer when that happens right at the end of a shift, isn't it?'

His blue eyes regarded her levelly. 'Well, this time it certainly was. I had no way of letting you know.'

Lindsey flipped a hand dismissively. 'We can fix that now, if you like.' She reached into her bag and pulled out her mobile and in a few seconds they'd exchanged numbers.

'So, we're good, then?' Dan's head came up in query and he returned his phone to his back pocket.

Lindsey swallowed unevenly. Running into him like this had been unexpected. And now it all seemed a bit surreal. And why on earth were they standing here? It was freezing. 'What are you going to do about some food?'

'I'm sure I'll find somewhere to get a takeaway if I look hard enough.'

Lindsey bit the edge of her bottom lip. She had the sudden vision of him going back to his place, sitting alone, eating alone. After the kind of brutal day he'd appeared to have had, the mental picture was awful. The fact that it bothered her so much took her by surprise. She lived only a few minutes away. She could offer to feed him. An invitation hovered on the tip of her tongue...

'Do you have the weekend off?' Dan asked.

Lindsey snapped her thoughts back to reality. 'Yes. You?'

'Back on an early tomorrow.'

Lindsey made a face. 'Make sure you eat, then.' She cringed inwardly. She'd sounded like his grandmother.

'Thanks for caring.' His eyes held a penetratingly blue honesty.

'Mmm...' Lindsey's mouth went dry.

'I haven't exactly been fun to work with.' Half turning, he dragged a hand through his hair, leaving a few dark strands drifting across his forehead. It gave him a faintly dissolute air.

Lindsey scrunched her fingers through the folds of her scarf, suddenly shaken by the intensity of emotion that just standing next to Dan generated throughout her entire body. 'Maybe we should appoint a laughter coach for the ED.'

Dan felt disconcerted for a second. Her mouth was smiling. Just. More a tiny upward flick at the corners. He smiled back and, for just a moment, a blink of time, there was a connection of shared awareness. Sharp. Intense. And then it was gone, retracting like the sun under cloud. 'Take that idea to the board.'

'Would I have your backing?'

Was she serious? 'You bet. Laughter in the ED sounds... remedial.' And ridiculous. In fact, the whole conversation was verging on the ridiculous. Which only went to prove how out of touch he was with the ordinary stuff, like social interaction. Especially with beautiful women. The atmosphere was fraught again.

'If you're looking for a takeaway, the Chinese should still be open,' Lindsey offered.

He gave a one-shouldered shrug, moving restively as though he wanted to be away. 'Maybe I won't bother after all. I've food at home. I can whip up something.' *Or I could ask you to come and have a coffee with me.* His thoughts churned with indecision. He took the easy way out and said, 'You're OK getting home, then?'

'I'm parked just over there.' Lindsey indicated the small sedan the same make as a dozen others in the car park. 'Where are you?'

'Near the exit.'

Lindsey burrowed her chin more deeply into the roll collar of her fleece. This was bordering on crazy, standing here like two puppets waiting for someone to pull their strings and activate their mouths. She felt like chucking all her doubts and insisting he come home with her for a meal. Instead, she lowered her head and began fishing for her car keys in her bag.

Dan's jaw tightened as her hair fell forward in a shimmering curtain and it was all he could do not to reach out and draw it back and hold it while he pressed a slow, lingering kiss on her mouth…

'Got them.' Lindsey held up the keys triumphantly. Her gaze held his for a long moment. Expectant. Something… 'I guess I'll see you at work, then.'

Dan managed a nod. Whatever chance he'd had to further their…*friendship* outside the hospital had gone now. He'd stuffed it. 'Guess so.'

'Make sure you eat,' she reinforced, and they both took off in different directions.

'Hey, Lindsey!'

She turned. He was walking backwards and smiling. 'In case you were wondering, I *can* cook.'

'Never doubted it.' Lindsey's own smile carried her all the way home.

Wednesday, the following week...

'Told you he'd shape up.' Vanessa's voice held vindication, as they completed handover for the late shift.

'Andrew?' Lindsey feigned mild interest.

Vanessa gave an eye-roll. 'Our Dr Rossi. He's been exceptionally co-operative and I detected quite a nice sense of humour lurking somewhere there.'

'I've hardly seen him this week.' Lindsey made a pretence of checking the list of patients waiting in cubicles. 'His shifts have obviously been all over the place.' And she'd noticed his absence. Oh, boy, had she noticed.

'Well, if you're happy with everything, I'm out of here.' Vanessa hauled off her lanyard and scattered a handful of pens into a nearby tray. 'Andrew and I are going to a movie.'

'Well, fancy that...' Lindsey drawled. 'He's finally asked you out on a date.'

'Well, actually, I asked him. But he was all for it,' Vanessa added quickly.

'Good for you, Van.'

'Well, the opportunity kind of just presented itself,' Vanessa said modestly. 'But it just goes to show, doesn't it? Some men merely need a shove in the right direction.'

Was there a message somewhere in there for her? Lindsey's eyes were thoughtful as she set about triaging the patients on her list.

CHAPTER THREE

LINDSEY TURNED UP the music and did a rhythmic little rock with her shoulders as she drove. It was Friday at last and she was on leave. *Going home.* It was a good feeling. And perhaps back among the vines and the majestic blue hills she'd be able to sort out her feelings about a certain doctor. Was she wasting her time, though? Maybe. Maybe not.

She shut her music off. It was time to concentrate on her driving. Even though the country road was bitumen and usually well maintained, it was narrow. And it was just on dusk, visibility questionable to say the least, but she hadn't wanted to hang about in Hopeton. With the thought of home beckoning, she'd just wanted to be on her way.

Automatically, she concentrated her vision on the road ahead. The headlights of an approaching car were illuminating the horizon. Lindsey adjusted her own headlights in preparation. She noticed there was a vehicle behind her as well. But so far it was obeying the road rules and keeping a safe distance.

Dan's thoughts were very mixed as he drove. He hadn't managed to catch Lindsey much over the past week. And that had been a frustration. He'd wanted to reinforce the little progress he'd made in getting to know her. But his hours at work had been manic, only because he'd made himself available so as to accumulate a few days' leave after the wedding. The wedding was tomorrow. He hadn't prepared a speech so he'd speak off the cuff. He and Nathan had so much shared history, it shouldn't be difficult.

Abruptly, Dan was jolted out of his thoughts of weddings and speeches as he noticed the lurching drift of an oncoming car. *What the hell?* All his reflexes sprang into action. He reduced speed instantly, preparing to brake. For a split second he forgot to breathe, following the speeding car's trajectory as it plunged out of control, crossing the centre line and placing it on a collision course with the car in front of him. He felt every nerve in his body tense.

Surely, a crash was inevitable.

Lindsey hissed an expletive, all her defensive driver training coming into play. This couldn't be happening! Who was this lunatic of a driver? Her heart pounded, echoing in her ears. *Please, no!* She pulled hard on the steering wheel, feeling she'd dodged a bullet as the sports car shot past in a blur. She was safe. The relief was instant but short-lived as the vehicle clipped the rear section of her car, pushing her off the road. Her head snapped forward and then back, slamming into her headrest as her car spun and spun again.

Dan's jaw went rigid. This was a nightmare. He watched in horror as the sports car rolled before coming to rest right side up in a mangled mess of metal and broken glass. One headlight remained working, shining brokenly on the prostrate figure lying in the middle of the road.

It took a few seconds for the nurse in Lindsey to react. All thoughts of her own welfare fled. Pushing out of the car, she set her feet on the road. She felt woozy as she stood, swallowing back sudden nausea. She had to get to the injured person. She began running.

* * *

The sight of the female figure running towards the accident wrenched Dan out of his quagmire of disbelief. He brought his Land Rover as near as was safe to the accident site, switching his headlights to high beam. In seconds, he'd lodged a call for an ambulance. Seconds after that, he was out and grabbing his medical case, complete with oxygen and suction. He had a feeling he was going to need every last item in his kit. He took off at a run, noting the woman was already at the scene, crouching over the injured man. Dan frowned. Should she even be there? He'd seen how her vehicle had copped the impact of the sports car. 'Are you hurt?'

Lindsey startled at the brisk demand, raising her head. She blinked uncomprehendingly. 'Dan…?'

Sweet God. Dan let his breath go in a stream. 'Lindsey?'

For a mini-second they stared at each other in amazement and total disbelief. But the whys and wherefores had to wait until later. They had a life to save. 'Are you OK?' Dan rapped.

She frowned slightly. 'Think so…'

'Then let's see what's going on.'

The injured man looked in his sixties. Possible causes for the accident ran through Dan's head. Had he fallen asleep? Suffered a stroke or heart attack…? He was wearing bike shorts, T-shirt and hiking boots. Dan threw open his medical kit, snapping on a pair of gloves. Who was this guy—some kind of fitness nut? First things first, he decided, placing an oxygen mask over the man's face.

Lindsey hunkered down beside Dan. 'Ambulance coming?'

'Yep. They've diverted one. Let's hope it gets here in time.' Dan shook his head at the carnage. 'Glove up, please, Lindsey. I need your help here.'

She swayed a little then gathered herself, taking a deep

breath and then another, pulling on her gloves over shaking hands. 'Is he still breathing?'

'Just. Obviously he wasn't wearing a seat belt to be thrown out like that.' Dan did a quick head-to-toe check. 'Multiple contusions, by the look of it, fractured tibias.' He ripped out an expletive. 'Arterial bleed from his groin.'

Lindsey felt her stomach turn upside down, the sight of bright blood pulsing from the femoral artery almost making her gag. She took quick, shallow breaths, swallowing down the bitter taste of bile. Working like a robot, she grabbed whatever she could find in Dan's bag to absorb the flow of blood and pressed hard against the site. Pressure. They needed pressure. A tourniquet. An ambulance. A and E back-up. Her brain fogged. This was bordering on her worst nightmare. She'd attended dozens of accident scenes. What on earth was wrong with her...?

'Sure you're OK?'

Suddenly Dan was butted up against her. Lindsey felt the warmth of his hand anchoring hers. Her teeth began to chatter. 'Bit s-sick...'

'You're in shock!' God, why hadn't he noticed?

'I'll...be all right.' Lindsey forced herself to slow her breathing. In and out.

Dan scanned her face. Even in the dim light he could see she was as pale as parchment. 'Do you hurt anywhere? Lindsey, I need to know.'

She shook her head and winced as a spasm in her neck caught her unawares. 'Bit of...whiplash. I'll be OK. Just... get on.'

Dan hissed a non-reply. Within seconds, he'd wound a tourniquet into place.

Freed from the task of providing pressure on the wound, Lindsey pulled back. 'Do you have a collar?'

'No, damn it.' He shook his head at his lapse. Made a mental note to include one in his kit ASAP. 'We've got to stop that racket somehow,' he grated. They both knew their patient's airway was seriously compromised, his tortured breathing rattling into the stillness. He'd have to improvise. Dan's responses were running at top speed. He moved forward, kneeling so that the injured man's head was between his thighs. It was the only kind of stability he could offer for his patient's head and neck. Using gentle pressure, he extended the chin. The man's breathing improved marginally. It had to be enough until the paramedics got there.

Lindsey rallied, giving Dan the back-up he needed. She passed him the portable suction unit, automatically pushing the mask aside so he could place the sucker inside their patient's mouth. She felt black nausea pool in her stomach as blood tracked down into the tubing. Turning away, she retched onto the road.

'That's enough, Lindsey,' Dan ordered. 'I can manage from here.' He motioned backwards with his head. 'Go and sit in my car and wait for me. There's bottled water in an Esky on the floor. Drink.'

Wrapping her arms tightly over her stomach, Lindsey walked a bit unsteadily to the Land Rover. Opening the passenger door, she stopped, breathing away the coil of utter wretchedness. The few seconds' hiatus gave her some relief and she scrambled inside. Letting her head rest back, she closed her eyes and steadied her breathing.

It took only a few minutes for her stomach to settle. Feeling more in control, she leaned down and took a bottle of water from the Esky. She began sipping, feeling better after each mouthful. But now she was beginning to feel cold.

Dan's jacket was draped across the back of the driver's seat. Guardedly, aware she could overstretch her already sore neck muscles, she reached over and slowly managed to unhook the coat, draping it across her body like a blanket.

She felt herself relax, snuggling into its warmth, breathing in the faint scent of sandalwood and seasoned leather.

And him.

Out of nowhere, Lindsey felt a warm sensation down low, sensual tentacles humming through her whole body. She burrowed more deeply into Dan's coat. And felt connected to him in a way she could have only imagined.

Her mind flew ahead to something much more intimate and she snuggled deeper, as though taking his body warmth into herself.

Gradually, she became aware that the ambulance had arrived in a blaze of lights and a blaring siren, the police vehicle and a tow truck not far behind, the multi-coloured strobes looking like a weird kind of stage show. Lindsey watched through the windscreen, glad to be away from it all. Her tummy had settled but the feeling of it all happening to someone else persisted. Unfortunately, the reality was there in the ache of her neck muscles.

She could only hope the injured man would recover. And if he did, it was all down to Dan's skill as a doctor. He had been amazing.

Twenty minutes later the ambulance had gone. Lindsey registered the activity up ahead. The police had redirected the oncoming traffic. She wondered why there seemed quite a bit for this rather quiet road. But, then, it was Friday and lots of folk liked to get away for the weekend for wine tours and the B&B comfort offered by several of the vineyards around Milldale.

'How're you doing?'

Lindsey startled. The driver's door had swung open and Dan was there beside her. 'Much better.' She gave a wan smile. 'I borrowed your coat.'

'Good. I'm glad you had the sense to keep warm.' He sent her a perceptive look. 'I take it Milldale doesn't have a hospital?'

'Not even a GP. Why?'

'Why?' Dan frowned. 'Because I think I should take you straight back to Hopeton and get your neck X-rayed.'

'Oh, Dan…please, no.' Lindsey squeezed her eyes tightly shut in rebuttal. 'I'll be fine, honestly.'

'You can't know that for sure, Lindsey.' He seemed unconvinced. 'But I had a feeling you'd be stubborn so I managed to snaffle a collar from the paramedics.'

'No collars.' Lindsey was adamant. 'Look, it's whip-lash, resulting in a bit of muscle strain. I have some massage oil that works miracles. I'll attend to it the minute I get to where I'm going.'

Dan quirked a brow. 'And where is that?'

'Milldale. Home.'

'Home,' Dan repeated. 'I thought you lived in Hopeton.'

'I do, for work. But home for me is Lark Hill, the vine-yard where my parents live. Where I grew up. I'm start-ing a bit of leave.'

It took Dan only a few seconds to process all this. She still had some way to drive to Milldale before she could get relief for her neck pain. Was she fit to drive? Was her car even drivable? He came to a decision. He was a doc-tor, for God's sake. He could treat her. Here and now. 'Do you have your *miracle* oil with you?'

Lindsey looked uncertain. 'Of course I have it with me.'

'In your luggage?' Dan was slowly opening the driver's door. 'Tell me where to look and I'll massage it in for you. The sooner it's done, the sooner some relief will kick in for you.'

Lindsey's hands clutched the collar of his coat, pulling it higher as if to ward off the idea. She couldn't let him do that. It was too intimate…too…everything. She moist-ened her lips. 'If you get me the oil, I can rub it on myself.'

He snorted. 'And how high can you lift your arms without it hurting?'

Emotions began clogging Lindsey's throat. If she was honest, she was aching all over and suffering the aftermath of shock. It would be so lovely to let go of all her scruples and let Dan take care of her. 'My car keys are still in the ignition.'

'And your luggage in the boot?' Dan swung one leg out of the car.

Lindsey managed a small nod. 'Just bring my beauty case. It's black with—'

'Lindsey, relax,' Dan broke in gently. 'I know what a beauty case looks like. I'll find it.'

Lindsey closed her eyes. He'd told her to relax so she'd try. He'd taken over anyway. And right at the moment the idea sounded heaven-sent.

Dan was back. Not only did he have her beauty case but he'd brought along her shoulder bag as well. And her long woolly cardigan was draped over his forearm.

'You've thought of everything.' Lindsey managed a trapped smile.

'And I have something for your neck pain as well.'

'What are they?' She looked dubiously at the foil-wrapped tablets he handed her.

'They're standard painkillers,' Dan said. 'Nothing to send you off to la-la land.' He watched as she broke open the foil and then handed her a bottle of water. When she'd swallowed the tablets, he asked, 'Now, how are we going to do this?'

Lindsey blinked. He was obviously referring to her massage. She unzipped her beauty case and handed him the bottle of oil. 'I could probably just manoeuvre myself so my back's to you,' she said throatily.

'Or we could fold back the rear seat so you could lie down.'

'That's not necessary.' Lindsey was firm. 'Just take your jacket back, Dan, and I'll get my shirt off.'

Dan's eyes widened. His heart gave a sideways skip. 'OK…'

Lindsey undid the buttons and shrugged off the loose-fitting shirt to reveal a snug little vest top beneath. She sent him an innocent look. 'What?'

'Nothing.'

She managed a soft chuckle. 'Had you going there, didn't I, Daniel?'

'A guy can live in hope,' he countered, his mouth lifting at the corners. 'Now, give me that oil and we'll get started.'

Lindsey felt her body relax its tension as Dan's fingers began the gentle kneading of her neck muscles. It felt good, so good, and she wanted it to go on for ever…

Dan let his hands drift over the smooth column of her neck and then tease out the tense muscles at its base, almost hypnotised by the feel of her satin-smooth skin under his hands. 'It's Dante, by the way.'

'Really?' Lindsey's voice went high in disbelief.

'Really.'

'From the Italian poet of the Middle Ages?'

'At least you have the origin right,' he said. 'My sisters used to tell everyone I'd been named after a middle-aged poet.'

'Oh, poor you. Were you teased a lot?'

'Sometimes I felt like quietly enrolling at another school.'

'I think Dante suits you.'

'Hmm.' Dan was noncommittal.

'Is your mother a romantic, then?'

'No.' He sounded amused. 'It's an old family name. Apparently, it was just my turn to be lumbered with it.'

'That's pathetic,' Lindsey said mildly. 'It makes you different…*special*.'

He didn't reply.

'How does that feel now?'

Lindsey heard the guarded tone in his voice. Had her remark embarrassed him? Probably. And she wouldn't have continued with the banter if she hadn't been feeling so relaxed with him. Her mistake. 'It's much better, thanks. I'll be OK now.' She swivelled round to face the front again.

'If you're sure?' Dan recapped the bottle of oil and handed it back to her.

'I'm fine.' She stowed the bottle back in her beauty case then reached for her cardigan and shrugged it on.

Well, he'd stuffed that up. Dan locked his hands around the steering wheel and looked blindly out into the night. He'd stomped all over her light remarks and shut down. Now she'd be back to thinking he was some kind of unsociable cretin. God, he felt like an infant trying to stand upright and walk.

His jaw tightened. He had to fix things. 'I've...made things awkward again, haven't I?'

Her throat constricted. 'I wasn't coming on to you.'

'I know that. You were being sweet and funny...' He paused painfully.

'I've—been out of circulation for a while.'

Lindsey glanced at him, taking in his body language. Obviously, he'd been through something that had knocked him sideways. Something it was taking him time to get past. She felt a river of empathy run out to him. 'Do you want to talk about it?' As soon as she'd said the trite words Lindsey wished them back. Whatever it was that was bugging him, he'd probably *talked* about it until he was blue in the face. 'Sorry, scratch that.'

He blew out a controlled sigh. 'It's just stuff that's a bit hard to...revisit.'

'I get that, Dan,' she said softly.

His head swung towards her. Even in the subdued light-

ing in the car, the force of his undivided attention was like
a mini-riot inside her. They breathed through several beats
of silence. Until… Dan bent, his lips grazing hers. It was
the lightest of kisses but heady with the taste of promise.
For a long moment they stared at each other. 'That was a
bit…' Lindsey's voice faded.

'Unexpected?' Dan moved closer, so close she had to
tilt her head up to look at him. So close she could feel the
heat radiating from his body. 'Nice, though?'

His softly spoken question danced across her nerves,
creating a new wave of warmth to cascade through her.
She nodded, words simply escaping her.

Dan stroked her cheek with the backs of his fingers, his
body drenched in emotions he'd almost forgotten.

A gossamer-thin thread of awareness seemed to shim-
mer between them, until they drew back slowly from each
other, breaking the spell.

Lindsey began pulling her cardigan more tightly around
her. 'Um, do you think we could find a hot drink somewhere?'

'Oh, God—sorry!' Dan hit the heel of his hand on his
forehead. 'You're probably still shocky. I'm an idiot—'

'Dan, it's OK.' Lindsey bit back a half-laugh. 'I didn't
expect you to have a Thermos of tea with you. There's
a service station a few clicks further on. We could stop
there.'

'Right. Good. We'll do that. But we'll need to do something about your car first. From what I saw, it's not drivable.'

'Oh—are you sure?' Lindsey looked pained.

'I'm no mechanic but looks like you had a pretty big
whack. The back wheel seems out of alignment and I had
trouble getting the boot open. I could have a word with
the tow-truck guys for you?'

'No, it's fine.' She waved the idea away. 'I'll get on to

my insurance company.' She flicked out her mobile and found the number on speed dial. 'All sorted,' she said after a few minutes of intense negotiation. 'They'll arrange for my car to be towed for repairs and if I need it I can pick up a replacement vehicle from the garage in Milldale.'

'I'll drive you home, then,' Dan said.

'I don't want to take you out of your way.'

'You won't be. I'm going to Milldale myself. I'll get your personal stuff from the car, shall I?'

'I'll help.' Lindsey volunteered, making to get out of his vehicle.

'Hang on a tick.' He stayed her with the lightest touch on her wrist. 'I'll come round and give you a hand. Don't want you falling.'

'Dan, I'm fine,' she remonstrated.

'Humour me, all right?'

Lindsey gave a contained little sigh but waited until he'd come round to the passenger door. He opened it and offered a steadying hand. She took it gratefully. He'd been right. She did feel a kind of light-headedness.

'When did you last eat?' Dan asked, keeping his hand firmly on hers.

'Sandwich at lunch.'

'Then the sooner we get some hot food into you the better.' He reopened the boot and retrieved her suitcase and a canvas backpack.

'And would you mind getting that large plastic bin as well?' Lindsey asked. 'It has a lid so you won't spill anything.'

Dan hefted the bin out by its handle, almost staggering at its solid weight. 'What the blazes do you have in here—body parts?'

Her mouth crimped at the corners. 'Clay.'

'I…see.' Although clearly he didn't.

'It's potter's clay,' Lindsey explained, following him

back to the Land Rover. 'I have a wheel and kiln at home. I aim to make some pieces while I'm on my holiday.'

Dan tried to get a grip on his wayward thoughts, imagining *Lindsey the potter* with her dark hair wild and flowing, perhaps her feet bare, her body lithe and swaying as she threw her pots. A compelling new awareness, sharp and insistent, stirred within him. An awareness that hadn't been stirred in a long time. An awareness that he'd stomped all over on that first day when Lindsey Stewart had smiled at him.

'Do you think you should let your folks know what's happened so they won't be worrying?' Dan asked as they settled back into the car. 'I imagine it'll be a bit late by the time we get you home.'

That sounded so thoughtful. Lindsey turned her head, slowly taking in his profile. It was almost sculpted. He'd make a perfect model. Her fingers began to tingle and she imagined carving out his features from a block of clay, pleating, smoothing, working her thumbs to form his cheekbones, a slow sweep to define his jaw, the touch of a finger defining the cleft in his chin. Definitely that. She pressed her thumb and forefinger together, almost feeling the slide of wet clay as she fashioned the curve of his mouth...

'Lindsey?'

'Uh—' She came back with a jolt.

'Do you need to ring home?'

'Actually, my parents are in Scotland, visiting my brother and sister-in-law. They've just had their first baby. Mum and Dad are away for a few more weeks yet.'

Dan started the engine and they began moving. 'So, who's at home for you, then?'

'I don't need looking after.'

'You've been through a trauma tonight, Lindsey. What if you need something—or someone?'

Heck! Was he offering? Lindsey pulled back from the flight of fancy. 'I should explain,' she said. 'We have managers for the vineyard, Jeff and Fiona Collins. Their cottage is quite close to the main house. Knowing I'm coming, Fi will have aired the place, stocked the fridge and left the lights on. I'll phone her when I arrive and she's around if I need anything.'

'I guess that's all right, then,' he said, as the bright lights of the roadhouse came into view.

'That was lovely, thanks.' Lindsey forked up the last of her omelette and then sat back, replete. 'So, why are you heading to Milldale?'

'Nathan Lyons's wedding.' Dan finished off his steak sandwich and casually swiped his mouth with the paper napkin.

'Of course. I can't believe I'd forgotten for the moment. It'll be a big do. Sami will have all the trimmings.'

Dan raised a dark brow. 'You know Sami?'

'For ever. Our parents' properties adjoin. We lost touch a bit when she relocated to Sydney but we've caught up again now she's back.'

'I'm Nathan's best man,' Dan said.

'I knew from the hospital grapevine you were mates.' Lindsey rested her chin in her upturned hand and looked at him. 'Are you looking forward to the wedding?'

'Yes, I am...' he said slowly, and realised it was true. 'They're a great couple.'

Lindsey gave a soft laugh. 'They're in love. It shows.'

'I suppose it does. Have *you* ever been in love, Lindsey?' he asked abruptly.

Wow! That was out of left field. 'In love. Out of love,' she sidestepped lightly. 'You?'

He gave a tight shrug. 'Same.'

They picked up their mugs of tea, each silently assessing the weight of their answers, each guessing that they hadn't exactly been lies but that they hadn't been quite the truth either.

'You're not Sami's bridesmaid, by any chance?' Dan asked after a minute.

'No. Her sister Caitlin's filling that role. She's just back from a modelling assignment overseas. Cait's the face of Avivia.'

'Which is…?'

Lindsey chuckled. 'Avivia is an international cosmetic company.'

'Ah.' He nodded sagely. 'But *you'll* be at the wedding?'

'Yes. I'll save you a dance,' she ventured daringly.

Dan's eyes flicked wide. The thought of dancing with her, *holding* her, sent a new chain of awareness shooting up his spine.

'I take it you *can* dance?'

'Yes, I can dance.' He gave a guarded kind of smile. 'In fact, I used to love dancing.'

'Used to?'

'It's been a while.'

'Oh.' Lindsey drew back in her chair. Out of nowhere, her body felt tingly with electricity. 'We'll have to catch you up, then.'

His chuckle was a bit rusty. 'Don't plan ahead too much. I think I'm supposed to dance with the bridesmaid a bit.'

'Well, only the first dance, perhaps.' Lindsey's eyes gleamed. She was enjoying this. 'Cait's engaged. She'll have her bloke with her.'

'So…' Dan considered. 'After the first dance, I'm off the hook?'

'Unless Nathan expects you to work the room.'

'Unlikely.' His mouth curved into a crooked moue that was almost a grin.

'That's good, then.' Suddenly Lindsey's breath felt fluttery. What was it about being with Dan that made her feel as though she was flying through space without a parachute?

And loving it?

CHAPTER FOUR

THE NEXT MORNING Dan was awake early. He got up, embracing a new sense of purpose, a kind of upbeat feeling, as he threw himself into the shower and then dressed in faded jeans and a long-sleeved navy T-shirt. He'd arranged to meet Nathan for breakfast.

He slipped quietly down the stairs from the upper floor of the pub and stepped out onto the street. So this was Milldale, Lindsey's family home. He could imagine her growing up here, he thought. A leggy country kid, bright as newly minted gold, a bit sassy, self-reliant... He shook the image away and continued along the quaint village street.

He checked his watch. He had time to spare for a walk and gain his bearings. Hope for something he couldn't quite define was springing up in his heart as he continued on his walk. The main street gave way to a few houses, a park and an unexpectedly steep hill. Full of energy, Dan climbed the hill to a viewing platform that overlooked the surrounding countryside. He leaned on the safety rail and looked out. The view seemed never-ending, timeless, stretching from the early spring greenness of the vineyards to the gentle rise and fall of blue hills beyond. Houses were dotted through the vineyards, a wisp of smoke drifting from one of the chimneys.

He took a cleansing breath so deep it almost hurt. Today was the first day of the rest of his life. He couldn't wait to see what it might bring.

'You're almost a married man,' Dan addressed Nathan as they sat over their traditional English breakfast.

'Can't wait.' Nathan added a curl of bacon to his egg. 'I'm sorry it didn't work out for you, mate,' he said quietly.

Dan gave a rough laugh. 'Well, the circumstances were hardly ideal, were they? Not like you and Sami. Even Lindsey remarked how "in love" the pair of you seem.'

'You mean it shows?' Nathan's face was lit with a goofy grin.

'Just a bit. Make sure it stays that way,' Dan said.

'Oh, man.' Nathan lifted his gaze briefly to the ceiling. 'You're not about to give me a *talk*, are you?'

'No. But I need to say something before we get caught up in all the hoopla. I can't count the number of times you've had my back, Nathan. You've been the best mate. The best. I hope you and Sami have the most amazing life together.'

'Thanks,' Nathan responded, a bit gruffly. 'That means a lot, Dan. But friendship is a two-way street. I'd like to think we've both had each other's backs over the years. Right, I could go another round of toast.' He broke what could have been an awkward male moment and hailed a passing waitress. 'Speaking of Lindsey...' he gave Dan an enquiring look '...how is she after last night's MVA? Have you called her?'

'It's a bit early yet.'

'And the injured guy?' Nathan asked.

'Induced coma. That's all they're prepared to say.' Dan placed his knife and fork neatly together on his plate. 'Uh—did you know Lindsey's into pottery?'

'Yeah. Lins is a seriously talented artist. When the

new maternity wing opened last year she gifted a mother-and-child sculpture for the foyer. You should take a ride to the fourth floor and poke your head in some time.'

'Maybe I'll do that,' Dan said, knowing he wouldn't. But that was his business. He poured a second cup of tea and gave himself permission to relax, to shuck off the negative thoughts Nathan's suggestion had set running.

Today was about new beginnings.

The wedding was wonderful, the best man's speech a triumph. Dan's remarks were warm and lively, with just the right amount of wit, nicely balanced with sincerity and in keeping with the significance of the occasion.

Lindsey joined in the applause as Dan resumed his seat. For some reason she couldn't define, she felt inordinately proud of him.

The remainder of the speeches were heartfelt but brief and the newlyweds took to the floor for the first dance. Almost as if her eyes were hotwired in Dan's direction, Lindsey saw him incline his head towards Caitlin. Caitlin smiled and they rose together. Obviously, they were about to join Nathan and Sami on the dance floor. Lindsey made a dry little swallow. Dan seemed very much at ease as he whirled Caitlin into an old-fashioned waltz. They looked stunning together. And Lindsey was swamped with jealousy. Taking up her glass, she took a gulp of her champagne and pretended not to care.

'Dance, Lindsey?'

Lindsey brought her head up sharply to find Eliot Swift, one of Sami's cousins, hovering. He'd come to Milldale for holidays when they'd all been in their teens. He'd had a bit of a crush on her then. Her eyes widened. 'Hi, Eliot. I didn't know you were here.'

He grimaced. 'Big crowd. You on your own?'

She nodded. Well, she *was*, wasn't she? Eliot held out

his hand and she took it and let him guide her across to the dance floor.

'Been a while.' He sent her a wry smile.

'Yes. What have you been up to?'

'Selling IT to the masses. Travelling a bit. You?'

'Travelling a bit as well. Presently nursing at Hopeton District.'

'Ah.' His eyes held a glimmer of humour. 'Found your niche, then.'

'I believe so.'

'Great summers back then, weren't they?'

'Mmm. But now we've all grown up. Are you married?'

'Nah.' He shook his head, and they took to the floor. 'Sorry, was that your foot?'

'One of them.' Lindsey laughed. She couldn't help herself. They could have been seventeen again and she could have been back on the Kellys' veranda, trying to teach Eliot to dance.

'I still can't waltz,' he apologised. 'But we can shuffle about until they change the tempo. Shouldn't be long. Ah, good.' He sounded relieved as the music changed into something slow and torchy and he gathered her in with style.

Dan frowned a bit, catching sight of Lindsey as she danced past. She was wearing a red dress, one smooth shoulder exposed, her hair loose and shiny. She looked... beautiful. Dan's interest intensified as he checked out her partner. They looked pretty cosy. And he was holding Lindsey far too close. Dan felt his gut curl into an uncomfortable knot. *He* was the one who should have been holding her.

For the next while Lindsey danced and mingled. She stopped to chat with Sami's mother, Marcia, and assured her it was a marvellous wedding. And, yes, she, Lindsey, was having a fine time.

'Oh—excuse me, love.' Marcia turned in response to some urgent hand gesturing from one of the catering people and took off.

Lindsey took a relieved breath. This was her cue to slip outside for some air.

It was a cool evening, and because much of the gracious old home's beauty lay in its outdoors, the verandas were spectacularly lit, fairy-lights peeped out of boxed hedges arranged beside the door, and glossy-leaved potted plants were decorated with love hearts and sparkly bows. Lindsey's mouth tipped into a wry smile. It seemed Sami had indeed got her trimmings.

Descending the shallow flight of stairs to the sweeping lawn beyond, she looked up and gave a little breath of delight. The fairy-lights sprinkled around in the trees gave a storybook feel. It was the perfect setting for a wedding, she decided, sitting down on one of the old-fashioned garden benches.

She rested her head back on the wooden slats, looking up to the clear sky and the twinkling necklace of stars.

The light strains of the music floated out on the night air. After a while she heard the change to the thump, thump of an upbeat rhythm. Was Dan still dancing with Caitlin? She'd heard a discreet whisper that Caitlin's engagement was off. Perhaps Dan would feel obliged to partner her for most of the evening. But from what she'd seen, it hadn't seemed much of a hardship for him. She shivered slightly. Obviously, he'd forgotten about *their* dance.

She closed her eyes.

'Hey…'

Lindsey's eyes snapped open. 'Dan!' She swallowed jerkily.

He sat beside her. 'I've been looking for you everywhere. I meant to call you but I got caught up. It's been like a circus all day and then the wedding...'

'Well, you had to expect that.' Lindsey gave a little shrug. 'You are the best man.'

'Last night was pretty rough.' Dan paused and looked at her. 'Did you manage to sleep all right?'

'Yes.' Lindsey turned her face up to his. Even in the half-light she could see the concern in his eyes. It unsettled her to realise how relieved she felt. She hadn't imagined the closeness of last night. It seemed he did care. 'In fact, I slept in. And Fiona's been like a mother hen all day.' She sent him a guarded smile. 'I'm fine.'

'You look amazing.' He lowered his head slightly, so close his chin was almost dusting her cheek.

Her breath caught on a stilted laugh. 'So do you.'

'I take it, then, we're both pretty amazing.' His eyes gleamed with intent.

Her stomach curled. He'd taken off his suit jacket, loosened his tie and rolled his sleeves back over his forearms. She took a breath, the subtle scent of his aftershave filling her nostrils. 'I thought you'd forgotten our dance.'

'Was that likely?' His mouth went to where her neck met her shoulder in the softest caress.

Lindsey's eyes drifted shut and she shivered.

'I had to have a couple of duty dances,' Dan said, 'with Nathan's mum and his Aunt Tilly.'

'The large lady in the purple pants suit? She looked formidable.'

'But a great dancer,' Dan proclaimed, his lips twitching. 'She runs a pub in Sydney.' His gaze went to Lindsey's mouth and lingered. 'Why are we having this crazy conversation? When we should be doing this...'

Lindsey swallowed, her heart banging out of rhythm. Racing. He was bending towards her, his blue eyes capturing hers with a magnetic pull. 'Dan...?'

'Don't talk…' In an almost imperceptible movement he slid his hands beneath her elbows and they rose as one.

Instantly, Lindsey felt her nerve ends tingling, her breathing uncomfortably tight. She lifted her head, searing her gaze with his.

'I need to do this again…' Dan reached up, sliding the tips of his fingers over her face, feeling the gentle throb of heat under her skin, the feminine, fragile line of her jaw. Even as his thumb lifted her chin his fingers were seeking her nape, drawing her to him.

He lowered his head slowly, giving her the chance to end it, if that's what she wanted. But she didn't, and her lips gave a tiny sigh of welcome as his mouth brushed hers, settling over its softness with touch-and-retreat little sips, feeling the instant response and teasing her lips into a more open kiss.

Lindsey was drowning in feelings she hadn't experienced for the longest time. Dan's mouth on hers felt right, their kiss pure and perfect. So dazzlingly perfect. He drew her closer and she opened her mouth as though to savour and hold onto the magic of his kiss, walking her fingers to the curve of his neck and into the soft strands of his hair.

And she didn't let herself think for one second whether any of what they were sharing had a future. She was just amazed that they should be kissing at all and that she'd so longed for it without even knowing why…

'You have the sweetest mouth,' Dan murmured much later, moving his hands to her shoulders and then cupping her face in his hands.

She licked her lips. 'Do I?'

'Mmm.' He bent to her again, pressing his forehead to hers. It seemed a lifetime later when Dan drew back. He took her hands, absently running his thumbs across her knuckles. 'I suppose we should get back in there.'

'Yes, I suppose we should.' Lindsey reluctantly withdrew her hands, swiping a fall of hair back over her shoulder. 'I imagine the bride and groom will want to get away soon.'

'Come on, then.' Dan held out his hand and they were linked again. As they made their way back indoors to Rosemount's beautiful ballroom, they saw the crowd gathering for the farewells. 'I'd better have a word with Nate,' Dan said. 'He looks like a rogue bull caught in the headlights.'

Nathan's relief when he saw Dan was almost palpable. 'Sami and I want to split. Any ideas for a quick getaway?'

'I'll alert the limo driver.' Dan pulled out his mobile, his eyes assessing a possible exit route. 'Have you said your private farewells?'

'All done. And, mate...' Nathan slung his arm around Dan's shoulders. 'Thanks. And I mean for the classic speech and, well, for everything.'

'It's been a great day.' Dan's jaw worked a bit. 'You and Sami have a fantastic honeymoon. Where is she, by the way?'

'Just here.' Sami materialised beside them and linked her arm through Nathan's. 'Are we heading off, babe?' She turned a very sweet smile on her new husband.

'As soon as Dan can find us an escape route.' Nathan bent and pressed a kiss into his wife's hair.

'Dan.' Sami let go of Nathan's arm and turned to Dan, kissing him on both cheeks. 'Thank you so much. You've been the best best man! Oops!' She put a finger to her smiling mouth. 'I think I've had a bit much champagne. But you know what I mean.'

'It's been fun, Sami,' Dan said. 'Take care of this big guy.'

'Take care of each other,' Lindsey chimed in, and hugged them both.

'Oh, Lins.' Sami whisked Lindsey aside. 'Keep an eye

on Cait, would you? She's a bit emotional about…well, you know…'

Lindsey nodded. 'Don't worry, Eliot's taken Cait under his wing.'

'Good old El.' Sami sent Lindsey an arch look. 'He still has a thing for you, you know?'

Lindsey just grinned. 'In your dreams, Samantha. Oh, look, Dan's beckoning. Grab Nathan and scoot.'

'Thanks for everything, guys!' Sami threw back over her shoulder as Nathan took her hand and urged her swiftly through the blaze of farewells and good wishes to the white stretch limousine in the forecourt.

Lindsey smiled softly as they watched the car drive out of sight. 'Wasn't it the loveliest wedding?'

'Yes, it was…' Dan's thoughts winged back to another time, another wedding…

'You OK?' Lindsey asked, realising he'd gone quiet.

Dan blew out a breath that untied the sudden knots in his stomach. 'Bit nostalgic,' he admitted, and threaded his fingers through hers.

'You and Nathan go back a long way, don't you?'

'First day at uni. Shared a house through our training…'

'Parties and girls,' Lindsey surmised, and smiled at him.

He gave a half-shrug. 'All that. I'm immensely happy for him.'

'So, you believe in marriage, then?' she said casually, although her antenna was tuned for his answer.

His look became shuttered. 'Well, people seem to be still doing it.'

And that, decided Lindsey, was no answer at all.

They headed back inside. 'My duties as best man are all done,' Dan said. 'The band is on a break, so perhaps we could find somewhere less noisy and have a drink? I believe the champagne is still flowing.'

Lindsey made a small face. 'I think I'd actually prefer some tea.'

* * *

They made their way through to a kind of garden room where a helpful waiter organised their pot of tea. Lindsey poured, saying, 'I'm assuming you have the rest of the weekend off?'

'Actually, I have a few days' leave.' Dan took the cup she handed across to him. 'I pulled some extra shifts to make it happen.'

'Oh.' The tip of Lindsey's tongue roved her bottom lip. So that was the reason she'd kept missing him at work. He'd been off when she'd been on. 'You must be running on empty, then, with the wedding on top of everything.'

He shrugged. 'I'll recharge quickly.'

Lindsey's heartbeat picked up a notch and an idea began forming. 'So…what are you doing with your time off?'

'I haven't quite decided yet. I have the use of an apartment at the Gold Coast whenever I want it. Maybe I could catch some waves. A bit of sun. A bit of fun.'

Fun? Lindsey dropped her gaze. Did that mean a holiday fling while he was at the coast? That idea didn't gel at all. She tilted her head back to look at him properly. 'Do you have friends at the coast?'

'No.' Dan's eyes seemed to track over her features one by one before he went on. 'I'm used to being on my own. It doesn't bother me.'

Well, it should. Lindsey's fingers spanned her teacup. Was Dan Rossi a loner by choice? She didn't think so. She'd seen how much he'd enjoyed the social interaction at the wedding. And he hadn't been faking it. He'd been warm and funny. And sexy…

However hard she tried, she couldn't remain detached. That assumption had been shattered like eggshells under a heavy boot the moment they'd tasted each other. She'd loved the way he'd kissed. So many men didn't know how to kiss, she thought. But Dan had it down in spades. Or maybe it was simply that their bodies were totally in tune, their chemistry perfect for each other. She felt her skin prickle at the thought. Suddenly she straightened in her chair. Like a spark on tinder, the idea turned into possibility. 'I have a much better idea. You could spend your days off here in Milldale. With me.'

Dan looked up, startled. 'With you,' he repeated.

'Well, not exactly *with me*,' Lindsey explained. 'What I meant to say was that we have several holiday cabins at the vineyard. You could have one of those—if you wanted to, of course.'

'Uh-huh.'

Oh, God, she thought as her heart began pattering. She couldn't believe what she'd just done. It was so unlike her. She'd jumped in boots and all and had probably put Dan on the spot. But he was a grown-up, she justified. He could say no. 'There are hiking trails if that appeals, heated pool and spa up at the house. Soft blue sky days and the quiet just seem to settle around you. There's no feeling quite like it. It kind of all ties together; the peace and the feeling you can let go and just...*be*.'

Be. Dan's breath jammed in his throat. One tiny word with a thousand connotations. Her eyes had turned almost silver. Here I am, they seemed to say. So why on earth was he hesitating? Unless his instincts were leading him astray, Lindsey Stewart was the real deal. Lovely, exciting. Sexy. He felt a wild heat in every part of his body.

And he hadn't had a feeling like this about a woman for the longest time.

Somehow their hands had met across the table, their fingertips touching.

'That sounds excellent,' he said almost formally. 'I'll be happy to accept your invitation, Lindsey.'

Lindsey watched as his mouth quirked with humour and acknowledged the almost painful lurching of her heart as it thundered out the heated rhythm of physical attraction. 'Oh, ha-ha.' She took her hand away, realising she'd worried about nothing. 'You're taking the mickey, aren't you?'

His grin unfolded lazily, his eyes crinkling at the corners. 'You looked so earnest selling me your idea, Lindsey, when in reality you didn't have to sell it to me at all.' Reaching across, he took her hand again, slowly interlinking his fingers through hers. A tiny pulse flickered in his cheek. 'I'd love to spend my days off with you.' He fiddled with the gold filigree ring she wore on her middle finger. 'Perhaps we could just *be* together?'

Her eyes slanted, their expression sultry and soft. 'Perhaps we could.' She reclaimed her hand gently. 'Now I'm going to call it a night.' Picking up her clutch bag, she held it against her chest. 'You know the way to Lark Hill so I'll see you tomorrow, shall I?'

Dan was immediately alert. 'How are you getting home?'

'Cab. I imagine all of Milldale's taxi fleet is on duty tonight.'

'My car's here. I'll drive you.'

'Dan.' Lindsey shook her head. 'It's not necessary. You've had a long day—'

She watched his mouth firm.

'I'll drive you home.'

CHAPTER FIVE

LINDSEY WOKE WITH a start on Sunday morning. She grabbed her phone off the bedside table and fell back against her pillow. It was just eight o'clock. Dan probably wouldn't be here for ages yet.

A smile touched her mouth and widened to a full-blown grin. The good Dr Rossi thought he'd played the cool card but she knew her invitation had rattled his composure. She was still a little amazed that she'd asked him to spend his leave with her. But the invitation had bubbled out from somewhere deep within her.

And just maybe it was all meant to be.

When her phone rang she was still hugging the thought. Checking the caller ID, she felt a thrilling reality. 'Dan, hi.'

'Ms Stewart, I presume. Are you up?'

'Of course.' She hastily levered herself upright and swung to the side of the bed. 'Are you?'

'Yes.' He didn't tell her he'd already been to Hopeton and back to collect some extra clothes for his impromptu holiday.

'Are you still at the pub?'

'Actually, no,' he said easily. 'I'm only a few minutes away from you.'

'You are!' Lindsey almost squeaked. Abruptly, she ended the call and sprinted to the bathroom.

What to wear? Back in her bedroom, she shuffled

through the clothes she still hadn't unpacked from her suitcase. She took out her soft jeans, a white T-shirt and, because she felt a lingering chill of winter in the air, she shrugged into a little cropped-style cardigan. Now shoes—

As the sound of the old-fashioned door knocker echoed along the hallway, she spun to a halt. He was here! And she felt only half-dressed. Hastily, she shoved her feet into ballet flats, finger-combed her hair and went to let him in.

'Dan...' She blinked out into the early-morning sunlight and felt a soft shiver like a slipstream of desire feather all the way down her backbone. He looked so early-morning sexy with the beginnings of a dark shadow along his jaw and the simple male thing of the collar of his check shirt all askew under his navy jumper. She made a little sound in her throat.

Just the sight of her curled a wild kind of excitement through Dan's gut. She had no make-up on. No lingering smell of perfume. But she exuded a kind of femaleness that was...intoxicating. A bubble of pure want exploded inside him. He took a step forward.

In a second they were leaning into each other.

Dan's mouth moved against hers, shaping her name as their bodies aligned. And then he kissed her, a gentle, sweet, slow kiss that tingled all the way down to her toes, before he let her go. 'Good morning,' she said softly.

He lifted a strand of her hair and wound it around his finger. '*Now* it is,' he said.

She gave him one of her wide smiles, activating the dimples beside her mouth. 'Come through. Have you eaten?'

'I had a coffee earlier.'

'Let's see what the pantry can yield up, then,' she said, leading the way along the hallway to the kitchen.

Dan took a quick inventory of the timber benches and

the navy blue and white tiles. 'Big workspaces,' he commented. 'Do you cater for your guests as well?'

'The cabins allow for self-catering,' Lindsey said, 'but sometimes we provide breakfast baskets if anyone requests them. I'll fix something for us now. What would you like?'

'Anything is fine. Surprise me.'

She flipped him a cheeky grin. 'I think I have already.'

She had. And his mind still couldn't quite grasp the fact that he was here with her. In her home. About to share breakfast with her. His gaze jagged across her face. 'I can't believe I'm actually here.'

'Of course you're here.' Her lashes swooped, eyeing him from head to toe. 'Otherwise who have I just kissed?'

Dan gave a gravelly laugh and looked around the room, his gaze lighting on the sun-catcher crystal that dangled from the window in front of the sink. 'Nice *feng shui*.'

Lindsey raised an eyebrow at the abrupt change in conversation. 'You a follower, then?'

He shrugged. 'Parts of the philosophy appeal to me.'

Who'd have thought? Now he'd surprised *her*. Lindsey loaded crockery and cutlery onto a tray and set them on the bench.

'What can I do to help?' Dan asked.

'Let's eat outside on the back deck,' she said, handing him the tray. 'Could you set the table?'

'I think I can manage that.'

Male distraction gone for the moment, Lindsey set about preparing breakfast. She juiced oranges and deftly arranged portions of melon and a variety of other fruit on a glass platter. That would do for starters, she decided, picking up the plate.

Dan was leaning over the railing, looking into the distance. He turned to Lindsey as she came to stand beside him. 'This is God's own country,' he said, a faraway look in his eyes. 'How can you bear to leave it and go to work in a casualty department?'

She sent him a pained look. 'Now you're talking like a tourist. Running a successful vineyard is extremely hard work, Dan. You can't sit around, admiring the scenery.'

His mouth quirked. 'And that's what you do in Casualty?'

She made a face at him. 'That's the creek down there.' She pointed out an unbroken line of willows. 'Sami, Cait, my brother James and I had some fun times there when we were growing up.'

'I can imagine.' Dan sent her a soft look. 'James is your brother who's in Scotland, right?'

'Yes. He and his wife, Catherine, are physiotherapists. Their baby daughter, Alexandra Rose, is just three weeks old.'

'Nice name.' Dan felt an uncomfortable tightening in his gut and breathed it away. 'And the cabins?'

'There are four. See, over there to your left.' She indicated the weathered timber structures nestled into the side of the hill. 'You can get settled in later.' She touched his forearm. 'Shall we eat, then?'

'So, how come the name Lark Hill?' Dan asked, as they each took a selection of fruit. 'As far as I know, we have no larks as such in Australia.'

'Long story short,' Lindsey said, popping a sliver of golden kiwi fruit into her mouth, 'my great-grandparents came from England. When they came to Milldale to begin farming, the bird calls reminded them of the larks back home. But of course they were our magpie larks, better known as peewees. But they'd already registered the place as Lark Hill so it just stayed.'

'Fascinating,' Dan said. 'So your family are literally pioneers of the district.'

Lindsey lifted a shoulder. 'It just feels like we've always been here, I suppose. What about the Rossi family, then?'

Dan's mouth puckered briefly. 'I don't think we're pioneers of anything—except maybe passing down old names.'

Lindsey *tsked*. 'I really meant whereabouts are you from?'

'Melbourne.'

'You mentioned sisters. Any more siblings?'

Dan shook his head. 'I suppose you want a rundown.' He gave a resigned lopsided grin.

'Of course. Then I'll know where to put you in your family.'

Dan lifted an eyebrow and helped himself to a sliver of melon. 'My dad is a linguistics professor at Melbourne Uni. Mum is a director of early childhood education.'

'Wow.' Lindsey lifted a hand, casually swinging her index finger through a long curl as it fell against her throat. 'I'll bet some interesting conversations happened there.'

'Mmm.' Dan sucked the sweet juice of the melon deeply into his mouth. 'They're both pretty passionate about learning. I think the girls and I could read before we could walk,' he joked.

'And your sisters,' Lindsey asked interestedly. 'Younger? Older?'

'Younger.'

'And what are they—lawyers, doctors?'

'No.' He gave an amused chuckle. 'Juliana trained as a teacher-librarian but now she runs a combined bookshop and coffee corner in downtown Melbourne. Reg—Regina—is married to Christoph. They're both professional musicians, violinists with the Melbourne Symphony Orchestra.'

Lindsey drank the information in. 'So, you're rather an arts-related kind of family, then. Rich in good conversation, music, books and so on.'

'I suppose.'

So, in fact, quite similar to her own background, Lindsey thought. 'But you obviously broke the mould and opted for the sciences and medicine. How did that happen?'

'My uncle Robert, Dad's brother, is a physician,' Dan explained. 'He arrived late in their family so to us kids he was more like a big brother than an uncle. I hung out with Rob a bit. And with his skeleton,' he added with a smile. 'I was always fascinated with the idea of becoming a doctor.'

'You weren't daunted by the study involved?'

He shook his head. 'Couldn't get enough of it.'

'It's a real calling for you, then.'

'Becoming a doctor? I guess it was.' Dan chased the last piece of fruit around his bowl and thought with something like amazement that it had been an age since he'd talked so freely about himself. But then again Lindsey seemed to have that effect on him. There was an openness about her that called to him to respond in a similar way. He leaned back in his chair, eyeing her thoughtfully.

'What?' Lindsey flicked him a startled look. His gaze had gone all smoky.

'Just thinking. This is good, isn't it?'

'This?' Her eyes widened and lit.

'This. Us. Here.'

Lindsey tipped her head on one side and looked searchingly at him. His voice had held slight wonder. 'Yes, it is,' she said, and thought that on a personal level they probably still had a few mountains to climb. But what was a mountain or two when Lark Hill was beginning to work its magic already...

'Well, come on, Ms Stewart.' Dan broke into her thoughts. 'That's me done. What about you and nursing?'

Lindsey batted the question away. 'There's not all that much to tell. I actually thought seriously about medicine but I'm a hands-on kind of girl. I figured it would be ages before I could do anything useful as a doctor, whereas nursing offered the chance to get stuck in fairly quickly,' she summed up with a smile. 'And here I am.'

Dan's gaze softened. 'Indeed you are.'

Deflecting his scrutiny, Lindsey hurriedly got to her feet and began collecting their used dishes. 'Shall we make some toast? Fiona's left one of her special wattle-seed loaves.'

'Sounds interesting.' Dan pushed himself upright and took the tray from her and they made their way back to the kitchen.

An hour later they were on their second pot of tea and still talking. About anything and everything. And it had all seemed as natural as breathing, Lindsey thought. In fact, so engrossed had they become, neither heard the sound of the front door opening and closing or the soft footfall along the hallway until, 'Yoo-hoo. It's only me. Are you there, Lindsey?'

'It's Fiona.' Lindsey put a finger to her lips. 'Be prepared to be well looked over. On the deck, Fi,' she called.

Fiona, cropped greying hair and with the suntanned complexion of her outdoor lifestyle, came out onto the deck and stopped, her clear blue gaze running assessingly over them. 'Not interrupting, am I?'

'Of course you're not.' Lindsey sought to put the older woman at ease. 'This is Dan Rossi. He's a friend from the hospital.'

Dan rose courteously and they shook hands. 'Nice to meet you, Fiona.'

'And you, Dan.' Fiona's gaze widened as something clicked. 'You're the doctor who kindly brought this one home after the accident, then?'

'That's me.' He shot a slightly mocking look at Lindsey. 'I think she'd have tried to walk home if I'd let her.'

Fiona shook her head. 'Independent to a fault. Always has been.'

'Hey, you two,' Lindsey protested. 'Do you mind?' She beckoned Fiona to a chair. 'Tea's still fresh.'

'No, thanks, love.' Fiona sat. 'I really just popped in to tell you I've let the last cabin.'

'Oh—OK… Who are the new people?'

'Young couple, Scott and Amy Fraser. Having a few days' holiday before the birth of their first baby.'

'A babymoon.' Lindsey smiled. 'That's so sweet.'

'They arrived last night,' Fiona said. 'Just saw them a while ago. They're off picnicking.'

'Well, it's a beautiful day so let's hope they enjoy the peace and quiet.' Lindsey looked at Dan. 'We should get out and stretch our legs too.'

With Fiona gone, they went inside, washed up and put the kitchen back to rights. Dan shoved the last of the cutlery into the drawer. 'I'll go back and stay at the pub tonight.'

'Why would you do that?' Lindsey hung the damp tea towel near the AGA to dry.

'Fiona said she's let the last cabin.'

'Stay here, then,' Lindsey countered practically. 'There's a guest bedroom you can have. It has its own en suite so you can be as private as you want to be.'

'Ah…' Dan swiped a hand across his cheekbones.

Watching his body language, Lindsey gave a little huff of disbelief. 'Surely you're not obsessing about propriety?'

He frowned through a beat.

'That's so sweetly old-fashioned.' Leaning back against the benchtop, she let her eyes rest softly on him. 'You're so well brought up, aren't you?'

Dan snorted. 'Give me a break. It's a small community. You and your family obviously have a certain…status.' And he hadn't missed Fiona's overt curiosity in his presence.

'Dan...'

'What?'

She stepped closer to him, her green eyes almost translucent as she met his gaze. 'We're grown-ups, aren't we?'

'I'd say so,' he murmured gruffly. 'Very grown-up...' he added, as he wound her hair loosely around his fingers, using the impetus to draw her closer and find her mouth.

They kissed long and hard until Dan let her go with a last lingering touch to her lips. 'Ah, Lindsey...' His fingers lifted her chin, his mouth only a breath away as he said her name again. 'Lindsey...'

'That's me.' She reached out to stroke his face, feeling his skin faintly, deliciously rough.

'I'll stay here then.'

Watching his mouth, so sexy in repose, Lindsey felt her heart pick up speed. 'I'm glad you've decided that. Now I won't have to put my fallback plan into action.'

He raised a brow in query.

'I was going to wrestle you for your car keys.'

'What's with you Milldale women?' Dan shook his head. 'Nathan said Sami was prone to wrestling *him*.'

'Must be something in the wine we grow,' Lindsey challenged, laughing, as Dan spun her away, as if they were about to dance. She shimmied back to him and locked her arms around his waist.

Dan's gaze heated. 'Now what...?'

She lifted her hand and traced the outline of his lips with her finger, recognising there was a new awareness beating its wings all around them. 'A walk perhaps?'

Or seventeen cold showers, Dan thought darkly, his mouth achingly sensitised by her touch.

Or he could give in to the avalanche of emotions engulfing him. And take her to bed.

Suddenly, making love with Lindsey seemed a natural progression from where they were now. The last step in intimacy. But perhaps he was fantasising. It had been so long since he'd been this close to a woman.

Had wanted to be this close.

So…all things considered, a walk, preferably a long one, would probably be a better option.

'Go get your stuff from the car,' Lindsey said, her gaze alight. 'I'll sort out some bed linen.'

CHAPTER SIX

'THIS IS GOING to be magic,' Lindsey said, as they walked through the vines, and then she showed Dan the creek and the rock pool. 'Next time you come, we'll swim here,' she said.

'So, I'm coming again…?' Dan held her loosely, looking deeply into her eyes.

He'd spoken quietly, his voice so husky it had made Lindsey shiver. 'Of course you are.' Wrapping her arms round his neck, she stepped closer to him so that they were hard against each other. And they kissed.

'So…' he said, when they'd broken apart.

'So…' she echoed.

'Funny how things turn out.'

'Mmm.'

They linked hands and continued on their hike. 'Should we be on the lookout for snakes?' Dan queried.

'Only elephants,' she deadpanned.

'I see.' Dan did a little sidestep away from her then pulled her back in. 'I've taken up with a joker.'

Further on, she challenged him to walk across the old bush log that spanned the deepest part of the creek. Dan obliged, easily and gracefully, arms held out like a tightrope walker to keep his balance. He gave a bow when he reached the other side and she made a face at him, before stepping lightly across the length of the log and joining him on the other side.

'Now where?' Dan asked as he gathered her in and spun her round.

'Up there.' Lindsey pointed to the highest point of the paddock. 'It looks steep but it's really a steady climb and then you get a great view.'

'And survey your domain,' he teased as they wandered off again.

'This is as far as we go,' Lindsey said when they reached the top of the hill.

Dan stopped and wheeled her round, linking his arms around her from behind. 'Ah...*bella vista.*'

'Pretty special, isn't it?' Eyes half-closed, Lindsey placed her hands on his forearms, almost absently stroking her fingers over his skin. She tipped her head back to look at him. 'Makes you feel good to be alive, doesn't it?'

'That—and being with you,' Dan added, a throaty edge to his voice.

They sat in a patch of dappled shade beneath a leopard tree, easing back against the trunk, their shoulders touching. For a long time they did little else other than absorb the gentle landscape and breathe in the air that was heady with the scent of wattles that edged up the hill and along the walking tracks.

'So, why New York, Dan?' His head jerked up as if she'd activated a string and she added quickly, 'Am I being too nosy?'

'No...' He pulled off a blade of grass and began shredding it with his fingers. 'I'd been there a couple of times on holidays, loved the buzz. When the chance came to work there, I grabbed it. The rest, as they say, is history. What about you?' He changed conversational lanes deftly. 'Travelled much?'

'Quite a bit.' Lindsey smiled up at him. 'The UK, of

course, seeing that James and Catherine live in Scotland. That was brilliant. We did some of Europe together. And last year I went to Japan for the snowboarding.'

'You're a snowboarder?' There was admiration in Dan's voice.

'Did you travel with a group?'

She shook her head. 'It probably would have been better if I had. I went with my boyfriend at the time.' She pulled her knees up to her chin and looked out into the distance. 'The day after we arrived he hooked up with one of the tour guides.'

'Ouch.'

Lindsey rolled her eyes in disdain. 'He described her as *cute* and said it was just a holiday fling. That it needn't change anything between us. The awful part was that it was all going on under my nose. How dumb was I?'

'I wouldn't call it dumb,' Dan said quietly. 'You trusted him and he let you down.' He brushed his fingers down her cheek. 'His loss, I think.' A long beat of silence until, 'I got married in New York.'

Married. The word fell like the thud of a stone into a deep pool. Lindsey's stomach began turning cartwheels. If he'd been going for shock value, he'd got it. She hesitated before asking, 'Are you still—?'

'No.' The word was snapped out. And then more or less on a sigh, 'We crashed and burned.'

Lindsey raised her gaze to look at him. That sounded awful. But he couldn't drop a major detail like that into the conversation and expect her to leave it there without comment. 'Do you want to tell me about it?'

Dan eased his back against the trunk of the tree, unaware his eyes had assumed a bleak look. He clamped his jaw and agonised over whether now was the time to tell Lindsey everything, but his gut did a somersault at the thought of resurrecting it all. He rubbed a hand across his cheekbones, feeling the familiar tightening in his throat, but he realised that if there was any chance of deepening his relationship with Lindsey, he had to plough on. 'Caroline and I met at a party. She was from out of state, an attorney, new to the city as I was. We began dating, doing stuff together…'

'OK. Fast forward all that. Obviously, you fell in love and got married.'

Dan averted his eyes quickly but not before she saw the pain in them.

She held out her hand to him. 'Sorry…that was glib.'

He took the hand she offered, pressing her fingers tightly as if to gain strength from the contact, then let it go. 'I imagine you've heard of the expression about your life turning on a dime?'

'Is—is that what happened to yours?'

'More or less.' There was silence as if he was searching for the words and then he began to talk very quietly and measuredly. 'When we met, we were both in crummy apartments so it seemed reasonable to move into something better and share the rent.'

'As a couple?'

'Well, it didn't start out like that and it wasn't something we'd planned.'

Lindsey frowned a bit. That didn't sound like the love affair of the century so why had they got married? Unless…?

'Caroline got pregnant.' His voice flattened. 'Down to a glitch in her contraception. She was panic-stricken. Her parents were…protective, ultra-conservative in their outlook, so totally proud of their only child when she'd got a place at one of the city's prestigious law firms, convinced she'd make partner in a few years. She was fearful of telling them about the pregnancy, distressed she'd let them down in some way. She said if she could tell them we were getting married, it would lessen the shock.'

Lindsey could hear the thudding of her own heart. She paused and frowned. 'And you married her?'

Dan registered her look of disbelief. 'It was my child too, Lindsey,' he justified. 'And I thought…well, if we put our best into the relationship, we could make it work. Then life began throwing us curveballs. We found out Caroline was carrying twins and that was scary enough but then we discovered they were mono-mono.'

Lindsey's breathing faltered. She interpreted what he was saying, that the babies had shared the same amniotic sac and the same placenta within the mother's uterus. 'That's extremely rare, isn't it?'

'Only in one per cent of pregnancies.' Dan looked out into the distance. 'The survival rate is not great. Cord entanglement can happen at any moment.'

Which meant the babies' oxygen could be cut off. Lindsey tapped into her medical knowledge, fearing what Dan was about to tell her. 'Do you want to stop now?'

He gave the ghost of a smile. 'What would be the point? You need to know and, God knows, I need to start gaining some perspective about it all.'

'OK…but I imagine, as a doctor, you knew the scenario you were facing and obviously you tried to shield Caroline about the extent of your fears.'

He dipped his head. How did she know that's exactly how it had been? 'I tried to keep positive for Caroline's sake but it was like living with a time bomb. At sixteen weeks the scan showed they were girls. Their heartbeats were strong and they appeared to be growing well. Caroline was being monitored by an ob team, of course, and they had protocols in place for the babies to be delivered by C-section at the earliest viable date. We dared to hope…' He stopped, his jaw working. 'They died in utero at twenty-two weeks.'

Lindsey heard the pain in his voice and tears welled in

her eyes but she said nothing, just sat with her arms locked around her middle and waited until he carried on.

'We had amazing support from the hospital and my family flew over. And Nathan.' His throat moved convulsively as he swallowed. 'Seeing Nate was hard. Brought it home the reason we were all there. I'd kept it together until then… But I was so damn glad to see him.'

Lindsey felt drenched in emotion, breathing harder as if a thumb pressed on her throat. 'Dan… I'm so very sorry this happened to you.' She looked at him, blinking away the scattering of tears. 'How on earth did you move forward from such heartache?'

'In a fog mostly.' He made an attempt at a twisted smile. 'I'm certainly in no hurry to experience fatherhood again. In the end, you do what has to be done. Caroline didn't want to be around me.' He shrugged. 'She was hurting.'

'And you weren't?' she queried softly.

'Caroline maintained there was nothing holding us together any longer. She quit her job and went home to her parents. I completed my contract at the hospital and then went to Florida. Did some training with a search and rescue team. After that, I came back home to Australia.'

'And you're not in touch with Caroline at all?'

'I tried a few months after I'd got home. She said she'd moved on and she hoped I'd do the same.' He paused. 'It's been two years now.'

Lindsey let the revelation hang for a moment. 'I imagine it's been pretty hard—trying to let it go, I mean.'

'I'm slowly getting there.' He gave a hard laugh. 'Except when it's a significant memory—like on the day I lost it in Resus.'

'I wondered…' She bit her lip. 'You said you were having an off day. But it wasn't the day, was it?' she stated with some perception. 'It was the *date*.'

'Yes, it was,' he said, his voice hollow. 'It was the date I met my babies. And the day I said goodbye to them.'

For a long time they stayed sitting under the tree. Dan had his arm around her, her head buried against him. Finally, he said, 'Thanks, Lindsey—for listening.'

'I hope it helped a bit,' she said, her voice scrappy.

His arm tightened and he pulled her closer.

And he figured only time would tell whether that was true and whether he could start taking more steps forward than backwards from now on.

'Hey.' He gave her a little shake. 'Want to race me home?'

She pulled back. 'I don't know about that.' Raising her arms, she lifted her hair and let it tumble down. 'One of us would probably break our ankle.'

'If it was you, I'd be on hand to patch you up,' he declared manfully.

'Then you'd have to carry me.'

Dan looked unfazed. 'You look like you don't weigh much. I think I could manage to hoist you over my shoulder in a fireman's lift.'

Her mouth turned down. 'I'm too tall for that. I'd be all dangly.'

He gave a deep-throated laugh. 'Dangly you would never be. A gentle jog, then,' he suggested, unwinding upright and taking her with him. 'Let's go.'

When they got home, Lindsey declared, 'You must be starving. What about a club sandwich?'

'Sounds good.' Dan got lemon squash from the fridge and poured them both a tall glass.

Lindsey began setting out the ingredients for their sandwiches. 'Perhaps, later, we could go into Milldale. The country markets are on all day on Sunday.'

'Again, that sounds good. But don't think you have to entertain me, Lindsey.'

She sent him a look of dismay. 'Is that how it seems?'

'Of course not. It's been the most brilliant day I've had in the longest time. And just *being* with you…' He shook his head, still poleaxed by the complete wonder of it all.

'Oh, Dan.' She sent him a misty kind of smile. 'Me too.'

'I think I'll change,' Lindsey said as they finished their impromptu lunch. 'The weather's warmed up.'

'So it has.' Dan hauled off his jumper. He sent her a quick smile. 'Don't be long.'

In her bedroom, she divested herself of her cardigan and T-shirt and stepped out of her jeans. She had managed to hang up a couple of dresses yesterday and she pulled one off its hanger. It was dotted with tiny flowers.

Longish and floaty. I feel like spring, she thought happily.

It was only a ten-minute drive to the village.

'You know, I haven't been to one of these for years,' Dan said as they roamed the market stalls, picking up and putting down various items.

'You should get out more, Dante.'

'Cheeky.' He sent her a lazy grin. 'So, are we looking for anything specific?'

'We are.' Lindsey urged him towards a stall decorated with flags from many nations. 'I like to support this group. They donate to several primary schools in one of the developing countries. Oh, recycled paper!' She pounced on the pale green and speckled box. 'It's Mum's birthday soon, she's a compulsive letter writer. And I must get some of this herbal mixture that helps to heal bruises.'

Dan looked bemused. 'Are you expecting some— bruises, I mean?'

'I work in Casualty, Dan,' she reminded him drily.

'I'm learning so much here,' he said.

Not sure whether he was being serious or not, Lindsey sent him an eye-roll. 'I just need to get some of the fair-trade tea and coffee and I'm done here.'

'I'd like some of that too.' Dan stayed her hand as she was reaching for her purse. 'I'll get this.' He handed over a note of a large denomination, waving away the change.

'That was a nice gesture.' Lindsey swung her carry bag lightly as they strolled on.

'Hardly philanthropic,' he mocked himself. 'But perhaps it might go towards funding some story books for the kids or a bit of sports equipment.'

'Happy thought,' Lindsey said. 'But the hard reality is it might help to pay for someone to keep the kids safe on the way to and from school.'

His mouth tightened at the bleak thought. 'We take so much for granted, don't we?'

'Not always,' Lindsey countered gently. 'I like to think most of us do what we can for others less fortunate. But for some folk it could never be enough.'

Dan looked at her with something like awe. 'You're such a wise woman.'

'So better not mess with me, then.'

He returned her grin. 'I think we need some ice cream.'

'Now let's have a wander through the art gallery,' Lindsey suggested, as they finished off their ice-cream cones. 'Check out the work of the local artisans.'

'Are you among them?' Dan asked.

'I've had a few pieces shown from time to time but nothing lately. I need inspiration.' She paused, her bottom lip puckering, considering. 'Would you sit for me, Dan?'

'No.'

They entered the gallery with its clean lines of black and white space and a striking mullioned window through which the afternoon sun was streaming.

'Just—no?' Lindsey stopped to look at a painting.

'I'm not that narcissistic, Lindsey.'

'That's pathetic reasoning.' She shook her head.

They continued their tour of the gallery and Dan held the door open for her as they left. 'I'd only need you for a couple of hours just to get the basics down,' Lindsey pleaded her case.

'It's not something I'd do. Count me as a firm no!' He softened his abruptness with a smile that spread his lips wide and Lindsey found she was biting down on hers. He looked so sexy, unshaven, a bit rumpled. So…perfect for her.

'Spoilsport,' she muttered, and stepped out into the street again.

Dan wound her fingers through his as they continued up the street. 'I saw a plant nursery when I took a walk yesterday. Would they still be open?'

'Probably. Sunday trading is the go in the village. Lots of tourists about. What do you need a nursery for?'

He squeezed her hand and swung it gently. 'Need to get some flowers for my lady.'

A few minutes later, Lindsey looked at the flowers she held. Dan had given her long-stemmed irises, their colour a rich and gorgeous violet, deepening to amethyst. 'Let's make tracks now,' he said, as they left the shop.

'Thanks for these, Dan,' Lindsey said when they were back and seated in his car. 'But why irises? Any special reason?'

He thought for a moment. 'Because they're extremely special and lovely…like you.' His fingers went to her nape and stroked. 'And brave-looking somehow, with their tall, straight stems.'

She turned to him, her heart beating so heavily she could feel it inside her chest. 'Today's been so amazing, hasn't it?' she said softly.

'Oh, yes…' His mouth lowered to her throat, his lips on the tiny pulse point that beat frantically beneath her chin. He looked at her, an unfulfilled yearning, as sudden as a lightning strike catapulting into his veins. 'I think we need to take this home, don't you?' His voice caught as he swallowed.

She nodded. No further words were needed.

Dan kissed her again before they got out of the car. Then, gathering up their parcels, they went inside. Somehow they found themselves back in the kitchen.

'We seem to end up here, don't we?' Lindsey gave a strained laugh, reaching up for a jug and putting her flowers in water.

'I like kitchens,' Dan said. 'They're friendly places.'

'The hub of the home.' Lindsey felt her nerves jangle, achingly aware of the almost tangible expectation hanging in the air between them. She turned to him, crossing her arms against her chest. 'Tea, then? Glass of wine, anything?'

A beat of silence.

'Dan…?'

He was very close. Unlocking her arms, he slid his hands down to her wrists, holding them gently. They waited there a moment, staring into each other's eyes. He took her wrist and raised it to his mouth. 'We haven't had our dance yet. Do you have some music?'

'I do—heaps of music.' Lindsey felt caught in a bubble. The world had faded and there was just the two of them. She could already feel the surge of heat between them. She swallowed drily.

They went through to the lounge. Lindsey slid a disc into the player and music, slow and smooth, filled the room. She looked up expectantly and saw that Dan had gone to the picture window and was looking out. She crossed to his side and saw what he did. Spears of red and orange shot across the western sky. 'Day's almost done.'

'We still have the night…' His voice was husky on the words as he turned and took her in his arms. Lindsey raised her face for his kiss, her whole body seeming to melt when their lips met. His hands stroked her back, encircled her hips, burning through the soft fabric of her dress as if his fingers were on fire.

Entwined, swaying together, almost lost in the throb of the music, they danced. And danced, wheeling and whirling around the room and all the way down the hallway to his bedroom.

They went in and Dan closed the door behind them. The curtains were partially drawn, the bed turned down. Dan pressed her to his side. 'When did you do this?'

'A bit earlier.'

'For us?'

The softest smile edged her mouth. 'Do you mind?'

He shook his head and paused. 'Ah, Lindsey…'

'What is it?'

'There's no chocolate on the pillow.'

'Silly.' She smiled mistily. 'That's for later.'

At her words, Dan's fragile control shattered and he took her in his arms. Then he stepped back, and without taking his eyes from her face slowly ran his fingers down between her breasts, unbuttoning her simple cotton dress, sliding it in one movement from her shoulders.

Then he was tugging off his own clothes and Lindsey was doing the same. 'This is us,' she whispered, as Dan drew her down with him onto the bed. She wrapped her bare legs around his, her arms reaching up to pull his head down, sighing deeply as she felt the slickness of his skin on hers, felt his body tensing with the effort to control it.

'This is us,' Dan echoed as his mouth ravished hers, hungry, demanding, tasting her everywhere.

Lindsey shivered, inhaling the scent of his naked skin, losing herself, returning his passion with her own kisses, hardly registering when Dan pulled back, pausing to protect her. 'Where were we…?'

'Don't stop…' She held onto him for dear life, his pleasure feeding hers.

Dan had no intention of stopping. Not until he had taken her with him all the way, higher and further, to a place beyond thought or reason. Only when release came, wave flooding upon wave, did they realise how very high and far they had climbed.

Together.

For a long time they lay replete, turned on their sides so they were facing each other. The soft light of early evening fingered the pale walls and ceiling. Outside the window a wood dove called to its mate and a burst of cicada drumming drenched the stillness.

Lifting a hand, Dan lazily combed his fingers through her hair. Something real was happening here. He could do nothing other than feel amazed. 'I'm lost for words…'

Lindsey sighed, sated, wrapping herself around him with the contentment of a purring cat. She gave him an indulgent look from under half-closed lids. She knew exactly what he meant. Freeing a hand, she ran a finger along his jaw and into the slight cleft in his chin. 'I've never wanted to be with anyone the way I wanted to be with you, Dan.'

He felt his heart contract. He could so easily fall for her—if he hadn't already. He could say, *Me too*, and mean it. But it was Lindsey and he needed to spell it out.

He brushed her lips once, twice. 'Without exception, this has been the happiest day of my life. It's been like a day out of time.'

'That's exactly how I feel.' Lindsey stopped and thought.

'It's a pure kind of happiness, isn't it? Like opening a mail-order parcel and finding everything just right.'

He gave a soft chuckle, his breath stirring her hair. 'I'll go with that.' He half spanned her waist with one hand, stroking a lazy pattern on her skin. 'I thought the spa looked pretty inviting earlier. Should we try it?'

'Perfect.' Lindsey rubbed her toes against his in anticipation. 'Then I'll fix us some dinner.'

'Uh-uh.' With exquisite sweetness, Dan claimed her lips. '*I'll* fix dinner.'

CHAPTER SEVEN

'Can I do anything to help with dinner?' Lindsey had arrived in the kitchen to find Dan well under way with his meal preparations.

He sent her a very sweet smile. 'A glass of your finest might be the go. I didn't know where to look.'

'Oh, that's easy.' Lindsey went to a door in a recess of the kitchen that led to a proper climate-controlled cellar. 'Red?' she called.

'Mmm, think so. I'm doing pasta.'

Lindsey took glasses and poured the wine and then watched as Dan expertly tossed onions, tomatoes and herbs in a pan. 'That smells wonderful.' She picked up her glass, lacing both hands around it. 'You really do know your way around a kitchen.'

'Would I lie?' He grinned, touching his glass to hers. 'Nathan would have cheerfully existed on takeaways if one of us hadn't cooked. I think he's a bit more interested these days. Sami has probably had some influence there.'

Lindsey made herself comfortable on one of the high-back stools and watched Dan at work. He was such a handsome man. With such an *air* about him. Perhaps it came from good breeding, she pondered. Or from a world of experience in so many ways. Her eyes took their fill. He was wearing a long-sleeved black cotton shirt outside his jeans and he'd shaved.

Her thoughts wandered off, unwinding the last hour. They'd had their spa and then instinctively gone to their separate bathrooms. Lindsey had been glad about that. Her emotions were in overload. She guessed Dan's had been the same. She'd had a long shower and shampooed her hair, spritzed perfume in the air and walked through it. Then, dressed in soft jersey pants and a ruby-red top with a crossover neckline, she'd come to find Dan. She took a mouthful of her wine.

'I took the liberty of lighting the fire in the lounge room,' Dan said. 'OK?'

'Very.' She parked her chin on her upturned hand. Her eyes lit softly. 'There's a little gate-legged table we can set up and eat our meal in front of the fire—if you like?'

'Of course I like.' He picked up his wine, his eyes caressing her over the rim of his glass. 'A perfect end to our perfect day.'

They erected the table and Lindsey set out the place-mats and cutlery.

'We should have some music.' Dan selected something from her collection, flooding the room with rich, mellow sound.

Lindsey was curled against Dan on the sofa. They'd ended their meal with Irish coffee and she'd raided the stash of dark chocolates her mother kept for special occasions.

'Are we fulfilling our brief to just *be*?' Dan smudged a kiss against her temple.

'Passed with flying colours.' Lindsey turned to meet his lips. They were still kissing when the phone rang, startling them apart. 'That's the landline,' she said, levering herself upright. She sent Dan a wry smile. 'Probably Mum from Scotland. She knew I'd be here this weekend.'

'You'll be a while.' Dan got to his feet as well. 'I'll sort this out and start the dishwasher.'

'Thanks.' Lindsey took off down the hallway to the room they used as an office and where their home phone was located. Contrary to what she'd expected, it wasn't her mother at all. 'Oh, Lord,' she murmured, after she'd ended the call and replaced the handset. She had to tell Dan what was happening. Full of misgivings, she hurried along to the kitchen. 'It was Fiona on the phone.'

Dan glanced at his watch. 'At this hour? What's up?'

Lindsey suppressed the urge to run to him. Hold him tighter than tight. 'It's the young couple from the cabin, Scott and Amy. They've just rung Fiona. They don't know what to do.'

'About what?' Dan felt his guts go into free fall. He had a fair idea. And he didn't need this. He really didn't. 'Is it the baby?'

'Amy's waters have broken.'

Dan let his breath out slowly. 'Well, there should be plenty of time to get her to Hopeton. Have they rung for an ambulance?'

'Fiona tried. And they'll get one to us as soon as they can. But there's been a major road trauma twenty Ks out of Hopeton on the Sydney highway, a semi-trailer and two cars. All the ambulances are there.' Lindsey felt her throat tighten. 'Amy's already getting strong contractions.'

In an instant Dan felt as if he was drowning in a sea filled with sharks, waiting to tear him to bits. And there was no escape. He saw the pleading in Lindsey's eyes and turned away, gripping the edge of the bench top until his knuckles turned white. And stared out into the night. He had to get it together. Be professional.

So, sort the logistics. The baby was probably well on the way. They had no history. What if the baby was breach? What if there was a bleed? *Sweet God, he hadn't signed on for this!* He spun back to Lindsey, a truckload of emotions churning through his mind. 'So, where have you left things with Fiona?'

'I've said we'll call her back as soon as we have a plan in place.'

Dan flexed a shoulder dismissively. 'We don't have much choice, do we?'

Lindsey shook her head. If there had been any other way around this, she'd have gone with it. She wouldn't have wished this emergency on Dan for the world. She just had to hope and pray everything would turn out all right for Amy and the baby. And Dan as well.

'The best plan would be to get Amy up here to the house and see what's going on.' Dan's voice was clipped and professional. 'The lounge room is probably the warmest. We'll set up as best we can in there. If you'll call Fiona, I'll get my bag from the car.'

They left the kitchen together, Dan striding ahead down the hallway to the front door.

'I don't suppose you have a birthing kit on board?' Lindsey called after him.

Was she nuts? Of course he didn't have a birthing kit! Without answering, Dan opened the door and stepped out into the crisp night air. He looked up at the tumble of stars and pulled in a deep breath that almost hurt. He had to centre himself.

Or go under.

Why on earth had she asked that damn fool question? Lindsey berated herself. She guessed Dan was feeling hijacked, pushed into a situation he'd rather have avoided. Delivering babies was certainly not on his agenda. And who could blame him?

Dan returned with his medical case and they began getting things ready. The sofa could be converted to a bed. That done, Lindsey went to search for some kind of plastic sheeting, resorting to a roll of garden bin liners she found in a utility cupboard. She came back with her booty plus sheets and cotton blankets. 'Amy could be a bit shocky,' she said, as Dan helped her prepare the sofa bed for their patient.

Well, he knew that. Dan's mouth tightened. Once the waters had broken, many women experienced a kind of delayed shock, shivering uncontrollably. 'I'll stoke up the fire,' he said.

'I'll warm some linen in the dryer,' she said to the back of Dan's head as he hunkered down at the grate. He grunted a non-reply and she shrugged and went off about her business. If the ambulance didn't get here in time…? She felt a curl of unease in her stomach. She'd delivered babies before but not away from the back-up of a fully equipped hospital.

When Lindsey returned to the lounge room, Dan was just putting his mobile away. 'I called Midwifery at Hopeton. Amy's not booked there.'

So no chance of any history. 'Fiona will have an address,' Lindsey said. 'I could check…'

'Bit late for that.' Dan swung round. 'Sounds like them now.' He managed a smile of sorts, softening the tension around his mouth. 'We'll just have to wing it.'

Dan flung the door open. The young couple stood there, Scott supporting his wife. Introductions were quickly made and they were ushered inside. Dan helped Amy onto the sofa bed.

'I feel so c-cold…' Amy was shivering, her teeth chattering.

Lindsey produced one of the cotton blankets warm from the dryer and tucked it over her. 'Try to relax now, Amy.' She placed a hand on the girl's shoulder and rubbed gently. 'Just breathe in and out. That's good.' Lindsey smiled. 'Bit better?'

'Mmm.' Amy blinked rapidly. 'The baby's not due for another three weeks.'

'That's neither here nor there,' Dan said. 'I'm sure your baby will be fine.' And, please, God, able to breathe, he added silently. Don't go there. He clamped his jaw, dragging his thoughts to the present. He turned to Lindsey. 'Could you get Amy ready and I'll see how she's doing.'

Lindsey quickly prepared Amy for Dan's examination. 'Scott, perhaps you'd like to sit over here close to Amy.' She smiled at the young husband, who was looking helpless and overwhelmed.

'We brought the bag Amy packed for the hospital.' Scott looked around awkwardly. 'Where should I put it?'

'I'll take it. And good thinking,' Lindsey said.

Dan bent to his patient. 'I'll be as gentle as I can, Amy.' His examination was painstaking. He was leaving nothing to chance.

'What do you think, Doctor?' Amy bit her lip and grimaced.

'I think your baby isn't waiting, Amy.'

Amy whimpered. 'Scott…?'

'I'm right here, babe.' Scott held tightly to his wife's hand.

Dan took Lindsey aside. 'She's fully dilated and the baby seems small.'

Small? Lindsey felt a lick of unease. 'We're not going to have a problem, are we?'

'Shouldn't think so. Foetal heartbeat is strong. I'd say she's been in labour most of today and not realised it.'

Lindsey stared into his blue eyes. She knew it had probably taken a Herculean effort but he looked in control. Confident. She gave a mental thumbs-up.

'Oh, help,' Amy moaned from the bed. 'I can't do this…'

As if they'd worked together in a birthing suite for years, Dan and Lindsey began talking Amy through each contraction. Dan checked his patient again. 'Not far now, Amy,' he encouraged quietly.

They had only seconds to wait before Amy began moaning again.

'OK, sweetie, big push.' Lindsey helped Amy into a more comfortable position as she bore down, eyes squeezed tight, her fists clenched.

'Head's crowning. We're almost there.' Dan looked down at his hands. The infant's head lay there, streaked and glassy, the dark, perfect curls pressed wetly against the tiny skull. His throat tore as he swallowed. 'Gentle push now, Amy—fantastic. And one more.'

Amy pushed and the rest of the baby slid into Dan's waiting hands. 'You have a daughter.' Dan had unconsciously steeled himself for a baby almost translucent, fragile, but little Miss Fraser was offering up an offended squawk, already pink and beautiful.

'Well done, you,' Lindsey murmured, handing him some cord clamps.

'Did I have these in my bag?' Dan looked bemused.

'Must have.' Lindsey unfurled one of her smiles. 'I didn't find them in the kitchen drawer.'

Dan felt his throat jag again as Lindsey handed him a warm towel to wrap around the infant. He passed the baby to her mother. 'Take great care of her,' he said, his voice not quite steady.

'Nice sound,' Lindsey said a little later, giving a nod towards the top of the bed where the young couple were clucking over their newborn.

Dan refrained from commenting. He felt stretched, hollowed out. 'I'm about to deliver the placenta,' he said. 'Can you find something to bag it? We'll send it to hospital with Amy. They'll need to check to make sure it's complete.'

'Plastic bags I can do.'

Lindsey went along to the kitchen, finding Fiona tip-toeing through the back door.

'Fi!' Her eyes went wide. 'You didn't need to come back. You OK?'

'I didn't like to intrude,' Fiona whispered. 'Is the baby—?'

'Delivered safely. Little girl.'

'Oh, thank goodness.' Fiona put a hand to her heart. 'I felt so responsible for all this. I should have checked how far along Amy was—perhaps recommended they stay closer to the hospital or something...'

'Fi, that's not your brief,' Lindsey said kindly. 'Scott and Amy made their own decision. And fortunately it's turned out fine. Mainly thanks to Dan. He was amazing.'

'Then what a blessing he was here,' the older woman said. 'That both of you were here,' she added, her gaze thoughtful and a little curious. 'Now, should I make some tea?'

'That would be wonderful.' Lindsey searched out the plastic bags Dan needed. 'And some toast as well, please. Amy, especially, must be famished. Oh, do you know if Mum still has Gran's cane-washing basket?'

'Hanging where it always has,' Fiona said. 'On the laundry wall.' She frowned a bit. 'What do you need that for?'

Lindsey smiled. 'It'll make a temporary bassinet for the baby.'

'Oh, bless.' Fiona was almost purring. 'What a sweet idea. Anything else you need me to do?'

'Perhaps you could check on the progress of an ambulance for us. But tell the base everything's under control here so the guys know they're not coming to an emergency.'

Laden with stuff, Lindsey went back to Dan. 'Ambulance has just left Hopeton for us.'

'Good. Placenta's almost out,' he said, continuing to massage Amy's tummy gently.

'As soon as we're finished here, I'd like to give Amy

a little tidy up,' Lindsey said quietly. 'Do you think you could organise a bit of privacy?'

Dan nodded. 'I'll need to write a few notes to send with the ambulance.'

'Use the office,' Lindsey said.

'OK. I'll take Scott with me. That do?'

'Nicely, thanks.'

Her basin of warm water at the ready, Lindsey passed Amy a sponge.

'Oh, that feels heavenly,' the new mother said.

'So, you're not from round here, then, Amy?'

'Further west, Shackleton. Scottie does contract farm work and we have a cottage in town.'

'We'll send you along to Hopeton District when the ambulance gets here,' Lindsey said. 'They'll check you and the baby over and maybe keep you a day or so. Will that suit your plans?'

Amy nodded. 'It'll give Scott time to trade the ute for something more practical for a family before we head home.'

'That sounds like a great idea,' Lindsey approved. 'Now, I'll just raid your case here and get you feeling fresh and beautiful.'

'Come on, let's get this lot cleared away.' Lindsey was looking purposeful. The ambulance carrying Amy and the baby had gone. Scott would follow later when he'd packed up their things from the cabin.

'Damn!' Dan surveyed the chaos in the lounge room and gave a short hollow laugh. 'Do you believe any of this actually happened?'

'Yep.' Lindsey began bundling sheets. 'There's a new little member of the human race to prove it.'

She glanced up. Dan sounded tired and the eyes that lifted briefly to hers were guarded and shadowed. He'd spent the past few hours on an emotional roller-coaster. He must be feeling wrung out.

She made a quick decision. 'Let's leave all this for now,' she insisted. 'Dad usually has some decent Scotch around. Fancy a dram?'

'Lead on.' Dan's agreement was heartfelt.

They were back in the kitchen again, sitting side by side at the breakfast bar. Lindsey had dimmed the lights and the big clock ticked on the wall.

'You're quiet,' Lindsey said as they sat over their drinks. 'You OK?' Her eyes scanned his face, looking for clues.

'I'll do.' He gave a trapped smile. Just, he added silently.

'I'm sorry you had this emergency thrust on you to-night.' Her voice was low, hardly there.

'It was out of your control, Lindsey. Don't stress about it.' He lifted his glass and finished his drink in a couple of mouthfuls.

'Another?' Lindsey offered.

He shook his head. 'I'm good, thanks.'

Lindsey had barely touched her drink. Where did they go from here? she fretted. Where? 'Do you want to...talk?'

'No...not really.' He covered her hand with his. 'Shower and bed, I think.' His eyes locked with hers, dark in shadow, tender in their caress. 'Come with me. I don't want to sleep alone.'

They made love slowly and with great care for each other. The soft mingling of their sighs and murmurs sprinkled the silence until the fire of their passion reignited, driving them before it until there was no escape and they tumbled into a blinding oneness, wrapped in each other's arms.

Lindsey woke to find the room suffused with morning light. At once snatches of their lovemaking flooded her mind and she reached out to touch Dan, but he wasn't there. Her heart fell. Dragging a sheet off the bed, she wrapped herself in its folds and scooted along the hallway to her bedroom. Hastily, she pulled on track pants and a jumper and went to find him.

She headed for the back deck. She had a feeling he'd be there and he was, looking out over the fields, focusing on the clouds of early mist already pierced with gold from the first rays of the sun. He was still. Absorbed.

Almost as if he was looking at it for the first and last time.

'Dan?'

He spun round. 'Hey…'

'Hey…' she echoed. Her eyes widened and she frowned. He was dressed in dark trousers and a charcoal-grey business shirt, his hair still damp from the shower. 'Have you been called in to work?'

'No.' He shook his head. 'Let's sit down. I need to talk to you.'

'OK.' For the first time she noticed his laptop open on the table. They each pulled out a chair and sat opposite each other.

'I'm going to take off,' Dan said bluntly.

'Oh.' Lindsey linked her hands on the table in front of her. He looked jaded, the fatigue lines around his eyes and mouth in sharp relief. 'What's going on?' she asked, her voice catching in her throat.

'I'm flying to Melbourne to see my family—well, my parents at least. I haven't been home since I got back from the States.'

They breathed through a beat of silence.

'You feel the need to be with them,' Lindsey said with some perception.

He was silent for a long moment and then he let his

breath out in a ragged sigh. 'We haven't really had an opportunity to talk properly since the twins... Their grief was as real as mine. They lost their first grandchildren. We need to connect, talk about the babies. Share the loss.'

Which he *should* have been able to do with Caroline. Oh, the unfairness of it all. Lindsey bit hard on her bottom lip. 'Last night...the birth...'

'It sharpened everything all over again. Stuff I'd thought I'd come to terms with—' He stopped, his expression set hard as if anything else would weaken his resolve. 'I'm hoping talking to my parents will give me a way forward. They'll understand.'

Understand, as she'd been unable to. Was that what he meant? She pushed the thought away. 'Would you like me to come with you? Not to your parents' obviously—but just for support?'

He hesitated, as if thinking it through. 'I need to do this on my own, Lindsey. But thanks.'

'When are you going?'

'Soon.' He flicked a hand towards the laptop. 'I'm booked on a flight to Sydney at ten. That'll get me on a connecting flight to Melbourne pretty well straight away.'

And in his mind he was already there, the monumental intimacy they'd shared nothing but a pleasant memory. Lindsey got to her feet, her insides suddenly twisting with the sad truth. 'I'll make some coffee, then.'

'Don't on my account. I'm packed. I should get going.'

She shook her head. 'Why didn't you wake me so we could have had time to talk about this?'

His brows twitched into a frown. 'I'm not following you.'

Damn right you're not.

'You're just...disappearing.'

He looked taken aback. 'With respect, Lindsey, what is there left to talk about?'

Lindsey flinched as though he'd slammed a door in

her face. Suddenly the magic of their lovemaking seemed a figment of her imagination. The carefree, wonderful man she'd discovered had gone. The amazement of their connection all but broken. 'You should get moving, then.'

Lindsey did a frenzied clean of the lounge room after he'd gone. Something in her heart scrunched tight and lodged there. *He should have held me this morning while he told me he was leaving*, she thought sadly. *He should at least have done that. I would have understood. But he'd chosen to walk alone. Well, I don't need you, Dan Rossi.* She kicked the off switch on the vacuum cleaner with the toe of her shoe.

She'd go back to being her own person. Depend on no man for her happiness.

Dan's thoughts were in turmoil as he travelled the thirty kilometres back to Hopeton. He couldn't believe how badly he'd handled things with Lindsey.

He hadn't slept. But that was no excuse for the stuff-up he'd left behind. He could turn round and go back. Sort it quickly. Take Lindsey with him to Melbourne. He glanced at his watch and the faint hope that had flared died. If he did that, he'd miss his flight. And he was pushed for time as it was. He had to be back tomorrow to begin a roster of night shifts.

His thoughts flew back to Lindsey and the way she'd made him feel plain glad to be alive, the way she'd made him laugh. He swore under his breath, disgusted at his lapse this morning. He should have been more caring. But right now talking with his parents had to be his priority. For his own sanity. And if that didn't work, then he had nowhere left to go to feel whole again.

Lindsey spent the afternoon venting her anger and frustration on her clay. She moulded, spun pot after pot and then trashed the lot of them. A bad end to a bad day, she decided grimly, making her way up the stairs from her studio. As she came in from the deck, the home phone was ringing. Dan? Her heart spun out of rhythm and she hurried to answer it, her expectations crashing when the caller proved to be Caitlin Kelly.

'Hey, Lins,' she said. 'I wasn't sure you were still at Lark Hill.'

'I'm taking a bit of leave.' Lindsey perched on the corner of the desk. 'How're you, Cait?'

'Bored.' She gave a half-laugh. 'Actually, I'm driving back to Sydney tomorrow. Wondered if you'd like a change of scene and come with me.'

'To Sydney?'

'Mmm. My apartment's right on the beach at Bondi. It'll be like old times. We could do some galleries for you, some clubs for me and shopping for both of us—are you in?'

Lindsey paused only infinitesimally. To heck with Dan Rossi and his machinations. She owed him nothing. 'You bet I am. What time?'

'Is six too early for you?'

'Honey, I work shifts,' Lindsey pointed out drily. 'My body clock is in permanent disarray. I'll be ready.'

CHAPTER EIGHT

THE FOLLOWING SUNDAY, Lindsey sat up in bed and blocked a yawn. Checking the time, she groaned. It was already well into the afternoon and she must have slept almost the entire day away. But she'd been late home last night, after flying from Sydney then picking up her newly repaired car in Hopeton.

She threw herself out of bed and showered, dressing in jeans and a dark green top. Gathering her hair up, she let it fall haphazardly around her shoulders.

She blocked another yawn on her way to the kitchen, filling the kettle and setting it to boil. That done, she went out onto the back deck.

So much for spring, she decided, leaning on the railings and looking across the landscape, seeing jigsaw pieces of darkening sky between the trees. Unless she was mistaken, those were storm clouds scudding across the mountaintops as if in a hurry to be elsewhere. But Lindsey knew about these kinds of storms. They came in fast and usually dropped their quota of rain and left just as quickly. She hoped it was one of those but even as she watched, the wind had begun whipping through the trees, swirling their foliage into a mad dance, while a streak of lightning snaked its way across the sky.

Lindsey felt a wave of unease. She'd better prepare in case there was a power cut later. She ticked off her to-do list—first locate the torches, make sure the batteries were viable. She'd just opened the cupboard where the lantern torches were kept when the front doorknocker sounded. Probably Fiona, she thought, come to check she was OK. She hurried along the hallway and opened the door.

'Oh—' Lindsey felt goose bumps break out all over her. Dan stood at the outer perimeter of the veranda, his hands jammed in his back pockets.

'I'm not taking anything for granted,' he said.

Lindsey's fingers tightened on the doorknob. You'd better believe it, she vented silently. Swinging the door wide open, she stepped back and with a small inclination of her head she said, 'Come in.'

For a second Dan's blue gaze faltered. 'Are you sure?'

'Sure I want you to come in?' Lindsey tilted her head in question. 'Of course. Lark Hill welcomes all strangers.'

Dan felt if she had struck him. Was that what he was now? A stranger? Well, he'd asked for it. The lady wasn't going to make it easy.

'I was about to make tea,' she said shortly. 'Come through.'

Dan stepped inside, noticing the carrier bags on the hall table and spilling onto the floor. His eye caught some of the big-name fashion brands, none of which were available in Hopeton. 'Been away?' he asked.

'Sydney, with Cait.' Lindsey sent him a look over her shoulder.

'Good trip?'

'Magic. Cait threw a huge party. Met lots of new people. Just what I needed.'

'Well, that's what holidays are about,' Dan felt compelled to say. But thought darkly that if she was sending a message that she'd moved on and that what they'd had was already history, then he'd got it.

'Looks like a storm coming,' Lindsey said, as she made the tea. 'Are you staying long?'

'Why?' he shot back immediately. 'Do you need to be somewhere?'

Lindsey looked taken aback. 'No...'

Dan's sigh was audible. Lifting his hands, he linked them behind his neck. 'You're still ticked off with me. And I understand that,' he added in response to her elegantly raised eyebrows.

'So at least you agree I have reason to be.'

'I was in overload.'

'And that's your excuse?' Lindsey snapped. 'For the whole weekend we were on fire for each other and then...' She palmed a hand and shook her head. 'You left me feeling...'

'I know... I wanted to turn round and come back but there wasn't time.'

Lindsey felt herself softening. She proffered the mug of tea.

'No tea, thanks.' Dan shook his head. 'I've been on nights. I'm in tea up to the gills.'

Lindsey swallowed. 'Would you like something else, then?'

A tiny pulse flickered in Dan's cheek. 'Just to talk—is that possible?'

She nodded, unable to speak. Every nerve in her body began tightening. What he had to say now would prob- ably make or break them. She flicked a hand towards the kitchen table and they sat facing each other.

'I don't want you to think I'm some kind of messed-up loser.' Without warning his hand reached out and covered hers.

'I would never think that.' Lindsey stared down at the hand covering hers. She took a deep breath and let it go. 'But you do get the prize for behaving with the sensitiv- ity of a block of wood.'

His mouth pulled down. 'Don't hold back on my account.'

'Dan, you all but dismissed me! That was pretty low after everything we'd been to each other.'

He tilted his head back and dragged in air. 'You're right,' he conceded without rancour. 'And I apologise. My only excuse is I wasn't thinking straight.' Abruptly, he pulled away, leaning back in his chair. 'I would never have wanted to leave you feeling hurt and questioning that what we'd had had been anything but entirely special. And *ours alone*,' he emphasised.

Lindsey took a shaky breath and asked the question that needed to be asked. 'Did talking with your parents help, then?'

'Their wisdom astounded me.' His voice roughened. 'I finally realised that I wouldn't be dishonouring my babies if I let them go.'

'Oh...' Lindsey's voice was a thread. 'Oh, Dan...'

'Yeah.' His smile was slightly wry. 'Took me a while to get there. But I have. I hadn't grieved properly. Hadn't said goodbye properly. It was as though there was a chunk of ice inside me that needed to thaw. And it was you who started the thaw, Lindsey. Only you.'

Lindsey's eyes pricked. 'I really just listened.'

'No.' He shook his head. 'You did a lot more than that. You brought something fresh and wonderful to my life. And I realised I had to break out of the mental straitjacket I'd put myself in. That's when I decided that talking to my parents might be the answer.'

Lindsey looked at him earnestly. 'So, what now?'

'For us?' Dan swallowed hard. 'I'd like it if I could hold you, if we could hold each other...'

He'd given her a look so warm Lindsey felt a quicksilver flip in her stomach. She swung up from her chair. 'So why are you still sitting there, then?'

Their kiss started gently but in a second they were desperate for each other. Dan lifted her hair, exposing the side of her throat. Lindsey felt his breath warm against her skin and then came the slight rasp of his tongue.

'Dan…' She gusted his name on a shaken breath and sighed when his mouth felt its way to the corner of hers.

'I've so missed you…' Dan made a muted sound in his throat. It was like the growl of a lion, shuddering through his whole length. 'Missed us.'

'I've missed us too,' she responded, shifting against him, her hands moving in a sweep under his T-shirt, taking him to her.

Where their kisses might have ended, they weren't about to find out. A clap of thunder ricocheted through the house, sending them springing apart. Lindsey put her hand to her heart. 'I don't like the feel of this, Dan.'

'Don't panic,' he said. 'A bit of thunder can't hurt us.'

'It's not that,' she countered. 'Around this valley, it's the wind. It can wreak havoc. The power lines can go down and knock out anything electrical. Is your mobile fully charged?'

He frowned. 'Ah—think so.'

'I'd better call Fiona.' Lindsey took off down the hallway. 'See who's at the cabins.' She was back in a few minutes. 'Thank goodness, there are no guests. The last ones left this morning.'

'One less thing to worry about, then. Do you have torches?' Dan asked.

Lindsey nodded. 'I was about to sort all that just before you arrived.' She got the torches and set them on the kitchen bench, testing them one by one. 'They seem OK.' She looked at Dan. 'When are you back on duty?'

'Late shift tomorrow.'

'So…' She bit her lip. 'You can stay tonight?'

He lifted his hand and stroked his knuckles down her cheek. 'If you'll have me...'

Lindsey pretended to think about it for a moment. 'Oh, I think I probably could.'

'Thank you.' He pulled her into his shoulder for a lingering hug. 'Now, what else do we have to do before the storm hits?'

'Just make sure the windows are secure, I guess. I'm so glad you're here, Dan.' Another crack of thunder sent her snuggling in against him. 'I think I'll make us an early dinner while we still have power,' Lindsey decided. 'Quick frittata, OK?'

'Fantastic. I'm starved. While you're doing that, I'll take a look outside. Might give us a clue if the storm is heading in our direction.'

Lindsey had no doubt it was. She went quickly about her task, sautéing onions, mushrooms and zucchini, fluffing eggs, and scattering fresh herbs and cheese across the top as she poured the mixture into the pan. In two seconds it was under the grill. She raised her eyes in question as Dan came back into the kitchen.

'It's really whipping up a frenzy out there,' he said. 'Actually feels a bit spooky.'

Lindsey punched him lightly on the arm. 'Not scared, are you, Dr Rossi?'

His mouth folded in on a dry smile. 'I thought perhaps you were, Ms Stewart.'

'Milldale girls don't scare easily.'

Dan felt a swell of desire as her lips made a soft little pout. Hell, she turned him on. In a reflex action he swept her up and swung her round and round, ending up in the centre of the room.

'Put me down, Dan,' Lindsey protested, laughing hard and hanging on tightly to his arms. 'That's if you want to eat tonight.'

They ate their meal, one eye on the weather as they glanced up constantly through the big kitchen window. The wind had now begun roaring, the rain falling sleet-like and icy. 'Glad we don't have to go out in this,' Dan said.

'Oh, me too.' Snuggling up in bed sounded like a much better idea.

Dan leaned across, his fingertips making long, shivery strokes down her forearm. 'We have a lot of making up to do, don't we?'

Lindsey made a tiny sound like a purr and felt a strange lightness as if love and desire had rolled into one high-voltage surge, sweeping through her body and out to the tips of her fingers. 'Should we do the dishes?' she ventured coyly.

'Are you serious?' Dan pretended outrage. 'Some matters are vastly more important than others. Don't you agree?'

Lindsey's laughter was sweet and clear. 'I agree.'

CHAPTER NINE

Wednesday, the following week...

FIRST DAY BACK from leave and Lindsey went in to work early.

She hadn't seen Dan since the storm but now she was back in town...the prospect of seeing him every day curved a smile around her lips, a flood of desire pooled into a warm ache inside her. It was a rainy, dreary morning yet she felt she was standing beneath a sunbeam.

It was good to catch up with her team, Lindsey thought as she stowed her bag and finger-waved around the staff lounge. Making a coffee, she joined Vanessa at one of the corner tables that looked out onto a rock garden. This morning the big succulent plants were dewy with rain-drops.

'Well, aren't you the chirpy one?' Vanessa said. 'I take it you had a nice break?'

'Fantastic.' Lindsey's hands spanned her coffee mug. 'But it's good to be back all the same.'

Vanessa gave an eye-roll. 'You *must* be on a high.'

Lindsey laughed good-naturedly. 'How're things with Andrew?'

'I think *cautious* must be his middle name,' Vanessa said darkly.

'Well, he's at a crucial stage of his training,' Lindsey

pointed out gently. 'Perhaps he's not into making commitments just yet.'

'Oh, *yawn*.'

Lindsey gave her contemporary a quick dry look. 'If you think he's worth waiting for, Van, cut him a bit of slack.' She glanced at her watch. 'Who's been the charge on nights?'

'Brooke Bartholomew.'

Lindsey's full lower lip pursed. Brooke was relatively new to the casualty department. She'd seemed nice enough during the casual encounters Lindsey had had with her.

'I don't get her,' Vanessa said frankly. 'She's not on for a chat when things are quiet—well, only with Dan. She kept bringing him cups of tea!'

'Well, that's not a crime.' Lindsey felt a lick of unease she couldn't explain, her pool of happiness shrinking ever so slightly. 'How come you were on nights anyway?'

'Anita Rayburn's little boy was sick. She asked me to swap a couple of shifts.'

Lindsey didn't wait to hear any more. She finished her coffee quickly and stood to her feet. 'I guess I may as well get a jump-start and take handover.'

'OK.' Vanessa helped herself to one of the mini-muffins someone had brought in. 'I'll rouse the team shortly and see you out there.'

'Oh, Lindsey.' Brooke Bartholomew looked up startled from the computer and blinked a bit. 'You're early.'

'I'll take handover, if you like,' Lindsey offered. 'Then you can get off. Are you OK?' She frowned as she looked at the other woman. 'You look a bit rocky.'

'Night shifts…' Brook's nostrils pinched as she breathed in. 'I hate them.'

'Have you been busy?'

'Swamped.'

'Right, who's still waiting for triage?' Lindsey's trained eye flew over the list. One name sprang out and rang warning bells. *Mia Roche.* She turned urgently to Brooke. 'Where is this child now?'

'I was about to get to her. We'd had an MVA and a gunshot wound...'

'Mia Roche is registered at the asthma clinic.' Lindsey was on her feet. 'You should have flagged it.'

'I know. She would have been next. I'll get to her now.'

'No.' Lindsey was definite. 'Page the registrar to Paeds Resus. And, please, Brooke, sign yourself off but don't go anywhere until I've sorted this.' Lindsey's request left no room for argument as she took off at speed to the waiting area. 'Erin!' She located the mother of the sick child and held out her arms for the toddler. 'How long have you been here?'

'A while... I tried to give Mia a drink but she vomited. She's so ill...'

Lindsey could tell that. Mia's little body was radiating heat through her cotton pyjamas. She pressed the back of her hand to the child's forehead, long experience telling her Mia's temperature was far too high for safety. 'Come with me,' she instructed, tight-lipped. With relief she saw her team assembling at the station. 'Vanessa, you're in charge. Jess and Gail, I'll need you both in Paeds Resus.'

Newly graduated, Jess bit her lip. 'I haven't done much paeds.'

'You'll be fine.' Lindsey hardly slowed her stride. 'Gail, you know what to do.' Gail Smith was one of their mature assistants in nursing, an absolute gem in this kind of situation.

The nurses all knew Erin from her attendance at the asthma clinic. Gail placed a guiding arm around the distraught young mother. 'It's OK, sweetheart. Mia's in good hands now.'

Lindsey quickly placed the toddler on the resus trolley. 'Erin, go with Gail now,' she said kindly. 'We'll take great care of Mia.'

'But…' Erin hesitated, her mouth trembling out of shape. 'Shouldn't I…?'

'Best if we leave it to the doctor and nurses now,' Gail said. 'You must be exhausted. Have you been up all night with the bub?'

Lindsey let out a relieved breath as Gail led the young mother from the room. She turned to Jess. 'Get me a Hudson mask, stat. We need Mia on a hundred per cent oxygen. Move!'

Jess moved. 'She's burning up, Lindsey.'

And they were running out of time. They could only hope the little one didn't start fitting. And where was the damned doctor when you needed him? 'Help me hold her, Jess.' Lindsey's calm request held nothing of her inner disquiet. 'I need to get some readings here. Come on, baby, hold still for me,' she pleaded. 'OK, all done… Thanks, Jess.'

'So, we'll give paracetamol next?' Jess had begun to step up into her role.

'Yes.' Lindsey placed what looked like a small piece of dissolvable paper under the little girl's tongue. 'Let's hope it'll start getting her temp down.'

Dan moved at speed through the casualty department. He'd barely pulled into the doctors' car park when he'd been bleeped. And by rights he shouldn't be here at all, but with Martin going home sick he was back on take for the early shift and straight into an emergency.

He pushed through the doors to Paeds Resus. 'What do we have?'

Lindsey spun her head up, expecting to see Martin

Lorimer, and went perfectly still for a beat. 'Dan!' She tamped down a slather of mixed emotions.

He gave a perfunctory nod. 'What do we have?' he repeated.

'Mia Roche, eighteen months old,' Lindsey relayed. 'Ongoing patient at the asthma clinic. Temperature forty-three, oxygen sats seventy-eight, pulse one-seventy. I've given oral paracetamol.'

Deep concern catapulted into Dan's eyes. One glance told him the child was rapidly becoming cyanosed. They'd need to move fast. 'Let's get an IV up and running. Smallest cannula, please, Lindsey. I'll need to crack a vein in Mia's foot.'

They sprang into action, Jess restraining the distressed toddler as best she could while Lindsey assisted Dan.

'Left foot, I think,' he said tersely, gloving quickly. 'I see a vein that might work for us.'

Lindsey's heart twisted. Tiny child, tiny veins. She prayed Dan's skill would be enough. 'I have a cut-down tray ready just in case.'

'We're short on time so let's hope not.' Dan's fingers were deft and sure. He secured the cannula on the first attempt, slapping down a dressing he'd stuck on the back of his left hand in readiness.

'Nice work,' Lindsey murmured, moving in to secure the site with a paediatric bandage.

Dan's expression lightened fractionally. 'Let's run five hundred normal saline and adrenaline five, please. We need Mia on a Ventolin nebuliser. And, Jess, keep checking the sats, please.'

'Yes, Doctor.' After a few minutes the junior reported, 'Sats up to eighty.' Jess looked up hopefully. 'That's a good indication we've got her in time, isn't it?'

Dan looked at the tiny, perfect fingertips. They were beginning to lose their blueness. 'A way to go yet but looking hopeful.' He flicked up his stethoscope. 'I'll have a listen to her chest now. See what that tells us. Left lobe a bit suspect,' he said finally, straightening Mia's little pyjama top. 'She's not allergic to anything, is she?'

'No,' Lindsey confirmed.

'Then we'll start with benzyl penicillin.' He picked up Mia's chart and began scribbling the dosage. 'Plus Maxolon to keep things settled down. Both delivered IV.'

Lindsey prepared the medication, relieved beyond words Mia would pull through this episode and that it had been Dan who had been around to treat this special little girl. Even if he wasn't aware of it, he had a natural affinity with kids. The thought made her happy.

'You did really well,' Lindsey said as she and Jess tidied up. 'Want to debrief later?'

'Thanks, Lindsey. That'd be awesome. Should I get back to the ward now?'

'Yes. Van will have need of you, I'm sure.'

'Excellent work, Jess.' Dan added his congratulations. 'Thanks for your help.'

Jess slipped out.

'I'll hang around until we can safely transfer Mia to Paeds ICU.' Dan pulled up a stool and parked himself beside the bed. 'Parents here?'

'Mum is—Erin,' Lindsey said.

Dan's eyebrows twitched into a query. 'Left it a bit late to bring the child in, didn't she?'

'No, she didn't.' Lindsey felt nettled. 'Erin is extremely up to speed regarding Mia's health. Very unfortunately, triage protocols were not followed here. Mia was kept waiting. I took over as soon as I got in. But I'm going to have to report it to the DON.'

Dan eyed her sharply. 'Who was the nurse on triage?'

'Brooke Bartholomew.'

Dan went very still, all his energies reined in. This

could have dire consequences for the department if he didn't speak up. 'Brooke is battling with some personal issues.'

Lindsey felt wrong-footed. 'How well do you know her?'

Dan hesitated briefly. 'We were thrown together on night shift. She needed to talk so I listened.'

Suddenly the air was taut with tension. 'So, what are you not saying, Dan?'

Dan was quietly monitoring his small patient. 'Brooke spoke to me in confidence, Lindsey. I advised her to ask for a transfer to another department urgently.'

Lindsey frowned. 'If she's not fit to work, she shouldn't be here.'

'You're right.' Dan's look was cool. 'But Brooke was competent on the shifts I worked with her. So what could I do except counsel her to act in her own best interests? Unfortunately, it appears she hasn't. I would have spoken to you about it but you were on leave. So do what you have to do.'

Lindsey shook her head in dismay. She hated having to report another nurse. 'Will you speak with Erin now?'

Dan didn't look up. Instead, he dragged in a weary breath and let it go. 'Yes, of course.'

With Mia finally transferred, Lindsey went back to the station. 'Everything OK here?' she asked Vanessa.

'Everything's under control,' Vanessa said shortly. 'How's Mia?'

'She'll be fine—eventually.' Lindsey paused, swallowing back the swell of emotion that rose in her chest. This was so unlike her. Normally, at work she was clinical and objective. But the thought that things could have just as easily gone drastically wrong for Mia... 'Keep covering for me, please, Van. I need to speak with Brooke.'

'Good luck with that,' Vanessa huffed. 'Don't get me wrong. I feel sorry for her. But the hospital's good reputation could have been put at risk. We all work too hard for that to happen.'

Lindsey's mouth tightened. She'd begun the day with such happiness in her heart. Now she was stuck with Brooke's mess to clean up. She looked at Vanessa. 'I asked Brooke to wait for me. Do you know where she is?'

'She disappeared pretty fast.' Vanessa picked up the phone as it rang. 'Staffroom perhaps?'

Lindsey decided she'd go there first. She just hoped Brooke hadn't cut and run. If only she knew the woman better. And why was Dan suddenly in the mix? she fretted as she pushed open the door to the staffroom. 'Brooke...' Lindsey took a steadying breath. She'd play this by the book. 'Thanks for waiting.'

Brooke took off the black-framed spectacles she'd been wearing and closed the magazine she'd been reading. 'How is the child?'

'She'll recover.' Lindsey pulled out a chair and sat down. 'You know I'll have to report this to the Director of Nursing, don't you?'

'Am I going to lose my job?'

'If there are mitigating circumstances, you won't lose your job. But it's not up to me, Brooke.' During the awkward silence that followed, Lindsey took stock of her contemporary. Brooke had changed out of her uniform into denim overalls and a simple white T-shirt. Her fair hair was out of its knot and flowing freely around her shoulders. She looked curiously vulnerable. 'Is there anything you want to tell me?'

Brooke's chin came up defensively. 'About what?'

'Did you feel ill during your shift? Headache—anything that would have clouded your judgement?'

Brooke worked her bottom lip as if searching for words. Words that wouldn't come.

Lindsey sighed audibly. 'Look, I'll do everything I can to advocate for you. But I'm in the dark here.'

'I was seconds away from getting to Mia.' Brooke tried to justify her actions. 'We were swamped.'

Lindsey kept her cool. 'You were on triage, Brooke. It means you're the first contact. You follow very set protocols.'

'Don't you think I know that, Lindsey?'

'OK.' Lindsey pulled back in her chair and said quietly, 'I'd urge you to be completely upfront with Clarissa. You'll be supported, Brooke, but sadly there may have to be an inquiry.'

Brooke pressed a hand to her temple.

'No one is ganging up on you here,' Lindsey said. 'But we have to follow the rules. Otherwise there'd be chaos throughout the hospital.'

The nurse didn't reply, yet somehow her silence was deafening. 'Are we done now?'

'Yes, we're done.' Lindsey got to her feet. 'Clarissa will be in touch.'

'I'm on days off.'

'But you'll be available on your mobile?'

'Yes.' Brooke stood abruptly. Snapping up her shoulder bag from the back of the chair, she walked out.

Lindsey's mind was churning as she made her way back to the station. As the song said, some days were stones. And today she felt like chucking her job and going to work in the scented serenity of a florist shop. 'Van, a word, please?'

Her friend nodded and came over. 'What happened?' she asked curiously.

Lindsey *tsked*. 'You know I can't talk about that, Vanessa. But I need some air. Can you keep holding the fort for a while longer?'

Lindsey left the hospital by the rear staff entrance. The rain had cleared and the sun was strafing pools of light and warmth across the car park. Leaning against the brick wall, she tipped her head back, breathing in the pure, crisp air. Ah, that felt better. Then she lowered her head and levelled her gaze.

And that's when she saw them.

Dan and Brooke standing beside a silver sports car—obviously Brooke's—their heads very close together, one so dark, one so fair, absorbed in conversation. At least Dan was the one doing the talking while Brooke seemed drawn towards him, her hand on his arm, listening as though her very life depended on it.

Lindsey felt the drum-heavy beat in her chest align with the sudden recoil in her stomach. She dragged in a shallow breath, hurt and anger in equal parts clogging her throat. Not again!

Sick with uncertainty, she spun on her heel and dashed back through the doorway.

Dan found her in the staffroom barely seconds later. 'Lindsey!'

Go away! she felt like screaming as she filled a paper cup at the sink. She took a gulp of water and then turned to face him.

He moved forward, wanting to take her by the shoulders, but caution held him back. Something in her face, her eyes. 'Don't go reading anything into what you just saw in the car park,' he attempted.

Lindsey shook her head. She wouldn't dignify any of this with a response. 'I have no idea what you're talking about, Dan.'

'Look.' Dan spread his hands in a plea. 'It's complicated.'

Lindsey's mouth felt stiff as she took another sip of water. 'What is?'

He frowned. 'Don't pretend you didn't see me with Brooke.'

Lindsey threw professional caution to the winds. 'Don't treat me like a fool, Dan. What the hell are you playing at?'

'I told you before, Brooke is dealing with some personal stuff,' he said, censure in the coolness of his tone. 'She needed a friend.'

'How touching.' Lindsey actually managed a jagged laugh. 'Dan the *go-to* man!'

A muscle at the corner of Dan's mouth pulled tight and flickered. 'This is all a bit juvenile, isn't it?'

'Let's get professional, then.' Lindsey swung round, tossing her paper cup into the bin. 'Are you protecting Brooke?'

'Oh, for God's sake.' In a gesture of a man almost at the end of his tether Dan jabbed his hands to the side of his head and hung on.

'Why can't you give me a straight answer?' Two spots of colour glazed Lindsey's cheeks.

'Oh—hey guys…' Vanessa popped her head around the door, her smile fading as she picked up on the thick tension in the room. 'I was just looking for… Is everything OK?'

'Everything is…fine.' Dan was the first to gather himself.

'Which one of us do you need, Van?' Lindsey swallowed, her throat aching from the brutal exchange with Dan.

'Well, Dan, actually,' Vanessa said carefully. 'We've a two-year-old with an inhaled foreign body. It looks a bit tricky. Andrew would like some guidance. If you wouldn't mind?'

'Where the hell are the paeds people when you need them?' Dan growled.

'Well, we've only one on staff and she's on her honeymoon. There are a couple of others in town but they're in private practice,' Vanessa supplied helpfully. 'No one is conducting a clinic here today. They usually do Monday and Thursday.'

Oh, Van, your timing is appalling, Lindsey gritted silently. Please, just stop the inane chatter and go away.

'Give me a minute,' Dan said. 'Tell Andrew not to do anything until I get there.'

With Vanessa gone, the tense atmosphere heightened again. Lindsey and Dan were left scoping each other. Dan was the first to speak. 'Are you saying I haven't been upfront with you, Lindsey?'

Lindsey felt sick to her stomach. The thought that he might have divided loyalties only increased her unease. '*You* work it out, Dan.'

Tension crackled between them as brittle as spun sugar.

Dan felt his heart surge to a sickening rhythm. God, he didn't want any of this. He felt racked with fatigue, having been dragged back on duty when he should have been on days off. Days he'd been looking forward to when he could spend some quality time with Lindsey after her shifts. Now it was all out the door like the garbage collection. But he had to try to salvage something. 'Look.' He pressed a hand to the back of his neck. 'If this needs to be sorted, let's sort it. But not here and not now. If I can get out of here at a decent hour, I'll come over to your place. And we'll talk.'

Lindsey lifted a shoulder indifferently. She didn't want to be patted down like some kind of recalcitrant child if that's what he was offering. Either they were equals or they were nothing. And right at the moment, she'd put her money on nothing. 'Please yourself.' She walked to the door and turned. She gave a sad little shake of her head. 'I thought I could trust you.'

For a second Dan felt poleaxed. 'You can,' he said. But his words were lost in the vacuum of her leaving.

Working alongside someone you had a personal relationship with was the pits when it all went wrong. Lindsey's throat constricted as she made her way back to the station. Or maybe she was just rubbish at relationships. She looked at the clock on the wall and sighed. It was still hours until the end of her shift.

Dan felt like ramming his fist through the wall. Being at odds with Lindsey felt as bad as having a cartload of gravel dumped into his guts. He swished back the curtains on the paeds treatment room, vowing he would sort things, whatever it took.

The day wore on and Lindsey couldn't believe how bad it felt to be offside with Dan. But there was no going back and she couldn't see a way forward. 'What is it, Jess?' Lindsey looked up sharply as the junior nurse approached the counter.

'Eighty-year-old male, Lewis Gaines,' Jess, who was gaining experience on triage, said. 'He's very frail, seems quite dehydrated and his pulse is thready. I've given him water and told him to keep drinking. But I think he needs to be seen.'

'Let's see what we can do, then.' Lindsey scooted down the list to see where she could juggle patients. 'Is someone with Mr Gaines, a relative?'

'No. He's on his own. He had to come to the hospital on the bus!' Jess was mildly outraged. 'Someone should have cared enough to be with him, Lindsey.'

'In an ideal world, you'd hope so. Right…grab Michelle. She's just back from lunch.'

'Oh. OK.' Jess hesitated.

A jaded sigh left Lindsey's mouth. She knew what this was about. Unfortunately, Michelle had a habit of being offhand with the junior nurses. It left them feeling unsure of their role and devalued as a result. Lindsey realised it was a personality thing with Michelle but they were *supposed* to be a team. 'Take your patient along to cube one, please, Jess, and wait with him. I'll ask Michelle to attend.'

As she made her way through to the cubicles, Lindsey let her pent-up breath go in a stream. It was turning out to be the shift from hell.

It was almost the end of the shift.

'Hey, Lins, want to come for a drink after work?' Vanessa came back to the station and propped herself at the counter.

'Sorry, not today.' Lindsey threw her pen aside and stretched. 'I just want to get home and have a long, long shower.'

'How did your meeting with the DON go?'

'Clarissa took her usual laid-back approach. If Brooke speaks up for herself, it will all probably blow over. I couldn't do anything more than tell it as I found it.'

'You're always scrupulously fair,' Vanessa declared supportively.

'I just want today over,' Lindsey said with feeling. And she still had to deal with Dan this evening. That's if he even showed up.

'Rotten first day back for you,' Vanessa commiserated. 'Why don't I do handover? Then you can take off and get that shower.'

'Oh, cheers!' Lindsey let her shoulders drop as if sloughing off a huge weight. 'That's the best offer I've had all day.'

* * *

Sweet God, how had all this happened? Slumped at his desk, Dan shaded his eyes with his hands. He had to fix things with Lindsey. She was keeping out of his way, delegating the other nurses to assist him.

He was still considering a plan of action when his mobile rang. Sitting back in his chair, he activated the call and then sat bolt upright as he listened.

'You've done what?'

Lindsey's thoughts were deeply focused as she made her way from the station to the staffroom.

'Lindsey…' Dan appeared out of nowhere and closed in beside her.

'Oh!' Lindsey drew to an abrupt halt. She brought her head up in question.

'Martin is back on deck.' Dan got straight to the point. 'He'll be in a bit later. I'll be off duty. We can talk. I'll come to you or we can meet somewhere neutral if you'd prefer.'

There was a wavering in her eyes, a sign of hesitation. Finally, 'My place is fine. Come when you get off.'

Dan felt relief course through him. 'I should be out of here by six. Could I bring a takeaway?'

Lindsey looked up and saw the sheen of appeal in his eyes. 'Thanks, but no need. I'll fix us something. Just one thing, Dan.'

His brow rose briefly. 'Name it.'

'We sort this. Truthfully. No double-talk.'

A tiny pulse flickered in Dan's cheek. His eyes softened, taking in the brave set of her head, the soft curve of her cheek, the sweet, very sweet fullness of her mouth. 'You've got it.'

'Do you have the address?' she asked, almost formally.

'You gave it to me on Sunday night. Remember?'

She did. Soft heat flooded her cheeks. She'd told him when they'd been snuggled up in bed during the storm and she'd foolishly thought that nothing or no one could touch their newfound happiness. Now they were both hurting and she hated it. In a gesture of fence-mending she put out her hand and he took it loosely. 'See you later, then.'

'As soon as I can make it.'

Lindsey couldn't keep still. When would Dan get here? She just hoped he hadn't had an emergency at the last minute. She had her stir-fry ready to just throw in the wok and she'd cooked rice to go with it. Taking a deep breath, she let it go. It felt like a first date all over again. She spun round from the kitchen bench, a little tumble in her stomach as the doorbell pealed.

Dan waited for Lindsey to open the door. Mentally, he was wiped. Today in Casualty had been one that took years from a health professional's life. Add the stress of that to the personal stuff that had gone down...the thought of that made him go cold. Everything between them had so nearly run off the rails today.

Lindsey opened the door. 'Hi...' She met his gaze almost hungrily. 'Come in, Dan.'

He nodded and stepped inside, realising he'd crack wide open if he didn't hold her. Properly. With no agenda. And she had that gleam in her eyes. The one that could send a sweep of sensation down to his toes, igniting all the parts of his body in between. He held out his arms and she melted into them, wrapping herself tightly around him, feeling his chest rise and fall in a broken sigh. 'God, I thought I'd lost you. Lost us.'

She reached up to bracket his face with her hands, her heart in her gaze. 'I hated what happened today.'

'Don't go back there.' Suddenly he looked uncertain. 'Tell me I'm not dreaming. I am actually holding you?'

'You're not dreaming, Dan.' Slowly she became aware of his palm resting warmly at her nape, the tips of his fingers playing gently with the strands of her hair.

'Could we delay *talking* and just go to bed?' he asked throatily. 'I need to put things right.'

CHAPTER TEN

'THAT WAS WONDERFUL.'

'I gathered it must have been.' Lindsey looked on indulgently as he forked up the last of the stir-fry from his bowl. 'You had two helpings.'

'Didn't eat much today,' he offloaded with a grin.

Lindsey looked across at him. 'Today was pretty bad, wasn't it? In all kinds of ways.'

'Just marginally,' he underplayed. 'For most of it I felt as though I had a knife jammed between my ribs. How about you?'

'No knife.' Soft humour shone in her eyes. 'But I wanted to just jump in my car and head back to Lark Hill and never set foot in a casualty department again.'

'That would be a terrible shame.' Dan swallowed the sudden razor-sharp emotion clogging his throat. Today could have all turned out so differently. 'You're an amazing nurse, Lindsey.' His blue gaze shimmered over her face. 'An amazing lover...'

She reached out her hand and they touched fingertips. 'Only with you...'

Her mouth suddenly dried. What they'd found together was still so new. And wonderful. *I think I love you.* Only she didn't voice that thought out loud.

She took her hand back and got to her feet. 'Coffee?'

'Oh, yes, please.' He looked up and thanked her as she took his bowl.

'How long have you had this place?' Dan asked interestedly. They were relaxing on Lindsey's big comfy sofa, their coffee and a plate of orange shortbread, compliments of Fiona, on the low table in front of them.

'I bought it ages ago. When I decided this was where I wanted to be.'

'For always?'

Lindsey looked startled. 'I hadn't thought about it like that. But my job is here. And my family.' She frowned a bit. 'Do you think that's…odd?'

'No.' He gave her a long, intense look. 'Knowing what you want, what makes you happy, sounds wonderfully… grounded.'

Lindsey felt a glitch of uncertainty. 'Not boring?'

'Is that even worth an answer?'

Probably not. 'The house was once a miner's cottage,' Lindsey went on. 'The structure was pretty sound when I bought it and I just refurbished it to my own taste as I went along.'

'You've certainly put your own stamp on it.' He looked around at the unmistakable *Lindsey* touches. 'Some of your work?' he asked, flexing a hand towards the table lamps with their blue and white ginger jar bases.

'Some of my early pieces.' She leant forward and poured their coffee. 'I found the fireplace at an auction. It was in an old post office they were pulling down.' She handed him his coffee. 'I offered twenty dollars to get the bidding started and came home with it.'

Dan gave one of his lazy smiles. 'I'm impressed.'

'You should come with me some time.' Lindsey pressed her head against his shoulder.

'To an auction?'

'I'm guessing you've never been to one. Am I right?'

'Guilty as charged.' His mouth tipped at one corner.

Lindsey took one of the tiny shortbreads and bit into it thoughtfully. 'Are you still in the hospital accommodation?'

'One of the flats. They're not bad and close enough to the hospital to make getting to work on time less hassle.'

'Nathan had a flat there as well, didn't he?'

'Still has. He didn't entirely move out before he and Sami were married. Living there suits me for the present anyway.'

And then what? Lindsey wondered. She knew he had a work contract with the hospital and Dan, being Dan, would honour his contractual arrangements whatever it took. But when his commitment to Hopeton District ran out, then what? Would he go elsewhere? *Then what about us?* she wanted to ask. But couldn't. Possibly because neither of them knew the answer.

Dan's chest rose in a long, uneven breath. The faint drift of Lindsey's distinctive floral shampoo was already escalating into the reality of her head on the pillow beside him earlier. And the completeness of their loving. It came as something of a shock to him that he'd never felt remotely like this before. The thought made him want to go forward with new purpose. Leave no room for doubt or misinterpretation. Lindsey deserved that. He expelled a rough sigh. 'If you're up for it, I guess we should talk about the elephant in the room.'

Well, no second-guessing there. 'Brooke?' Lindsey felt her heart beating in double-quick time. 'I heard back from Clarissa. They had a long talk. At the end of it Brooke decided to resign. She's left the hospital.'

'She's left town as well. She called me.'

So Brooke had his mobile number. Lindsey felt that sense of unease return. Suddenly her nerve ends were tingling, her breathing uncomfortably tight. She lifted her head, searing her gaze with his. 'Is she in love with you?'

'No.' In a kind of releasing gesture Dan raised his hands, ploughing his fingers through his hair. 'It's a bit of an involved story. But now Brooke's gone…' He stopped and considered. 'I don't think it would hurt if I told you. But before I do I want you to know there was nothing going on in the car park when you saw us.'

Lindsey was far from mollified. 'She was practically welded to your groin!'

He gave a reproving look before his mouth twitched into a transparently smug grin. 'I can't help it if women flock round me.'

'Oh, get over yourself, Dr Rossi,' she countered drily. 'I was probably mistaken anyway.' She spread her hands in a shrug. 'Go on with your story.'

Dan looked serious for a moment. 'It's off the record, Lindsey.'

'Of course. And before we go any further, I feel really sorry for Brooke. It was a rotten thing to happen but it did and there were consequences.' When Dan remained silent, she asked, 'Why did she come to Hopeton?'

'Spot on the map,' Dan said. 'As random as that. And there were vacancies advertised at the hospital. It had been a while since she'd nursed but she took a chance and applied. She was offered a position in Casualty. She hadn't wanted to begin there but she needed a job.'

'But it seems as though she was far from comfortable, working there. What kind of training did she have?'

'She was well qualified to work in Casualty. Brooke was in the ADF. She'd done two tours in Afghanistan.'

Lindsey frowned. 'She was an army nurse?'

'She was dedicated. And decorated.'

She blinked uncertainly. 'So, what are you saying?'

'In my opinion, Brooke is suffering from PTSD.'

'Oh—that's awful.' Lindsey felt a flow of sympathy. 'Because of her time in the Defence Force?'

Dan nodded. 'Her fiancé was a soldier. They were both attached to the same company when they were overseas. He was wounded. Brought in when Brooke was on duty.'

'Oh, Lord...' Lindsey squeezed her eyes shut. It got worse and worse. She swallowed heavily. 'Did he survive?'

'No. They airlifted him out but it was too late. Brooke went with him. Not that it counted for much in the end.'

'And Brooke told you all this on night duty?'

'We had long stretches when it was quiet,' Dan replied. 'I'm pretty tuned in to mental fatigue.' He didn't add he'd done advanced training in stress management as part of his search and rescue course. 'I sensed something about her. I put out a few feelers and she responded. I urged her to be upfront with Clarissa and ask for a transfer to another department. Anywhere but Casualty. I think she was getting around to it.'

'But not soon enough.' Lindsey looked thoughtful. 'Did she say what triggered her meltdown this morning? Why she didn't react when Mia was brought in?'

'The ambulance base had called and said there was a gunshot wound coming in. Brooke admitted she freaked.'

Lindsey shook her head. 'Where did all her training go, her protocols?'

'Lindsey, we can't have any real idea of Brooke's mental state at that moment. We hadn't been through what she'd been through. Obviously, she wasn't thinking straight. She spun out at the mention of guns. In any event, it turned out it was only a superficial wound. Some idiot out spotlighting feral pigs had misfired and shot himself in the side of the foot.'

'And in all the carry-on Brooke forgot about Mia.'

'Well—momentarily anyway.'

Lindsey felt her stomach churn. The incident could

have all been avoided if Brooke had just signed off and gone home and let someone else deal with the emergency. 'When did she tell you all this?'

'I watched for her to leave this morning and followed her out to the car park. I reiterated what I'd already told her. Suggested she get counselling as a priority.'

'Instead, she's left town.' Lindsey's eyes looked troubled. 'Where will she go?'

'When she called me she said she was going back to Sydney. She'll have family support there. And I've linked her up with a good shrink. She promised to follow through. Today has been a huge wake-up call for her. She'll get the help she needs now and life will get much better for her.'

'Oh, Dan…' Lindsey scooted up the sofa to him.

'I know.' He gathered her in and placed a soft kiss on her mouth. 'If we all had hindsight, the world would be a much better and kinder place.'

'Brooke kept to herself a lot. It was difficult to offer any kind of friendship.'

'Don't beat up on yourself,' Dan said. 'In our job we can only do what we can do. What people will *allow* us to do.'

'I'll scotch any rumours,' Lindsey promised.

'That'll be good.' He gave her a quick hug. 'You didn't really think I had something going with Brooke, did you?'

Lindsey felt his smile on her skin as he touched his lips to her throat.

'I admit to a smidge of jealousy.'

He looked into her green eyes. An intensity of emotion he'd never felt swamped him. 'You're all I need, Lindsey. So…with that in mind, am I staying the night?'

Lindsey drew in a shaken breath, feeling the sweet sting of anticipation tingle up her spine. 'Where else would you go?' A smile flickered around her mouth. 'But just so you know, I'm on an early tomorrow.'

'Ah.' His eyes caressed her tenderly. 'And I'm on a day off.'

'Then I'll leave it to you to make the bed and tidy the kitchen, shall I?'

He reached out a finger, his touch feather-like along her bottom lip. 'I think I can manage that.'

'Hey, I'm kidding.' Lindsey smothered a laugh. 'I wouldn't expect you to do that.'

'I'll do it anyway.' Carefully, he scooped up a wayward tendril of her hair and tucked it behind her ear. 'I'm really quite house-trained. I thought you knew that.'

'I probably did.' She snuggled closer. 'So, what are you going to do with your day off?'

His mouth quirked. 'I'm going to a talk on beekeeping.'

'Well, that makes sense—not.' Lindsey chuckled. 'Where are you going to do your beekeeping, may one ask?'

He sent her a pained look. 'It's good to have a hobby. And who knows, I may invest in acreage one day.'

Next morning Lindsey drove to work with a new resolve. Surely there had always been a sacred bond among nurses? Perhaps if Brooke had been more open… Lindsey turned into the car park. From today she'd make extra sure her team knew they were valued and supported.

It wasn't long into the shift when Vanessa pounced. 'Did you hear?'

Lindsey lifted her gaze in query. 'If this is about Brooke, Vanessa, yes, I heard. She's resigned.'

'I heard she got the sack.'

'Well, she didn't,' Lindsey said firmly. 'She decided Hopeton wasn't for her and she's gone back to her family in Sydney.'

'Will she be all right?'

'Let's hope so. Brooke was in the armed forces.' Abruptly,

Lindsey decided she'd tell Vanessa just enough to settle the wild supposition that was probably on speaker phone around the hospital already. 'She did a couple of tours in Afghanistan. Apparently, it was pretty rough.'

'Wow…' Vanessa sobered. 'What went down—personal stuff?'

Lindsey nodded. 'Very personal. Someone very close to her was killed.'

'Oh, that's awful.' Vanessa blinked quickly then straightened her shoulders resolutely. 'If anyone starts spouting rubbish about Brooke being sacked, I'll quash it.'

Lindsey's mouth kicked up in a resigned smile. 'Diplomatically, please, Van.'

'Of course I'll be diplomatic.' Vanessa looked wounded. 'By tomorrow it'll all be a non-event anyway.' She picked up the phone as it rang. 'Bound to be something more juicy come along.'

Continuing with her new resolve, Lindsey drew Jess aside when she got a chance later in the shift. 'How did things turn out with Mr Gaines yesterday?' Lindsey knew she could have pulled the notes and found out for herself but it would be helpful for the young nurse's professional development to let Jess debrief.

'Oh, Michelle admitted him,' Jess said earnestly. 'He was exhibiting early signs of pneumonia.'

'So, you made a good call, then.'

'Think so.' Jess's mouth curved, a tiny dimple showing in her cheek.

'Are you getting on all right with Michelle?'

Jess went pink. 'She can be a bit daunting. But yesterday she included me in Mr Gaines's treatment plan and that felt really professional.'

'Good.' Lindsey smiled.

'And Mr Gaines has a nice neighbour who brought some

pyjamas and things in for him,' Jess went on. 'And I got some toiletries for him as well. And some batteries for his little radio.'

'But I hope not out of your own pocket, Jess?' Lindsey pressed the point. Patient care only went so far. And while Jess was very committed to her role, shelling out for patients' extras was not part of it.

'Oh, no. Mr Gaines was very upfront with his money. And Michelle had a chat to him about his living arrangements and apparently his granddaughter from Sydney would like to come and live with him.' Jess continued enthusiastically, 'Grace, that's her name, has a little three-year-old, Liam, and her husband is a FIFO worker. Fly-in, fly-out,' Jess enlarged.

Lindsey hid a smile. 'I know what it means, Jess. So that would seem a good arrangement if they're both keen.'

'Well, Grace is a bit lonely and so is Mr Gaines and he seemed really chuffed to think it might all happen. Michelle's handed everything over to Declan,' she said, mentioning the hospital's social worker.

'Well, good outcome,' Lindsey approved.

'Um…' Jess looked a bit uncertain. 'Is it OK if I run up to Medical to see Mr Gaines now and again? In my break, I mean.'

'Of course.' Lindsey smiled. 'I imagine it would brighten Mr Gaines's day as well. Just realise, though, that in Casualty we're just the jumping-off point. We can't give holistic care, no matter how much we'd like to. You're really enjoying your nursing, aren't you, Jess?'

'More than I thought.' Jess considered. 'And it's nice when your patient says thank you and when you've made a positive impact on them.'

'Perhaps we could nominate you for Nurse of the Year,' Lindsey said teasingly. 'The local Lions Club gives an annual award with a cash prize.'

'Wow—I didn't know that.' Jess's hand went to her heart. 'That'd be so cool—to be nominated, I mean. But I guess one of the midwives would be sure to win.'

'They do seem to have all the fun,' Lindsey agreed. 'Next time we have a staff meeting, I'll run it past the DON.' She touched Jess briefly on the shoulder. 'You know I'm always available if you need to discuss anything work-related, Jess. Or anything personal, for that matter,' Lindsey added, thinking of Brooke again. 'Confidentiality guaranteed.'

'Thanks.' Jess bit her lip. 'Could I extend my time in Casualty, do you think? I really like being part of our team.'

'Just keep doing what you're doing,' Lindsey said. 'That's probably the best way to go.'

Lindsey leaned over the counter to replace a file, deciding that if yesterday's shift had been hell on wheels, today's had been relatively uneventful.

'How was your meeting?' Vanessa looked up from the computer.

'Quick for a change.' Lindsey gave a wry smile. 'Apparently, we're getting a new senior nurse for the department.'

'Mmm, I heard.' Vanessa stretched languidly. 'Charlie Weston, thirty-two, divorced, shared care of four-year-old Poppy.'

Lindsey shook her head. 'You take my breath away sometimes. How do you know all this?'

An imp of mischief danced in Vanessa's eyes. 'Oh, I have my ways. And I like to keep ahead of the game.'

Lindsey cast her eyes down. She wondered how long she and Dan had before their involvement was *out there*. She gave a mental shrug. They'd deal with it when it happened. As it undoubtedly would.

'It's ages since we've had a male nurse in the department,' Vanessa said chattily. 'Do you think he'll come on to our team?'

'We'll have to wait and see, I suppose.'

'We'll lose Annie Logan soon when she takes her mat leave.' Vanessa considered. 'So possibly we'll get Charlie to replace her.'

'Possibly.' Lindsey came round and joined Vanessa at the desk. 'I'll give handover. Take an early mark, if you like.'

'Ta, Lins.' Vanessa was already on her feet. 'I'm off to the gym.' She bit down on her bottom lip around a quick smile. 'Andrew kind of said he might be there.'

Lindsey watched her friend leave. Privately, she thought Vanessa was chasing shadows. If Andrew had wanted a closer relationship with her, he would have acted ages ago, not left her wishing and hoping for something he wasn't capable of giving.

Thank heavens Dan had known what he wanted and gone after it. Lindsey's gaze turned dreamy. She wondered whether he'd be there when she got home. Would he stay again tonight…?

'Afternoon, Lins.'

Lindsey's head swivelled round as charge for the late shift, Greta Ingram, joined her at the desk.

'Oh—hey, Greta.' Lindsey brought her thoughts smartly back to reality.

'How are things?'

'Pretty good, thanks. And with you as well, I imagine.'

Lindsey's eyes opened to questioning wideness.

'You and your new man? I heard you and Dan got off together after Nathan's wedding. Looking very much an item, according to my cousin Alison.'

When Lindsey remained speechless, Greta gave a chuckle and went on. 'You've obviously forgotten Ally works in Nathan's department. Her mum made the wedding cake.'

'Well, I saw Alison there, of course,' Lindsey flannelled. 'But there was a big crowd so I didn't…' She picked up some paperwork and held it against her chest. 'Who else knows?'

'Well, I haven't said anything,' Greta said calmly. 'But would it matter?'

Lindsey thought for a minute. 'I suppose not. You know, in all my years of nursing I've never become involved with someone I worked with.'

'Well, that doesn't make you *odd*!' Greta insisted. 'I didn't date work colleagues either.'

'Kind of ironical then, wasn't it?' Lindsey teased, 'That you actually met your husband-to-be in a hospital setting.'

Greta's husband, Harry, was a painter and decorator. When they'd met, he'd just started his own company and had won the tender to refurbish the entire Hopeton casualty department. 'I thought he needed looking after.' Greta sank onto a chair, looking amused. 'I kept bringing him big mugs of tea.'

'I remember.' Lindsey's laugh tinkled. 'Poor guy. No wonder he was in and out of the men's so much.'

'Oh, he never was!' Greta chuckled and flapped her lanyard in protest. 'Now, what do you have for me?' She moved closer to the computer.

When Lindsey arrived home from work there was no sign of Dan, but he'd left a note on the kitchen counter. It said simply that Nathan and Sami were due back that evening and he was meeting their flight. He'd see Lindsey at work tomorrow.

And he hadn't taken the spare key she'd left him. It was placed pointedly on top of the note.

Now, what was she supposed to read into that? Lindsey fretted as she stripped off and threw herself under the shower. Suddenly her mind was a whirlpool of jumbled thoughts and emotions. Well, obviously Dan didn't trust what they'd found together at all. She'd assumed. And *he* hadn't liked it. Vigorously, she washed her hair and let the shampoo puddle round her feet. Did they have yet another elephant in the room? It seemed so.

As Lindsey towelled dry, she gave a bitter little laugh. Where understanding men and their motives were concerned, she'd obviously been as naïve as Vanessa.

As soon as she saw Dan arrive at work on Thursday morning, Lindsey went straight to his office. There was a knot in her stomach and tension in her muscles as though she'd run a marathon, but she wasn't about to let him retreat to some place in his head and leave her outside.

Knocking briefly on his door, she popped her head in and then the rest of herself. Turning, she closed the door and looked across at him. 'Hi.' She managed a smile. 'Got a minute for me?'

'Of course.' Dan got to his feet slowly, meeting her where she'd stopped at the front of his desk.

He parked himself against the edge of the desk, folding his arms and crossing his feet at the ankles. He sent her a narrowed look, drawn by the intensity of her expression. 'You OK?'

'Fine.' Lindsey shoved her hands into the pockets of her trousers. 'How was your day off?'

'It was good.'

'And the talk?'

'It was interesting.' A tiny flicker of amusement appeared behind his eyes. 'I learned the queen bee mates with fifteen males in mid-air and then flies back to the hive to lay her eggs.'

'Wow! That's quite an impressive gene pool they have going.'

'Mmm.' Dan rubbed his chin. 'I felt a bit sorry for the males, though. They're history after they've mated.'

'That's nature, I guess.' Lindsey hardly gave the statement head room. She had to do what she'd come to do now or let it fester for the rest of the shift. She tilted her head higher and sent him a very frank look. 'So...the key. Too far, too fast?'

He frowned a bit. 'Sorry?'

'I left you a spare key to my home. Clearly, you didn't want it.'

Dan felt the wind taken right out of his sails. He'd hoped for opportunity and the right time to explain his motives but it seemed he wasn't going to get it.

'We hadn't talked about it and I didn't want to presume anything.'

'In other words, you thought *I'd* taken far too much for granted.'

'Hell, Lindsey...' He lifted his hands and scrubbed his fingers impatiently across his cheekbones. 'I don't know what I thought. It just seemed a bit...awkward.'

'Oh, Dan...' Lindsey shook her head. It appeared they still had a long way to go. A long way. 'I left the key as a kind of no-strings invitation,' she flannelled, going all-out to save the situation as best she could. 'I just thought you might have wanted to come back after your talk, relax a bit, even though I wasn't there.' She took a tiny swallow. Even to her own ears the whole scenario sounded less than plausible.

Dan felt the unease in his gut begin to unravel. How had he got it so wrong? Lindsey was everything he'd ever dreamed of in a woman. He'd accepted almost greedily everything she'd offered in the bedroom. Why had he got all stiff-necked about her offer of a damned key! It made his stomach twist. 'I'm an idiot.'

'Well, maybe the jury's still out on that.' She managed a smile of sorts and stepped away. 'Oh.' She turned at the door. 'How were the honeymooners?'

Dan cracked a crooked grin. 'Still in love, by the look of them. They had a great time.'

'Oh, bless. Where did they go?'

'One of the Barrier Reef islands.'

'Fantastic. Ever been?'

He looked a bit sheepish. 'Very remiss of me, I know. Never seemed to get the time.'

'Poor excuse.' Her green eyes lit briefly. 'We'll have to remedy that.'

Why on earth had she made that ridiculous comment? Lindsey gave herself a mental ticking off as she made her way back to the station. The way things were going between her and Dan, they had about as much chance of making a romantic trip to the Reef as being in Edinburgh for lunch on Sunday.

Back at her desk, she buried herself in paperwork.

'You OK?' Vanessa gave Lindsey an assessing look when the two caught up during a quiet moment.

'Yep.' Lindsey gathered her paperwork and tapped it into a neat pile. 'Oh, by the way, Greta left a flyer. Harry and the Rotary need some helpers for a community project. Working bee at the kindergarten. Could you bung it up in the staffroom, please?'

'Sure.' Vanessa scanned the bright yellow notice. 'Oh, it's at the kindergarten that caters for differently abled little ones. I'll be off that weekend, so I'll go along. Perhaps Andrew as well…'

'Did you meet up at the gym?' Lindsey asked casually.

Vanessa made a face. 'He didn't show. I hung around until I'd made myself dizzy on that stupid walking thing. And then I left.'

'Do you think—?' Lindsey stopped. How to be diplomatic here? 'Tell me to mind my own, but do you think it's really working with you and Andrew?'

Vanessa blinked a bit and shrugged. 'Obviously, *you* don't.'

'What do I know about men and their *ways*?' Lindsey snorted.

'Are you and Dan...you know?' Vanessa rocked her hand suggestively.

Lindsey sat back in her chair. Why keep up the secrecy? 'We've been seeing each other a bit.' And wasn't that the understatement of the year?

'You were into something pretty heavy yesterday when I walked in on you.'

'That was entirely work-related.'

Vanessa rolled her eyes. 'And if I believed that, I'd believe someone's just given us the rest of the day off!'

'Oh, hush up, Van,' Lindsey responded mildly. 'It's sorted, OK?'

'You know,' Vanessa said thoughtfully and with a seemingly new-found maturity, 'I'm starting to believe that trying to have a personal relationship with someone you work with is doomed from the outset.'

'Well, perhaps it depends on the *someone*,' Lindsey countered. 'But whatever, it's certainly a minefield,' she added darkly, picking up the phone as it rang. 'MVA coming in. Grab whoever you can and I'll meet you at the ambulance bay.'

He should be certified.

Dan gave vent to a groan of frustration as he drove home. And placed in lockdown, he gritted silently.

What the hell was wrong with him? Why couldn't he just have accepted the key to Lindsey's home with grace? Because deep down he knew it had been a loving gesture from her. And, however much she'd denied it, loaded with expectation. And that fact was what had almost brought him out in a cold sweat.

He made a sound of disgust at his pathetic handling of his relationship with Lindsey. She was lovely, her femininity enthralled him. And she was sweet and clever. And she made him laugh. Put simply so that even an idiot could understand, everything about her called to him. So why couldn't he have sorted things when she'd come to his office? Told her he wanted to take things slowly—for both their sakes. God, after his stuff-up with Caroline—

He shook his head. *But surely to God he could have just taken a step forward and wrapped his arms around Lindsey. Reassured her.*

His jaw tightened, the regret almost numbing him. And he didn't wonder any longer why all day his arms had almost ached with the thought of the lost opportunity.

His introspection was cut short when he responded to an incoming call on his hands-free mobile. 'Rossi.'

'Hey, mate.'

'Nate.' Immediately, Dan's mood lifted. 'How're things?'

'Yeah, great. Are you by any chance on your way home?' Nathan asked.

'Almost there.'

'Any plans for tonight?'

Dan grimaced. He could have had plans but he'd well and truly scuttled those. 'No, I don't have any plans. What do you need?'

Nathan chuckled. 'You know me too well. Actually, I need a hand to shift the last of my stuff out of the flat. Some other dude wants to move in over the weekend.'

'What kind of *stuff* are we talking about?' Dan asked cautiously. 'I don't need extra health cover for a broken back, do I?'

Nathan snorted. 'It's only a few books and things.'

'What books? Those massive medical tomes you've been carting around for years?'

'It won't be that difficult,' Nathan justified. 'I've hired a trolley thing. I just need you and your car boot. It'll be sweet.'

'What's in it for me, then?' Dan shot back.

'Hang on, I'm thinking.'

'Yeah, I can hear the cogs.'

'Fish and chips for dinner,' Nathan offered gallantly. 'Plus a very smooth bourbon.'

Dan cracked a laugh. 'Fair enough. I'm two minutes away.'

CHAPTER ELEVEN

Friday...

CASUALTY WAS BUSY. Lindsey thanked her lucky stars it was. It gave her less time to begin thinking. Analysing. Had she come across to Dan as too organised about their relationship? Too calculating? Pushing too hard? She shook her head. She hadn't meant to give that impression at all.

She wondered how he'd spent last night. Had he stayed home and thought about her? About them? Maybe he'd gone out on the town. Not that Hopeton had much of a night-life during the week but still...

'The police just brought in two old chaps, drunk as.' Vanessa came round the corner of the station and slapped her notes on the desk. 'They politely or impolitely vomited all over the floor and now the waiting room smells like—well, you know.'

'Get the cleaners in,' Lindsey said patiently.

'I tried.' Vanessa's mouth twisted comically. 'They're on a tea break.'

'What's wrong with your patients, besides needing something for their hangovers?' Lindsey asked.

'Cuts and bruises mostly. When the pub shut they spent the rest of the night in the park. A couple of low-lives rolled them this morning. Stole their wallets.'

'What's the place coming to?' Lindsey frowned. 'Are the police looking into it?'

'Dunno. Dan spoke to them.'

'I imagine their ID and social security details were in the wallets.'

'Declan's on it,' Vanessa dismissed. 'For the present, the old boys are *resting* in the side ward. I guess we'll do what we always do. Patch them up, give them something to eat a bit later and send them off.' She flopped into a chair. 'You can't help wondering how people's lives disintegrate so drastically. I mean, they must have been young and hopeful once. I wonder where they'll sleep tonight.'

Lindsey looked at her friend sharply. It was not like Van to be introspective. 'Perhaps Declan will be able to arrange some sheltered accommodation for them. Are *you* OK? You still have some leave due. Maybe you should take it? Get away from the place for a bit.'

'Maybe.' Vanessa managed a jaded smile.

'By the way, Annie finished last night. Her ob wants her to rest up. Our new man is starting on Monday on an early.'

'Oh, joy.' Vanessa brightened. 'On our team, then?'

'For the moment. Uh-oh.' Lindsey sighed as she picked up a call from the ambulance base. She listened to the report and then shot off a few questions of her own. Putting the phone down, she turned to Vanessa. 'Ten girls from St Faith's College coming in from a school camp, suspected food poisoning. ETA twenty minutes.'

Quickly, Lindsey found Dan and relayed the details of the emergency.

'Right, this is where the rubber hits the road, people. We'll need everyone on deck,' Dan said when the team had assembled at the station. 'We'll wait to ascertain the extent of the illness and go from there.'

'And be ready with basins, please,' Lindsey said. 'Some of the students could still be vomiting.'

Within minutes two ambulances had arrived, followed by one of the teachers who had helpfully offered his Land Rover to transport several of the young patients to the hospital.

'Let's get some triage happening, shall we?' Dan came in authoritatively. He half turned his head. 'Lindsey?'

Lindsey ran her eyes over the assembled group. 'This is going to need everyone's co-operation. Some of the students appear quite ill so, Gail, where you can, would you begin taking names, please? And liaise with the accompanying teachers about letting the parents know.'

'How do we work this patient-wise?' Andrew cut in, throwing the question at Dan.

'We'll see the kids on stretchers first. You team with Jess. Michelle, you team with Vanessa. Anything you're uncertain about, don't dither. Give me a yell. Now let's go.'

Accompanied by Dan, Lindsey went into the first cubicle. Their patient, a sixteen-year-old student, looked pale and clammy. Lindsey placed her hand on the youngster's shoulder. 'What's your name, honey?'

'Katherine Enders.'

'And when did you start feeling ill?' Lindsey smoothed the girl's long fair hair away from her cheek.

'Soon after breakfast.' She bit her lips together and went on. 'The other kids were sick too.'

'Katherine,' Dan said gently, 'I just need to feel your tummy.' His mouth compressed as he palpated. 'Right.' He stepped back and drew the sheet up. 'That's fine. Have you had any diarrhoea?'

'Some. Oh…'

Lindsey noticed the girl's sudden pallor. 'Do you want to vomit, Katherine?'

The girl blocked a tear with the tips of her fingers and sniffed. 'I feel so awful.' She swallowed convulsively and tried to sit up. 'My little sister, Alix, is really sick…'

'Shh… It's OK,' Lindsey hushed gently. 'She'll be looked after. Let's just try to get you settled.'

That wasn't going to happen.

'Oh, help!' Katherine gulped and gave a little moan. 'I want to be sick…'

Lindsey grabbed a basin. They were in for a morning and a half with this lot.

'Someone's head should roll over this.' Dan was grim-faced. 'Let's run ten milligrams of Maxolon stat, please, Lindsey. That should settle her nausea.'

Quickly Lindsey secured the drip and taped it down. 'Lomotil for the diarrhoea?'

Dan nodded. 'Start with two orally and cut back to one after each bowel movement. She's dehydrating. I'd like her on four per cent glucose and one-fifth normal saline IV. Sips of water only. Could you take her blood sugar levels as well, please? Anything below three, I need to know.'

And so it went on for the next couple of hours.

'I don't know about you, but I'm starving.' Dan followed Lindsey into the staffroom. They'd just done a round, re-checking all their young patients. And releasing most of them into the care of their parents.

'I have sandwiches, if you'd like to share?' Lindsey offered.

'Hmm…' Dan considered his options. 'I think I'd like something hot. Let's go to Leo's.'

'Oh.' Lindsey hesitated. 'OK. I'll just make sure Vanessa's around to mind the station.'

'What about Alix Enders?' Lindsey asked as they crossed the street to Leo's. 'How long will you keep her?'

'I'd like to leave her drip in a bit longer. She was seriously dehydrated.'

'Did you get any clue as to what may have caused the food poisoning?'

'Probably something dodgy they ate for breakfast, seeing they were ill so soon after. The guys from Health and Safety will suss it out, send whatever they come up with for analysis.' Dan pushed open the door to the café and they went inside.

'I'm not usually out for lunch.' Lindsey took the chair Dan held for her. 'I shouldn't be away from the hospital too long.'

'You're entitled to your break.' Dan had no such qualms. 'And we're only five minutes away if we're needed.'

'I suppose.' She ran her gaze over the short menu. 'I think I'll have the fish.'

'I'll have the beef stroganoff.' Dan placed the menu beside his plate. 'I had fish last night. An impromptu dinner with Nathan and Sami.'

So that's where he'd been. Lindsey looked up as Leo arrived to leave water and take their orders. How pathetic, she berated herself, waiting for any crumb that would let her a little further into Dan's world. While they waited for their food, Lindsey poured them each a glass of water. Suddenly she was aware the silence had extended for too long. 'So... Nathan and Sami settling into their new place all right?'

'New *old* place,' Dan countered drily. 'It's Georgian in design, huge garden, built in the eighteen thirties, according to Sami. She's already on a roll, talking in terms of topiary, stone walling and hedge laying.'

'How's Nathan feel about that?'

'Terrified.' Dan's eyes glinted with soft amusement. 'Sami's been to the historical society to get details of the house as it used to be. She found the front hedge was originally clipped into a whimsical line of marching elephants.'

'Are you serious?' Lindsey spluttered a laugh. 'That girl is totally priceless. But I don't know why I should be surprised. Sami has always known what she wanted and gone after it. I guess that's what Nathan loves about her.'

'I'm sure...' Dan paused. 'Oh, while I think of it, I've been given time off on Monday to attend a refresher training day in search and rescue. If you're pushed, Nathan's back on Monday. He'll come down. And Martin's in at noon.'

Lindsey nodded. 'Thanks for letting me know. Where do you have to go for your training?'

Dan lifted a shoulder. 'Locally.'

And that seemed to be that. Within seconds they were facing another wall of uneasy silence.

It was Dan who broke it.

'Would you like to go out for dinner tomorrow? Perhaps somewhere we could dance as well?' He'd made himself aware of Lindsey's roster, knew she was on an early tomorrow and then off on Sunday, and had decided he could work around that as well.

Slowly Lindsey raised her gaze. Her throat constricted. 'That would have been...good. But I'm heading straight out to Lark Hill after my shift. Mum and Dad are due home next week. I want to make sure everything's looking nice for them.'

It was on the tip of Dan's tongue to ask if she'd like a hand—his for preference—but it was clear she wasn't about to issue an invitation. It was also clear she was making a statement. She didn't want him there. He took a mouthful of water and placed his glass back on its coaster. 'Something's obviously bugging you, Lindsey. Why don't you just hit me with it?'

She didn't pretend to misunderstand him. 'I like clarity in my life. That's how I am. I don't seem to be getting it from you, Dan.'

They stared at each other.

'Let's be frank, then.' Dan's blue eyes glittered. 'You're still ticked off with me because I didn't accept the key you left for me.'

Lindsey hated confrontation but there was no backing down. 'I was hurt at your reaction,' she admitted.

'I acted like a jerk.' His mouth straightened into a grim line. 'Your leaving the key was spontaneous and sweet. I could have called you and sorted it, instead of leaving that pathetic note.' He gave a mirthless laugh. 'God, I can't believe I did that!'

Lindsey raised an eyebrow. 'But you did. And I was left wondering whether every move I make in the future is going to be the right one. If you want out of this relationship, then tell me. Let's end it cleanly.'

End it? Dan felt a cramp in his chest. Was that what *she* wanted? He let his breath go in a stream. He'd been the luckiest man alive, finding Lindsey. Lindsey with the generous spirit, the forgiving heart. But everything had its limits and her patience with him must be running low. 'Are you saying there's no hope for us?'

Lindsey drew back sharply. 'I'm not saying that at all.' She spread her hands in appeal. 'But I can't be myself around you any more.'

Dan felt his heart beating hard against his ribs. 'OK. I hear what you're saying. I don't want to lose you, Lindsey. Lose *us*.'

Lindsey could see the sudden tight set of his shoulders. She didn't want to put pressure on him. Push him to do things he wasn't ready to do. But they couldn't have gone on the way they had been, neither knowing what the other was thinking half the time. 'I don't want to give up on *us* either, Dan.'

'OK, we won't, then.' His blue eyes held an appeal. 'So this is the new, improved me, communicating. If I wouldn't be intruding, I'd like to come out to Lark Hill on Sunday. We could spend the day together.'

'That would be good,' Lindsey said guardedly. 'And definitely a step in the right direction.'

'More like thirty Ks in the right direction.' There was the slightest waver in his eyes. 'So we're back on track, then.'

'Come early on Sunday.' Lindsey tilted her head and reached out a hand across the table. 'I'll put you to work.'

Dan took her hand, shackling her wrist. 'I want to kiss you,' he said softly.

'No chance.' She ran her tongue along her lips. 'Here's Leo with our food.'

'Sunday, then?' Dan leaned back in his chair.

She nodded.

And so it was settled.

They ate quickly and went back to the hospital. As they approached the station Vanessa called out, 'There you are! We've an MVA coming in. Collision between a car and one of those double-cab utilities. Woman reversing out of her gateway into the main road. Guy in the ute didn't have time to swerve.'

'What kind of injuries do we have?' Dan asked calmly.

'Terry Ryan said the woman's pregnant, ten weeks or so. She's a bit shaken but nothing broken. Ute driver's an older man, shocky, possible ribs and seat-belt injury. It happened just out of town a bit so they'll be here directly.'

'Right.' Dan said, 'Anything else happening?'

'No.' Vanessa shook her head. 'We've been quiet.'

'OK.' He glanced at his watch. 'It's nothing Michelle and Andrew can't handle between them. I have a meeting with the board. Lindsey, will you deal?'

'Go.' Lindsey shooed him off. 'Do we have names, Van?'

Vanessa checked her notes. 'Rebecca Brannon and Graeme Ley. Did you have a nice lunch?' she sidetracked deftly.

'Yes, thanks.' Lindsey busied herself at the computer. 'Can't remember the last time I was at Leo's. OK.' She whirled off her chair. 'Van, would you grab Jess and make sure the resus room is ready, please? And check the radiographer's on hand. At some stage there'll need to be an ultrasound done on the pregnant woman.'

'Got all that.' Vanessa took off.

The ambulance siren could be heard outside as Lindsey briefed the junior doctors. She addressed Andrew. 'Which patient do you want?'

'I'll take the ribs,' he said emphatically. 'I've a bit to learn yet about pregnant women.'

'Better smarten up, then, if you're aiming to be a family practitioner,' Lindsey suggested, her tone dry. 'Jess will assist you. Michelle, I'll be with you.'

'Perhaps we should get the ob down?' Michelle looked a question at Lindsey as they made their way to Resus.

'You're the doctor,' Lindsey said. 'It's your call.'

'On the other hand, he'll be grumpy if we call him down for nothing untoward. We'll play it by ear and see how we go, I think.'

Lindsey shot her a discerning look. 'You're OK about treating this patient?'

'Mmm. Yes, of course.' Michelle gave an awkward little laugh. 'I know I've not been the easiest to work with but I'm finally getting the hang of working in Casualty. It's like running a marathon every day.'

'Maybe. But you'll learn a lot here.' Lindsey pulled back the curtain and they went into the resus cubicle. 'Hi, Rebecca, I'm Lindsey. This is Michelle. She'll be your treating doctor. How are you feeling?'

'A bit scared...' Rebecca was shivering, her eyes wide in trepidation.

'Have you felt any bleeding?' Michelle asked.

'No. Don't think so.'

'Well, we'll make sure anyway. Lindsey, would you check Rebecca, please?'

A few moments later Lindsey was able to report, 'So far, so good. But we'll pop a pad on you, Rebecca, so we'll be able to monitor any change.'

Rebecca took a shaky breath. 'I don't want to lose this baby.'

'We'll do everything we can to stop that happening,' Michelle interposed gently. 'Now, I want to check your tummy for any injury from your seat belt.'

Michelle's hands worked their way methodically across her patient's abdomen, palpating, checking and rechecking. Finally, she lifted her head and smiled. 'You seemed to have escaped any spleen damage. Now, let's see what the rest of you is doing.' She turned to Lindsey, her brows raised in silent query.

'BP and pulse within normal range.'

'Thanks.' Michelle shone a torch into Rebecca's eyes to check her pupils were normal and reacting. 'OK, that's fine,' she said. 'Now, I want you to squeeze my hand as hard as you can and then I'll check your legs and feet. Excellent.' She smiled. 'You're doing great.'

'Are you ready for the Doppler now?' Lindsey asked from behind Michelle's shoulder.

'We certainly are.' Michelle ran the special obstetric stethoscope over Rebecca's slight bump. For several seconds she concentrated, listening. Shifting the stethoscope slightly, she listened again.

'Is s-something wrong?' Rebecca's eyes flew wide in concern.

'Nothing at all.' Michelle gave a reassuring pat to her

patient's arm. 'Your little one's heartbeat is ticking away very nicely.'

'Oh, thank God.' Tears spilled from Rebecca's eyes and down her cheeks.

'Thank you so much, Doctor.'

'I don't think you've anything to worry about,' Michelle said. 'But to make absolutely sure, we'll do an ultrasound as well.'

'Are you booked here to have your baby?' Lindsey spread a blanket over the young woman.

'No…' Rebecca bit her lip. 'I'm from Sydney, here visiting my nanna. It was her car I was driving. It's a bit different from mine. I had trouble adjusting the seat belt and then I think I may have put on too much speed as I reversed. Is the driver of the ute all right?'

'We'll find out for you,' Lindsey said. 'In the meantime, could we contact someone for you—your husband perhaps?'

Rebecca shook her head. 'Dean's away on business. I'll call him later.'

'What about your nanna?' Michelle plonked herself on the corner of the bed.

'She's not been too well. I was actually on my way to get a scrip filled for her.' The young woman gave a funny little grimace. 'She's probably thinking I've gone shopping or something. I…suppose I should let her know…'

'That might be a good idea. I'll speak to her as well, if you like,' Michelle offered. 'Just to reassure her.'

'Thanks…both of you.' Rebecca's eyes flicked between the doctor and nurse. 'For being so kind to me and everything…'

'That's what we do.' Michelle scribbled quickly on her patient's chart. 'Now, if you give me the name of your doctor in Sydney, I'll make sure he or she gets your notes. And I'd like to keep you here for a couple of hours, just to make sure you and your bub are fine. We'll pop you on a saline drip and a little later we'll take some blood. That'll tell us whether your haemoglobin levels are where they should be.'

'OK…' Rebecca pulled herself higher on the pillow. 'Could I have my bag, please? I'll dig out my phone and call Nanna.'

'How's the side ward looking?' Michelle turned to Lindsey. 'Perhaps Rebecca would be more comfortable out there.'

'Should be fine,' Lindsey said. 'Most of our youngsters have been discharged.' She smiled at their patient. 'Now, what about a cup of tea?'

Rebecca gave a little tearful nod of appreciation. 'That sounds like heaven.'

Sunday at Lark Hill…

Hands resting across the railing, Dan and Lindsey were on the back deck, looking down at the patch of newly mown lawn. 'Thanks for doing this, Dan.'

'It's fine.' He sent her a wry smile. 'Anything else you'd like me to do?'

'Well…if you wouldn't mind, I'd like the wood brought in for the fireplace. Even though we're eventually heading into summer, the nights can still get quite cool. Jeff would have seen to all these jobs but he's a bit off-colour at the moment.'

Dan hooked a questioning brow. 'Should I look in on him?'

'Do you have your bag with you?'

'Of course. I'll get it.'

'Dan—stop!' Lindsey smothered an embarrassed laugh. 'I'm kidding. Fiona will have everything in hand.'

'Ah. I see.'

He lifted a hand, stroking the back of his index finger

gently over the curve of her cheek and across her chin. 'You're playing the joker again. Is this something you do only at Lark Hill, Ms Stewart?'

'Must be...' She tried to laugh again but the laughter caught in her throat. His body was very close, his mouth closer still. 'Got you in, though.'

'Payback, then,' he murmured as his mouth came down and closed over her tiny sigh.

While Dan brought in the wood, Lindsey prepared lunch. 'I've made burgers,' she said, when he came through to the kitchen. 'But not your usual kind.' She gave him a quick, hopeful look. 'They're sweet potato and quinoa. And don't look like that.' She flicked him playfully with the tea towel. 'I promise they won't be bland. I've made a chilli yoghurt dressing to go with them.'

Dan washed his hands at the sink. 'So we're on a vegetarian kick today, are we?'

Lindsey put her health professional's hat on. 'It's good to have a change from an all-meat diet.'

'Hey.' He held up his hands in mock surrender. 'Did I say anything to the contrary?'

'No, you didn't.' The dimple in Lindsey's cheek came into sharp relief as she smiled. She loved him like this. Light-hearted. Fun to be with. And the look in those glinting blue eyes sent her insides melting.

They assembled the lunch tray together. 'There's some feta to crumble over the burgers,' Lindsey said. 'Interested?'

Dan's mouth pursed as he considered. 'Think I'll pass. But I'll have some of those black olives, please.'

'And there's rocket from our own veg patch.' Lindsey separated the delicate green leaves from their stems.

'Mmm. Fantastic.' Dan hefted the tray. 'Are we eating on the deck as usual?'

'Why not?' She gathered glasses and a jug of water. 'It's kind of our special place.'

'And I love being here.'

And I love you, he could have added, and wondered why he couldn't voice it.

Because saying it would cause repercussions as wide and deep as the ocean. Was he ready to leave the safety of the shore, take Lindsey with him and set sail to an unfamiliar destination? He deliberately steadied his breathing, tightening his fingers on the edges of the tray and pulling himself back to sanity.

As they neared the end of their informal meal he asked, 'Would you mind if I ran a work-related matter past you?'

'Fire away.' Lindsey refilled their glasses and waited.

'Michelle's evaluation is due. She's about to move on to her next rotation.' He paused. 'Professionally, I wondered how you've found her.'

Lindsey considered her answer. 'Is that a reasonable request, Dan? Michelle's evaluation is surely down to you and Martin.'

'I know all that. But the fact of the matter is the nurses work day in and day out with the junior doctors. And I trust your judgement entirely.'

'Well, in that case...' Lindsey met his gaze, seeing the crease in his cheek as he smiled, the action activating the persuasive gleam in his eyes. 'Michelle's attitude towards the junior nurses has been off-putting for them. They need to gain confidence just as much as the junior doctors do. But things have improved markedly.'

Dan's lips twitched. 'Since you had a quiet word.'

Lindsey gave a shrug. 'She seems to have finally got the message that she's in Casualty as a member of a team. And, believe me, from the nurses' point of view, that's a whole heap of progress.'

'Clinically, she appears very sound. Would you agree?'

'Yes. I've made it my business to work with her a bit more lately. She seems confident in her diagnoses and treatment. And I should charge you for this consult, Dr Rossi,' she added drily.

'Oh, I'll see to it you're well compensated.' His voice was low, deeper than deep, whispering over her skin and right into her heart.

She looked at him mistily. Making love in the afternoon had a lot going for it.

'So, what are you thinking?' Dan's eyes were tender.

'That we have such a lot going for us.'

'We do. I think you're wonderful. And beautiful. And perfect. And damn,' he deadpanned, 'there's my mobile...'

Lindsey sent him an eye-roll, packed up their lunch tray and left him to his call. A few minutes later Dan joined her in the kitchen. He looked serious. 'Everything OK?'

'Hope so. That was the SES.'

Lindsey stopped what she doing and waited for him to explain.

'There's an emergency situation at Mt Rowan. It's near here, I believe.'

'A few Ks up the road. What's happened?'

'Apparently, it's an abseiling group from one of the churches—seven young lads, one leader and one parent.'

'And?' Instinctively, Lindsey moved closer.

'The last of the boys to descend pushed out too far. He came back in at an angle instead of front-on to the cliff and appears to have slammed against some kind of projecting rock. And knocked himself out. Fortunately, his locking device has activated and that's saved him from further injury.'

'Oh, poor kid.' Lindsey looked uncertain. 'But why are the SES calling you?'

'Because I've made myself available this weekend. With my training in search and rescue, volunteering for the SES seems a natural fit. And as I'm relatively close to the accident scene, I said I'd attend. It might be some while before the base can muster a team.'

'Then I'll come with you,' Lindsey said. 'Just give me a minute to change.'

Dan clocked her quick response. 'You're not thinking of abseiling?'

'Of course.' She made a motion of brushing him aside. 'I've done heaps. What about you?'

'As you say. I've done heaps.'

'We're a team, then?'

'We seem to be.' Dan shrugged his acceptance, meeting her hand in a high-five salute. 'Now, get a wriggle on.' He tapped her backside. 'I'll close up the house.'

'Do you have your own ropes and things?' Lindsey asked.

'Yep. Luckily, as I've this training day tomorrow I put together what I thought I'd need for any emergency. See you outside.'

Toby Marshall, the team leader, was waiting for them at the cliff-top. 'Boy, am I glad to see you, Doc,' he said grimly as Dan shook hands and skimmed over the introductions.

'So, do we have a name and how far down is the lad?' Dan asked, already beginning some warm-up arm and shoulder exercises for the physical task ahead.

'Riley Dukes, aged sixteen. By my estimation, he's about twenty metres down.' Toby looked keenly at Dan. 'Obviously he's going to need medical attention, so it's you for the drop, is it, Doc?'

'We'll both go,' Lindsey said firmly. 'I'm a nurse. I'm Dan's back-up.'

'And you've abseiled before?' Toby queried.

'Lots of times.'

'OK, then. The sooner we get this under way, the better

for young Riley. And, Doc, I realise you have your own gear, but I'll need to check what you're wearing. We don't need any more mishaps.'

'Sure.' Dan was compliant. 'No worries.'

'And I'll be your anchor at the top,' Toby said.

Dan showed Toby the special sit-in retrieval harness he'd be wearing, pointing out the sturdy shoulder straps and leg loops.

'You realise you're going to have to attach Riley's harness to yours to get him down?'

'These are the clip gates I'll use for that.' Dan's hands closed around the metal locking devices. 'This type is the best and easiest to operate in case I have only one hand free. And I have a sheathed knife to cut Riley's line away once I have him secured to my harness.'

'Right, you seem well equipped,' Toby said approvingly. 'Don't forget you'll have Riley's extra weight on your line so be aware of the sudden impact when you cut the line away. But I'll have you firmly anchored and it should be fairly smooth sailing down to the base. And hopefully by then the SES team and ambulance will be there. Meanwhile, take this radio. It'll connect you with me. Any problems, yell.'

Meanwhile, Lindsey had climbed into her own harness, tightening the waist belt above her hips.

'You set?' Dan touched her shoulder.

'Yes.' She swallowed the dryness in her throat, checking the trauma kit's bulk, which she'd anchored at the rear just below her bottom. 'Let's do it.' Her eyes met Dan's and clung. She hadn't done this for quite a while, but she wasn't about to tell Dan that. What they had to do would be tricky, to say the least. He would, of necessity, have to keep focused. She didn't want him distracted and worrying about *her* safety.

* * *

Bouncing down the granite face of the cliff, Dan felt the familiar adrenaline kick in. The hard slog of his training in Florida had been well worth this feeling of achievement. Cautiously, he cast a look downwards, just able to glimpse their quarry in his bright yellow sweatshirt. 'We're nearly there,' he called to Lindsey, who was slightly above him and to his left. 'Slacken off.'

'I hear you.' Little by little, Lindsey began paying out her rope, moving on down the rock face until she was alongside him.

'Right—this'll do us.' Dan signalled and together they swung in as closely as they could to the boy. 'And Eureka...' His voice held relief as they landed on a ledge of rock and he began testing its viability. Finally, he managed to position his feet so that he was more or less evenly balanced. 'This should hold both of us, Lindsey. Close up now.'

'I'm with you...' She edged in beside him.

Dan's gaze swung to her. She looked a bit pale. A surge of protectiveness shot into his gut. 'You OK?'

'Piece of cake.' Her brittle laugh jagged eerily into the stillness.

Riley was hanging in space, quite still. But the top part of his inert body had drooped so far forward he was almost bent double into a U-shape.

Dan swore under his breath. Another couple of centimetres and the kid would have turned upside down. They had no time to lose. 'OK, Lindsey, let's reel him in.'

Lindsey looked doubtful. 'Can you reach him from there?'

'Just about, I think. I'll give it a good shot.'

She felt her stomach knot, fearing for Dan's safety as he edged perilously along the ledge, making the most of his long reach to grip the boy's waist harness and guide him in close to the cliff face. Riley's colour was glassily blue. Her nerves pulled even tighter. Were they already too late?

'Lindsey, listen,' Dan instructed firmly. 'I want you to
position yourself to receive Riley's torso and support his
head, OK?'

Lindsey was put on her mettle. She reached out her
arms. 'Right, I've got him!' Immediately, she began to
equalise the position of Riley's head and neck, which
would automatically clear his airway. 'How's his pulse?'

Dan's mouth screwed tight. 'It's there but it's faint. And
no breath sounds. Damn.' He dragged in a huge breath and
in one swift movement bent to deliver five quick mouth-
to-mouth breaths into their patient.

The silence was deafening; seconds felt like hours
as they waited. And then they heard Riley's roughened
cough. 'OK, he's breathing but still well out of it. Grab
me the torch, Lindsey.' Automatically, he took their patient's weight so Lindsey could access the torch from the
trauma kit.

Dan's face was set in concentration as he flicked the
light into the boy's eyes. 'Equal and reacting,' he relayed,
feeling the tightness in his temples ease fractionally.

So, no bleed to the brain, Lindsey interpreted silently.
'His knee seems at an odd angle.'

'I had noticed.' Dan began feeling around for the clip
gates attached to the runner looped over his shoulder. Riley's injured knee was an added complication. The sooner
they got the kid down and treated, the better. His gaze lowered to where Riley's injury was just visible below the coloured band of his shorts. The matter of the scraped skin
was of little concern but Dan's instincts were telling him
that the puffy state of the boy's knee plus the blood seeping from the wound from the rock were a worry. 'He's obviously hit the rock with some force.'

'Do you think he's banged his head and lost control?'
Lindsey voiced her own concerns tentatively.

'Quite possibly. Whatever, I can't do much from here.

We'll need to get him down so I can look at him properly. Right, I'm about to try to anchor Riley to my harness.'

Lindsey felt unease crawl up her backbone as she realised the logistics. It seemed a very big ask. Dan was going to try to align Riley's body to his, chest to chest. 'In practical terms, how do you want to work it, then?'

'Slowly and carefully. We'll endeavour to manoeuvre Riley upright now. I'll help as much as I can but I'll have to concentrate on getting him adjacent to my own body so I can link our harnesses together. OK, let's do it.'

It was useless. Lindsey shook her head in despair. It was like trying to steady a ton weight balloon with a piece of string. Riley was a well-built young man, his unconscious state only adding to their difficulties. And in their precarious position, it was nearly impossible to co-ordinate the lift so the two harness belts were close enough to link.

'This isn't going to work,' Dan said concisely. His shoulders slumped and he shook his head. 'This was a hare-brained idea.'

Lindsey sensed his anguish but they couldn't give up now. Riley's young life could well depend on their teamwork. She pushed down her fears. 'Give me the clip gates, Dan.'

'That's ridiculous!' His brows shot up. 'Riley's way too heavy and you're not wearing the right kind of harness.'

'I didn't mean I'd try to take Riley's weight,' Lindsey pointed out. 'But we have to find a resolution here. What we're doing is not working—when you're steady, Riley's either too high or too low.'

Dan swore under his breath and slumped into his harness. 'We'll just have to wait until the SES guys get here. They can drop someone. Between us, we'll be able to attach Riley and get him down.' He reached inside his vest for the radio transmitter.

All that could take precious time. Lindsey thought

swiftly. It was time they didn't have. Her confidence in her own capabilities kicked in. 'Wait a minute. Could you try linking your hands under Riley's behind and lifting him to your waist level? Then I could make a grab for his harness and snap you together.'

Dan's jaw tightened so hard it felt like snapping. He hated not being in control. Hated and loathed it. Nevertheless, he did what Lindsey had suggested, gripping Riley and lifting him as high as he could, his muscles straining with the effort.

Lindsey's nerves were stretched like the strings on a bass fiddle. She had only the barest window of opportunity to hitch the two harnesses together before Dan's strength gave out and he'd have no choice but to abort his hold on the injured boy. She steadied her breathing, conscious of almost choreographing her movements.

'Do it now, Lindsey…' Dan gasped, pulling his torso back so Lindsey could use what little space there was between him and the boy. 'Now!' he yelled.

'Do it—or I've lost him!'

In a flash, remembering everything she'd been taught, Lindsey used her feet in a technique called smearing, where most of the climber's weight was positioned over one foot to reduce the overall load on the arms. Twisting slightly, she turned her upper body so that her arm closest to the rock face could counter-balance her movement and give her other arm maximum extension. It took barely seconds to execute.

But to Dan those same seconds felt like hours. The muscles of his throat and around his mouth were locked and sweat pooled wetly in his lower back. His mind was so focused he hardly felt the nudge of Lindsey's fingers as she secured one then two more clip gates to link Dan to his patient.

'Done…' Her voice was barely above a whisper.

* * *

Lindsey hardly remembered how they got down. She only remembered the relief she'd felt when Dan had cut Riley's rope and they'd been able to begin their descent.

And there were plenty of hands to help them once they were safely on the ground. A subdued cheer even went up. Riley was released from his harness and placed on the stretcher.

Lindsey divested herself of her own harness, vaguely aware her legs felt as unsteady as a puppet's. She swallowed back the taste of bile. Surely she wasn't about to disgrace herself and throw up here in front of all these macho men. Someone from the SES handed her a bottle of water. 'Nice work, Lindsey. You're a beauty.'

She managed a weak smile before swallowing several big mouthfuls of water. Her equilibrium steadied and she pulled her thoughts together. Removing her safety hat, she shook out her hair and began making her way across to where Riley's stretcher had been placed in the shade and Dan was bending over him.

Dan looked at her briefly. 'He's come round. You'll be fine, mate,' he reassured his young patient. 'Take it easy now. We'll get you on some oxygen.'

The portable oxygen unit appeared as if by magic. And a space blanket.

'How is he, Doc?' Toby Marshall hovered uneasily. He'd have some explaining to do to the kid's parents over this.

Dan folded his stethoscope away. Riley's breathing was a bit raspy but this wasn't the place to be passing that information along. It would right itself as the oxygen kicked in. 'Riley has a fractured kneecap and possible lower rib injury. We need to get him to hospital.' He turned to the paramedic and took him aside. 'I'll leave Riley in your capable hands, Terry. Cane it in, mate. His parents are probably wearing out the floor in the ED.'

'No worries, Doc. Scratch us a few notes to take and we'll be out of here.'

Late afternoon and the vivid sunset was rapidly being overtaken by the sweep of pearly grey evening sky and the wind that had risen had the sharpness of a whip crack. One of the SES crew had given Dan and Lindsey a lift back to the cliff-top and Dan was rapidly sorting his climbing gear and stowing it safely in his Land Rover.

Arms wrapped around her middle, Lindsey stood watching him. It had been the oddest kind of day.

Dan closed the tailgate on his SUV and turned, his gaze narrowing. He frowned a bit. She looked shattered. 'Why didn't you go and sit in the car?'

'I wanted to wait for you.'

'Aw…' He gave a goofy grin. 'Need a hug, then?' He opened his arms and she ran to him. She cuddled into his embrace and he held her. And held her. 'You were amazing.' He looped back a strand of hair from her cheek. 'I couldn't have done it without you. You had no fear at all, did you?'

Lindsey bit back a snort. If only he knew. But a girl was entitled to warm herself in his male look of admiration for just a little while. 'Climbing is practically a religion around here. We did lots of it when we were growing up and we were taught properly from the beginning. Today was the first time I've had to assist in an emergency situation, though.'

Dan frowned and then said slowly, 'Then I hope you never have to do it again, Lindsey.'

She pushed her hands up under his T-shirt, feeling the

clean sweep of his skin. And loving it. 'I didn't enjoy it much,' she admitted. 'But I was impressed by *your* skills.'

'You were?' His eyes glinted with dry humour. 'You're just saying that.'

Lindsey bugged her eyes at him. 'Stop fishing for compliments, Dante, and take me home.'

'I'm going to have to head straight back to Hopeton, I'm afraid,' Dan said as they neared Lark Hill. 'The training day starts at six a.m. tomorrow.'

'And you need all the sleep you can get. I'm heading back myself. I'm on an early tomorrow and we've a new member of staff joining us. I'd better look at least as though I'm awake and functioning.'

Dan picked up her hand and raised it to his lips. 'I would much rather have lain with you and held you all night.'

'That sounds really poetic...' Lindsey rested her head against his shoulder and smiled. 'Perhaps you do take after your namesake.'

He spluttered a laugh. 'And perhaps not.'

'And here we are,' Lindsey said as they pulled into the Lark Hill driveway and Dan coasted to a stop. Almost simultaneously, they released their seat belts and reached for each other. They kissed long and slowly, savouring every last stroke of the tongue, each lingering taste of each other.

'I won't come in.' Dan pressed his forehead against hers. 'Will you be OK?'

'Mmm. I just have to throw my stuff together and take off.' She moved to open the door. 'Just one other thing, Dan.' She bit her lip. 'I don't know what kind of crazy stuff you'll be expected to do tomorrow. But...please... be safe. For me?'

Dan felt his insides twist, the sudden swell of emotion

hitting him like the force of a king tide. His heart was over-flowing with love for this woman. He reached out, slowly drawing her gaze up so it was level with his. 'I promise I won't do anything reckless. And I'll come back to you safely, Lindsey. For no other reason than I need to.'

CHAPTER TWELVE

LINDSEY LOOKED OUT at the landscape the next morning. It was raining lightly, the gentle, soaking kind that would have the farmers smiling and the mothers of young school children dredging up an endless supply of patience as they pushed reluctant little arms into raincoats.

She pulled a face, making her way slowly from her bedroom to the shower, her leg muscles protesting all the way. So much for the abseiling lark yesterday, she vented silently.

Arriving at the hospital, she went through to the staffroom.

'Well, get you!' From her table near the window, Vanessa looked up, her eyes wide in laughing disbelief. She rattled the pages of Hopeton's daily paper.

'You and daring Dan in a cliff rescue. What else did you get up to, Ms Stewart?'

'Oh, show me.' Lindsey gave a *tsk* and leaned over Vanessa's shoulder to read the report on the incident. 'Why on earth would they have thought this was newsworthy?' she dismissed.

'Because the kid you rescued just happens to be the grandson of Angus Whittaker, the local MP. He was here at the hospital only last week, doing what they euphemistically call "a guided tour". Ring any bells?'

'No.' Lindsey slammed the paper shut. 'He didn't come to the ED.'

Vanessa's mouth turned down. 'Bit too confronting for him, I guess. I heard he went to Midwifery. He wanted to tell them personally he'd got funding for a new birthing suite.'

'Well, bully for them,' Lindsey huffed. 'I could have given him a long list of things we need in Casualty.' She made a cup of tea and came back to the table. 'Riley's surname is Dukes,' she said, wanting to get things straight in her head. 'So his mother must be Whittaker's daughter.'

'Correct.' Vanessa pushed the newspaper aside. 'So, what's to prevent you from popping in on Riley at visiting time? I'm sure his mum would like to meet one part of the rescue team who got her son down from the cliff.'

Lindsey's eyes widened. 'Are you suggesting I should go armed with my list for the casualty department?'

'Well, not quite. But you could start opening doors, so to speak. If you get my drift? I mean, Mr Whittaker's bound to be visiting his grandson some time or other.'

Lindsey grinned. 'You should be working for the UN. But I'll definitely think about popping up to see Riley.'

'Now, what about the second part of my question?' Vanessa wasn't about to be put off.

Lindsey's shoulders lifted in a resigned gesture. There was no use prevaricating. When Vanessa sensed intrigue, she was like a terrier with a bone. 'Yesterday Dan spent the day with me at Lark Hill. He's volunteered for the SES. They called him about the abseiling incident. The rest, as they say, is in the local paper.'

'So...' Vanessa moved her head closer. 'You two are a couple, then?'

'Yes.' Lindsey took a mouthful of her tea and wondered what else you could call it. 'Your hair looks amazing, by the way,' she diverted skilfully.

'Oh, thanks, Lins. Mimi's had a cut-and-colour special.' Vanessa swung her new choppy style as if to emphasise the all-shades-of-blonde highlights. 'I thought I needed an update.'

'Well, it's gorgeous and it suits you.'

A beat of silence and then, 'Oh. My. God.' Vanessa's gaze was riveted on the doorway and the male who hovered there. 'Now, that's what I call a body...'

Lindsey swung round. And blinked a bit. *Wow.* 'That must be our new recruit.' She got swiftly to her feet. 'Let's make him welcome.'

'Wait for me.' Vanessa almost catapulted out of her chair.

'I'm in the right place, then?' Charlie Weston's sea-green gaze tracked between the two women after introductions had been made.

'And on time as well.' Vanessa took the lead cheekily.

'Awesome. I've brought muffins,' Charlie said, with a kind of eager-to-fit-in look.

'Apple and blueberry?' They were Vanessa's favourite.

'Tuna and mustard,' he deadpanned.

'Perfect,' Vanessa shot back, already on the same quirky wavelength. 'Come and I'll show you where to put your stuff.'

Lindsey just shook her head at the pair of them and went to take handover.

When the team assembled, Lindsey allotted jobs, adding, 'Vanessa, I'll leave Charlie's orientation in your capable hands. Yell if you need me.'

'Thanks, Lins.' Vanessa all but batted her eyelashes. 'I'm sure we'll be fine.'

Watching the two walk away, Lindsey noted that Charlie's longish sun-bleached hair was neatly tied back in a ponytail. And she'd already clocked his hands and nails were well kept and scrupulously clean. Good, she thought with satisfaction. He'd do nicely.

By mid-afternoon Lindsey could hardly keep her eyes open. She discreetly blocked a yawn. Yesterday's escapade had obviously taken more out of her than she'd realised. She wondered how Dan was faring.

Dan took some deep breaths, mentally clearing his thoughts for the umpteenth time. He could have done all this stuff standing on his head. But when in Rome…

They'd completed all the physical training and now he just had to sit in on a lecture about handling hazardous materials, dealing with oil spills, chemical leaks and more. Then he'd be out of there. Tonight he and Lindsey were going to dinner with Nathan and Sami. And on Saturday he was going to Lark Hill to meet Lindsey's family. It seemed they were *out* as a couple. Dan was amazed how good it felt.

Friday…

'Are you going to Greta's working bee tomorrow?' Vanessa propped herself on the counter at the nurses' station.

Lindsey glanced up. 'I'll come for a while. Dad's just turned sixty. We're having a celebration dinner for him at Lark Hill.' And Lindsey had invited Dan. It was time he met her family.

'From what I hear, it'll be a good turnout for the working bee,' Vanessa chirped. 'Charlie's coming along too. He's brilliant at DIY.'

Lindsey gave her friend a long look. 'And you know this how?'

Vanessa went pink. 'He's taken over Nathan's old flat. I've been helping him tart it up a bit before Poppy arrives. He's made such a cute job of her bedroom.'

'You and Charlie have really hit it off, haven't you?'

'He's fun.' Vanessa shrugged. 'And I can be myself around him. It's…nice. Uncomplicated.'

And he's so different from Andrew, Lindsey interpreted, happy for her friend. And for Charlie as well, for that matter. Van was a gem.

A week later…

OK, so this was crunch time.

Dan braced himself. He had clearance from the board. He was packed. Now he just had to tell Lindsey. He knew she'd hate it but it was something he needed to do.

He looked at his watch. Still early. But she'd be up and he didn't have much time.

The sound of her doorbell roused Lindsey. She sat up groggily. What the heck?

She sat for a second on the side of the bed and felt around for her dressing gown. Oh, why bother? She was decently clad in long pyjama pants and a T-shirt. Shoving her feet into a pair of slip-on sandals, she clacked to the front door. 'Dan…' She blinked, her gaze uncertain. 'Is something wrong?'

'Morning.' He gave a contained kind of smile. 'Nothing's wrong. May I come in?'

'Of course.' She stood back to let him in.

'Did I wake you?' He looked concerned.

Lindsey finger-combed a fall of hair from her forehead. 'I'm on a late. I just felt like a sleep-in. Come through. I'll make some tea.'

'I'll make it,' Dan offered.

He felt guilty. She looked whacked.

'Thanks.' She gave a wry smile. 'I'll wash my face and wake up a bit.'

After she'd changed into jeans and combed her hair, she felt more in control, more like herself. She headed into the kitchen, where Dan was making himself busy.

'So, what's up?'

He handed her a mug of tea and she saw he'd made toast as well. She took long mouthfuls and looked at him above the rim of her mug. Waiting.

'I have something to tell you.' Dan was hunched over his tea mug.

She forced her lips into a smile that felt stiff and uncomfortable. 'Better get on and tell me, then.'

Dan hesitated as if searching for the right words. 'Have you been watching the TV news at all over the last twenty-four hours?'

She shook her head. 'Why, have I missed something important?'

'A category-three cyclone has hit parts of New Guinea's coastline, and particularly a little island to the north. It's called Cloud Island. There's huge damage and their resources are poor. The ADF are organising to send supplies and personnel as we speak. They need MOs on the ground. I've volunteered. I'm flying out at noon today.'

'Oh.' She moistened her lips and took a long controlling breath. 'How dangerous will it be?'

Dan shrugged. 'It's hard to put a classification on it at this stage. But there'll be protocols in place. We'll just follow orders mainly and do what we're trained to do. In my case, I'll be helping to set up a field hospital and treat the incoming casualties.'

Her throat closed tightly. 'Are there many people injured… do you know?'

Possibly hundreds, he could have told her, but refrained. 'Well, the gurus at the weather bureau are calling it a natural disaster so I imagine there'll be a bit of tidying up in all directions.'

'How long will you be gone?'

'Don't know yet. Possibly not more than several weeks. Once the hospital is up and running, the army will start taking things over, bringing in more of their own personnel. But right now they need as many trained boots on the ground as they can get.' A muscle pulled in his jaw. 'And I *am* trained for this kind of emergency, Lindsey. I can't just sit on my hands and do nothing.'

Her heart did an odd tattoo. One part of her was inordinately proud of him but the other part... She looked at him, her eyes unguarded. 'I guess there's nothing to say other than take care of yourself.'

'Of course I will.' Dan reached out and took her hand across the table. 'You take care as well while I'm gone.'

She gave a jagged laugh. 'I'll be just going to work and coming home. I can't get into much trouble.'

'Will you come out to the airport and see me off?'

Lindsey stared at him for a moment, then suddenly and clearly, saw things from his perspective. He had to go. And she was glad and proud of his humaneness and the depth of his commitment to medicine and his willingness to use his skills in whatever way and wherever they were needed. 'Of course I will.'

'You're not taking much.' Lindsey saw he had only a carry-on bag. They were in Hopeton's airport lounge and holding hands tightly.

'We'll be issued with everything. I'll try for a video hook-up so you can see me in my army fatigues.'

'And handsome as all get-out.' Lindsey tried to joke but it was hard. She swallowed. 'So when you get to Sydney, what then?'

'I'll meet up with the rest of the contingent. We'll fly out in a Hercules later today, I imagine. Look at the TV news tonight. There's bound to be a camera or two record-ing our departure. I'll send you a wave.'

'And I'll be bound to see it,' she said drily, looking out through the glass wall of the passenger lounge to the air-strip, where the luggage was being ferried across for load-ing. She felt a wrench to her heart. He'd be gone soon. The line of her mouth trembled for a second.

Watching her, Dan took stock, finding it hard to be-lieve the avalanche of emotion that swamped him. He, Dan Rossi, had fallen headlong in love with this beauti-ful woman. And what he had to say couldn't wait a mo-ment longer. 'I love you absolutely, Lindsey Stewart. Will you marry me?'

Dazed, her mouth opened and closed. She couldn't speak. She just bit her lips together and nodded. Then smiled as if her lips might crack. 'Oh, Dan...'

'So that's a *yes*?' Dan's eyes locked with hers.

'Yes! Of course, yes! I love you, Dan. How could you think I didn't?'

Dan's heart began clamouring. He heaved in a long breath and let it go. Joy, clear and pure, streamed through him. Oblivious to the crowd around them, he pulled her close and kissed her—hard. 'When?'

Lindsey felt shaky and happy all rolled into one. She fiddled with the button on his shirt front. 'As soon as you like. As soon as you come back from your tour?'

'Yes.' He nodded eagerly. 'In the meantime, think about what kind of wedding you'd like and I'll do the same. And we'll do it,' he added softly, as if making a promise to him-self, a promise to both of them. His eyes clouded for a sec-ond. 'And you don't mind all my baggage?'

She placed her fingers on his lips, her gaze clear and untroubled. 'What baggage? This is *us*, Dan.'

He took her hands and held them against his chest, as if reaffirming their commitment. 'It's about time I got that into my head. After I get back, I never want to be away from you again.'

'You won't have to be,' she said, knowing it as surely as she knew her own name. 'We'll be together.'

'Oh, my Lindsey...' Dan leaned into her, kissing her softly, tenderly.

'This is the best day of my life.'

Lindsey's smile was tremulous. 'And mine. Oh.' She lifted her head and listened. 'That's your boarding call. Do you have everything you need?'

His face worked for a minute. 'Everything but you.' He gave her one last, fierce kiss. 'That'll get me through the tough times,' he said, and picked up his bag.

Lindsey watched as he jogged across to join the end of the queue of boarding passengers. Suddenly, he turned. He began walking backwards and smiling. 'I love you!'

'And I love you,' she echoed, but he was already out of sight.

Two weeks later...

'Have you heard from Dan recently?' Vanessa asked as she and Lindsey met up in the staffroom before work.

Lindsey made a face. 'The mobile reception is pathetic. I've had a few phone calls. But Dan said the army techs are hoping to have a satellite up and running shortly so that will make communication easier.'

Vanessa propped her chin on her hand. 'You look a bit wan, Lins. You're really missing him, aren't you?'

Lindsey nodded and bit her lip. 'Every day seems like a month.' She paused. 'Dan asked me to marry him as soon as he gets back.'

Vanessa's mouth fell open. 'Get *out*. Oh, Lins—that's amazing! And you said yes? Of course you did. Oh...' Vanessa's hand went to her heart. 'A wedding. How could you have kept that kind of news to yourself? I'd have been doing a shout-out all over the ED. What plans have you made?'

'Well, none, really.' Lindsey was still feeling stunned to some extent. She needed Dan's presence to make things real.

'I'll help you,' Vanessa said promptly. 'We'll make a list. All you need is the date, time and venue. And your dress, of course. And the guest list. Oh, and flowers...'

Lindsey managed a shaky laugh. 'I need to think about it a bit more, Van. But thanks.'

Vanessa batted a hand. 'What kind of wedding does Dan want?'

'We left it open-ended. We'll decide on something when he gets back...'

'But you could get a jump-start,' Vanessa pointed out excitedly. 'Guys usually go along with whatever the bride wants anyway. I'll dash out on my break and get the latest bride books. Lace is so *in*. But you'll look stunning in whatever you wear,' she summed up happily.

Lindsey locked her arms around her stomach. Butterflies as big as doves were looking for a place to land. Vanessa's enthusiasm had been like an avalanche, drowning her in excitement. And the faintest trepidation.

Later in the day, Lindsey was surprised to receive a phone call from Sami.

'Is it OK to call you at the hospital?' Sami asked.

'Of course.' Lindsey swung away from the computer. 'If I'm elsewhere in the department, you can always leave a message and I'll get back to you. Is everything OK?'

'It's wonderful.' Sami gave a throaty laugh. 'Look, Lins, I know Dan is away and you're possibly a bit at loose ends so I wondered if you'd like a little catch-up after work—cup of tea or something?'

'What a good idea. That sounds just what I need. Where?'

'You know where my cubbyhole is in the main street? There's a tea room newly opened a few doors down. It's called Browne's. I'll pop along and keep a table. See you when you get there. All right?'

'Fantastic.' Lindsey smiled, glad for once she'd brought a change of clothes to work.

'Over here!' Sami's blond curls bobbed as she waved Lindsey across to the table. The two friends hugged briefly and settled themselves in the old-fashioned high booth. 'Now, what are we having?' Sami scanned the menu. 'Pot of tea?'

'Oh, yes, please!' Lindsey smiled and ran her tongue along her lips. 'I'm parched.'

'And something to go with it…' Sami made a moue of conjecture. 'Everything looks a bit buttery and I'm so off sweet stuff. What about cucumber sandwiches?'

'Lovely.' Lindsey tossed back her head and laughed. 'We can pretend we're having high tea at the Ritz.'

Sami cackled. 'Have you done that too?'

'A long time ago with James and Catherine.' Lindsey looked up as the waitress arrived to take their order.

'So, what news do you have for me, Lins?' Sami asked, placing the menu back in its folder.

'Dan's asked me to marry him,' Lindsey blurted. Once she'd told Vanessa, she'd been bubbling with a queasy kind of happiness all day.

'He did?' Sami gave a subdued squeal. 'That's brilliant!' She pressed her hands together in a praying motion under her chin. 'Oh, help… I feel a bit teary. Dan's so lovely. And you're so right for each other. So, are we invited to the wedding?'

'Of course, you dope.' Lindsey blinked a bit and thought

she may as well start making concrete plans. 'In fact, I wondered whether you'd be my matron of honour…'

'Absolutely! I'd be delighted. As long as it's relatively soon so I'll fit into my dress.' Sami's look grew misty. 'I'm pregnant, Lins…'

It was Lindsey's turn to look stunned. The outline of Sami's face went out of focus and then righted itself. 'Ooh…' She let her breath go in a sigh. 'That's so sweet. Congratulations!'

'Thanks. It's a bit sooner than we planned but…you know?' Sami looked coy.

Lindsey felt her own tears welling up. 'I'm so thrilled for you and Nathan. Are you feeling OK healthwise?'

'Pretty good, actually. Off the sweet stuff, as I said, but so sleepy I can't believe!'

Sleepy. Lindsey's stomach heaved alarmingly. Warning bells like the peal of a carillon resounded in her head.

'Mum said she could fall asleep at the drop of a hat when she was expecting Cait and me,' Sami went on happily. 'I've been so looking forward to getting our house in order and now we've a nursery to plan. And Nathan's on cloud nine. He'll be such a *dad.*'

It can't be. Lindsey clasped her hands on her lap, then unconsciously spread them over her tummy. *I'm imagining things. I have to be.* She'd had a period. But it had been lighter than usual. Much lighter, she corrected. It didn't mean anything untoward. She lifted her cup and swallowed a mouthful of her tea. She had to leave. But she couldn't, not yet. Instead, she half listened to Sami. Gave answers when she had to and Sami was on such a roll she hardly noticed anything amiss. Except when they got up to leave.

'You know, Lins, you're looking pale. Working in that hospital environment does absolutely nothing for your complexion.'

Lindsey laughed the comment away and felt as though her lungs had flown into her throat. Sami blew air kisses and they parted, promising to meet again soon.

As Sami had said, they had dresses to choose and a wedding to plan.

Would there even be a wedding now? Lindsey felt shaky as she reversed out of the parking bay. She'd go to one of the busy big chain pharmacies where no one would recognise her and buy a pregnancy testing kit. She swallowed. It was absolutely the last thing she'd expected to be doing when she'd got up this morning.

When she arrived home, she went straight through to the bathroom. Removing the box from the chemist's wrapping, she felt as though she was handling a time bomb.

And it may as well be. An explosion that would surely blow her and Dan's plans for their future to smithereens. He'd said that after the tragic outcome with his twins he was in no hurry to experience fatherhood again. She couldn't do it to him. Present him with a fait accompli like Caroline had done. No way I'll do that to Dan, she vowed, preparing herself for what she had to do.

The test was positive.

Lindsey felt all the strength drain from her legs as she sank down on the side of the bath. *I'm having a baby.* We're *having a baby.*

She sat there for a long time. Then, surprisingly calmly, she got up, had a shower and shampooed her hair. Out of the shower, she towelled dry and dressed in a pair of her softest cotton pyjamas, then went through to the kitchen and put the kettle on. She gave the ghost of a smile. Perhaps she'd have to stop drinking so much tea. She called in sick for work next day. She needed time to herself. Time to start planning hers and her baby's future.

Next day...

Lindsey was amazed she'd slept so soundly but as the day wore on she was aware of a slow crawl of panic overtaking her. She so wished Dan was there so she could have told him, got everything over and done with. And if he walked, so be it. She'd manage on her own. She could even go to Scotland, to James and Catherine. Have her baby there. Her thoughts flew wildly ahead.

The ringing of the doorbell startled her out of her introspection. She sighed, hoping it wasn't Vanessa with her wretched bride books! She went to the front door, flinging it open almost impatiently. And took a breath so deep it almost hurt. 'Dan!' She'd already begun steeling herself for when he'd get back, running over little speeches in her head, but seeing him standing there in the flesh, still dressed in his army fatigues, all her carefully prepared words flew away like leaves in the wind. 'When did you get back?' she croaked.

Dan gave the briefest smile. 'Flew into Sydney in the early hours this morning. Had to hang about for a debrief. There wasn't a flight to Hopeton until God knows when, so I got a cab.'

'You got a cab from Sydney!'

'Needed to see my girl.' He followed her inside to the lounge. 'I rang the hospital. They said you were home sick so I came straight here.' His gaze flew over her. She certainly looked under the weather, not like his bright, beautiful Lindsey at all. And surely she'd lost weight in the time he'd been gone. He put out his hands and took hers. 'Are you actually sick?'

'No—not really.' Just *worried* sick more like. 'I felt like a day to myself, that's all.'

'Ah.' His eyes burned like brilliant sapphires. He grinned. 'Well, you won't be getting that now, will you?'

Suddenly, like a dam breaking, Lindsey burst into tears.

'Hey…what's up?' Dan guided her down onto the sofa. Hell. He felt his heart beating hard against his ribs. What was wrong here? He held her until at last she took several shaky breaths and regained control.

'Oh, Dan…' She curled her face into his neck.

'It'll be OK, Lindsey.' He stroked her back. 'I love you. Whatever it is, you can tell me.'

That's just it, she thought despairingly. I don't know how to.

'Have you gone off me?'

'What?' That brought her to her senses in a flash. 'Of course not.' She sniffed, reaching for the box of tissues on the coffee table. 'This is so unlike me.' She gave a watery smile and made use of the tissues.

'Better now?' His eyes were so close she could see the faint specks of silver in the blue.

She nodded.

'OK, then.' Dan stretched his arm along the back of the sofa behind her. 'I can't keep guessing, Lindsey. Just spell it out. Please.'

His voice was gentle but it couldn't free her from the stomach-caving fear that this was all too difficult, and even now, when he'd told her he loved her, she still couldn't guarantee his reaction would be one of…gladness?

His fingertips stroked the back of her neck. 'I'm going nuts here, sweetheart. What the hell is it?'

Lindsey drew in her breath and let it go. 'I'm pregnant. We're having a baby.'

A beat of silence, absolute and prickling with awareness and disbelief.

A baby. Dan felt his heart double in size. For a second he felt his life spinning out of control and then it slowed and came right. And he was able to think. 'We always used protection.'

'Well, we obviously slipped up. It happens.'

Another beat of silence.

'Have I ruined your life?' he asked quietly.

Lindsey looked at him uncomprehendingly.

'Do you want to be pregnant?' he asked in the same quiet manner.

She jerked upright. 'Are you asking if I want your baby, Dan? *Our* baby? Perhaps I should be asking you if you want it. Because if you don't—'

His kiss cut her off. Rough. Then gentle. Sweeter than sweet. She felt his chest rise and fall in a broken sigh. 'Give me a break, Lins. I think I'm in shock. But I also think I'm ecstatic.'

'Really?'

'Did you think I wouldn't be? Our own baby.' His hand smoothed over her tummy as if he hoped there might already be changes. 'When did you find out?'

'Just yesterday.' She went on to tell him about Sami and Nathan's news and how she'd identified with some of Sami's symptoms.

Dan chuckled. 'Nathan a dad! What a stud, eh!'

Lindsey slid her hands around his neck. 'Our babies will grow up together. Won't that be a laugh?'

He pressed a kiss into her hair. 'What about you? Are you feeling all right?'

'Think so,' she murmured.

'Do you have an ob you prefer?' Dan's mind skipped to professional matters.

'Therese Gordon.' She paused. 'And don't take this the wrong way, Dan, but I don't want you hovering.'

'Oh.' Dan felt his throat suddenly dry. A thousand reasons why he *should* be hovering juxtaposed in his head. And who could blame him—after last time? But there was nothing to indicate that Lindsey's pregnancy would be anything but perfectly straightforward. He had to get that through his head. 'OK.' He took a deep breath and let it go. 'I promise I won't be neurotic about things. But I would like to be there for your scans and ultrasounds.'

'And I'll *want* you there,' Lindsey hastened to reassure him. 'Like any normal expectant dad.' She brushed a kiss across his mouth. 'I love you, Dan, but this is *us*.'

And thank heaven for that. Mentally, Dan kicked all his uncertainties to oblivion, resolving to leave them there.

Lindsey snuggled closer. 'I'm so glad you're back.'

'Me too.'

'How was it?'

'A bit taxing but we managed. Things are quickly getting back to normal. That's why they chucked out the civilians and got their own medics in. Have you thought what you'd like for our wedding?'

'Sorry, no.' She ground her bottom lip. 'I just couldn't seem to get my head around it and then when I found out about the baby…'

He cupped her face in his hands. 'Surely you didn't think I'd do a runner?'

'I hoped not…' She took a deep breath. 'Prayed not. But you were adamant about not wanting fatherhood again.'

His gaze deepened and darkened. 'I was still angry back then. And I hadn't realised I'd just met the love of my life.' He shook his head as if it still amazed him. 'Could we pull a wedding together pretty soon?'

Lindsey looked into his eyes, seeing the sheen of tenderness. 'I think we could. But we'll need a licence.'

He tapped his breast pocket. 'I already have one. Picked it up in Sydney this morning. It's amazing how fast you can get things done when you're in uniform.'

'Oh, Dan,' Lindsey chided. 'Did you let them think you'd been posted?'

He shrugged. 'I suppose I might have given that impression. I just looked a bit helpless and they fell over themselves cutting red tape.'

Lindsey fisted him on the chest. 'You couldn't look helpless if you tried. But back to the wedding. Where? Any preference?'

'Lark Hill? That's if it's all right with your folks. Something intimate and all about us. What do you think?'

'That sounds perfect. There's a wonderful spot amongst the vines where we can make our vows. Reception up at the house. We don't want a crowd, do we?'

He shook his head. 'Just your lot and mine, a few mates from the ED and Nathan and Sami to stand up for us. Easy. Can you take a couple more days off?'

'I guess so. What do you want to do?'

'I still have a few days' leave up my sleeve. I'd like us to fly to Melbourne tomorrow so you can meet my family. We'll take them all to dinner and you'll be wearing your ring.'

'Oh…' Lindsey reached out and placed her palm against his cheek. 'Are you buying me an engagement ring, then?'

'Absolutely. And we'll get matching wedding rings as well.' He smiled indulgently. 'I want to do things properly.' He added silently, this time.

CHAPTER THIRTEEN

A few weeks later, Saturday, a wedding at Lark Hill...

IT WAS MID-MORNING and a clear day. A bridal path had been especially prepared between the rows of vines.

A string quartet was playing softly.

Surrounded by a stunning display of old-fashioned bush roses and fruiting vines, Dan was waiting with Nathan. The guests were seated in bespoke chairs. It was an informal setting but the atmosphere was laden with dignity and purpose. And so much love for the happy couple.

Vanessa sat with Charlie. They were now officially *going out*. Or staying in, as Vanessa laughingly told anyone who would listen. Poppy was now living with her dad most of the time. She adored Vanessa and the feeling was mutual. Charlie leaned over and whispered, 'Is my tie all right?'

Vanessa gave it a quick straighten. 'It's fine. Why?'

'I looked everywhere for it this morning, then found Poppy had been using it as a lead for her guinea pig.'

Vanessa rolled her eyes. 'Why didn't you just wear another one?'

Charlie looked blank. 'I don't have another one.'

'Shh...the music's changing. The bride must be on her way.' On cue, the guests rose as one. Vanessa gripped Charlie's arm. 'Oh, bless...doesn't she look gorgeous? I knew she'd wear lace. And look! Dan's going to meet her. Oh…it's just too romantic.'

Daintily, Vanessa began tapping away the press of happy tears.

Charlie, wearing a goofy grin, handed her his big red hanky.

The newlyweds stepped into their reception, where the atmosphere was already bubbling with laughter and music.

'Dr and Mrs Rossi,' announced Nathan, who was doubling as master of ceremonies.

'I like the sound of that.' Dipping his head, Dan kissed his bride gently but thoroughly for all the world to see. 'You take my breath away, Lindsey Rossi.' His eyes held a gleam of teasing humour. 'I'm so glad you turned up this morning.'

Lindsey gave a shaky laugh, her heart cartwheeling with happiness. 'Of course I turned up,' she countered. 'This is our party. Our beautiful wedding day. Doesn't everything look amazing, Dan?'

It did.

The lovely old home was adorned with fresh garden flowers and a sumptuous buffet lunch was set out on the long table in the dining room. There was comfortable seating everywhere. Guests could wander out to the verandas or into the garden. The back deck had been cleared and the floor sanded and polished for the dancing later.

Lindsey directed Dan's attention to their wedding cake, lavishly decorated with meringue buttercream icing and a trail of blue forget-me-nots. A silver-spangled bauble on the top declared simply: *Love*.

'This is Fiona's gift to us.'

Dan looked smug. 'I knew she approved of me from the get-go.'

They wandered out onto the deck, where so much of

their courtship had taken place. Dan lifted Lindsey's hand and kissed her fingers and the sunlight caught her new rings, causing a beautiful rainbow of sparkles to reflect all around them. 'I love you,' he said for the umpteenth time. 'What about dancing with me?'

Lindsey looked at him through a haze of happiness. 'I think we're supposed to wait until after the speeches and we've cut the cake.'

Dan looked unimpressed. 'It's our wedding, we can do what we like.' He spun her away and she sashayed back to him, draping her arms around his neck.

His eyes lit with satisfaction. 'Happy?'

'I am.' Lindsey smiled serenely. 'You're a very nice man, Dan Rossi.'

Dan gathered her closer. His beautiful Lindsey had come to him today as his bride. He had no doubt their marriage would be good and true. He had to be the happiest man alive.

'And not a bad dancer,' he said.

EPILOGUE

'PANT THROUGH THE BREAK, LINDSEY,' Jenna Metcalf, the midwife, coached.

'I can't…'

'Yes, you can,' Dan encouraged.

'The lights are too bright,' she whined. 'Dan…?'

'Head's almost out,' Jenna said. 'One more push…'

'One more push,' Dan echoed. 'Come on, Lins, he's almost here.'

Lindsey gave a long sound of effort, one that thrust her head back hard against Dan's chest as he held her. They wanted pushing? Well, she'd give them pushing!

'That's it. You're amazing.' Dan kissed the top of her head. And prayed as he'd never prayed before.

'Gently now. Almost there,' Jenna called encouragingly. 'Looking good. Head's out. I'm delivering one shoulder. Wow.' She laughed. 'We have a strong little guy here. He's very anxious to meet his mamma and daddy, aren't you, gorgeous?' In seconds, she held the baby up, his little body all wet and slippery.

Dan made a noise that came from deep within his chest. *Born.* Their son was safely born. His eyes stung and filled as baby Rossi cried lustily and waved tiny fists.

'Oh, Dan, look…' Lindsey's voice cracked. 'He's so beautiful. And perfect.'

'Perfect,' he whispered throatily. Almost in a daze he

cut his son's umbilical cord. 'Jen, thank you.' He felt his throat clear and he swallowed. 'You were brilliant.'

'Uh-uh.' Jenna shook her head. 'Your wife was the brilliant one.' She expertly wrapped the baby and handed him to Lindsey.

Dan moved to sit beside Lindsey, his whole heart in his eyes. 'Put your hands beneath mine,' she said, pressing her cheek against his shoulder. 'And we'll both hold him.' She smiled mistily. 'He looks like you.' Gently, she unwrapped their infant son and they looked in wonder at the perfection of his tiny limbs, fingers and toes. 'Happy?' Lindsey looked at Dan, knowing how special this moment was for him.

Dan nodded, too full for any words—well, any that would make much sense. He felt a surge of love and protectiveness for his beautiful Lindsey and their little boy. They were a family. They had been truly and magnificently blessed.

Lindsey stroked the gentlest finger around the baby's cheek, watched as his little mouth moved instinctively in a suckling motion. Tipping her head back, she smiled at Dan and their gazes locked in sweet understanding.

Lindsey placed the softest kiss on her husband's mouth and then bent to look again at their son. Pride and a kind of triumph filled her. 'This is *us*,' she said.

* * * * *

LET'S TALK
Romance

For exclusive extracts, competitions
and special offers, find us online:

f facebook.com/millsandboon

🐦 @MillsandBoon

📷 @MillsandBoonUK

Get in touch on 01413 063232

For all the latest titles coming soon, visit
millsandboon.co.uk/nextmonth

WANT EVEN MORE
ROMANCE?
SUBSCRIBE AND SAVE TODAY!

'Mills & Boon books, the perfect way to escape for an hour or so.'

MISS W. DYER

'Excellent service, promptly delivered and very good subscription choices.'

MISS A. PEARSON

'You get fantastic special offers and the chance to get books before they hit the shops.'

MRS V. HALL

Visit millsandboon.co.uk/Subscribe
and save on brand new books.

MILLS & BOON
A ROMANCE FOR EVERY READER

- **FREE** delivery direct to your door

- **EXCLUSIVE** offers every month

- **SAVE** up to 25% on pre-paid subscriptions

SUBSCRIBE AND SAVE

millsandboon.co.uk/Subscribe

MILLS & BOON

THE HEART OF ROMANCE

A ROMANCE FOR EVERY KIND OF READER

MODERN

Prepare to be swept off your feet by sophisticated, sexy and seductive heroes, in some of the world's most glamourous and romantic locations, where power and passion collide.
8 stories per month.

HISTORICAL

Escape with historical heroes from time gone by. Whether your passion is for wicked Regency Rakes, muscled Vikings or rugged Highlanders, awaken the romance of the past.
6 stories per month.

MEDICAL

Set your pulse racing with dedicated, delectable doctors in the high-pressure world of medicine, where emotions run high and passion, comfort and love are the best medicine.
6 stories per month.

True Love

Celebrate true love with tender stories of heartfelt romance, from the rush of falling in love to the joy a new baby can bring, and a focus on the emotional heart of a relationship.
8 stories per month.

Desire

Indulge in secrets and scandal, intense drama and plenty of sizzling hot action with powerful and passionate heroes who have it all: wealth, status, good looks…everything but the right woman.
6 stories per month.

HEROES

Experience all the excitement of a gripping thriller, with an intense romance at its heart. Resourceful, true-to-life women and strong, fearless men face danger and desire - a killer combination!
8 stories per month.

DARE

Sensual love stories featuring smart, sassy heroines you'd want as a best friend, and compelling intense heroes who are worthy of them.
4 stories per month.

To see which titles are coming soon, please visit

millsandboon.co.uk/nextmonth

JOIN US ON SOCIAL MEDIA!

Stay up to date with our latest releases, author news and gossip, special offers and discounts, and all the behind-the-scenes action from Mills & Boon...

 millsandboon

 millsandboonuk

 millsandboon

It might just be true love...

GET YOUR ROMANCE FIX!

MILLS & BOON
— blog —

Get the latest romance news, exclusive author interviews, story extracts and much more!

blog.millsandboon.co.uk

MILLS & BOON

True Love

Romance from the Heart

Celebrate true love with tender stories of heartfelt romance, from the rush of falling in love to the joy a new baby can bring, and a focus on the emotional heart of a relationship.

Eight True Love stories published every month, find them all

millsandboon.co.uk/TrueLove

MILLS & BOON
MEDICAL
Pulse-Racing Passion

Set your pulse racing with dedicated, delectable doctors in the high-pressure world of medicine, where emotions run high and passion, comfort and love are the best medicine.

ight Medical stories published every month, find them all at:

millsandboon.co.uk